"*A Mile from Sunday* is a … journalist's quest to exp… Kadlecek's gripping storytelling abilities make you want to keep turning those pages, her in-depth characterization makes you want to pause for a laugh and a chocolate chip cookie with Jonna, the brave yet humble heroine. A great read that leaves you wondering, *What will Jonna's next adventure be?*"

—BECKY FREEMAN, sports journalist

"I became attached to Jonna Lightfoot MacLaughlin, the authentic, contradictory, smart, funny, real-life woman of this book. Jonna lives in today's world with grown-up problems, hopes, and dreams, and her relationships and life tell the gospel in a unique, compelling way that both Christians and non-Christians will enjoy. The suspense of the story lines made this a page-turner, and now I can't wait for the next book in this trilogy."

—SHIRLEY V. HOOGSTRA, attorney;
Christian college vice president

"Jonna Lightfoot MacLaughlin and I became fast friends from the moment I began reading *A Mile from Sunday*. Her wisdom and wit spoke to my heart and soul as I lived each moment with her. Jo Kadlecek is a talented writer who masterfully connects you to life in the kingdom. Don't miss it!"

—JANE ALBRIGHT, women's basketball coach,
Wichita State University

"I love Jonna Lightfoot MacLaughlin. She's clever, intelligent, faith-filled, and heartwarmingly vulnerable, yet wholly unique. Meet her and you'll love her too. Highly recommended!"

—GAYLE ROPER, author of *Allah's Fire* and *See No Evil*

::a mile from sunday

a novel

jo kadlecek

NavPress
P.O. Box 35001
Colorado Springs, Colorado 80935

ISBN 1-60006-028-5

Cover design by StudioGearbox.com
Cover image by Andreas Pollok/Getty
Author photo by John Decker, www.DeckerProductions.com
Creative Team: Terry Behimer, Traci DePree, Darla Hightower, Arvid Wallen, Kathy Guist

Published in association with the literary agency of Alive Communications, Inc., 7680 Goddard Street, Suite 200, Colorado Springs, CO 80920 (www.alivecommunications.com).

Library of Congress Cataloging-in-Publication Data
Kadlecek, Jo.
A mile from Sunday : a novel / Jo Kadlecek.
p. cm. -- (Lightfoot trilogy)
ISBN 1-60006-028-5
1. Reporters and reporting--Fiction. 2. Clergy--Fiction. 3. Denver (Colo.)--Fiction. I. Title. II. Series: Kadlecek, Jo. Lightfoot trilogy.
PS3611.A33M55 2006
813'.6--dc22

2006016255

Printed in the United States of America

1 2 3 4 5 6 7 8 9 10 / 10 09 08 07 06

For Nanci and Dad,
and, of course, Chris

If the Divine does not make us better, it will make us very much worse. Of all bad men, religious bad men are the worst. Of all created beings, the wickedest is the one who originally stood in the immediate presence of God.

—C. S. Lewis

Summer 2003

::Chapter One

God called me on the phone this morning.

Unfortunately—or fortunately, depending on your perspective—I hadn't gotten into the office yet. My alarm forgot to go off again. So he left me a voice mail telling me that "the world was a violent and evil place, full of all kinds of unnecessary suffering because human beings had deteriorated into dreadful leeches of self-centered greed."

"Well, you don't need to be God to figure that out," I mumbled right before I swallowed a lukewarm blend of 7-Eleven coffee and swished it around my mouth. The newsroom was buzzing this morning, so I pinched the phone closer to my ear, scratched my head with the tip of my pencil, and listened to the rest of his message. His voice sounded more like a whiney child than that of the Almighty:

> *People must turn to me, Jenny. They need me, Jenny. And so, this Saturday morning at sunrise, in the shelter of the Boulder Canyon, just outside that wretched city, I've invited many, many beautiful female beings to come and worship me. When they arrive, they will be delivered. You need to come, too, and cover it for your newspaper so more in the world might know, Jenny.* Click.

"First things first, pal," I said to the phone. "It's Jonna, not Jenny."

I logged on to the computer. You'd think God would get my name right, but then again most humans always seemed to struggle with it too. I'd been Jane, Jan, Jolene, anything but Jonna. Once I was even Jonita. I didn't mind that one really because the woman who called me "Jonita" was ninety-three years old, every inch of her a wrinkle, and her favorite neighbor a long, long, long time ago had been Jonita. She patted my shoulder when she said her neighbor's name, and her tiny brown eyes got cloudy. I didn't correct her.

She, however, was the exception. To the rest of the planet I always made sure they knew the gorgeous, magical name my hippie parents gave me twenty-seven years ago when I was born, the same year the United States of America turned two hundred years old, 1976: Jonna Lightfoot MacLaughlin.

Jonna because I was a girl after my three brothers were born, and my parents—who smoked a little too much "groovy stuff" in the 1960s—really liked the names of the music groups they listened to, like Peter, Paul, and Mary, or Crosby, Stills, Nash, and Young. They figured they must have heard Matthew, Mark, Luke, and John doing some tight harmonies somewhere on Haight Street in San Francisco and the names just stuck. Of course, they improvised on the last one when I was born a girl, so we became: Matthew, Mark, Luke, and me, Jonna.

Lightfoot because they were "conscientious objectors" to how Native Americans had been treated and decided that by giving their children Indian middle names—Matt BigBear, Mark RunningWind, Luke EagleWing—native traditions would be kept alive. Of course, they never had a drop of Cherokee or

Apache in their blood—that would've been hard to explain to three generations of Irish clan who had shipped over from County Clare after the Great Potato Famine.

Which explained *MacLaughlin* on my dad's side and *O'Connor* on my mom's. And why names were so important in our tribe. They meant something.

You'd think God, of all people, would understand that, especially since he had been, more or less, in the "naming" business. So if he was going to telephone the religion reporter at the *Denver Dispatch* daily newspaper to tell her about some spiritual love-fest in the Rocky Mountains, you'd think he'd get her name right.

Jonna Lightfoot MacLaughlin. Don't forget it.

By the time I'd finished checking the other messages on my voice mail—a Methodist minister, a Catholic volunteer, and one ex-Baptist leader—it was 9:34 a.m. I jotted down their phone numbers, and aside from thinking "God" had a serious credibility problem with me right now, I wondered if I should call the Boulder Police Department to warn them about Saturday's potentially wacky gathering.

I replayed the message and realized "God" had failed to tell me where exactly the sunrise extravaganza would be in the canyon. I was not about to get up early on a Saturday morning for nothing, let alone tip off the Boulder police that some potential cult leader was lurking around Boulder. They got those types of phone calls all the time. Their beat might as well have been dubbed New Age Headquarters, what with all the meditation gurus, spirituality centers, psychics, and animal communicators in town. For some reason, Boulder had always attracted a variety of believers and seekers, mystics and philosophers, activists and kooks. And since it was only forty minutes or so from downtown Denver,

Boulder was considered part of my territory to cover.

No shortage of story possibilities there.

I swirled coffee against the inside of my cheeks and considered my next move. At the bottom of my plastic IN-box I had tucked away half a Hershey's bar yesterday before the staff meeting. Maybe that would help. I broke off a square and waited.

"Ask the boss," a voice inside my head told me. I blinked. "Not *that* one. The one who edits your stories and signs your paychecks, not the One who runs the universe."

"Skip, I got a voice mail from God," I said, pushing the door open into his office.

"Again? Remind me to stand next to you the next time we're in a thunderstorm." Skip Gravely grinned as he said it and looked up at me from the papers on his desk. It was the same grin he had thrown my way two years before when he first recruited me to be the *Dispatch*'s "Number One Religion Reporter." I was too fresh out of college to know that I would also be the *only* religion reporter. But since I'd been covering obituaries, the police blotter, and an occasional city hall meeting—the kind of sleepy assignments every rookie reporter got at every newspaper—I was ready for something a little more sizzling, something that exercised my brain muscles. So when he said the job title with such Pulitzer Prize-winning intonations—"Number One Religion Reporter"—I'd be lying if I said I hadn't been interested.

I'd never forget it. April, 2001, Denver was getting dumped on in another spring snowstorm, and I was freezing by the time I'd gotten to my desk in the newsroom that morning. I picked the snowflakes out of the curls in my hair and tried to get a comb through the mass of frozen frizz on my head. It was not going there. So I thawed and decided to go with the natural woman, white-girl 'fro look, hoping the rest of the day would be a little more tame than my hair.

Once I had tossed my bag into the drawer beside my desk, I saw Skip's note taped to my computer screen: "See me. Now!"

I tasted the backwash of hazelnut coffee. What had I done? Maybe yesterday's obituary was terrible. Maybe I had bogged it down with too many poetic, and consequently, unnecessary details trying to make the poor guy sound halfway decent. Or maybe he hadn't really died and we were getting sued for printing a bogus obit. I thought I'd checked my facts.

Then I glanced over to the sports desks — the reporters weren't there. Maybe they were sick and I was the only reporter around to cover the Colorado state high school wrestling tournament. The last thing I needed was to watch a bunch of half-naked adolescent boys sweat onto each other's skin. I had suffered through years of wrestling tournaments watching all three of my brothers trying hopelessly not to get pinned in high school matches. The agony was too much to bear. It didn't help that Mom and Pop always gave them a positive lecture on nonviolence and good karma and told them how proud they were of "passing on peace and joy to their opponent."

"No, God, anything but wrestling," I'd prayed. Aloud. I reread Skip's note. Boy, I wanted a cigarette. Since I didn't have time, I popped a few chocolate drops into my mouth instead and walked into my editor's office as the snow fell outside his window. I put on my thin, wiry glasses, hoping they would make me look smarter, or at least older than twenty-four and a half.

"MacLaughlin, glad to see you this morning," he said. Skip was a tall, thin man whose patience translated into biblical proportions. He wore pin-striped suits that were as wrinkle free as his attitude. The man never appeared flustered, no matter how many stories were breaking and driving the rest of his reporters and editors mad. Skip was, as they say, a calming presence. Chamomile tea with a trimmed beard.

"Mary Virginia Blake has just told me she's calling it quits," he said, still typing on his keyboard as the screen above it changed colors each time his fingers moved.

"Mrs. Blake? The lady with the white hair and paisley sweaters? The one who actually says 'good morning' when you walk by?" I sat up straight in the chair as more questions popped out of my mouth: "I mean, she covers religion and stuff like that, doesn't she? Hasn't she been here a while?"

"Since before Moses chiseled out the Commandments." Skip laughed, thinking his joke was funny. I faked a chuckle too and tried not to snort. Then he looked away from his screen and straight at me.

"Know anything about church, MacLaughlin?"

I swallowed a morsel of confidence. "As a matter of fact, um, I do," I noticed that the fluorescent lights above his desk made for terrible atmosphere. "I try to go each week, that is, when I'm not working on a story. It's a little Presbyterian church just behind the capitol; my brother and his wife told me about it when I moved here last year from Summit County. We're about the only members who don't get the senior citizen discount when we hit the Sirloin Buffet after services, but I don't mind."

"Uh-huh. That's what I thought," he said, still staring. "What do you think of it?"

"Think of it? You mean of church?"

Skip nodded, pushing his eyebrows forward as he waited for my answer. He folded his hands together on the desktop and smiled kindly at me. I relaxed.

"Actually, since you asked, I think a lot of it. My parents sort of *found Jesus* when I was in high school, and believe me, that was *big* in our family." I snorted and held my hands out wide like I was showing him the size of the fish I'd just caught. "They had tried all sorts of religions when I was growing up, but Jesus, well, he stuck. Then they went to Costa Rica to work with coffee farmers through a Christian mission, so we haven't seen them for a while."

I wasn't sure how much more I should tell him, but his eyes suddenly got real big and he leaned forward. "Go on," he said.

And so I did. I told the same editor who'd hired me right out of Mountain State College all about my wonderful and weird parents: of their years as flower children in San Francisco; of their decision to raise my brothers and me among Mother Earth a.k.a. Colorado's ski country; and of their dabbling in Buddhism, Judaism, Hinduism, Humanism, Altruism, and all the other "isms" they explored throughout our lives. I told Skip about the environmental protests they took us to on family vacations, the organic cigarettes and biodegradable laundry soap we sold door-to-door—or condo-to-condo—at ski resorts, and the books my parents read to us every Sunday night during family time throughout our lives because they thought having a television was an "appalling symbol of capitalism." And I explained to him that because my parents told us *Jesus* was what they'd been looking for their whole lives, my brothers and I now chatted regularly with him, too, and read the Bible when we remembered (though my brothers were better at remembering than I was).

When I finished, Skip unfolded his hands, crossed his arms, and gave me *that* grin.

"You, MacLaughlin, have been training all your life for the job I am about to offer you. How would you like to be the *Dispatch*'s Number One Religion Reporter?"

That was it. I was thrilled, hooked, and nervous when I said yes, shook his hand, and walked back into the newsroom. I grabbed my bag, took the elevator down to the lobby, and walked out to the entrance of the *Dispatch* to have a smoke. In the snow. And though I knew all the surgeon general's warnings and everything, I had to admit, *that* cigarette *that* day in the freezing cold of the Mile High City was one of the best I'd ever had. At least it was organic.

I'd been on the job barely five months when the World Trade Center was attacked, and suddenly, religion stories seemed more important than ever for news outlets like the *Dispatch,* with people trying to make sense of foreign beliefs and national tragedies. I ran myself ragged trying to keep up. But now, two years and ninety-seven features, news series, and profiles later, I was still the Number One—and only—Religion Reporter at Denver's number two daily newspaper.

I'd had a couple of phone calls from "God" before, but the message this morning bothered me more than the others had for some reason.

"Really, Skip, the guy sounded, I don't know, scarier than usual. Talked about recruiting beautiful women and *delivering* them," I said, slouching in the same chair I'd sat in that morning I'd been promoted. Skip never had done anything about the fluorescent lights.

"What else are you working on?" My dear, calm editor asked the question more for my sake than his—he knew I was always juggling about five stories at the same time.

"The Unity Church in Cherry Creek is about to split, the Southern Baptists are coming to the Mile High Convention Center in a few weeks for their annual shindig, which—I don't need to tell you—is a priority for the *Dispatch*, and, you know, the usual other inspirational stuff." Out of habit, I scrunched my hair up toward my ear hoping to give it a little more body. It didn't.

"You found your *good news* story?" Skip looked hopeful and sipped his coffee.

"Well, not really. But I keep praying," I said, meaning it. Ever since I took this job, I thought it would be a good opportunity to write something inspiring for our readers, to print some good news sprinkled among the bad of the daily world calamities. "Positive karma," as my parents would have called it in their hippie years.

But rarely had I found the good news I wanted to cover. I had voiced my dream to my boss when he first gave me the promotion. "After all," I said to him, "isn't religion supposed to be good for you, for everybody, sort of like oatmeal and exercise? Aren't Christians and Buddhists and Jews supposed to be nice and moral and conscientious? Don't religious people make better citizens and nicer neighbors?"

Skip had simply smiled at me, and after two years on the beat, I knew why. I had met only a few who reflected my naive perception of religion. The rest, well, they were more human than they were religious. Or maybe it was the other way around.

Anyway, Skip kept reminding me not to despair, telling me my writing and reporting skills were being put to good use, even if they weren't yet covering any *good* news in the world of religion. And especially since September 11 with the gloomy treatment of religious fundamentalism getting gloomier, people actually were reading *my* stories. In fact, Skip announced in a staff meeting one morning that religion news was all the more important since the Twin Towers fell. I believed him, too. He was the type of newspaperman even conservatives, Republicans, and sportswriters respected.

"Are you really worried?" he asked as he rubbed his beard between his thumb and fingers.

"Something didn't sound right in his voice. I can usually handle the Boulder crowd, you know, the New Agers and new religions and all. I get it because I sort of grew up in it. But this guy . . ." I took the pencil from where I'd stuck it in my curls and doodled around on the notepad where I'd taken notes from the voice mail.

"Why don't you call Frank Murphy just in case?" Skip was flipping through his Rolodex, looking as serious as he did during staff meetings.

He scribbled down the phone number of the Boulder County detective, ripped it off the pad, and held it out for me.

"Be careful now, Jonna. Fanatics are rarely saints." He stood as he spoke. He was a good six inches taller than I was, but then, most people were. He grabbed his coffee mug and walked down the hall with me. He said he had a cranky advertising manager to meet with. I had a cup of coffee and a deadline waiting for me.

At my desk, I gulped my coffee and popped another piece of Hershey's to get that near-mocha experience in my throat. I scrolled through my e-mail. Conference announcements, pastors retiring, special church services—most of the thirteen e-mails were like most I received on a daily basis. Each was a lead to a potential story as more and more people paid attention to my religion coverage in the local news.

I felt a hand slap my back.

"Got a treat for me, Lightfoot? I'm a little desperate this morning," Hannah said, with her usual morning cheer. Hannah X. Hensley was one of the few other women journalists in the newsroom, other than the lifestyle reporters and obituary interns. She sat at the desk beside mine, an immense woman—more in presence than in pounds—a few years older than I was, but with more energy than any teammate I had had on the college ski team. Her skin was the color of an almond bar, and I always found it wonderfully ironic that that was also her favorite snack whenever we went downstairs to the cafeteria for a break.

Hannah also loved experimenting with perfumes and lipstick shades, both of which were common fixtures around her cubicle. As female reporters in a male-dominated industry, we had developed a connection from the day I first plopped down in my desk beside hers. True, our mutual devotion to chocolate helped, but there was an ethnic activism that also bound us together. She valued the *X* in her byline in the same way I did *Lightfoot*. She used the capital letter as a reminder to readers that most "African Americans really don't know any name but the one their slave owners gave them. And honey, don't nobody own me, so X is my way of taking it back."

I raised my fist in solidarity each time she gave her Black Power speech. And then, within earshot of the news guys, we'd ruminate about how our feminine powers could work wonders in getting sources to trust us, open up, and spill all. Or at least help get conversations rolling. Our banter across cubicles about story angles and reporting strategies confounded some of our colleagues and kept the sports guys at bay.

"Well, do ya, Lightfoot? I've got to interview the mayor in an hour, and my head is groggy." Hannah sunk into her chair.

"Oscar de la Renta?" I sniffed, tossing her the last of my Hershey's.

"Left over from yesterday. I like it." Hannah unwrapped the candy, placed it all in her mouth, and closed her eyes while it melted onto her tongue. Her hair and makeup were a perfect complement to her natural features, a feat I could never quite figure out for myself. This morning, her eye shadow and shoes matched her teal suit. Exactly. I sighed at the smudges on my clogs and the wrinkles across my skirt and clicked on a new e-mail with the heading, "Waiting." At least I hadn't yet spilled coffee down my blouse this morning.

"What's new?" Hannah asked me as she opened her eyes and began flipping through her notepad and the morning edition of the *Dispatch*.

But I was engrossed. "Waiting" was from one of those free e-mail accounts, and as I read it, I knew it was from the same guy who called me this morning. Now I *was* nervous:

"The WORLd is dooMed, Jenny, like I told you this morning in my message. So you better come worship Me Saturday. AS the Sun rises on the wretched city. —God."

"God's on the loose again, Hannah," I said, picking up the phone.

"Should I tell the mayor?"

"Hold that thought." I waved to her like I was stopping traffic and punched the numbers on my phone. The ring turned into a beep and then a scruffy recorded voice: "This is Frank Murphy, Boulder County detective. Leave me a message, and I'll call you back when I can."

I hung up the phone, not exactly sure how to leave a message about an anonymous man who thought he was God and was holding a sunrise service next Saturday. I tucked Frank's number into my notebook and picked up the phone to make another call. It rang before I could.

"Hello, Jonna Lightfoot MacLaughlin here."

"Little Sister!" Matt was calling from his office at Denver College. "How's my favorite religion reporter?"

"Holy, righteous, and in the process of saving the world. How's my favorite oldest brother?"

"Up to my eyeballs in grading papers. Ugh. You should teach these kids how to write, Jon. Anyway, I have this colleague who teaches English . . ."

"Well, don't waste any time with small talk, my Brother! Let me guess, Matt. This colleague of yours is single, right?"

"You're good. How about dinner with us Saturday night?"

"He's seminormal?" I had to ask. The last time Matt set me up with a colleague was a year and a half ago during spring break. The guy was nice enough, a visiting physicist at the college researching nuclear fusion. I couldn't understand one single sentence he said over dinner. I didn't know what my brother had been thinking. At least he had waited before trying again.

"Of course he's normal. I think he teaches American literature or researches something like that, so he can't be all bad, right?"

I coughed, leaned back in my chair, and thought about it.

"If I make it through the week and the world hasn't ended by then, I'll show up with bells on. Your place?"

"Righto, Sis. Have a good one, okay?"

"You too!"

I hung up the phone and smiled at the picture I'd taped to the bottom of my computer: Matt and his stunning wife, Mary; Luke and Sarah, his fiancée; me; and Mark, who was in between girlfriends at the time. The photo had been taken last January on top of Copper Mountain, by the same slopes we always conquered as kids. Mark had flown in from Alabama and Luke and Sarah from New Jersey for our annual family ski trip. Our parents couldn't afford to leave Costa Rica, but my brothers thought we should get together anyway. Even with our ski parkas and boots, you could pick out the MacLaughlins in the picture. Each had the same short stubby bodies and brown curly heads, just in different sizes and lengths. No one could confuse my family. And the MacLaughlin brothers—who were notorious for looking out for their little sister—beamed around the women in the picture. I sighed, hoping Matt's colleague might at least have potential.

"Whatever," I said aloud.

"Big brother's setting you up again? It's about time." Hannah spun around in her chair toward me, arms across her chest as if expecting a full report. The single life and our perpetual search for a decent guy were also interests Hannah and I shared.

"That is scary. How do you know those things?" I asked, pushing around the papers on my desk like pieces in a puzzle.

She tilted her head and rolled her eyes. "Lightfoot, you forget I come from a line of African warriors," Hannah said. "I'll want all the details after the date." She swiveled back toward her computer.

I punched another phone number and waited. The Methodist minister in Arvada, a suburb west of Denver, told me about a potluck dinner her church was hosting Friday night for the community and thought I might find it an interesting event to cover. I was certainly invited, the minister said to me. I politely thanked her for the information without committing to coming.

If I had a Snickers bar for every potluck I'd been invited to since becoming a religion reporter, I'd be a blubbery advertisement for the candy bar company. But I wouldn't have written a single story. Potlucks were nice and all, and religious folks loved them, but with all due respect, there wasn't much news in Mrs. Smith's meatloaf casserole or Betty's "sinfully delicious" brownies.

As I was trying to hang up with the Methodist—who was now reading me the menu of what each family was bringing—Hannah tapped me on the head. I turned and watched her lip-speak to me that she was on her way to the mayor's office and would meet me later for lunch at Pete's Kitchen. I nodded and scanned the list of calls I needed to return when the Methodist stopped talking.

Terry Choyce was my next caller. His voice was low and rich, soothing even, and his tone assured me I was not about to be invited to another food festival. He introduced himself simply as one of the volunteers at the Catholic Outreach Center in the Five Points neighborhood and wondered if I would be interested in finding out more about their after-school program for children from low-income families. I paused. There was a hint of inspiration in this story, the potential for good news on a day when "God" had been making me anxious. I scanned my Day-Timer and decided to rearrange a few things before finishing my story on the now-divided Unity Church, which had a 4 p.m. deadline.

"I could come by in the next hour. Would that work?" I asked. There was silence on the phone.

"Mr. Choyce?" I asked. I swallowed the last of my coffee, which was now cold, and waited.

"Forgive me," he said softly. "I guess I was expecting you'd be too busy for our small program." I liked this man.

"Oh, ye of little faith," I said to him. We both laughed, and I scribbled the directions to the Center, thanked him for his invitation, and hung up. I grabbed my notebook, cell phone, and bag, sent a quick e-mail to Skip letting him know my plans, and left.

The Denver sky was a metallic blue, and the thin air was soft across my face. Colorado summers could get hotter than fire, but my brothers, Luke and Mark—the experienced travelers in the family—informed me that the dry heat was friendlier than the East Coast or the Deep South where each lived respectively. Today there was even a playful breeze.

I turned up Twenty-third Avenue and headed north, past the Mexican restaurants and newly renovated warehouses-turned-loft apartments and into the neighborhood that was once known as the "Jazz Capital of the West." Downtown Denver and its surrounding neighborhoods had seen quite a comeback in the past fifteen years, and now it was hip to live close to the city again, instead of retreating to the tired suburbs of the foothills.

I drove by a few housing projects, parked in front of the Center, and walked up the adobe red stairs.

"Hello. *JoAnna*?" A stunning man about Matt's age was waiting as I walked into the lobby of the old building. The sound of his voice sliding over the syllables was so gorgeous I considered for a moment changing my name. The music of it matched the melody in his eyes, and his broad firm shoulders made me remember that it had been seven months, two weeks, and three days since I'd had a real date. Since, in fact, I'd been around any males other than reporters, story sources, or my brothers. I was suddenly quite interested in the work of the Catholic Outreach Center, thinking it might provide me what I had long been looking for since coming to Denver: good news *and* a good man. Maybe I would even volunteer.

"It's, um, Jonna. Lightfoot. MacLaughlin," I heard myself saying, feeling the pink of my Irish cheeks fill out. I looked at my feet and shook my head at the stains on the toes of my clogs. Then I tried to smooth out the wrinkle in my skirt with my hand and adjusted my bag on my shoulder.

"How embarrassing," he said. "I knew that. My apologies, *Jonna*." It was a magnificent name, rolling off *his* lips. A stunning, glorious name filled with possibilities for wonder and devotion. He might as well have handed me a valentine. "I'm Terry Choyce." He held out his hand, and I glanced at the other hand, noticing it had no gold band on the ring finger, and smiled. I shook it and sighed.

"Thank you for coming," he said. "Let me show you around." I followed. Terry's hair was blond and wavy, his jaw firm and perfect. As he talked about his program, his arms directed an invisible orchestra with the same kind of passion my eldest brother, Matt, showed when he talked about teaching. When he escorted me into the new computer room, his eyes brightened. This room was particularly exciting to him, he said, because it would give "so many kids a step up in preparing them for the future." I jotted down his comments in my notebook and was considering whether it would be unprofessional to ask if he was dating anyone, when my cell phone rang. A sure sign of divine intervention.

"Excuse me," I whispered to this handsome Catholic. He nodded politely and walked over to the corner of the room so I would have privacy. A gentleman, too, I thought. This call better be important.

"Jonna Lightfoot MacLaughlin," I answered, testily.

"Jonna, it's Skip. Just got a call for you. The Buddhist temple on Colorado Boulevard is on fire. Right now." He paused, cleared his throat, and continued, "The fire chief doesn't know yet if it was arson or if one of the priests left the incense burning a little too long." He said it as if he'd just sipped his morning tea. I marveled again at the lack of emotion my editor displayed, even when a building was burning down, and wrote the details in my notebook.

"I'll be right there." I flipped off my phone and dropped it in my bag, found my car keys, and hurried over to Terry. "I'm so sorry. I've got to get across town right now. Could I take a rain check?"

His eyes opened into empathy as he held out the door for me.

"Of course. I understand. Call me when you can; we'll be here for a while," he said, laughing, as he waved to me from the steps. The sun glistened across his face, and I assured him I would do just that.

I waved back from behind the steering wheel and pulled onto the street, watching him in my rearview mirror until he went back inside the center.

Whoever said religion was boring was obviously mistaken.

::Chapter Two

Black smoke tunneled its way into the blue Colorado sky. I could see it almost a mile away before I turned onto the street and saw its source.

A brawny police officer was directing traffic. I smiled at him as I slowed down to hold out my press pass from the window. Stone-faced and bulked-up, he glanced from the laminated ID card to my face, grunted as he inspected my beat-up little Datsun, and then simply waved me away from the neighborhood traffic toward the "authorized" vehicles lined up across the road.

Fire trucks were parked close to the Mile High Zen Buddhist Cultural Center, and firefighters were spraying it with arms of water as a few flames shot from its roof. Much of the building's interior had been devoured by the fire, leaving a skeleton frame of metal and shattered windows. A flood of ash and smoke fell over an adjacent section, which I found out later was living quarters for the monks. I shook my head at the awful mess in front of me and felt a lump in my throat when I read the charred but still legible temple mission on the sign in front: "For The Innocent, The Faithful, and The Suffering."

I got out of the car, pen and notepad in hand. The smoke slapped my nose and throat, and I put a tissue across my face so as not to breathe in the fumes. When I looked up for a fresh breath, I noticed three men standing shoulder to shoulder a few yards away, watching the firefighters with teary eyes. I couldn't tell if they were crying from sadness or from the smoke. They wore brown cotton robes down to their feet, which reminded me of dyed bed sheets, and each had a black square patch hanging across his chest that made me think of the bib on a farmer's overalls. The men's shaved white heads were turning pink in the summer sun.

I walked back to my car and grabbed a fresh bottle of Leadville Springs Water from my stash in the backseat. The monks were thirsty and did not seem to mind drinking from the same bottle as they passed it to each other. I stood quietly as we watched the firefighters struggling to save the main building of their cultural center. The monks were probably all in their midthirties. The tall one had the kind of European-American face that told me he probably grew up somewhere in Texas or California playing baseball, attending Mass, and studying business in college before becoming disillusioned with the world and joining the Center. The two shorter men pushed black professorial glasses in front of their eyes when they finished their drink. The tall one had long skinny lines above his eyebrows as he stood lost at the sight in front of him.

"I'm really sorry for you, Brother," I whispered. The monks with glasses stared ahead, stoic, but my words seemed to break the spell on the other.

"Thank you," he said, turning to me with the look of an altar boy who'd rather be outside playing catch. "Y'all can't imagine how crushing this is." The trace of a Southern accent confirmed my assessment of his background. I held his gaze, offered him a half smile, and instinctively patted his wrist. His eyes filled.

"It must feel terrible to lose such a sacred place," I said. Then

I held out my hand to him.

"I'm Jonna Lightfoot MacLaughlin, religion reporter with the *Denver Dispatch* newspaper," I said, slightly louder than a whisper. "I'd like to report on this, if you think it'd be all right with your community."

I had learned early on in the world of religion reporting that because people were often passionate about their beliefs, it was generally better to ask permission *before* writing about them, than to ask forgiveness *later*, although it certainly was not a hard-and-fast rule in the world of journalism. Nonetheless, most human beings I'd encountered liked the power of giving someone else permission to do something. They weren't nearly as strong on the forgiving part, let alone with reporters who didn't get something right. Or worse, who actually told the truth about them. That could get sticky.

The monk looked up at me and shook my hand as if it were a greasy hamburger and he was clearly a vegetarian. That is, until an epiphany seemed to erupt in his soul, and suddenly my hand, wrist, and arm were shaking like a carrot juicer.

"Really? Jonna Lightfoot MacLaughlin? I have read your stories and believe you have spiritual understanding," he said, tapping his colleagues' shoulders and whispering something to bring them into the conversation.

"I try," I said, pulling back my arm to make sure it was still attached. I flipped my notebook open and looked up.

"I am the spiritual director of the Center, a Dharma of Robert James Toshiti." The monk with the darker glasses was speaking to me in a monotone voice that oozed peace and tranquility. "The cornerstone of Buddhism is the observance of the precepts. We concentrate our practice on ethics and conduct, right action and right livelihood, right speech and compassionate deeds. We come together to embody the true sense of Buddha: to work and live in harmony with all beings."

He watched my hand move across the pad as I wrote what he said, in a MacLaughlin version of shorthand.

At that moment it occurred to me why Buddhism was the shortest religious experiment my mom and pop ever tried when I was growing up. They had a short fuse when it came to rules. And all the things their Zen teacher told them they had to do to achieve the "awakening of their True and Original Mind," the self-discipline and physical denial and all that, well, it just was not fun for them. Lord knew, my parents wanted a good time from the minute they were born.

Years later when they became Presbyterians, Mom and Pop did occasionally reinstate their Buddhist meditation skills to "meditate on the Lord." But mostly they liked the freedom that the Westminster Confession offered them: "Glorify God and enjoy him forever." They'd always been particularly fond of the concept of *enjoyment*.

The Dharma stopped talking when he saw I'd stopped writing. I didn't particularly feel the need for a lecture on the ins and outs of the ancient Eastern tradition from a converted middle-class American shortstop. Besides, what I didn't know of Zen Buddhism I could find in my doorstop copy of *Cromwell's Encyclopedia of World Religions* back in the newsroom, an amazingly dull but massive and illuminating gift left over from my predecessor, Mary Virginia Blake. And if I still couldn't find the necessary Buddhist information buried somewhere between the book's 2,173 pages, I could hunt it down on the Internet. I was supposed to be part of the techno-generation, after all.

I tried to redirect the spiritual director.

"Tell me about *your* temple. How many attend?"

"Numbers are not important to those who benefit from the calming and centering of the mind. Our aim is to transcend the delusional notion of a separate ego, or self, and realize the inner being that has always been there, so as to be one with all that is. That quite transcends mere numbers, you see."

I nodded.

I was about to toss out another question when he continued. His face was getting sweaty. "Our training school attracts a different number of seekers with each session." He took a deep breath, and his brothers followed suit. "Our lectures are open to the public so our attendance tends to vary . . ."

"Especially if a Hollywood celebrity is speaking," the Southerner interrupted.

He received a severe glance from his leader, who continued, "We teach that through awakening we have nothing fundamentally to gain or to lose, and we can gradually relinquish the *need* to grasp and cling, as well as the fear and hostility that accompany *this need*."

He stopped, his voice a static line across an invisible screen that made me anything but eager for more spiritual direction. I tried to be patient as he finished. "For chanting and daily meditation and private yoga instruction, and all the other activities I have mentioned, many hundred children of Buddha participate and practice with us."

Skip would let me get away with "many hundred." I looked up from my notes and tried to appear "enlightened" by relaxing my shoulders and bobbing my head. Then I asked, "Do you know how the fire started?"

The Southern monk stepped in when he heard this and said, "We have no idea why or how such things happen or why our holy center should experience such darkness. We simply accept it."

"Yes, but is it possible someone set the fire . . . intentionally?"

"Are you suggesting arson, Miss MacLaughlin?" the Dharma asked, in a way that hinted to me that he actually did have blood circulating through his veins.

"I guess I am. Isn't that possible? Did you see anyone suspicious around when the fire began this morning?"

The three monks looked at each other.

"No one suspicious," the elder said. "I cannot imagine anyone would want to burn down a peaceful temple of transcendence and harmony."

"Maybe someone else didn't see it that way," I said, scratching behind my ear with the eraser on my pencil. I smiled and nodded as if there might be more we didn't know. The three men stood silent. The Southern monk began to rock back and forth and hum quietly.

I cleared my throat.

"Okay, forgive me if I wasn't clear. I'm on your side, so any information you could give me about what happened will help the Mile High Zen Buddhist Cultural Center." They stared. I waited. More humming and staring.

Then I took a deep breath and shifted strategies. I'd throw out a last resort and see what happened before hunting down another source. So I stepped into their personal space and whispered in a stern, monotone voice, "Remember, I have spiritual understanding. Come, enter into my sphere of understanding, relinquish the need to grasp and cling to the self. Let us end the fear and hostility and concentrate on ethics, right action, right livelihood, and especially right speech . . . right now. What do you say?"

A siren suddenly sounded, and all four of us about jumped off the sidewalk as we watched a truck speed away. By this time the firefighters had controlled the last of the flames and were beginning to put away some of their gear so the cleaning process could begin. I stepped back into the monk's space.

If I was going to file this story for tomorrow's morning edition, I needed a few basics from those on the inside of the Center: what time they first called the fire department, whether anyone was hurt, what they planned to do now. I threw out the questions and waited, tapping my pencil against my notebook.

The siren must have inspired a bit of "centeredness" in the Dharma because he quickly obliged. The other two stood beside him, one still rocking while both stared transcendentally at me. Tiny sweat beads formed on their now sunburned heads. I gave my business card to each of the monks and decided to forgo my usual custom of handshaking.

"I really am sorry for your loss," I said, looking straight into their faces before stepping again just inches from their eyeballs. "Please call me if there is any other realm of transcendent knowledge I should acquire." The director looked back at me, tilted his head, and offered me a holy nod. The others imitated him.

They breathed in deeply and closed their eyes.

"So, I'm going to go away now, okay?" I said, not quite sure what state they had entered and not wanting to startle them out of it. They nodded, which relieved me, and I waved as I walked toward some of the firefighters. They didn't wave back.

I needed a cigarette. In fact, I thought I had clearly earned one after the morning I had just endured, what with a scary "God" incarnate on the loose, a blow-by-blow potluck solicitation, a missed opportunity for marital bliss with a hunky Catholic man, and now this. I would have sat down right there and then, yoga-style, to light up, but something in me said it would be sort of sacrilege to strike a match and smoke a cigarette with the charcoal ruins of a Zen Buddhist Cultural Center still smoldering a few feet away.

Instead, I swallowed eight ounces of Leadville Springs and bumped into Freddy Stephano, a fire inspector I'd met when I covered a small bombing at one of the city's mosques in the aftermath of September 11. It had been a gruesome time, and I prayed I'd never have to do something like that again. It had, however, connected me to some good people who could also be good sources, one of whom was Freddy. I asked him what he thought of the fire that had now died but still smoked behind us. He took off his orange and blue baseball cap, ran his fingers through his curly red hair, and shook his head from side to side. Then he spit on the dirt, just to the side of his right boot.

"Doesn't make much sense, Jeanie," he said. Inspector Stephano was a nice enough guy but not very good in the social skills department, which I guessed was probably because he worked mostly with buildings and not people. "Thank God—or Buddha in this case—nobody was inside when it happened."

He chuckled to himself, spit again, and turned serious.

"But that's the weird thing. Usually on Tuesday mornings they've got all sorts of yoga classes and group chants. The last two days everything had been cancelled for repairs. Guess they hoped to fix up a few things and instead got a fire that busted just about everything." He spit one more time, pulled a handkerchief from his back pocket, and blew his nose hard into it.

"Hate these allergies," he mumbled.

I stepped back from his "allergies" and scribbled a few of his details into my notebook. "It does sound strange, Freddy. I'm assuming it's up for inquiry."

"You got it, Jeanie." He shoved the hankie back into his pocket.

"Well, keep me posted, okay?" I stepped over his saliva collection on the ground to hand him my card. He read it and put it in the same pocket he'd just stuffed the hankie.

"Oh, and it's Jonna, not Jeanie," I said cheerfully as I turned toward the street.

"Right. One more thing," he called after me. I looked over my shoulder at him and waited. "For the record, we are *not* treating this as a hate crime. There's no evidence of that. So simply put, it ain't one. You got that, Jeanie, I mean, Jonna?"

"Got it, Inspector. Thanks for your help." I waved at him and wished him good health—for the sake of other reporters who might need to track him down later.

When I drove away with my left hand under the wheel, I kept digging with my right hand and struck gold when I found a pack of Marlboro Lights. I was out of organic. I felt guilty for a second—since last month I had promised Matt I was going to quit. But, I reasoned with myself, I *would* be quitting soon. Just not today.

I pulled a smoke from the pack and let it dangle from my lips while I waited for the lighter to pop out of my dashboard. I pulled the rearview mirror in my direction and could not find a part anywhere on my head—frizzy curls were flying everywhere. I tried to smooth them over to the side and hoped they would cooperate.

Twenty minutes and two cigarettes later, I was standing

in the entrance of Pete's Kitchen hoping to find Hannah at our usual table in the back. I spotted her teal self and pressed my way through the lunch crowd to join her.

"Sorry I'm late, Hannah. And even more sorry I've got to get my food to go," I said, sliding into the seat across from her. She was just finishing a meatloaf sandwich and a side salad. I caught her midbite.

"Heygirldsjwewoemf," she said, mouth full.

"Does someone have the interpretation, please?" I asked, looking around the noisy room. She swallowed and grinned.

"I said, 'Hey, Girl, what took you so long?'" She took a long slow slurp of iced tea.

"The Buddhist temple was on fire." A waitress approached, and I ordered a turkey and alfalfa sprout pita pocket to go and a large coffee.

"The Buddhists were on fire? Literally or spiritually? Either one could be page one material," she said as she pushed the salad in my direction.

"Funny. It's fishy because no one seems to know how it started," I said. I picked up a fork and speared a cherry tomato.

"Arson? Wow, that's some deep karma." Hannah wiped the sides of her mouth with her napkin, pulled out her lipstick from her purse, and outlined her lips.

"This one's called 'Winter Rose Garden.' Well?" She pushed out her lips so they formed a bright, frosted "O." She lifted her eyebrows for effect.

"Nice if you like the afterglow of a cherry Popsicle," I teased as the waitress brought my order and check.

"You're just jealous, Lightfoot." Hannah put away her lipstick, tucked a ten-dollar bill under her glass, and stood up.

"You're right, Hannah X." I sighed. When I stopped to think about it—which I didn't really have time to do today because of my deadline—I *was* jealous. I was envious of any woman who carried herself like Hannah did: poised, regal, beautiful. I rarely felt any of those. Confident, sure. Smart, you bet. But pretty? Poised? Regal? Rarely. In fact, some days I wondered if my face and body could give television sitcom writers plenty of material for seasons to come.

I didn't mind admitting that I had a way to go in each of the regal and poised departments. Some days I attempted primping. I occasionally even applied mascara and blush, though I could never quite see the point. My eyelashes were already thick and brown, and my cheeks turned pink at the slightest sign of embarrassment anyway. My nose took up too much space on my face, and my chin drooped into my neck. Though my brothers, parents, and the ladies at church always told me they thought I was "the most beautiful girl they knew," sometimes even calling me "cute" or "interesting looking," I simply smiled at their well-intentioned but surely uninformed compliments.

Of course, on bad days, I wanted to believe them.

Most of the time, though, I was never quite sure what it meant to be "beautiful" for single career women like me who were pushing thirty and wondering if Prince Charming even existed, let alone was on his way. If beauty was wearing a size-three dress with parted, controlled hair and luscious rouge across Victorian cheeks, well, I hardly felt qualified.

This day, however, I hadn't had time to powder my nose, let alone consider an entire makeover on my feminine features. I grabbed my pita pocket and coffee and walked with Hannah. As we stood at the cash register, I rested my elbow across the corner of her shoulder and whispered, "I've *always* been jealous of you, Hensley. Always will be."

"The girl's got her priorities down," she said to Pete, the owner of the place, who took my money and tucked it into his cash drawer. He smiled at us, as though he had no idea what we were talking about, and told us he'd see us later.

By the time we got back to the newsroom, it was two o'clock, and I had exactly two hours to write the story of the temple fire. Hannah was already halfway finished with her story about the mayor's new convention site plans, partly because she had the uncanny ability to write in her head as she drove so that once she got back to her computer, the words just gushed out of her. My process was a little more like my hair: scattered, out of control, and thick with misguided details.

Still, what I'd gotten from the monks and from Freddy today was enough to relay the story while leaving the door open for a follow up if any new information surfaced with the investigation. I signed on to my computer, set up a new file, and began:

> *Most mornings at the Mile High Zen Buddhism Cultural Center on Colorado Boulevard are peaceful, calm, and transcendent. Just after sunrise this morning, however, the Buddhist community of several hundred participants experienced its worst trial to date as a two-alarm fire spread throughout its two-story center, leaving only its adjacent building intact. According to . . .*

My phone rang. I stared at the sentences I'd just written and tried to ignore the noise. Instead, it continued to annoy me until finally I couldn't concentrate and picked it up.

"Jonna Lightfoot MacLaughlin," I said with a short edge in my voice.

"Ms. MacLaughlin, it's Jedediah Sundae. I called you earlier and don't know if you got that message or not, so I wanted to check back in." I had gotten the message. He was the ex-Baptist who'd left a message just after "God." I simply hadn't had time to call him back.

"Mr. Sundae, yes, I did get your message, but you know what? I'm on deadline. Would you mind if I called you back? Say around 4 p.m.?" I reached for my pen to jot down his number.

"Well, this will just take a minute— " he began.

I rolled my eyes and interrupted, "I'd rather give you as much time as you need, so how about if I call you back in a few hours? What's your number again?" I waited.

No sound.

"Mr. Sundae?"

"It's not about the convention next week, just so you know. It's about something much more important."

That got my attention, since most Baptists thought convention was just shy of heaven. My computer stared at me as I heard the man cough.

"Sorry, but I still missed your number."

"Hmm. I'm sorry, but I'll have to call *you* back," he mumbled and hung up abruptly. I gulped my coffee, wondered what that was all about, and went back to the screen. I typed: "According to Fredd . . ."

The phone rang again.

"Oh, for Pete's sake!" I hollered. Hannah shot me a teal-raised eye.

"Jonna Lightfoot MacLaughlin."

This time it was Betty, the secretary at the Unity Church of Cherry Creek. We'd developed a friendly rapport during the weeks that her congregation had considered their divided future, and I liked her. Today, though, her voice was so shaky and tense I felt funny dropping the same request to her I'd just asked of Mr. Sundae. Instead I clicked on the "Unity" file on my computer and asked what I could do for her.

"It's more what you won't do," she said. She told me the board was meeting tonight, and there was a "very good chance" that the Unity Church might in fact stall its "divorce" and stay together. That night, they'd be discussing the same issues that had forced them to consider splitting in the first place: military support, organized peace rallies, and Girl Scout troops using their building.

"I think we'll finally be able to come to a consensus. Could you hold the story until tomorrow, just in case?" she whimpered slightly.

"God has smiled on you, Betty, because the story got bumped anyway," I said, typing in a few of her quotes, saving the document, and clicking it off.

"Oh?" She sounded both relieved and hurt.

"Yes, a Buddhist temple burned this morning, and I've got to get that story in."

"Terrific," she said, less shaky. Then she caught herself. "I mean, terrific about the story waiting, not terrific for the Buddhists."

"I'll say. Be glad you still have a building to meet in." I was winding the conversation down. She thanked me and hung up.

At exactly 3:58 p.m., I filed a 533-word story on Denver's Buddhist temple going up in flames. They say journalism is the first draft of history, and I felt both a twinge of satisfaction for capturing a piece of Buddhism's American dream on paper and a tug of sorrow that its nightmare had happened at all. I wondered how the dream would shape up from here.

By 5:25, Mr. Jedediah Sundae still had not called me back, and though I found his comments curious, they were not enough to cause me to stick around too much longer. I was tired and determined to get a good night's rest. I checked with Skip to see what edits he'd made on my story before I left, and as usual he'd made me look like a better writer than I really was. My stomach growled as I read the copy until I realized I'd never eaten my pita sandwich. I grabbed my lunch and drove to my apartment before I—or Skip—found something else to do at the office.

When I got home, I kicked off my clogs and collapsed, sprouts in hand, on my couch. I loved the quiet refuge of my living room—the bookshelf underneath my stereo, the photographs and paintings I'd collected at street fairs or thrift shops, the Goodwill floppy chair and footrest. I stared out the window of my second-floor apartment at nothing in particular as the sun set on the Denver skyline.

By the time I finished my dinner/lunch, I smacked my lips and got inspired. I scoured through my cupboards and found just enough ingredients for a batch of chocolate chip cookies. So I tossed them in the oven and breathed in their hypnotic aroma.

The magic of chocolate—in any form—is that it actually tastes better when you eat it *with* someone else, an experiment I had confirmed millions of times throughout my life. So I grabbed a plate and knocked on Mrs. Rodriguez's door across the hall in 5A.

Her face expanded when she saw me *and* the cookies. "Juana, you good girl!" She pulled me into her apartment, pointed to the spot on her couch beside where she'd been sitting, and got me a glass of milk. She was a compact woman whose English was better than my Spanish, but she had welcomed me to the building when I first moved in three years ago. We'd been friends ever since. Her long white hair still had a few black strands in it, and her face was filled with a lifetime of hardworking—but happy—lines. She loved her grandkids, bean burritos, Saturday night Mass at the Cathedral, and me.

Like two little girls, we munched through a half dozen cookies as the nightly news came across her tiny black-and-white TV. I took a sip of milk and was just putting down my glass when the story of the burning Buddhist temple came on. I was stunned by what I saw: I was being scooped by the local television station on a religion story! Unless it was a major scandal, the television news *never* covered religion.

Then my Dharma came on, sunburned and savvy, looking straight into the camera as the reporter asked him about what happened, the skeleton frame of the Center smoldering behind them. He gave the same answer to her that he had given to me, but the more I watched, the more I realized something wasn't quite right. There was a strange sparkle in his eye that did not match the grief of his words. He *sounded* distraught that his temple was in shambles behind him, but his face reminded me less of sorrow and more of mischief.

Mrs. Rodriguez squeezed my whole being when I said good night and strolled back to my apartment across the hall.

I crawled into my bed with the copy of Oswald Chambers' daily devotional *My Utmost for His Highest* my parents had given me for the Christmas before they left. The author's insights always made me feel like I'd just had a long, soothing spiritual bath.

And though his words on being devoted to Jesus lingered in my head the next morning, the image from the television news of the Dharma stayed front and center.

Even when I got to the office, that strange juxtaposition of the burning temple behind the sparkly monk wouldn't leave me alone. I dropped off a Ziploc bag of cookies on Skip's desk and Hannah's, grabbed a copy of the morning edition, and made a note on my to-do list for the day to call Freddy Stephano to ask about the investigation of the fire. Then I picked up the phone and heard the worst and the best voice mails I could get for a Wednesday morning.

"Jenny, it's me again. The world is doomed, and I am its only hope." This time "God's" voice was strained and gloomier than the last time he'd called, but he still made no reference to where he was holding his Saturday session. I gulped my coffee and called Frank Murphy. The Boulder detective ought to know about this guy, but again I got his machine, so I left a generic message asking him to call me back as soon as he could.

The second message made my spine tingle. I even had to set down my coffee. It was a beautiful, rich voice, and its melody carried the sincerity of a faith and gentlemanly-ness I'd always believed existed somewhere in the world. He said he was really glad to meet me yesterday and wondered if there was a time this afternoon I could finish the tour at the Catholic Outreach Center.

It was Terry Choyce, and my schedule was suddenly quite free.

::Chapter Three

No matter how much I liked to think of myself as a spiritual woman, sometimes only a cigarette had the power to calm my soul. This morning, I felt anxious. The combination of a cute Catholic, a dubious Buddhist, and a potentially cracked cult leader lurking in the Boulder Canyon kicked my nicotine cravings into high gear.

Since I was a little girl, my mother had told me I "internalized too many of the world's perplexities." And depending on her spiritual state at the time—this was pre-Presbyterianism—she'd sit me down on my yoga mat and help me "channel the dark vibes back from where they came," or "release the negative energy into the cosmos." As a nine- or ten-year-old, I could barely sit still, let alone channel or chant, so she'd just smile at her only daughter, kiss my curly head, and send me outside to play with my brothers and to "find my own way with Mother Earth guiding me."

When she became a "Bible-loving, grace-filled, prodigal daughter"—as she liked to call herself—my mother had offered daily prayers for me as well as Scripture-laden letters, both of which had the power to reduce my natural tendency to take on too much. They helped remind me for the ten thousandth time that there already was a Compassionate Maker of the Universe who was pretty good at running the world, so I didn't have to.

My brain knew I didn't need to worry. But this morning, as much as I *wanted* to believe, the spirit was weak, and the flesh was more than willing to indulge.

I sucked in a long slow drag of my Marlboro Light, closed my eyes, and silently apologized for liking—really liking—the taste of tobacco even when I knew what it might be doing to my lungs.

I leaned against the wall at the entrance of the *Dispatch,* ignoring the honks of traffic on the street, and turned my face toward the morning sun. I was lost in my smoky reverie, enjoying the image in my head of Terry Choyce while pushing out the weird footage of burning temples and roaming gurus. In another few hours, I would see Terry's gorgeous and holy face in real life, escorting me on a tour of his blessed building and looking more like my future husband with each step we took.

"And you call yourself religious!" The voice was prickly but playful. A distinctly feminine aroma floated toward me.

"Morning, Hannah X.," I said, without opening my eyes.

"I don't know why you do that. Those things are so nasty, stinkin' you all up and everything." Her passion was cause enough to lift my eyelids, and I laughed when I realized she was more concerned about how I smelled than if I died of lung cancer. I took a final drag, careful not to exhale onto her freshly perfumed self.

"Disgusting!" she said, punctuating her aromatic point with a wave across her nose. She shook her perfectly coifed head at me as if she were considering another scolding but then apparently thought otherwise. Her orange silk dress hung just above her knees and as usual, her pumps matched. So did her eye shadow and lipstick, though both were lighter shades that offset her African queen features. Scolding, I was sure, would have messed up something.

Instead, she turned my shoulder toward the building and led me inside. In the elevator, she pressed the "10" button and flicked the headline on the newspaper in her hand as if it was a fly.

"Nice job, Lightfoot. Buddhism goes page one," Hannah said with little emotion but enough for me to know she was proud of my story.

"Bittersweet. I hate the idea of fire, especially in peace centers. That's just wrong," I said. I glanced toward the numbers as they lit up the higher we went.

"You know what your problem is?" Hannah asked, her face suddenly inches from mine. Here came the scolding after all.

"Which one? I have hundreds."

"Today's. Your problem, Lightfoot, is that you've got too much of a conscience to be a hard-nosed, cynical journalist . . . like me."

Ding. The 10 was green and the elevator doors slid apart.

"That's funny," I said. "I thought a conscience might come in handy covering religion." Hannah whisked me out of the elevator and hurried down the hall. I struggled to keep up with the orange blur, who was by now a good ten yards ahead of me.

"It won't win you a Pulitzer, Sugar," she hollered back to me. Hannah tossed her bag on her desk as she rushed by, no doubt determined to get Skip's ear before the other reporters could. I watched her rocket into his office, swinging the door behind her and leaving a perfumed trail in the hall. She smelled good. She looked good. She *was* good.

I, on the other hand, reeked of nonorganic tobacco, had a frizzy hairstyle that never cooperated, and wore thrift-store outfits that told the whole world I had never outgrown the habit of shopping secondhand, which my "conscience" told me was not always such a bad thing in this crazy materialistic culture. At least my shoes matched each other. I shrugged and considered heading back downstairs for round two with my evil, smoking alter ego.

Too late. My phone was ringing, and I knew I needed to get moving, to get my mind off of the anxiety and into the work, onto something I could manage. I dropped into my chair, clicked on my computer, and answered my ringing phone all at the same time.

"Jonna Lightfoot MacLaughlin," I said as I reached for my coffee.

"Jedediah Sundae here. I don't want to waste your time, Miss, but I'm not sure I'll be able to call you again after this." *Ah, the stars must be aligned.* Another human besides me was having a tense morning.

"Mr. Sundae. I'm so glad you called back. I worried when you didn't." A lukewarm blend of Kona and hazelnut tempered my nerves. "I am sorry I didn't have time to talk with you last night. Crazy deadlines. But I'm free right now."

"I understand. Well, I'm glad to hear you're free now because a lot of folks in this town are not." His voice was serious and deep, with enough restrained emotion in it to make me pay attention.

"Excuse me?"

"Free. Certain so-called 'Christian' circles around town are holding people in bondage even as we speak. I ought to know."

I slumped in my chair at the sound of more bad news and took a full breath. When I let it go, I reached for a pen and notepad, flipped to a blank page, and scribbled: "No Freedom for Sunday."

"Tell me about it. It's S-U-N-D-A-Y, right? And we're on the record?"

"It's Sundae with an *e*, not a *y*. Yes. On the record. Get the word out there, Miss MacLaughlin, before more damage is done."

"Please call me Jonna. And what damage?"

Jedediah Sundae spent the next fifteen minutes talking while I held the phone between my chin and shoulder like a violin, listening and writing. He had left the East Coast and the American Baptist denomination about ten years ago—"too legalistic for my liking"—came west and joined Denver's "Into the Fields Fellowship," a nondenominational group of new churches that sounded increasingly like a denomination the more he talked. Into the Fields Fellowship—or IFF—used converted rock bands for its worship hours, and apparently the small group of leaders, mostly ex-ministers disappointed with other denominations, were determined to start their own countercultural evangelistic ministry. Only problem, according to Mr. Sundae with an *e,* was that they grew so quickly that after six years, Into the Fields Fellowship was now so much like the organized churches they'd been trying to avoid, you couldn't tell the difference. Except IFF was "out of control."

"Maybe I'm missing something, but isn't church growth a good thing?" I asked. I stretched out my fingers to keep them from stiffening, set down my pen, and took another sip of coffee.

"With all due respect, Joan, you *are* missing something. That's what's kept me up nights, wondering if I should call you." Now he really had me confused. I couldn't tell whether it was IFF's sudden popularity or my thick brain as "Joan the Journalist" that had forced him to lose sleep. Or something else altogether.

I was just about to correct him in the name department when he continued, his voice a blend of Southern televangelist and jazz DJ. "It's one thing if a church grows because people are genuinely worshiping God. It's another if they're told they'll only find him when they give all their money for the 'Lord's work in the Fellowship' and then *aren't* allowed to leave."

I paused to let the words sink in.

"Wow. Religious slavery?"

"You could call it that. The IFF leaders are taking hard-earned money from their people and telling them all sorts of new 'ministries' will come from it. Only problem is . . ." He hesitated and coughed. "Only problem is . . ."

Jed Sundae seemed unable to continue. Emotion clogged his throat, and he suddenly went silent. I heard a muffled sound, as if he was putting his hand over the phone, but I could tell what was happening. He'd begun to weep into the phone.

Something about hearing the sobs of a grown man—however stifled—always got to me. My eyes began to water as Jed Sundae paused and murmured something unintelligible in my ear. I felt a few knots twist in my stomach. Hannah had been right about me—I was a pushover, destined to blemish the stone-cold face of journalism.

I looked out the window at the Colorado sky, grabbed a tissue, and got a grip.

"I'm sorry for whatever is happening, Mr. Sundae. But I'll only be able to help if you answer a few more questions." He sniffled and mumbled an apology.

"No, *I'm* sorry. Didn't think it still got to me like this," he paused. "Yes, of course. Anything. What do you need to know?"

"For starters, your role?"

"I *was* a deacon in the first IFF church with Pastor Jeff Whitman. I really believed that this was the next great way to reach the world with hope. Boy, was I wrong. Dead wrong. I think that's all you'll need to know about *me.* What else?"

Okay. The man was not much for small talk. I could respect that.

"Well, how about other names, addresses?" I wrote frantically as Jedediah Sundae provided me the list of names, brief bios on each, and a couple of addresses for the three sites where IFF met each week for services. I made a note to visit this Sunday—noticing the pun—scribbled the phone numbers he blurted out, and assured him I'd look into it. If people were being robbed and enslaved in the name of Jesus, well, I couldn't ignore that. I knew it wasn't a rule for a good journalism to take a story personally, but I tended to feel invested in these types of misrepresentations.

Mr. Sundae spoke again, quietly, as if he didn't want someone to hear. "I'm glad we talked. But you need to know, they're not going to like this. They don't like to be challenged." And before I could ask him what he meant or how I could reach him, he thanked me for my time and hung up.

Immediately, I did a search on my computer for Into the Fields Fellowship. Nothing came up. I could understand how an old congregation—like the Presbyterian one I was a part of—was not yet web savvy. But it seemed to me, a six-year-old countercultural Christian group would use every modern means possible to recruit the nontraditional folks out there. High-tech was the ticket for these organizations. That was, unless they didn't want people to know they were out there, which would seem to go against their mission for attracting new believers. And unless Jedediah Sundae hadn't told me everything, which I was sure he hadn't . . . Come to think of it, hadn't he said no one was allowed to leave IFF? How then could he? What did he want me to find out?

The phone rang. I literally jumped two inches off my chair at the sound, knocking over my coffee mug, which thankfully was empty by now.

"Jonna Lightfoot MacLaughlin," I said, recovering from the intrusion and reaching again for my pen and pad.

"Frank Murphy here, Ms. MacLaughlin."

Frank Murphy? Sounded familiar, but for the life of me I could not remember who he was. I reached for some brainpower in my bag and bit off a piece of a chocolate chip cookie.

"You called?" he said.

I did? Oh, brother. I tapped my pen on the desk in a nervous rhythm and tried to remember. I began to write "F-R-A-N-K M-U-R" but my pen ran out of ink by the time I got to "P." I tossed it in the trash and stretched across to Hannah's desk for a new one.

"Yes, uh, thank you for calling me . . . back," I said, stalling. I was an easy read, though, and he laughed.

"Boulder County Detective's office? You left me a message this morning? Hey, how's Skip these days? Good grief, I haven't seen that old bag of bones in a couple of years." His voice was friendly. In fact, he sounded more like a dentist you were visiting for the first time trying to make you comfortable than a detective, about the exact opposite of what you'd expect to hear from a man whose daily job probably was not pretty.

"Of course! Sorry about that. It's been a little strange around here this morning," I said, clicking on my computer file titled, "'God' in the Canyon."

"No problem. Strange is normal routine around my office. What can I do you for?"

I told him about the e-mails and messages "God" had left me, about Skip's insistence that I call to alert the Boulder County

Police, and about the general uneasiness I was feeling about this guy. I told him I had worked on a few other cult-leader stories in Boulder, but they all seemed pretty harmless. There was something creepy, though, about this message from "God."

"Yup. This *is* important information. You've done the right thing. I'll tell our officers and put our Saturday morning shift on it," he said with the same kind of emotion I'd imagine he'd have if he were talking about filling a cavity. "Hey, forward me the e-mail from this guy, too, will ya? That'd be good for us to have here. And tell Skip I said he owes me one."

"Will do. Thanks, Detective." I hung up, feeling a few pounds lighter from the morning's burdens, that was, until I ate two more of last night's cookies, the last of my stash, though I did eye the bag I'd left for Hannah. At least these were justifiable pounds.

Chocolate, I had long believed, was good for human consumption, full of antioxidants that fought off every type of disease and depression, and full of the kind of nutrients that kept blood pressure down. So of course, I was thrilled when an old college roommate sent me the recent studies confirming the fact that regular intake of dark chocolate even reduced the risk of heart attacks. That was good enough for me. Never mind that it was the chocolate industry that funded the research, my brother Matt liked to remind me whenever we got into it.

"Hey," I'd say. "We all have our vices."

I just about ran into Hannah as I walked down the hall to get another cup of coffee.

"Treat waiting for you on your desk," I said about the cookies I'd left for her.

Since I had just eaten the last of mine, I figured hers would be fair game if I didn't tell her they were waiting for her.

"Whatever," she said, tossing the word in the air along with her hand as she hurried by.

I stopped still, letting the tornado pass. Obviously, her meeting with Skip hadn't gone as well as she'd hoped. Sometimes the two went at it when she was hot on a story's trail, especially when it concerned Denver's black mayor and black leaders.

Not that Hannah wanted to defend them—just the opposite. She was one of those "Affirmative-Action-Was-A-Great-Thing-Whose-Time-Has-Gone" kind of woman who wanted to be judged on the content of her character—as well as her stories—and not on the color of her skin. She made no bones about acknowledging the pioneers of the past, but today's was a different playing field, she liked to tell anyone who'd listen, not exactly level though it was on its way to seriously flat.

Because of this, she tended to be harder on minorities than Skip was. He was the one who often had to reel her back in to keep perspective. Judging from her face and the whirlwind she left as she disappeared down the hall, I guessed she'd been a bit "reeled." It was that kind of morning for everybody.

Which was confirmed again once I arrived at the coffee machine and noticed the black crust on the bottom of the pot. The last desperate reporter had claimed the dregs and failed to make a new brew while also forgetting to turn off the machine.

"Of course," I said to an empty employee room and went to work. I threw out the old filter and grinds, put in a new batch as well as the replacement pot, and clicked the *brew* button. This was one of those ingenious machines hooked up somehow to a water pipe so you never had to fill it with water. Every day it worked I deemed it a miracle—it was my right as a religion reporter.

Besides, the smell of freshly brewed coffee was transcendent. While the pot filled, I stood at the white Formica counter and flipped through the morning paper to see what my reading options were.

Then I did what any honest writer would do: I reread my story before I read anyone else's:

> *Most mornings at the Mile High Zen Buddhism Cultural Center on Colorado Boulevard are peaceful, calm, and transcendent. Just after sunrise this morning, however, the Buddhist community of several hundred participants experienced its worst trial to date . . .*

I stopped and looked up at the black gold filling the glass coffeepot. Something Freddy Stephano had said to me yesterday suddenly dropped into my memory: No one had been in the Center the morning of the fire, though most mornings, all sorts of "enlightened" motion were filling the place—classes, meditation, yoga. It seemed strange—and awfully convenient—that not one "awakened soul" had been anywhere near the building when the fire started and spread. And why had the temple's Dharma smirked so on the news last night? Did he know something about the fire he hadn't told me?

I made a mental note to call Freddy about the investigation that afternoon and then remembered what else was in store for me: Terry Choyce. Maybe the cosmic alignment—or at least the Almighty—was smiling on me after all.

"Well, well, our resident psychic. What's the news from the other world, Lightfoot?" Tony Thompson was helping himself to the coffee I was still waiting for.

I shook my head at the veteran sports reporter. "I have good sources who say your name just came up in a séance," I said, pushing my cup under the drip. "The Ouija board does not lie, Tony." He reached across me for the sugar and cream, laughing so hard that the paunch bulging over his belt jiggled. I'd heard once that Tony had been a decent athlete in his younger days. Now his forty-year-old body seemed allergic to any kind of movement other than getting up from his desk for coffee.

Ever since Skip made me religion reporter, Tony had given me a hard time. He just didn't get it. To him, the only news worth knowing included scoreboards and game times. To him, athletes, coaches, and umpires were miles above preachers, priests, and rabbis on the spiritual food chain.

"I'll put ten bucks on the fact that more Denverites read my story on Coors Field's new hot dog distributors than your 'thing' on the Buddhists." He was smirking now, almost guzzling his white coffee as if it were a pint of ale, maybe hoping it was. Tony's hair was as tousled as his blue cotton shirt was wrinkled, and I secretly wondered if sports reporters were born this way or if some old jock-god made the stereotype something to aspire to.

"Hey, I've always said Denver sports fans are way more religious than all our Catholics and Protestants combined," I said as I picked up my cup, hoping to get out of this conversation. "Besides, Tony, you have better things to do with ten bucks. Why, you could even put it in the offering plate this Sunday!"

He rolled his eyes, laughed again, and was just about to strike back when someone screamed down the hall. "Thompson, phone call! Waranowski is being traded to the Jets!"

"What the . . . !"

I was surprised—and slightly impressed—at the creative litany of profanities that Tony strung together and spewed rapid-fire in my direction. Then as if he'd suddenly become aware of the paper's religion reporter standing a few feet from him, he hollered, "No offense, Lightfoot!" and took off down the hall. It was the first time I'd ever seen Tony move so fast, jiggling and splattering white liquid behind him in a Hansel and Gretel trail. I had no doubt he would find his way back to the coffee and vending machines.

"Let's do this again, Tony!" I hollered. He raised his hand straight in the air to me just before he turned a corner out of sight.

I wiped the counter off where he had spilled, picked up my cup, and strolled back to the more peaceful meadows of the newsroom. I could be just as delusional about my job as the sports guys.

By the time I was ready to drive to the Catholic Outreach Center, I had polished off two more cups of coffee, nibbled on a bit of leftover salad I'd actually remembered to bring in this morning so I could feel sort of healthy, watched Hannah storm off to City Hall, attempted to tame my hair twice in the ladies' room, and read a few press releases. One was from the Southern Baptist Convention, which was coming to town next week for its annual conference and display of nice manners and hairstyles. Another from Betty the secretary, explaining that the Unity Church of Cherry Creek, in an emergency meeting last night, was "re-renegotiating" after all and trying to re-reconcile, so no split was imminent . . . yet. And the Arvada Community Methodist Church had e-mailed me the entire detailed list of who had signed up to bring what dish for their potluck community dinner this Saturday—just in case I was tempted to reconsider. Suddenly I remembered I had a dinner date with my brother, sister-in-law, and Mr. Single American Literature Professor. I regretfully declined the Methodists.

Maybe blind dates were redemptive after all.

Skip was wearing a forest green suit today and was deep into his computer screen by the time I poked my head into his office to tell him where I was going.

"Good news and bad news, Boss," I said, trying to lighten the mood in case Hannah's meeting had altered his normally calm disposition. He simply glanced up at me as if I were delivering his favorite ice cream, and everything in me wished I were.

"Lightfoot! Loved the cookies. You're too good to me," he said, smiling over the now-empty bag he picked up from behind the pile of magazines on the corner of his desk. "The bad news first," he said.

"Strange call today about a nondenominational group that's become a denomination and that, as one disheartened ex-member claims, is a big fat fraud." I tapped on the corner of his desk with my fingers as I spoke. "He gave me lots to check out . . . on the record."

"That's the bad news? I wish some of your colleagues could get sources like that on the record," he said, sitting up straighter. "And?"

"And I'm on my way to see a gorgeo—I mean a generous Catholic lay leader whose after-school program just might be my ticket to inspiration. An inspiring *story,* that is." I felt the curse of the Irish red fill my cheeks as the words fell from my mouth. Skip's smile grew and he leaned back in his chair, putting his elbows behind his head, reminding me of a big green bow tie.

"Well, you take real good notes, okay, Miss MacLaughlin?" I could spot an exit a mile away.

It was another spectacular Colorado summer day by the time I'd pulled up to the Outreach Center in the Five Points urban neighborhood. A cloudless sky, eighty-five-degree dry heat, slight breeze moving across the trees in the park. Some days, I missed living in the mountains, but the city and I were getting more and more familiar with each other. The place—and the adventure of urban living—was growing on me.

Terry's tall, svelte body stood on the steps as he talked with a priest. I looked at my reflection in the rearview mirror, wondering if some supernatural makeover might have happened on the way over. No such luck. I shrugged and went to plan B: Be myself. It was all I had to go on.

"Lordhavemercy," I pleaded, climbing out of the car and walking toward the finely sculpted male on the steps. The priest saw me coming and waved my way as he headed down the street toward the bus stop.

Terry looked toward me. He was wearing dark blue gym shorts, sneakers, and a plain white T-shirt, as if he'd just finished a workout.

"Jonna!" He spoke my name as though it were a song, and I had the sudden urge to ask him to sing it again.

"Please excuse my appearance," he said, extending his hand. I took it. "I just came back from a jog around City Park—the day was too beautiful to pass up, don't you think? Do you like jogging?" Tiny beads of sweat glistened on his forehead, and he looked just as stunning as he did yesterday, maybe more so.

"Jogging? Oh, I love it!" It wasn't a complete lie—I did love jogging, especially when someone other than me was doing it. I'd done a lifetime of exercise on the college ski team, so I figured I was excused. I pulled out my notepad and pen in hopes of changing the subject. "How about that tour?"

He pulled the door open for me, and we entered the lobby of the Center. Blown-up photographs of dozens of Latino and African-American children lined the walls. Funny, I hadn't noticed them when I'd visited before, maybe because I'd been looking at another face.

Below each photograph were the first names of the children in the pictures, most of whom were smiling or hamming it up for the camera. A large brass crucifix of Jesus hung in the center of it all, and the words, "Suffer the little children to come to Me" had been printed in a banner underneath it. The Catholic Outreach Center had a clear mission, and the images in its foyer made it an inviting place.

Terry pointed to the children in the photos by name, beaming over each of them with big-brother pride. Then he led me into a computer lab and explained how he'd gotten involved in the Center through a lawyer friend of his named Maddison Jones. He explained how his boss at the law firm where he worked was allowing him to be here two days a week as community outreach and how they'd raised money to buy the best equipment possible.

"These kids deserve a chance to get ahead," he said. "But when I visited the local elementary school, they didn't have a single computer." He shook his blond head in disbelief and continued. "This way, kids get high-tech training *and* spiritual input. Seems like a good combination, don't you think?"

I did think. And told him so. Then I went on to tell him that one of my first assignments at the *Dispatch* had been covering a local school board in Five Points, and I realized then that there didn't seem to be such a thing as "separate but equal" education, even in the twenty-first century.

The corners of his mouth turned slightly up, and his eyes gripped mine. "Are you Catholic?" he asked softly.

I suddenly considered converting. Until I remembered the faces of my senior citizen friends at Capitol Presbyterian Church, as well as my brother and sister-in-law who were members there before I was, and I felt a sting of loyalty.

"Presbyterian," I responded. "But I've always thought Christians have a lot more in common than they do differences, don't *you* think?"

Terry's face filled out into a beautiful wide smile, the kind that pushed his eyes upward into small half moons. He nodded in agreement at me and cupped my elbow as he led me on the rest of our tour. By the time we had seen the gym, a few other classrooms, offices, and a small kitchen, I had three brochures in my hand, a volunteer packet, and a firm invitation from Terry to come back when the kids were there.

"I think my editor is going to want photos for the story, if that's okay. How about if I come back tomorrow with a photographer?" Terry didn't have to know that *Dispatch* policy did not require reporters to accompany photographers, nor that Friday afternoons were tough to schedule photo shoots. He just needed to know I'd be back. And I would.

I couldn't help but whistle the old Sunday school song, "Jesus Loves the Little Children" in the car as I drove back to the *Dispatch*. It felt as good as the summer breeze to find a story that showed something positive was happening in the religious community that also improved city life a bit. And I was certainly not complaining that it happened to be run by a young, handsome, *and* devoted lay leader.

As Thursday afternoons went, this had turned into a good one after all.

When I got back to my desk, I decided to follow up on Jedediah Sundae's story and see what I could find out about his claims before calling it a night. I wasn't expecting the pastors he'd named to oblige me considering his accusations, but when I punched the numbers on my phone to call Pastor Jeff Whitman, the founding leader of Into the Fields Fellowship, I wasn't prepared for the response I got.

"I'm sorry, Miss MacLaughlin, but I don't recall anyone by that name. And Pastor Jeff's not in now," the secretary said in a voice full of sincerity. "Please let me know if I can be of any help in the future."

The second pastor gave me almost the same response, and though the third was out of the office, his secretary told me she was sure the name Jedediah Sundae "didn't ring any bells."

In terms of weirdness, the day was coming full circle. I typed Jed's name in our Denver database that listed all area residents. The computer came up with no matches.

It seemed Mr. Jedediah Sundae did not exist.

::Chapter Four

I wiggled my way into my favorite corner booth at The Pub of Saint Agnes, the table right next to the window and just across from the portable air conditioner, and pulled my notepad out of my bag. On hot July days or frigid January nights, Saint Agnes's had become a sanctuary for me. It was an unusually quiet bar, which probably had something to do with its décor: fake stained-glass windows, church pews, rosaries, and pictures of young Agnes bearing a palm leaf or holding a lamb that hung prominently on each wall. Locals had never really taken to the idea of drinking a beer in the shadow of the young Christian martyr. I guessed it wasn't easy guzzling a Coors—brewed just about ten miles away—when the patron saint of bodily purity was staring at you.

I, however, often felt inspired by Saint Agnes's story, which Michael MacNickels, or Mick, the owner of The Pub, had had scripted in a fancy old-English font, framed, and placed on the wall a few feet away from the dartboard. Apparently, during the reign of the Roman emperor—the one who had ordered the last great persecution of Christians—Agnes converted to Christianity and then decided not to marry. She was prepared to die for the sake of her faith and her virginity as the "bride of Christ" rather than become the wife of some big-shot Roman prefect. So she was martyred at age twelve, buried outside of Rome, and enshrined centuries later at the Basilica of St. Agnes Outside the Walls. Agnes's convictions had been inspiring young maidens—like me—ever since, but she obviously wasn't too good at drawing a bar crowd. Save the possibility of divine provision, I often wondered how The Pub stayed in business.

Mick, who'd grown up in Scotland celebrating the feast of Saint Agnes each January, liked the idea of opening a bar in her honor, even when friends tried to convince him that Denverites weren't too good at mixing religion with drinking. These were people of the West, after all, who had four very distinct seasons and therefore liked things neatly compartmentalized: religion on Sundays, work nine to five Monday through Friday, and drinking or sports—and in some cases, the sport of drinking—in between. That didn't bother Mick, though, who bought the old Masonic Lodge building in the Capitol Hill neighborhood and told people Saint Agnes was going to "redeem the place."

To keep with the theme, he hung Scottish poems written in that same fancy font, usually with images of the young saint right beside them, on the walls near the bathrooms and over the bar:

Saint Agnes, that's to lovers kind,
Come, ease the trouble of my mind.
and
Agnes sweet, and Agnes fair,
Hither, hither, now repair;
Bonny Agnes, let me see
The lad (or lass) who is to marry me.

It was a strange combination for a bar—beer, whiskey, church pews, and Scottish verses paying homage to one of the four great virgin martyrs of the Christian Church. Most of my colleagues at the *Dispatch* wouldn't come near the place; they said it gave them the creeps, even if Mick did serve the best shepherd's pie and corn chowder in town. Instead, they'd wander off to the Broncos Sports Lounge in LoDo—which stood for Lower Downtown, Denver's version of New York's SoHo—or to Buffalo Bill's Bar and Grill a few blocks east of the capitol on Colfax Avenue. Even Hannah avoided The Pub of Saint Agnes, but she claimed it had more to do with maintaining her figure than it did the atmosphere. I believed her. For me, however, this was the ideal place to retreat from the noise of the news and find a little perspective.

I asked Mick for a bowl of chowder and a half pint of Fat Tire—a sweet lager from a local microbrewery—and studied my notes. Jedediah Sundae with an *e* had been so clear and passionate on the phone—how could the leaders he'd named not have any memory of the man? Why wouldn't our own database come up with any of his records? Accusing a church group of fraud was no small thing, but it was a moot point if I couldn't confirm my source really was, well, a source.

I let it go for now, flipped back a few pages, and reread the notes I'd taken when the Buddhist Cultural Center was burning. The Dharma seemed determined to teach me the Buddhist precepts but not too intent on explaining what had happened that morning when they lost most of their temple, the morning no one was in the building. I was missing something; I knew that. And the more I pictured him on the television news last night, the less I believed him—though I had no viable reason to think a Buddhist monk would lie to me.

Mick set down my dinner, smiled at me, and nodded. His hair was a thick red mop, his eyebrows and mustache identical in color and mass. He was a tall man whose belly looked as if he sampled just about everything he made in the kitchen, which he might have, given that he was the chef, bartender, manager, and waiter of The Pub.

In an odd way, I considered Mick a friend, though we rarely exchanged words other than what I was going to have for dinner. Maybe it was because his hair always seemed less cooperative than mine, which of course, gave me a particular fondness for the guy. Besides, I was a sucker for those squiggly kindness lines that curved around any man's eyes. They reminded me of my dad's, whose face did so much smiling through the years that his skin sometimes looked like the boys in a high school play who drew pencil lines around their eyes to look like men. Mick's face was kind too. And he never asked me a single thing about my work—which was a good quality for a bartender and another reason I liked coming here. I knew I could sit and think in this holy little bar, without a noisy newsroom to interrupt my contemplative moment. I knew Mick and The Pub of Saint Agnes were dependable, and at the end of this strange Thursday, I wanted something I could count on.

Saint Agnes stared at me from the wall, and I took that as a reminder. I closed my eyes, bowed my head, and said aloud the mealtime grace my parents had taught us: "Hear this prayer from grateful sinners as we thank you for our dinners. Amen." The Fat Tire tasted sweet on my lips, the chowder a little thicker than usual. I flipped open my cell phone and pushed the speed dial. A firm but tired voice answered.

"Matthew BigBear MacLaughlin, this is your lucky day. I'm drinking a Fat Tire, about to eat some fine chowder, and hoping that my big brother and his lovely wife can be spontaneous and join me." I slurped my soup into the phone for effect.

"At Saint Agnes's, are you, lass?" He loved doing his *Braveheart* brogue. "Well, me beautiful wife, Marrrry, is working tonight at the library, but I rrreckon I've just finished here. I'll be there in five if you'll orrrder me the same grrrreat grrrrog you're drinkin'."

I grinned at my brother's impersonation and waved to Mick. The Pub was not crowded tonight, as usual. Only a few men in UPS uniforms stood at the bar, and an older couple sat at a table near the door. Two college-age guys in baggy jeans and Rockies T-shirts threw darts next to a painting of Saint Agnes. I sat alone by the window, watching the city whirl by, thinking of the nonexistent people I'd talked to on the phone and the tenets of Buddhism. Mick strolled over, picking up empty glasses on his way.

"Matt's on his way, Mick. He'll have the same," I said, noticing how green his eyes looked as the daylight faded outside. He nodded his red head at me and then at my half-empty glass as if the motion were a question.

"No, thanks, one's my limit. Any more and I'd be sleeping over," I said. He chuckled a laugh that moved his belly up and down, and then he walked to the kitchen as though he were taking an evening stroll in a Scottish garden. Though Mick always asked if I wanted a second round, I'd never been much of a drinker. Growing up, my parents occasionally enjoyed a glass of red wine at dinner—for medicinal purposes, of course, or to enhance a flavor from a particularly favorite vegetarian dish. They usually offered my brothers and me some as well, for the same reasons. But if my parents thought television killed a kid's brain cells, they were convinced anything harder than cabernet killed your emotions.

"There's so much to *feel* in life. Why numb yourself with

that stuff?" they'd lecture us, sometimes in unison, which, given the stories they'd tell us of their pot-smoking flower-power days in San Francisco, always made me a little confused. Nonetheless, their passion for "feeling," and the fact that the good Lord never gave me a taste for anything harder than lemonade, kept me uninterested in drinking throughout my teen years.

Thankfully, it spilled over into college life as well, earning me the nickname, D. D.—Designated Driver—because my friends knew I couldn't stomach the 13 percent stuff they were downing like candy. I'd just shrug at their increasingly silly behavior and revel in the money—and dignity—I'd save by not joining them. By then, I had come to believe what my dad always said about me: My taste buds were just like my soul—too sensitive for anything hard or tough. In his world, that was a very good thing.

But when microbreweries came onto the scene a few years ago, creating flavors I actually liked—cherry, licorice, raspberry—his perspective and my sensitive tastes were slightly challenged. In fact, for the first time in my nearly three decades of living, my no-drink habit began to change, due in part to my discovery of The Pub of Saint Agnes and Fat Tire. I became faithful to both on Thursday nights, just as I was to Capitol Presbyterian on Sunday mornings, partly because I found The Pub of Saint Agnes a fitting place for a reporter who covered religion, and partly because one pint of Fat Tire was a refreshing diversion from anything mystical or depressing.

Halfway through my chowder, Matt's face was pressed against the window and contorted so that he reminded me of a robber with pantyhose on his head. I rolled my eyes and shook my head, holding up eight fingers as though I were a judge at a skating contest. He flashed all ten fingers at me like a neon sign, jumped up and down, and then bolted inside.

My eldest brother never failed to live up to his middle name—BigBear. He hugged me so hard I could feel every ounce of air pop out of me, as well as my last bite of corn chowder. I wiped my mouth, took a gulp of my beer to wash the taste back down, and pointed to the seat across from me, though Matt was already settling in.

"That was worth a ten and you know it." He leaned his head back against the wood as if it were a pillow and smiled. Since the last time I had seen him—Sunday morning at church to be exact—he'd apparently lost his razor. His chin and jaw were well past a five o'clock shadow.

"Going natural, are we?" I rubbed my chin to reinforce my observation. Mick strolled over with chowder and a pint for Matt, nodded at my brother, and walked back to his bar. Matt held up his index finger signaling for me to hold that thought. Then he closed his eyes and said, "Hear this prayer from grateful sinners as we thank you for our dinners."

"Amen," I agreed. He took about three gulps and then answered my question.

"I was actually going for an Andrea Bocelli look. More artsy, don't you think?" Foam covered the top of his lip and turned some of his mustache yellow, reminding me more of a rugby player than an opera star. We mirrored a smile at each other. It was always good to see my brother.

"I wouldn't throw away the razor just yet, Big Brother," I said as we slurped chowder from our fat, wide spoons. "What's new?"

"Nothing is ever new in the world of American history, which can be a problem." He stared at his glass as though it were a crystal ball. He ran his fingers back and forth across his curly hair, pinched his eyebrows forward, and shook his head at me. I took another sip as he continued, "Honestly, Jon, each semester I seem to get more discouraged, and my students seem to get slightly more clueless. This morning in class I asked if anyone knew what distinguished the Reconstruction Era in American history, and one girl raised her hand and said, 'Botox and breast implants?'"

Fat Tire flew from my mouth and into my chowder. We laughed so hard our pews rattled, and the UPS guys looked over at us. Ever since I could remember, my brother had been fascinated by American history and had been able to convince me of both its importance and its fun. When we were little, he'd made our brothers and me act out stories of Native Americans helping the settlers in the West and then getting rounded up onto reservations. He'd insisted we memorize Frederick Douglass's abolition speeches and Susan B. Anthony's lectures on women's suffrage while we took turns pretending to be the crowds who were listening. In our family, it was always the outcasts who were the heroes, so I hated the times I had to play the cavalry or the presidents.

The older we got, the more Matt's love affair with history deepened. Now that he was a tenured professor at Denver College, he took it personally if his students didn't also fall in love with the terrible and noble past of the U.S. of A., but not so personally he couldn't laugh at himself or his students. My brother was good about laughing, scheduling it in several times a day.

When our snorting finally subsided and the delivery guys at the bar went back to their bottles, Matt spotted my notebook on the table and knocked on it as if it were a door. He wanted to know what was inside.

"What's new with *you,* Lois Lane?" he asked, pushing my notepad toward me. He took a few more swings of his brew and waited for my answer.

I sighed and scraped the bottom of my bowl for another spoonful.

"Oh, you know. The usual weird world of religion." I looked out the window, wondering if Matt would bite, until he thumped a packet of sugar against my arm.

"Okay, okay," I said. "Ever heard of Into the Fields Fellowship?"

"Hmm. I think our neighbors across the street went to their services, before they moved to Dallas. Pretty big Christian group, isn't it?"

"Right. A nondenominational group that's formed a couple of churches, I guess. Well, I got a strange call from an ex-member who had been involved with the first one, and now is calling Into the Fields Fellowship a scam, ripping off members left, right, and center." I pushed our empty pint glasses to the corner of the table and took a sip of water from what seemed a miniature glass in comparison. Mick wandered over to collect them as Matt ordered a second beer. He was always better at drinking than I was—a less sensitive soul, though I knew he rarely pushed his limits.

"A church ripping folks off—that's pretty heavy stuff. Have you checked it out?" Matt reached into his shirt pocket, grabbing his wiry glasses and pushing them onto his nose, giving him his professorial, albeit shaggy-beard, look after all.

"That's the problem. The source seemed upset enough by what was happening, but when I called the three pastors he'd accused, well, they said they'd never heard of the guy. And get this—" I paused as Mick set down Matt's second pint—"I looked for him on the *Dispatch* system and couldn't find a thing. No name, no address, no phone, nothing."

"What do you mean—he's nonexistent?"

"Exactly." I tapped my fingers on the table and reached for the spoon, hoping I'd missed a drop of chowder in my bowl. I hadn't. Just like Jedediah Sundae with an *e*, there was nothing there.

"There's got to be an explanation. Who knows how many invisible men there've been throughout the centuries? We call it selective history—where the powers that be provide only the information they want the people to hear, and then conveniently leave out all the rest. It's how the great American myth was made." This thought must have created quite a thirst for my brother, as he chugged half the glass in the next few seconds. I watched him guzzle his drink, studied his hairy chin, and considered what he'd said. If his theory was true, the IFF leaders had some explaining to do.

I scribbled a few notes on my tablet, reached into my purse, and pulled out a twenty and a ten-dollar bill. Mick saw my motion and brought over the check.

"Hey, nice job on the Buddhist story, by the way. It must have been terrible for them," Matt said, reaching into his jeans pocket for his wallet. "Let me treat tonight, Jon. Mary and I are worried you're not saving enough money."

"I'm not. But considering I make as much money you rake in each month as Mr. Big-Professor, I think I can manage," I said, handing Mick the money without looking at the check he'd given me.

"She always gets her way, Mick," Matt said, looking up at the tall red-headed man who stood over us. Mick chuckled as he wiped off our table and turned toward the kitchen. Matt pulled today's *Dispatch* from his backpack. He unfolded it to the first page where the picture of the Dharma and the Cultural Center in flames behind him beamed at us.

"Tsk, tsk, just more bad press for the religion world, isn't it?" he said, shaking his head at the story.

"Yeah, but something's not quite right there, either, Matt."

He looked up at me.

"Uh-oh. It's that gut-level, intuitive woman thing coming out, isn't it?" He pushed his glasses closer to his eyes and suddenly thought of something else.

"Hey, remember when we were Buddhists? Mark and Luke both wanted to shave their heads . . . like Dad . . . but I had a crush on Arlene Wiggins, and I knew the most popular girl in the sixth grade would never like a bald boy, no matter how much good karma I gave her . . . ?"

"Arlene Wiggins was not the most popular girl in the class, was she? I thought she was kinda weird. Didn't she wear a ski mask to school?" I asked.

"She was just getting ready for ski practice. Besides, she *was* the most popular girl . . . to me. I thought that mask was sort of . . . sexy." My brother's cheeks turned a mild shade of pink, and he glanced over at the painting of Saint Agnes. He had always been a hopeless romantic. I patted his wrist as though he were a patient in a hospital wanting to get better.

"Seriously, what's up with our Buddhist brothers?"

"Seriously, I don't know. I have a call in to the fire investigator—or at least I think I do." I picked up my pad and looked at my to-do list. *Call Freddy Stephano* was not yet crossed off—but I wasn't sure if that was because I had called him and forgotten to cross him off or if it was one of many follow-up calls I still needed to make. I might have been born with a sensitive soul, but my eldest brother had gotten the organizational skills.

"I mean, I'm going to call him tomorrow." I scribbled *Stephano* in big letters on my notepad and threw it in my bag.

We walked out into the mild Denver evening. The sky was at that in-between stage—dark purple and pale black—and a few tiny stars had begun to sparkle above the city skyline. Matt had locked his bicycle to the bus stop sign, and I stood beside a few older Mexican women who were waiting for their bus while my brother prepared his own ride. Helmet on, chain wrapped around his seat, backpack in place, Matt walked his mountain bike down the sidewalk with me toward my car. His bike was his transportation everywhere, and Denver's many bike paths sometimes made it possible for him to get around much quicker than if he were driving. Plus, he had indefinitely loaned his old car to his little sister when I first arrived a couple years ago.

"Still running okay?" he said, tapping the hood of his Datsun with the kind of affection guys usually had for their cars, one I could never quite understand.

"Good enough for me," I answered, looking at the traffic on the street and worrying about whether the cars would see him in the dark. "You're going to be okay riding home, right?"

He reached up to the top of his helmet and clicked on a small, flashing red light he'd attached.

"Course I will." He leaned over and kissed my cheek. "I'll call you when I get home, okay? And hey, we'll see you Saturday night, right?"

Oh, yeah. Saturday's blind date. I suddenly wanted a cigarette, but if I lit up now, I would also get a lecture. In the best girly voice I could muster, I said, "Oohh, I've got an appointment tomorrow to get my nails AND hair done."

He glared at me.

"Aw, Jon, he's a nice guy. We're just having dinner. Think of it as four brilliant adults enjoying a meal together, okay?" His brown eyes formed the same squiggly kindness lines that my father's had, and I relaxed a little.

"Okay, okay. Hugs to Mary!" I watched him ride off as I started my car. I told God that he had better get my brother home safely or I would come back to The Pub of Saint Agnes on a daily basis—and we both knew that would be a dangerous thing.

Then I whispered that I could not, would not, imagine life without my BigBear.

By the time I got home, the night sky had faded into the color of tar—not quite black and not quite gray. A few summer clouds had begun to form, so I couldn't see any stars. As I walked from the car toward my apartment building, I looked up at the night, but my eyelids felt heavy. The Fat Tire and the week's events were taking their toll.

When I turned the key to my apartment door, I almost stepped on the plate of brownies Mrs. Rodriguez had left for me on the floor. My phone was ringing. I picked up the plate and rushed inside.

"I'm home, Little Sis." Matt's voice was light. That was by far the fastest answer to prayer I'd had in a while. Maybe I should do that more often.

"Too bad for you. I just found a stash of brownies at my door."

"See? You are spoiled. Well, I just found a gorgeous brunette at my door." I heard Mary in the background, laughing at her husband.

"Does your wife know?" I teased, dropping my bag on the couch. "Thanks for calling, Matt."

"No problem. Gotta go—I'm about to be seduced by . . ." The phone clicked and I hung up, smiling. Mary was a very lucky woman.

Luckier than I'd ever be.

Where were my cigarettes? I shut the door, bit into a brownie, and scrounged through my bag for my Marlboro Lights. When I found them, I glanced at my answering machine, but the light was not blinking. No calls. Again. I struck a match and lit my cigarette. At least my professional life was busy.

I spent the next hour or so finishing most of the brownies and the last chapter of an Agatha Christie novel I'd checked out from the downtown library. Just as I turned to set down the book, I noticed a rank smell floating from the kitchen. I walked in and realized that I hadn't taken out the trash since last week. In fact, it had begun to grow something. So I snatched the bag out of the can, tied it, and walked toward the door. I stopped when I passed my reflection in the mirror on the wall.

Why was I still single? Maybe I *should* cut my hair. That would help me look . . . better. Maybe I should get Hannah to give me some tips on makeup. Maybe I should go to the gym more than once a week or pray more for my future husband or take up jogging like Terry Choyce.

Terry Choyce. I'd see him again tomorrow afternoon. I'd skip breakfast, maybe lunch, and wear something nice.

My mind was lost in tomorrow's meeting at the Catholic Outreach Center when I realized I had found my way instinctively to the huge garbage bins in the alley behind our building. I sighed, tossed the kitchen stink overboard, and turned to go back inside. But when I did, I froze. Spray painted on the wall of our building in thick silver strokes were the words, "The WorlD is dOOMeD, GoD was HerE and He WANTS YOUU!"

Though the air was hot, a chill burst through my bones. I shot back up to my apartment, grabbed a pen and paper, and came back to the alley to copy the handwriting on the wall exactly as it appeared. But I scribbled quickly, very quickly, before heading back upstairs where I slammed my door and locked it.

::Chapter Five

The morning sun was already fierce when I walked out of my apartment just before eight, making it feel more like high noon than the crack of dawn. Strange dreams of walking snowmen and stinky werewolves had interrupted my sleep, and this Friday morning felt more like the day after a college ski race than the end of a typical workweek. My body was slow, my head tired.

Mr. Donald Fink, our building maintenance man, was out sweeping the sidewalk by the time I got across the street where I had parked Matt's car. I dug for my keys in the bottom of my bag and pushed them into the driver's door. The handle jiggled but the door didn't budge. I looked down at the black T-shaped lock inside and realized I had just locked the door instead of opening it, which meant it was unlocked when I first came over, which meant I'd forgotten to lock it the night before. I sighed. Considering my alley fright, I made a conscious effort to lock my car door at all times from now on, even if the only things in it were a few past issues of the *Dispatch* in the backseat.

"Mornin', Mr. Fink," I hollered, glancing over the roof of the car when I finally opened the door. He stopped sweeping when he heard my voice, leaned on the broom, and nodded my way while studying his work on the sidewalk. "You're starting early today," I said.

Mr. Fink was in his midsixties, a little man, maybe five foot four, and one of the few people I knew who wasn't considerably taller than I was. Long-time neighbors like Mrs. Rodriguez told me he'd been the maintenance man on our block since anyone could remember. He could fix everything from a refrigerator to a light switch, though I had yet to get him to come by to stop my showerhead from leaking.

His nearly bald head glimmered in the morning light, and he wore a muscle shirt about three times too big for him, making his skinny arms look even skinnier. Come to think of it, I couldn't remember ever seeing Mr. Fink with sleeves, even when it snowed. A belt that reminded me of a bungee chord held up his baggy work pants. The thought occurred to me that his life probably wasn't filled with much besides maintenance.

"Them kids make a mess of this neighborhood, so I gotta get up," he said, not exactly yelling but loud enough for me to hear. I wanted to ask him about the graffiti on the back of the building, but when I saw his cheeks, already pink from the sun, turning redder at the thought of local teenagers dirtying his sidewalks, I decided he'd probably find out soon enough. My job was simply to inform Detective Murphy. Mr. Fink ran his wrist across his sweaty face, shook his head as though he didn't want to think about disobedient kids anymore, and went back to sweeping.

"Hope you have a good day, Mr. Fink," I called to him, as I rolled down the window in my car door to let the morning air blow through. Mr. Fink simply held up his hand to me without raising his head. When I pulled to the stop sign and glanced in my rearview mirror, Mr. Fink had stopped sweeping altogether. He was watching me drive away.

I tossed my hand out the window to wave at him, but when

he saw this, he turned around and began a furious sweep of the path he'd just come down. Mr. Fink might not be much for socializing, but I had to give it to him: He was a hard worker.

The radio news wasn't too interesting, so I flipped the dial and settled on an oldies country music station. Though I'd never been a devoted fan, I always admired the corny but raw emotion of country music whenever I did listen to it. This morning, some deep twangy voice was crooning about cheatin' hearts and cravin' love and feelin' blue.

I sighed. I didn't really want another reminder of my nonexistent love life, but suddenly I remembered the possibility that my afternoon appointment with Terry Choyce might change that.

I turned up the volume and pulled into Java Pit Stop, the drive-through coffee hut that had once been the attendant's booth in the parking lot across from the jail. Java huts were one of Denver's great features since the coffee craze hit the country—makeshift outlets all over town that provided a quick and full-flavor cup of joe for a few bucks. The mornings I couldn't endure a 7-Eleven cup that had been sitting on the burner all morning, I liked to treat myself to Java Pit.

"Mornin', Coco," I said to the lady whose nametag was as bright as the Colorado sky. "I'll have a double mocha grande deluxe with whipped cream and a chocolate chip muffin."

"A woman after my own heart," she said. She smiled as she took my five dollars, swiveled around to concoct the brew, dropped a muffin in a bag, and turned back to me with the goods in hand, all in the same thirty-second motion.

"Enjoy!" I gave her a thumbs-up and drove about twenty yards across the lot and parked, turning off the car and the country love songs. A grassy area with a park bench beside a lilac bush outlined the blacktop. Some summer mornings I liked to sit here before going into the office. It gave me a chance to wake up.

I pinched apart the muffin bit by bit, chasing each bite with a sip of mocha so that the extra chocolate flavor slid smoothly down my throat. The lilac bush was past blooming, but a hint of its scent still floated in the air, and I breathed it in. The sun felt warm and gentle on my face, and a few sparrows chirped from the telephone line above me. I was having a Zen moment.

Until the Lord's Prayer popped into my head. I sat up straight, and in between sips, I recited the prayer aloud, just like we did Sunday mornings at Capitol Presbyterian: "Our Father which art in heaven, Hallowed be thy name. Thy kingdom come, Thy will be done in earth, as it is in heaven."

I drank the syrupy part of the mocha, exhaled, and continued. "Give us this day our daily bread. And forgive us our debts as we forgive our debtors." I set the empty cup beside me on the bench, stuffed the muffin wrapper inside it, and paused before continuing. I wanted some of this ancient prayer to sink in, especially the forgiveness part, which I wasn't exactly an expert in.

A slight breeze moved across my face and I soaked it in. I felt stronger, or at least a little more awake. So I finished the prayer with as much passion as the country singers had their songs. "And lead us not into temptation, but deliver us from evil: For thine is the kingdom, and the power, and the— "

But before I could get out "glory"—let alone "forever and ever, Amen"—a siren was screaming down the street. Two fire engines bellowed by, disturbing the peace and reminding me of the last time I saw fire trucks: a few days ago when the Buddhist Cultural Center was burning down. My mind jumped into work mode, and I wondered again what I had missed the morning I interviewed those three monks. Maybe I would pay them a visit later this morning. I wrapped up the prayer, shut my eyes tight, and tossed in a few other requests about family and neighbors and colleagues.

By the time I got to my desk at the *Dispatch*, Hannah was already at hers. Friday was casual day in the office, but for Hannah that meant wrinkle-free linen slacks, a gorgeous blouse and jacket, whose designer I'd never heard of, but which she educated me on, and one-inch matching pumps instead of her usual two-inch. For me, casual day meant a faded jean skirt that dropped just shy of my kneecaps, Birkenstocks, and a lime-green Denver College T-shirt Matt had given me last year for my birthday. In fact, casual day was just about every day for me since I had yet to break the thrift-store fashion habit.

"Top o' the mornin', Hannah X. Hensley," I lilted in Irish form. She looked up from her notepad and smiled. Then Hannah's eyes scanned over me, from the Birkenstocks on up to my wild hair, which I couldn't remember if I'd brushed this morning. She shook her head like a teacher at a failing student, adding an occasional "tsk, tsk" to punctuate her disapproval.

"Lightfoot, just because you cover religion does not mean you have to dress like you just walked off the commune," she said, her head still circling back and forth. "Cancel your dates tonight because I am taking you shopping."

"Cancel my dates? And break the guys' cheatin' hearts?"

She sighed as if there was little hope in the world and said, "The mall for you, Girl. Six o'clock sharp."

"Yes, Ma'am."

"Ah, two of my top reporters." Skip had suddenly appeared at our cubicles. Today, our boss was wearing pressed black jeans and a golf shirt, looking less like the managing editor and more like he was about to tee off.

"Hannah, do you have a minute? The mayor's called again." Skip nodded at me, smiled, and then offered the same to Hannah, who did not return either nod or smile. She knew what his request meant: another complaint about her City Hall coverage. I didn't know how she did it, but it seemed Hannah was always on the verge of breaking some really ugly story on the local officials who liked to think they ran the city. Her stories made a point of reminding them just who paid their salaries, which meant she was not the most popular journalist at the *Dispatch*, though she was probably the most read. As a result, Skip took an earful from just about every elected—and nonelected—city representative.

Hannah picked up her pen and notepad and marched down the hall toward Skip's office, her head held high and a "don't even dare me" look on her face. When Skip turned to follow, I jumped in.

"Skip, the Buddhist Temple fire—"

"You're following up, right?"

"Well, I was thinking I should make a house call if you—"

"Great. Keep at it, Lightfoot, and keep me posted." He patted the top of my shoulder and hurried down the hall. Something big must be happening.

I heard the door to Skip's office shut and felt a hint of insignificance sift through my spine. For some reason, a memory popped into my head. I was watching my three brothers pose with their prom dates in our living room while my parents snapped their photos. Like then, I smiled at the situation, glad my brothers had nice girlfriends and just as glad for the direction Hannah was getting from our editor, but knowing I probably wouldn't get asked to the dance.

And except for Ralphie Snodgrass, the secretary of the math club, I didn't.

No matter. Religion reporting was important, I reminded myself. I replayed in my brain many of Skip's speeches defending my position to other reporters. Okay, so we all knew political news and sports were what sold newspapers, that politics made a journalist's career, which meant Hannah was doing something right since the mayor called the *Dispatch*'s managing editor. Again. So what if no one called much about religion, except the Methodists with potluck inquiries? That didn't mean it wasn't a big part of the newspaper, I said to myself. People didn't call about the horoscope, either, or the advice columns or the obits, but they'd call to complain the day they didn't find them in the paper.

At least, I hoped they would.

I poured myself a cup of coffee and tried to refocus at my desk. Did anyone besides Skip and Matt ever read my stories? Was that the reason I was a reporter? I stared out the window as if I'd find the answers there; then I remembered Mr. Texas-Buddhist monk, who told me how "enlightened" I was for writing the stories I did.

And then I realized what felt so wrong about their responses. It was as if they had been prepared for me, as if they knew I'd be coming to talk with them just as their Cultural Center was going up in flames. In fact, the Dharma recited the same speech on TV that he'd given me, as if someone had coached him and recognized a media opportunity when he saw it. Had they planned it this way?

I picked up the phone.

"Freddy Stephano, please."

Freddy told me he'd found some wires at the circuit breaker box that had been reworked, but when he checked on it, the Buddhists' records showed an order had been placed at "Charged Up Electric Repair and Installation" a week before.

"So what are you saying, Freddy?"

"Only that the wiring didn't start the fire, Jane."

Boy, did this guy have trouble with names. I asked Freddy to keep me updated and looked up the number for "Charged Up Electric" on my computer.

"It was a routine call," a scratchy, deep voice said when I called.

"What exactly is routine at a Buddhist temple?" I asked.

"Routine to get the place ready for conversion," the manager told me.

"Conversion?"

"Yeah, they were about to get an air-conditioning system installed, and that meant some electrical rewiring, you know, *conversion*."

"Of course." I thanked him, typed a few notes, and hung up. Then I glanced through my *Cromwell's Encyclopedia of World Religions* and read, "To achieve awakening, many Buddhist sects traditionally live as simply as possible, in line with the natural order of the universe. The First Noble Truth suggests 'there is suffering,' not 'I suffer,' and so followers must gradually relinquish the need to grasp and cling to their own sense of suffering."

I looked up the phone numbers of a few other Buddhist temples in town and called each one, asking only if they had air conditioning in their facilities. After listening to their proclamations of transcendence, peace, and good deeds, etc., each told me the Buddha helped his followers avoid anything that made them falsely comfortable.

"Would that include air conditioning?" I asked.

Most told me they "must let go of suffering and admit it into consciousness," which I took as a yes. So why would someone from Mile High Zen Buddhist Cultural Center have placed an order for air-conditioning installation with Charged Up Electric? And why did the monks seem to anticipate my coming?

I left a Snickers bar on Hannah's desk to encourage her to keep going, sent an e-mail to Skip, and drove to the Mile High Buddhist Cultural Center—or what was left of it. No one answered the door of the unburned annex. I rang again, knocked, and was walking around the building when Mr. Texas opened the door.

"Ms. Lightfoot!" he quipped with more enthusiasm than he should have. He recovered his Zen stoicism as soon as his elder appeared behind him.

"Hi, guys. I need a little enlightenment."

"That is what we are here for, to help realize the *inner being* that has always been there—being one with all that is."

"Uh-huh. May I come in?" I asked, peering down the hallway.

"No."

"No?"

"No. It is a morning of silence, and it cannot be disrupted."

"I think it just has been, hasn't it?"

A line of perspiration formed on the younger monk's forehead, and he looked toward the street to avoid eye contact with me.

"Okey doke," I said. "In fact, that's fine. Let's talk out here where it's a beautiful summer morning." They closed the door behind them and stepped into the morning heat. We glanced over at the ruins of their center. I fumbled for my notepad and pulled the pen from behind my ear.

"Okay, I guess I'm just a little confused about something." I paused. "It's a shame your building is . . . gone."

"Suffering is a path toward compassion. Buddha teaches us to harmonize with the reality of life; it is not contained in a mere building. Through awakening, we have nothing fundamentally to gain or lose."

"Right," I said, writing his words as he watched me scribble. When I finished a sentence, I looked up at the sky. "Whew, it's a hot one today, isn't it? How do you guys handle the heat in your robes? I wouldn't last a second."

"Ms. Lightfoot, suffering is a gift for all. We are not affected by natural discomforts but rather allow them to teach us of the enlightened path," the Dharma said. Though he wasn't as slick as when he was on television, he was convincing.

"How about that? Well, I guess that's part of my confusion. I just talked with Charged Up Electric Repair and Installation, and they told me someone had ordered air conditioning for the whole center about a week ago. Even sent a guy out to check on the wiring. Wouldn't that sort of eliminate a natural discomfort?"

The Dharma's eyes widened and closed. The younger monk coughed, looked at his leader, and followed suit, shutting his eyes tightly. They both breathed in and out in a slow rhythm, apparently having chosen this moment to meditate.

I could respect that. I waited, tapping my pencil against my notepad in sync with their breathing. Moisture formed above their lips and eyebrows. I grabbed a tissue from my pocket and dabbed my forehead, while the monks' breathing and meditation seemed to deepen.

Just as suddenly as they closed their eyes, both monks popped them open, in unison.

"It is a moment for peace and tranquility. Our meditation is required of us." And with that, the Dharma turned around and walked inside. For a second, his disciple looked at me as if some other spiritual insight wanted to come forth from his being. But he shrugged his shoulders and closed the door.

I walked toward the charred wood and stone that used to be their main center. The ground was black and ashy, and a few fresh flowers had been scattered across the building's burned foundation as though it were a grave. In a way, it was. I stared at the tombstone and wondered why a building like this should die. Many people would be affected by its passing, their lives disrupted, their religious devotion diminished.

The two monks seemed generally positive—as monks went—almost void of grief. I wondered how their daily routines would change now that their center was gone. When I looked back at the annex, I saw the Dharma standing at the window looking toward me like Mr. Fink had only a few hours earlier on the street in front of my apartment. The sun on the glass of the annex window, though, distorted the Dharma's image and gave me the impression of a mask across his face.

He was hiding something—that much I knew. I raised my hand to wave, but he moved away from the window. Tranquility was waiting for him.

On my way back to the office, I decided to make another stop. I pulled over to the side of the road, started to light a cigarette, and then felt guilty, thinking maybe today should be the day I'd quit, like I'd promised my brothers a million times. I remembered the "Lead us not into temptation" part of my morning prayer, put the cigarette back in its pack, and flipped through my notes for the office address of Into the Fields Fellowship.

A blonde-haired woman in her forties was sitting behind the desk, typing furiously despite her long pink nails. I had always marveled at the finesse any woman with long fingernails had for daily functions, let alone typing. The IFF office was neatly designed with beautiful leather couches, a glass-topped coffee table with religious or self-help books on top with a thick Oriental rug underneath, and classical music playing softly from an upright stereo system. It reminded me more of the reception area for a Fortune 500 corporation than a church office. The only difference was that in this office all the pictures on the walls, most of which were ocean or mountain scenes, had beautifully scripted Bible verses written across Mother Nature: "2 Corinthians 9:7: God loves a cheerful giver!" or "Acts 4:32: All the believers shared everything they had."

The Buddhist monks suddenly seemed a thousand miles away.

The woman smiled at me as I walked toward her, her scarlet lipstick forming a perfectly shaped "U" on her face. I glanced at her golden-engraved nameplate and read, "Delores Watson, Executive Assistant."

"Good morning. How may I help you?" she asked, her voice smooth with grace. She stopped typing and looked at me with hazel eyes highlighted by black mascara and blue-gray shadow. This woman was as well designed as the office.

"Hello, Ms. Watson. I'm Jonna Lightfoot MacLaughlin, religion reporter with the *Dispatch*. Is Pastor Jeff Whitman in?"

"Oh. Please, call me Delores. A journalist coming to our

office!" She clapped her hands together, careful not to click her nails. "This is a unique day!" she exclaimed, the smoothness in her voice sliding in and out of my ears. I felt my Irish cheeks give me away.

"Oh, well, uh, no big deal." I cleared my throat, enjoying the pleasure of what seemed like affirmation but trying not to admit it. "Is the pastor in?"

"Gosh, I'm afraid you just missed him. He's making hospital visits today." She tilted her head slightly while her U turned upside down, signaling her disappointment, all as her hazel eyes focused on mine. I handed her my business card and asked her to have him call me when he came back.

"Sure I will, Ms. Lightfoot." She jotted a note on a pink memo pad, stapled my card to it, and put it on a small stack of messages waiting for her boss. I was halfway across the hall of Scriptures when Delores spoke up.

"Was there anything *I* could help you with?"

I turned at the idea.

"It's about a Mr. Jedediah Sundae. That's Sundae with an *e*."

Delores's red smile retracted into a straight and serious line across her face, as if the monitor on a heart patient just went dead.

"Who?"

"Jedediah Sundae."

"Jedediah Sundae? Hmm, doesn't ring a bell."

"He used to be a deacon or an elder or some kind of leader here?"

"Well, goodness, I've only been here a few years. Maybe he was before my time."

"Maybe he was." I noticed her fingers fanning the top of

her desk, her nails silent at the touch. "Could you do me a favor, Delores? Could you give me some information on your church? I'm always looking for congregations to profile for the paper, and I think I'd like to learn a little more about Into the Fields Fellowship."

The smile returned. She handed me last Sunday's bulletin and an apology that their church information brochure was still at the printers. They'd recently had to update it, but once it was delivered, she'd be glad to drop one in the mail to me.

I thanked her for her time and left, reading again the verse from Acts 4 as I walked out of the perfectly ordered office. Something was wrong with so much neatness, I thought. Weren't Christians usually, well, a little less formal or tidy? No wonder Jedediah Sundae—if he did exist—decided to leave Into the Fields Fellowship; if their services were anything like their church office, not many real humans would fit in.

I decided to skip lunch, hoping it would help me look a little thinner later that afternoon when I visited the Catholic Outreach Center. Hannah—and the Snickers bar—was away from her desk when I got back to the office. Skip was out of his office as well, so I figured they were both breaking some world-changing story. I went over to the photo editor to confirm our shoot for the afternoon, but he was also away. I left a note on his desk, grabbed a water bottle from the employee room, and went back to my desk.

The afternoon was long, slow, and dull. I read every link from the BuddhaNet website and checked the *Dispatch's* morgue—or archive of past issues—for any Delores Watson, Jeff Whitman, or Jedediah Sundae, still finding nothing. How could there be not even a hint of information on any of these people? Surely it was too coincidental if they all just happened to attend IFF—at least at some point—or if they all just happened to change their names.

But the existence of these IFF-y folks was enough to hurt my brain at the end of the week, so I switched gears and thumbed through my latest edition of *ChocoLatte* magazine to see what new blends of coffees and chocolates were coming out in the upcoming months. I called Matt at his office but got his voice mail, read the headlines from today's *Associated Press* wire, and considered walking over to the sports department to talk with Tony Thompson about the weekend games until I realized I'd rather clean out my paper clip holder than talk sports and get a teasing about religion from Tony today.

By 3:15, I had detangled most of my hair so that it resembled a reasonable mop rather than a burning bush and smoothed out most of the wrinkles in my skirt. Wherever Hannah and Skip were must have been keeping them busy because they still weren't back in the office by the time I left for the Catholic Outreach Center. I e-mailed them both, grabbed my bag—and confidence—and headed for the car.

The temperatures had cooled to the low nineties, and a few afternoon clouds formed across the sky. I drove by Civic Center Park, which was lined with huge ceramic flowerpots full of white and yellow daisies. Groups of tourists were walking toward the capitol and the Denver Art Museum. I rolled down the windows of my car, hoping the air would cool off the dashboard. I was anxious, so again I chanted my morning prayer.

It wasn't every day I had an opportunity to meet a man who seemed both normal and spiritual, both handsome and interesting. Terry Choyce seemed to have all of that, and I confessed I was hoping to get to know him, even if it was under the guise of writing about his program, which I was going to do anyway. What harm could it do to take a little extra time with a single Catholic hunk who was about my age?

I reached for my cigarettes to calm my nerves but was afraid the smell would stay on my clothes, so I tossed them into the glove compartment. I turned on the radio and turned it off just as quickly when I heard, "You don't love me anymore." I hummed, prayed, meditated, sang, and did a number of deep-breathing exercises all the way past Coors Field, the artsy lofts, and Mexican restaurants until I pulled up to the Catholic Outreach Center at about the same time Jimmy Larson, the youngest *Dispatch* photographer we had, was parking his car.

We walked up the steps together to the Center. I prepped him on the photos I wanted to accompany the story: Shoot as many of the volunteers as possible with whatever kids have permission from their parents. And definitely snap as many shots of Terry Choyce in action as possible, from all angles and on all sides.

"You've got me for twenty minutes, Lightfoot, before I head to the Junior Rodeo to shoot the quarterfinals," Jimmy said, trying to sound older than he was. As soon as we entered the lobby, though, he was off and running. I looked around for Terry but saw only brown and white faces of ten-year-olds running through the halls. I strolled past the beautiful pictures of children in the hall and into the computer lab. A few volunteers sat with a group of girls in front of computers, working on designing a calendar and finishing a math program.

Jimmy took a few pictures and wandered into other rooms while I walked toward the gym. Seven boys in black T-shirts were running basketball drills while two older men stood watching and coaching.

"Excuse me, have you seen Terry Choyce?" I asked the coach without the whistle.

"Not today. Did you check the office?" He pointed back toward the direction I'd just left and smiled.

"Thanks." I turned around and walked toward the office, feeling a slight hunger pang flip around in my stomach. Kids were walking in and out of rooms, volunteers were talking to each one, and pictures of Jesus on the cross looked down at them kindly from the walls. It was an exciting work to be sure, especially in a neighborhood known more for its decline than the opportunity it offered its residents.

A regal white-haired woman with skin color the exact opposite of her hair was sitting in the office talking on the phone. She hung up when I walked in.

"Let me guess—you're Jenna MacLaughlin from the *Dispatch*, right?"

"Jonna. Yes, I'm looking for— "

"Aren't we all, Baby? Aren't we all looking for something?" She gave me a grandmotherly grin and sipped out of a straw from an orange plastic cup before she continued, "Well, hate to tell you this, but that was Terry on the phone, and he told me to tell you he is really sorry, but he can't make it in today. Had to go to court. He's a lawyer you know."

She sucked again from the straw while I watched, trying to let her words register.

"He's not coming?"

She stopped drinking and shook her head. Disappointment the size of those basketballs I'd just seen bounced in my gut. My stomach growled for some food.

"That don't mean, Sugar, you can't see what's going on here.

I'm Olivia Sampson, office administrator. Let me take you on a tour. Is your photographer here?"

"Thank you, but Terry took me on a tour yesterday when I . . ."

She didn't seem to hear me. Instead, she smiled, stood up, grabbed my elbow, and whisked me through the building, introducing me to countless children and volunteers, explaining this about that program and that about this one. She gave me the history of every picture we passed, every donation that paid for every computer, and every success story of every child who'd come through these doors. In between lectures, she'd dispense wisdom or hugs to particular children while I tried to keep up with her and write down all she said. Jimmy caught her in a few candid moments, waved good-bye to us, and hurried out the front door, changing film in his camera as he left.

By the time we got back to the office, Grandma Outreach Center, or Momma O as everyone called her, was handing me a volunteer application, a brochure about the programs, and a time slot to come back next Thursday to work with some of the girls in a reading club. Without really thinking, I told her I would, handed her my business card, and asked her to have Terry call me for a follow-up interview. She read my card, nodded, and grinned again.

"Oh, okay, Sugar. I'll have him call you, for a *follow-up interview.*" She winked at me as she spoke. Then the phone rang. She picked it up, laughed, and waved at me while I sneaked away.

I stopped in the entryway before heading back to my car, looked again at the photos of the children on the wall, and thought of the handsome man who'd helped get them to this center. Though I couldn't see his face, it wasn't hard to see his heart.

I tumbled to my car, tired from the blur of Momma O's tour as well as the ache I felt in my stomach from missing out on both lunch and Terry Choyce. I rolled down the window, reached in the glove compartment to pull out a cigarette, and lit it, breathing in the calming effect of nicotine.

"That's not good for you." A tiny African-American child with beaded braids in her hair was standing beside my car.

"Momma O and Mr. Terry says smokin' is bad for you." Her soft brown eyes were steady sermons directed straight at me.

"They're right. Smoking is bad for you," I said, trying to hide my cigarette and my guilt.

"Then, why you doin' it?" The child did not move as she spoke.

"Cuz I'm dumb. Dumb as a doornail."

"Doornails can't be dumb. And neither are you. Know why?"

"Why?"

"Cuz God made you. And he don't make nobody dumb. Momma O told me that, too."

I looked at the tender voice standing beside me. I smashed the cigarette in the ashtray and smiled at the child. Her face filled into a happiness that spilled out of her mouth in giggles. She jumped up and down, and I laughed with her.

"My name's Jonna. What's yours?"

"Keisha. I'm in the Readin' Club. I'm eight."

I held out my hand to her through the window, and she shook it with eight-year-old energy.

"Very nice to meet you, Keisha. Thank you for helping me today."

"That's okay. Where you goin'?"

"Back to work."

"Where you work?"

"At the newspaper." Her eyes got bigger. "Want to come visit the newspaper sometime?" She nodded and then hopped up and down again as if someone had just handed her a jump rope.

"I'll see you next week, okay, Miss Keisha?"

"'Kay. Bye, Miss Jonna!" She waved at me and ran back into the Outreach Center.

I drove slowly through downtown, past the capitol, and into the parking lot of the *Dispatch*. When I got out of my car, I grabbed the pack of Marlboro Lights and dumped it into the trash can at the entrance of the building. Since I was starving, I stopped at the hot dog cart outside the building. I was buying a chili dog when a tall, thin man with dark sunglasses suddenly approached me.

"Jonna Lightfoot MacLaughlin?"

I nodded and bit into the chili dog, which almost exploded, squirting strands of meat juice down my T-shirt.

"I've been waiting for you." He looked at my messy lunch and then glanced around, as if he thought someone was following him. "I'm wondering if you have some time to talk with me."

I swallowed, wiped my chest with a napkin, and noticed the worried face of this man. "Okay, we can talk. How about for starters you tell me your name?"

He glanced around again, leaned toward me, and whispered, "Jedediah Sundae."

::Chapter Six

Jed Sundae was slightly taller and older than I'd imagined him from the one time I'd spoken with him on the phone. Thinner, too. He wore a black, wrinkled sports jacket that looked as though he might have slept in it and gray slacks that hung just above his loafers. I couldn't see his eyes because his sunglasses were thick and dark, and his chin was in need of a razor, which seemed funny to me because his dark hair was neatly combed back from his forehead. For a summer day, the man seemed uncomfortably hot and clearly bothered.

"So you do exist?" I asked as I led him into the *Dispatch*. "I was beginning to wonder."

He stopped suddenly in the lobby, took off his sunglasses, and squinted at me. "What do you mean?"

I swallowed the last of my chili dog before answering, still battling the mess on my shirt. "What do you mean 'what do I mean'?" The question confused even me, though it had dropped out of *my* mouth.

"I *mean*, after we talked, I looked you up in the phone book, in the *Dispatch* databases, and in any city records I could access. You know what I found? Nothing. Nada. Zero. There's not a lick of information on 'Mr. Jedediah Sundae'—that's Sundae with an *e*. Not a doggone thing." I noted the irony as I tossed the wrapping of my lunch in the metallic can and looked up. The squint was widening. "But here you are." I smiled, hoping it would diffuse his obvious anxiety.

"Yes, Ms. MacLaughlin, here I am. Jed Sundae." His eyes flew down to his loafers, and he shifted his weight from left to right, then back from right to left. He reached into the pocket of his jacket, pulled out a folded piece of paper, and stared at it in his hand as if he were debating what to do with it before pushing it back into his pocket. He looked up at me with clear, brown eyes, a look that conveyed to me both gentlemanly sincerity and childlike pain.

"Would you like to come up to the newsroom, Mr. Sundae?" I asked. "I have a swell little cubicle that gives us virtually no privacy, but no one would bother us. The religion thing, you know. Journalists tend to avoid it." I tapped his arm playfully and chuckled, hoping to help him relax a little.

"No. No, thank you." He shifted his focus back to his shoes and scratched his head.

"Yeah, bad idea. How about if we just sit down right here?" I chose one of the square metal chairs that lined the wall of the *Dispatch* lobby. I'd never been quite sure why they were there to begin with, wondering who would ever want to sit down in the lobby of a newspaper as people hurried in and out. Now I knew.

Jed Sundae deliberated about the seat beside me, sighed, and finally sat down. Again he pulled out the piece of paper from his pocket, stared at it some more, cleared his throat, and kept staring. "Ms. MacLaughlin, there is a terrible thing happening at Into the Fields Fellowship."

"Tell me about it! I dropped into their office today, and the place seemed about as lively as a library. Don't get me wrong—I'm a big fan of libraries but . . ."

His stare jumped from the paper to my face. "You went to IFF?"

"I was in the neighborhood."

"And?"

"And the pastor was on hospital visits, so I only met Delores, the kind and perfectly dressed *executive assistant.* I don't know how she types with those nails. An amazing feat if you ask me."

"Ms. MacLaughlin— "

"Call me Jonna." I smiled again.

His face relaxed. "Okay then. Jonna. May I tell you something? I have been a good Protestant since I was twelve years old, been in and out of Bible-believing churches throughout my life, and even led one once as a pastor. I was a soldier in the army, watched my father die an alcoholic, had a marriage go bad, and worked in some pretty terrible businesses. But . . ." He looked away as the door to the lobby opened and a few sports reporters walked by, laughing and betting each other about the weekend games. The elevator opened and the lobby was empty—and quiet—again.

"But?" I whispered.

"But in all my experiences, I have never seen evil like I have at Into the Fields Fellowship." He pinched the piece of paper firmly in his hand and tapped it on his knee like it was an important envelope he was getting ready to open.

"Evil?" Except for adventure movies and fairy tales, I hardly heard the word anymore. Even in my line of work. I studied his face to make sure I had heard right.

"Evil. Pure, dark evil. And the worst part about it is they're using the Lord's name to do it."

"What exactly is it they're doing, Mr. Sundae?"

"Jed. Please call me Jed. It's short for Jedediah, you know." He paused, as if the mention of his whole name was as meaningful to him as mine was to me. I liked this man. "The evil they're doing, well, I think you already know, Jonna."

"I do?"

"Yes. Instead of giving people a second chance like a Christian church is supposed to do, they're taking people's lives away. Just like that." He snapped his fingers, scratched his chin, and flashed the paper in front of me. "This confirms it."

"It does? What is it?"

"This is a statement that all IFF members must sign to join the fellowship." He waved the paper in front of me, shooting me a look so serious and somber that something in my gut told me I'd better pay good attention. Then he brought it back to his lap, sat up straight, and looked silently at the door.

I followed his stare, but the only thing I saw was a big question mark hanging over the exit sign. I didn't understand. "You know what? I'm not having a very good day, Jed, and I'm feeling even more confused than I was earlier." I looked at his face while he stared toward the door. "What's the big deal about church members agreeing to a statement of faith to join a church? Isn't that common procedure?"

I picked up the hair off my neck and twisted it into a ponytail before letting it drop back onto my shoulders. Sometimes this slight rearrangement of my head seemed to unclog my brain and help me make sense of conversations.

Jed considered my question. "I suppose it would be normal if . . ." He stopped midsentence and closed his eyes.

He had me now. "If?" I prompted.

"If it were in fact a statement of faith." His voice turned shaky, like emotion was blocked in the back of his throat. "But that is not what this is."

With that, he opened his eyes and turned toward me. I could see they were cloudy. Oh, no. I'd be worthless if Jed Sundae began to cry right here in the *Dispatch* lobby. The day had already been fragile for me—if a grown man even let a trickle of a tear slip, I knew I'd be blubbering within seconds and finished for the day.

But he didn't. Instead, Jed Sundae simply stood up, glanced toward the door, put the piece of paper back in his pocket, and coughed. "I've probably said too much."

"Did I miss it?"

"I'm sorry to have taken your time, Jonna." He rubbed the back of his neck and shook his head.

"You haven't. In fact, I have lots of time. My schedule is completely free. Maybe we should go get a cup of coffee?"

Jed Sundae simply stared toward the building's entrance.

"Could I take a look at that statement of faith, Jed? It might help."

He looked back at me and slid his hand into the pocket with the paper. "Faith is one thing, Jonna," he said softly. "*This* is quite another."

"But until I see *this* document, I'll never know the difference, will I?"

His face went tight as if a raging debate were taking place behind it. Apparently, the protective side won out. Jed suddenly reached for his sunglasses, slipped them over his eyes, mumbled an apology to me, and bolted toward the door.

I followed him out to the hot dog stand, grabbed his elbow, and pulled him around.

"Look, Jedediah Sundae with an *e,* something about this church has obviously upset you, and in the process has *me* really confused and now, really curious. Why not tell me a little more so we can figure out our next steps?"

He paused, his eyes hidden again beneath his glasses. A truck honked across the street, drawing Jed's attention away from me. "Thanks for your time, Jonna. I'll be in touch. I've got to go." He tried to leave, but I held onto his elbow.

"But how do I reach you?"

"You don't. I don't exist, remember?"

"Well, I do exist," I said. "At least take my card—it's got all my numbers. Call anytime."

I watched the man in black fade into the crowd and disappear. I hoped he would keep the business card I'd slipped into his hand and wondered what in the world he was so afraid of.

I bought another chili dog and headed up to my desk.

Hannah was finally at hers and so lost in her computer screen that she didn't even lift her head when I walked by. She was completely deaf when I asked what she was working on. More amazing still, her nose had somehow shut down its sensory abilities because she did not seem to notice the waft of chili in the air. Deadlines had an amazing power over reporters.

I watched her for a few minutes and laughed. That was when it occurred to me that maybe Jed Sundae's piece of paper had that same sort of power, something that drew in IFF members so much that they got completely absorbed in whatever it was they were being offered and didn't even know there was a world outside.

The problem was, I had no idea what that "something" might be.

I looked at the bulletin from Into the Fields Fellowship that Delores, the Nail Lady, had given me and noted the time of services for Sunday morning. They didn't begin until 11 a.m., an hour after Capitol Presbyterian finished, so I decided this week I'd be a good Christian and a good religion reporter and attend both. I wanted to see for myself what could make someone like Jed Sundae so nervous, so sad, and so invisible.

Since Skip wasn't expecting any stories from me today, I flipped open my spiral pad to the notes I'd taken the first time Jedediah Sundae had called me. "It's one thing if a church grows because people are genuinely worshiping God. It's another if they're told they'll only find him when they give all their money for the 'Lord's work in the Fellowship' and then aren't allowed to leave."

A few sentences later I had scribbled something else he said. "The IFF leaders are taking the hard-earned money from their people and telling them all sorts of new 'ministries' will come from it. Only problem is . . . Only problem is . . ."

I remembered how Jed had barely been able to hold back the tears that day on the phone, as he had just now in the lobby. Something had broken this man's spirit. The fact that he was now coming to me with this information—confusing as it was—made me feel both responsible and helpless. If this was as serious as it was beginning to feel, well, I might be in over my head. After all, I was only a religion reporter.

Aside from the church's schedule of services, the IFF bulletin listed a few of their ministries for members to get involved in. "Field Works" called itself a "social outreach ministry," providing temporary jobs for Denver's homeless and unemployed. "Field Hands" was described as a service that "provided meals or house-cleaning to elderly friends who lived alone." And "Fields of Green" was a "youth sports mission that taught city kids everything from soccer and golf to baseball and cricket."

But each time I typed the name of one of these ministries into our database search, "No Match Found" appeared on my screen. I checked the website for Denver County records of nonprofits registered, and again I didn't see anything that might relate to the services listed under Into the Fields Fellowship. That was strange because usually I could at least find charter documents as well as tax status from the Internal Revenue Service for churches or religious affiliates I was covering. True, Colorado law exempted churches, certain religious organizations, and state and local nonprofit organizations from the annual filing requirement, but they were at least required to apply for status.

The more I kept looking, the more I kept finding absolutely nothing about any agency with "Fields" in its title. Maybe I was missing something. I even clicked onto the Council for Better Business Bureau and studied their information on giving to nonprofits. "Nonprofit organizations and companies, known as 501 (c) (3)s after their designation in the IRS code, have special requirements for filing and public disclosure that differ dramatically from requirements for regular companies."

Obviously, Into the Fields Fellowship was taking advantage of these special public disclosure requirements. But why?

My phone rang. I debated as to whether I should answer it and risk getting sidetracked from my search, although I wasn't finding anything anyway. I let the voice mail pick it up while I searched LexisNexis for any stories, business announcements, or public advisory notices that might have been written in the last six years on Into the Fields Fellowship. Still nothing.

How could an organized Protestant church, whose office I'd visited and whose Sunday bulletin I held in my hand, not be listed anywhere? And, more perplexing, why would they want to be so undetectable if their mission was to grow? I mean, no organization the size of IFF could escape every mention everywhere, especially in the information age. It would start to look *too* clean, like a murder scene that had been scoured with bleach to hide the evidence.

By 5:55 p.m., Hannah was still on the phone, typing frantically, immersed in whatever story she was working on. When I signaled to her about our shopping date, she grunted an apology and went back to scouring her notes before writing some more. I'd lived twenty-seven years already without a fashion field trip to the mall with Hannah, so I wasn't too disappointed if we weren't going now.

I decided to check my e-mail one more time before heading home. I saw the usual church bake sale, potluck, and conference announcements in the "New Mail" box. I ignored them and instead listened to my voice mail before leaving for the day.

"Jenny, I expect to see you tomorrow morning. The world needs me." Click.

A chill shot through my spine when I heard "God's" squeaky voice again. I pushed replay and listened again for any clues about where he might go. None. Now I wondered if I'd made the right decision not to pick up the phone, but I wasn't sure what I would have said if I had. In all my years of growing up watching "spiritual" gurus wander in and out of our house, I rarely came across anyone who seemed as pushy as this guy. It was safe to say, in fact, that "God" didn't seem to be operating with a full deck of cards. I was suddenly thankful for earthly protection like the Boulder

County Police Department. I picked up my bag and car keys and left the *Dispatch.*

On my way home, I decided to drive by the Catholic Outreach Center, just in case. If for no other reason, I could use a little inspiration. So what if it was two miles out of my way? Something about that place—and the man who ran it—lifted my spirit, which was no small thing in a week of wacky phone calls, secretive monks, and broken ex-church members. The good work of the Catholics for these neighborhood kids was a refreshing reminder that there still were some religious efforts that were authentic, honest, and genuinely concerned about people. That in itself offered at least one small piece of good news, and right now I would take what I could get.

As I turned the corner toward the Center, there, sitting on the steps in the evening sun, looking calm and handsome and normal, light glowing all around him, was Terry Choyce. Completely alone, completely inviting.

There *was* a God.

In that moment, I heard my dad's voice proclaiming in my head like he had done countless times at the dinner table, "There are *no* coincidences on this planet, Jon, only God working anonymously." I smiled.

"Jonna!" Terry called as I got out of the car.

He recognized me! This was getting sweeter with each second. I pushed my hair back and sucked in my stomach as I walked across the street.

"Hey, Terry," I said, sounding as calm as I could, though I felt sweat collecting in my armpits. "We missed you today for the photo shoot." My shoes felt clumsy on my feet as I made my way up the steps.

"Me, too. Sorry about that. Had to do the lawyer thing." He was smiling at me as he stood, and I noticed he was wearing a white T-shirt, faded jeans, and sandals—looking very hip, Colorado-style.

When I got to the top step, he extended his hand. I took it, my hand in his, flesh on flesh, and suddenly I forgot everything that had happened all week long. I sighed, still holding his hand. He gently pulled his back and I snapped out of my state.

"No problem," I said, recovering. "We managed to get some good shots anyway." I glanced down and saw the chili stain on my shirt. To deflect, I folded my arms across my chest and tried to look relaxed.

Terry's hair was bright, radiant even, like one of those paintings of the apostles sitting at the feet of Christ you see in the art museum. His nose was a perfect line between his cheeks, and his eyelashes curled up toward the sky. They seemed to glow, too. His mouth was positioned perfectly on his chin, and it danced with the rhythm of his beautiful masculinity. When his lips moved, his hands illuminated his story.

But I didn't hear a word.

I was still staring when I finally recognized some words midsentence, "and the kids were hiding behind the desks when I came in. You should have seen them!"

I nodded and chuckled with him, as if I completely understood what he had just said. I wiped my mouth in case I had drooled during his story and then looked away to get composure.

"So what brings you by the Catholic Outreach Center?"

I glanced at his face and wondered how in the world he could ask such a question. "Oh, was in the neighborhood, you know," I lied.

"Wow, twice in one day?"

"Well, although Momma O did give me a grand tour this afternoon— "

"Yeah," Terry interjected, "Ms. Olivia is great. Couldn't do this work without her."

"I can see why. She's a force to be reckoned with. But I knew I needed a few more questions answered from the leader of the pack himself."

"Sure. Pretty impressive—you're working on a Friday night."

Uh-oh. My nonexistent social life was on the verge of exposure. I scrambled. "Some stories can't wait," I said, grabbing paper and pen from my bag, pushing my hair around, and trying to look as though I was focusing.

For the next five minutes, I jotted down notes while Terry gave me answers to most of the questions Momma O had already covered. The sound of his rich, deep voice was as soothing as a Sunday morning liturgy, even though I was not exactly listening to the words he was saying. The more he spoke, in fact, the more my heart and my pen picked up speed. I suddenly felt inspired that I should indeed become an official volunteer for the reading group at the COC.

When Terry finished speaking and the music of his voice no longer floated through the air, I studied my paper and decided to dive in. I looked up. "So, how exactly did a talented lawyer like yourself become so, uh, compassionate? Isn't that an oxymoron?"

Terry laughed at my question, a sound sweeter on my ears than even his voice. He shrugged his broad shoulders and tilted his head. "Good genes, I guess," he said as he pushed his hair back from his face, the muscle of his bicep bulging in the process.

I was not prepared for what he said next. I was still staring at his build.

"And you? How exactly does one become a religion reporter? Talk about an oxymoron!"

I smiled at his comeback and tried to catch my breath. It wasn't often that a source actually asked me a question during an interview. Usually I was the one tossing out questions, but now Terry had turned the conversation back toward me. I viewed that as a very good sign.

"Guess I could say the same—it's in my blood," I answered, thinking of all the times my parents had converted growing up. Each religious experience they'd had was a news flash in our house. Sometimes they'd even go so far as to hold informal press conferences with their friends and neighbors while my brothers and I listened to them explaining the tenets of their new devotional life. Each time, we got completely absorbed in their storytelling and passion, following our mom and pop not because we had to but because we wanted to. They never forced us into believing anything. They simply invited us to the table or the temple or the altar, depending on the religion of the day.

Skip—the voice of *Dispatch* editorial wisdom—had been right when he'd first offered me the position. I'd been training my whole life for this job.

But just as I was about to dazzle Terry with the wild religious adventures of the MacLaughlin Tribe, a blue Volkswagen Bug pulled to a stop in front of the Catholic Outreach Center. A tall woman about my age climbed out of the driver's seat and waved at Terry. He waved back. Her hair hung smoothly over her shoulders, and her sleeveless dress hugged the curves of her trim figure. My eyes darted between her face and Terry's, then back again, and I felt like I was watching a tennis match. But from the look in Terry's eyes, I knew who'd won.

My interview was over.

The woman grabbed a pizza box from the backseat of her car and sauntered up the steps with an elegance that reminded me of Princess Diana. She handed the pizza to Terry, who had not stopped looking at her since she'd driven up. I dropped my notepad into my bag and yanked my car keys from the bottom. The urge to drive a million miles away from here swept through me with a fervor I hadn't known before. And I didn't even like driving.

"Hawaiian pizza with onions," the woman said. "Just what you ordered."

Terry opened the box and examined the pie with a hungry enthusiasm. "Thanks, Maddy. You're the best," he said, still looking at the pizza. I couldn't tell if it was the fading sunlight or the presence of this woman, but Terry Choyce's beautiful cheeks had turned a pale pink color. I coughed.

"Oh, sorry," he said. "Maddison Jones meet Jonna Lightfoot MacLaughlin." He waved his hand between us as we stood around him.

The smell of cheese, onions, and ham rose from the box, and I didn't know whether to run or to ask for a piece. I opted for the former. "Pleasure to meet you," I said, lying for the second time in the last hour and extending my hand to her.

Maddison Jones grabbed it with sincere emotion. Her brown eyes held mine. "Lightfoot MacLaughlin, the religion reporter?"

I bowed my forehead, fighting hard not to roll my eyes, especially when I noticed the chili stain still jumping off my shirt.

"No, it's a thrill for me," she said. "I read your work as

much as I can." She was smiling and nodding some more. At that moment, a vast army marched through my soul as Maddison Jones uttered her polite words. This stunning single woman was clearly the enemy, competing with me for Terry's affection. The last thing I wanted to do was like her.

"Really. I think what you're doing is crucial for readers in this town," she continued. "So few people see the important role religion plays these days. Denver's lucky to have a reporter like you."

That was a cheap shot. Hitting a reporter right where she's most vulnerable: her ego. My face suddenly felt hot, and the keys in my hand felt sweaty.

"When do you ever have time to read the paper?" Terry asked. Then he shook his head and looked at me. "Maddy is a colleague of mine at the law firm. I've never once seen her read the paper."

"That's not true!" she exclaimed. She swatted Terry's muscular arm with her palm and laughed. These two obviously had a quaint little something or other going on, and I wasn't about to stay and watch the show.

"Well, I'm glad to know people read the *Dispatch* from time to time," I said, though I doubted either heard my proclamation. "I better get going now. Thanks, Terry, for the interview. Nice to meet you, Maddison Jones."

As I turned to walk down the steps, Terry and Maddison stopped their little spat, looked at me, and smiled. The last of the sunlight glowed on their faces, though I was sure Terry's was brighter.

He extended his hand. "Thanks for coming by, Jonna. Let me know if you need any more information."

"Did I interrupt an interview?" Maddy asked. "I'm sorry."

"No problem. I was finished." I grinned and tossed my hand out. Then I shook Terry's quickly—not wanting to touch it for too long—and bolted toward my car.

I tossed my bag in the seat beside me, jammed the keys in the ignition, and drove off. When I glanced in the mirror, I noticed the happy pair sitting on the steps of the Center eating pizza. A gust of disappointment whirled around my head. I rolled down the windows to let in some fresh air.

I didn't bother to get my mail when I got to my apartment twenty minutes later. Instead, I went to the refrigerator and scrounged for dinner. Though I hadn't been to the grocery store in a few weeks, I did find an old Chinese takeout box half full of fried rice and grabbed a fork.

The quiet of my apartment was painfully louder than usual, reflecting every tired and scattered emotion I had encountered throughout the day. I lit my vanilla bean candle, hoping its aroma would be consoling since I was out of chocolate bars; then I plopped on the couch. Tomorrow I'd go shopping.

My eyes clouded when I thought of Terry and Maddy, and I sniffled at another potentially lost opportunity for love. So what that I had only met Terry a few times or that he had obviously been waiting for Maddison to arrive tonight when I drove by? Why else would he have been on the steps? Why did I wear this stupid chili-stained shirt? Why was my hair so ridiculous? What was I thinking, stopping by like that?

I wiped my nose with my napkin and acknowledged to myself that, yes, I was being overly dramatic. But sometimes it was downright easier to feel sorry for myself in moments like these than it was to "keep my head up and remember how much God loves me," like my dad always said whenever those "coincidences" didn't go as I'd hoped. I had never been very good at rejection, and long ago I'd discovered that sulking, smoking, or eating offered better and more immediate comfort even than spiritual truths. It was a dumb strategy, I knew, one I'd been trying for years to get over, but it was one that helped me manage for now. Jesus and I would work on a new one tomorrow.

When I woke up the next morning, I was shocked to see it was almost 10 a.m. But it was Saturday, a day when I usually caught up on apartment projects. My neck was stiff from falling asleep on the couch, and the summer heat filled my living room with a stuffy gust. I decided a walk to the Food-a-Rama neighborhood grocer would help work out the kinks and wake me up.

But when I got to the checkout aisle, the clerk was listening intently to a portable radio on her counter. She turned up the volume and I heard the news. "State troopers and Boulder County officials this morning in the Boulder Canyon apprehended a man they say has been threatening women in the area for months. Boulder Sheriff spokesman, Frank Murphy, declined to identify the man, though he did say they had taken him into custody for questioning as the— "

Static from the radio sizzled in the air, so I couldn't hear the rest of the story. But it didn't matter. I had heard enough.

::Chapter Seven

The light was blinking on my answering machine when I got home from the Food-a-Rama. I dropped my groceries on the kitchen counter, grabbed a Snickers bar, and pushed the play button.

"Hi, Jon. It's your biggest brother calling, reminding you about dinner tonight. One quick change: Our stove broke. Long story. Anyway, let's meet at The Pub of Saint Agnes instead, okay? See you around seven. No excuses, Little Sis!"

I inhaled hot morning air, let it go, and tossed my Snickers wrapper in the trash. After last night's loser-fest with Terry and this morning's radio announcement, I was not exactly excited to meet another member of the male species. If I didn't love my brothers and my dad so much, I'd think all men were alien beings interested either in manipulating women or breaking our hearts.

Okay, so I was feeling bitter. I knew I couldn't compete with the likes of Maddison Jones or even the Hannah X. Hensleys of the world. "Maddy" had probably won beauty pageants growing up, while I was rolling organic cigarettes and picking wildflowers in the mountains. In fact, she'd probably always had beautiful men like Terry Choyce drooling after her. And why not? Her hair was straight, her figure was perfect, and the worst part about her was that she was sincerely nice. Why did God make people like that?

I knew I needed an attitude adjustment, so I poured myself

a cup of coffee, plopped myself on the couch, and reached for the little green Gideon's New Testament someone had shoved into my hands six years ago when I was standing in line to register for college courses. Because it was no bigger than a pack of playing cards, I'd kept the miniature Bible with me all these years—fondly referring to it as "My friend Gideon"—usually in the bottom of my purse or backpack, knowing Gideon was there in case I needed a little dose of inspiration or direction. Like now.

I flipped Gideon open to whatever page he might fall on and found myself in the Gospel of Mark, chapter seven:

"[Jesus] answered and said unto them, 'Well hath Esaias prophesied of you hypocrites, as it is written, This people honoureth me with their lips, but their heart is far from me. Howbeit in vain do they worship me, teaching for doctrines the commandments of men.'"

I took a gulp of coffee and looked out the window to ponder the passage. It wasn't exactly the pick-me-up I had hoped for. In fact, Christ's words about hypocrites hit a little too close to home this morning. Here I had been trying to do some good for the world, looking for good news to report and all, when I couldn't show even an ounce of compassion to the nice but unjustly beautiful lawyer who was cozier with my current crush than I was. What a hypocrite I was, willing to write a good religion article or show up on Sunday for church but not too willing to love thy prettier-than-I-am neighbor as myself. Maybe I should have stuck with obituaries.

"Lord have mercy," I said. It was a prayer I'd learned during my parents' jaunt as Episcopalians, right before they joined the Presbyterians. I knew there was more to it, a longer version, but this simple phrase was all that seemed to stick in my head. And except for the Lord's Prayer, it was the only one I knew by heart. It seemed pretty all encompassing.

I gulped my coffee, exhaled my anxiety, and was just about ready to visualize Maddy's face so I could imagine myself forgiving her, when the phone rang. Instead of visualizing—or answering—I decided to let the machine pick up the call while I turned the page in Gideon.

It was the story of Jesus feeding the five thousand people, probably in a place equivalent to a Colorado state park in the mountains. I loved that while they were out enjoying nature, God made a feast from a couple of fish and loaves of bread for a crowd of people, with plenty left over for seconds. Now this was a story I could relate to. It was probably the first mass organic meal ever.

But the voice from the answering machine interrupted my culinary meditation.

"Jonna, it's Detective Murphy here. Sorry to bother you at home, but I wanted you to know . . ."

I set Gideon on the couch and jumped for the phone. "I'm here, Detective."

"Ah, right. Sorry to bother you at home."

"No problem. What happened?"

"Well, we've apprehended a man who might fit the description you gave us."

"I didn't give you a description."

"Don't get semantical on me. I mean, we have in custody someone who might fit the bill of the God-guy you told us about."

Semantical? I was sure he'd made up that word on the spot.

"I know," I said. "I heard it on the radio this morning."

"So we need to see if you could identify him." He sounded

gruff, as if he'd not had enough coffee this morning.

Since I could appreciate feeling that way, I tried to be polite. "Be glad to, Detective. Only problem is, I've never seen his face; I've never even talked with the guy. I've just listened to his messages."

"Yeah, well, it's about all we have right now," he said, and before I could argue with him or tell him I was busy, he yelled to another officer to pick up the phone and put it to the ear of the man they now had in custody.

"What?" a man's voice said.

"Tell me where you live," Detective Murphy said to him as I listened.

I heard the prisoner click his tongue against his teeth as though he was disgusted. "I wanna lawyer first." His voice was low and raspy.

"Where you live, Pal?"

"Why?"

"Answer the question."

He sighed. "I live in Loveland."

"Of course you do. How old are you?"

"Old enough to know I have a right to a lawyer."

"You make a habit of calling reporters at newspapers?"

"Huh?" The question seemed to throw him.

The detective prodded. "You ever call any reporters?"

"Why would I do that? Why would I care about reporters? I don't even read the paper. It's just a bunch of c— "

"Oh, yeah?" the detective cut him off. "Then what were you doing in Boulder Canyon?"

"Fishin'."

"Uh-huh. Without a pole?"

"I forgot it."

"So, what were you doing?"

"Waitin' for my lawyer."

"All right, I've heard enough," Detective Murphy said, before he hollered at the officer to take the phone away, and I heard a sudden crack on the other end. "Well, Jonna? You recognize him?"

"No way. That was not the voice of 'God.'"

"You sure?"

"I'd recognize God's voice if I heard it. I mean, the guy who called himself God was much more panicky, higher pitched, almost nasal. This guy sounds, I don't know, like he's a football player for CU. I've still got the messages on the answering system at work, Detective, if it would help."

"Probably would. Good thinking. Listen, I'll be in touch, okay?" He hung up as suddenly as he'd called.

I could tell by his voice that he and I both knew my answer meant only one thing: that whoever had left those creepy messages on my voice mail and e-mails, whoever had threatened to force women and the world to worship him, was still out there. Somewhere.

I spent the rest of the afternoon cleaning my apartment, napping on the couch, trying not to think about "God on the Loose," and snacking. I mulled over the phone conversation with the detective's prisoner, wondering if I'd missed something, but I was sure it was not the same man who had left me those messages. Which was even more disconcerting than if it had been.

When I was getting ready for dinner with Matt, Mary, and Mr. American Literature Professor, Mrs. Rodriguez, my neighbor, knocked on the door. One half of my hair had calmed down, but

I hadn't straightened out the other half, so when I answered the door I looked a little like a clown at the circus.

She laughed at me. She put her fingers through the ringlets on the wild side and shook her head. "Juana, you got such nice curls, why you not let everyone see how pretty you are?"

"Because not everyone is as, um, appreciative as you are." I waved her into my apartment and went back to the mirror.

She poured herself a cup of coffee and stood at the bathroom doorway where I was trying to get the brush through my remaining frizz. Her hair was pinned back into a bun—an obviously easier solution than mine. "Juana, you should let it go."

"I should do a lot of things, Mrs. Rodriguez. I should lose about twenty pounds. I should exercise more than once a year. I should think nice things about people I'm jealous of."

She laughed, her flower-print housedress swaying back and forth in the motion. She shook her head and pointed her finger at me, so I had to pay attention. "Mi amiga. You perfect as is."

The brush slipped out of my hand onto my neighbor's slippers. She laughed again, bent over, and picked it up. The wrinkles in her face filled out her cheeks as she placed the brush in my hand. When I reached for it, she set her coffee cup down on the sink and put her tiny fingers on top of mine.

"Juana. God no make mistakes. You his, uh . . ." She paused, looking for the words and waving her hands around my face as if to describe what she wanted to say. "Tu eres la belleza de Dios." Her tone was motherly and sincere, and I wanted to believe that whatever Mrs. Rodriguez was saying—and I wasn't really sure—was true. My eighth-grade Spanish helped me recognize a few words, something about being the "beauty of God." I nodded at the idea, though I wasn't feeling it.

Her wide smile relaxed me. Even though we had a language barrier, Mrs. Rodriguez always seemed to be able to read me.

We walked into the living room. I grabbed my purse and was looking for my car keys when it occurred to me that I didn't know why Mrs. Rodriguez had come by.

"Did you need something?" I asked, turning to her and admiring again the easiness of the bun in her hair.

She swallowed the last of her coffee, washed the mug, and put it in the dish rack in the small kitchen. "Sí. Juana, I go church with you mañana?"

Usually Mrs. Rodriguez went to Saint Vincent's, though sometimes, when her grandchildren weren't visiting her, she liked going to Capitol Presbyterian with me, probably because it was smaller and there were more parishioners her age. Then I remembered that I'd be going straight to the service at Into the Fields Fellowship.

"Que bueno. But I have to go from Capitol Pres to another church, too, okay? You can go with me if you want."

She seemed to understand, patted my shoulder, and strolled back across the hall to her apartment.

By the time I got to The Pub of Saint Agnes, the straight in my hair had gone curly again. I tried to smooth it down by licking my fingers and pasting it to my head as I looked in the mirror. But that worked about as well as throwing water on a plastic plant in hopes of making it grow. It was against the natural order of the universe.

I resigned myself to a world of frizz and walked into the pub, relieved when I saw my brother's equally frizzy head in the corner booth. He was admiring his wife's face, sipping a pint of beer, and holding her hand. Mary was smiling at her husband, nodding as they whispered to each other. But they were the only two in the booth. Maybe I could avoid the blind date after all.

"Okay, you two love birds. Enough of the public displays of affection," I said, dropping into the seat across from them.

"Hey! Well, it's the influence of Saint Agnes, you know," Matt said as he patted my wrist and then kissed his bride on the cheek.

She rolled her eyes at me and grinned. "Yup, it's true, Jonna. Love is in the air."

Mary was yet another beautiful woman who had brains to match. While Matt worked on his PhD in American history, she had been completing hers in English literature. They'd met in the reference section at the college library. He claimed that when he first saw her long brown hair *and* her pile of books in front of her, he was hooked for life. She claimed she just wanted to be left alone to study Blake's poetry, and the only way that was going to happen was if she said yes to his persistence. I thought of Terry Choyce and wondered if I'd ever be so lucky.

"So, where is he?" I said with as much enthusiasm as a vegetable. I motioned to Mick for a pint, feeling suddenly really thirsty as I looked around the nearly empty pub. Poor Saint Agnes. Even on Saturday nights she couldn't draw a crowd.

"Where is who?" Matt asked. Mary elbowed him. "Oh, *him*. Well, he called right as we were leaving the house— "

"Rejected already?" I said as Mick set down my Fat Tire and walked back to the bar. "I guess my reputation has preceded me."

"Relax, Little Sister. Like I was saying, he called right before we were leaving and said he was running a little late but that he'd be here by eight." A tiny foam mustache stayed on Matt's lip as he gulped his ale.

Mary dabbed it with her napkin, then turned to me. "Don't worry, Jonna. I even like this guy. I've made Matt run them by me first. He came for dinner a few weeks ago and was a perfect gentleman," she said with a protective smirk. Then she raised her glass and said, "To love!"

We clinked our pints in agreement, though I was not so sure the toast would do me much good. The cold smooth taste of Fat Tire did, however, make up for it.

For the next hour or so Matt and Mary rambled back and forth about studies, students, and research projects. I listened as if I were sitting in the front row of their classes, admiring their passion for their subjects as well as for each other.

They were completely absorbed in talking about Matt's research of a former slave family who'd lived in Denver in 1890, finding letters, deeds to their homestead, even tax records and a bill of sale from their last owners in Mississippi before they came west. He'd come across some of the items at an estate sale in Five Points, the historically African-American neighborhood of Denver. Now Matt was piecing together the documents to make sense of these people's lives during that time in the city's history. He planned to give the papers over to the Black America West Museum when he finished.

"If you could find deeds and records from a hundred something years ago," I said, "why am I having so much trouble tracking down even a phone bill for a guy who's still alive?" The two looked up at me as if they suddenly remembered I was sitting across the table from them.

"Well, maybe he didn't have a family who'd taken care of his records like this one has," Matt suggested.

"Then why'd his family give *you* such valuable stuff?" The

question seemed obvious to me.

"Well," Matt said, "for one, no one *gave* me anything. The woman who *sold* them to me seemed to think no one in the family saw their value anymore. She apparently thought I had a trustworthy face." He grinned, sitting up straight and raising an eyebrow.

Mary shook her head, then pinched Matt's cheek. "I'm sure that adorable face had everything to do with her handing over those documents."

"Well, it couldn't have hurt."

"Whatever, guys. I'm serious now," I said. "I'm working on this story where my main source is a guy who's claiming some pretty serious stuff about his church, or former church." I leaned forward and gripped my mug as if I were telling a secret.

"This the same guy you told me about last time we were here?" Matt asked, wiping the grin from his face and mirroring my actions. I nodded. "And you haven't made any progress?"

"Well, he came to see me at the *Dispatch*. That's progress. Except there's not a trace of him in any records or databases anywhere. If I hadn't seen him with my own eyes, I wouldn't have believed he existed at all."

"What's his story?" Mary asked.

I told her about Jed Sundae, about his claims that Into the Fields Fellowship was stealing from its members, and about his accusation that there was real "evil" at work there. Matt and Mary stared at me intensely, their eyes a straight line to my words. The wheels in their researching brains were turning—so much so that none of us noticed when David Rockley appeared.

He cleared his throat. All three of us looked up.

"Sorry I'm late. Couldn't get my head out of this document," he said, sitting down beside me. "You must be Jane." He extended his hand as Matt came to my defense.

"Jonna. David, this is *Jonna,* my little sister. Jonna, meet David."

He pulled back his hand, slapped his forehead with his palm, and laughed. "I knew that! Jonna. Sorry," he said as he glanced at me, then at Matt and Mary and back at me. His eyes were pale blue. Or were they green? I couldn't tell from the glare on his glasses.

"Hi," he said. "It's a pleasure to meet you." He looked nice enough, but thirsty.

"More like a *pressure*, don't you mean?" I asked. "I know my brother threatened you with your life if you didn't come tonight, right?" Matt glared at me.

"Only with a few research projects," David responded, turning to Matt. "Besides, Professor, I thought you were a pacifist."

"Not when it comes to my sister," Matt said, flashing that same grin he'd beamed minutes before. Then he rolled back the top of his sleeve, turned his arm sideways, and flexed his muscle, pushing it up a little with his other hand to make it look bigger. "See? I could really hurt you, Rockley. So watch out!"

David raised his hands above his head in surrender and laughed. So did Mary and Matt. I chuckled, too, more to go along with them than because I thought either was particularly amusing.

"I'll be good, I promise," David said. "Especially once I get some food. I haven't eaten since, well, since lunchtime!" He handed us menus from behind the salt-and-pepper-shakers and began reading his. I pretended to look at mine, though I already knew everything that Mick served. Without moving my head, I did a quick perusal of the man beside me.

David Rockley was about my brother's age, early thirties. He wore faded blue jeans, a green rugby shirt, and round glasses, the type that didn't seem to have a frame. His hair was dirt brown with streaks of black and red in it as if he'd either spent too much time in the sun or hadn't quite outgrown his punk rocker days. It was a tussle of wooly thickness, the kind that looked like a comb was not necessarily an easy option. I could sympathize. And, like Matt, David had grown one of those little mustaches and beards on the center of his chin, though the rest of his jaw was smooth. It must have been the style in academia.

When I decided he didn't look anything like Terry Choyce, I gazed at the already-memorized dinner menu.

"What looks good?" David asked. I didn't feel right answering that Terry Choyce did, but I wanted to. "This is my first time here," he continued. I sighed.

Mick appeared at our table, and Matt, Mary, and I all ordered the shepherd's pie. David ordered a cheeseburger and a Coors.

This was going to be a long night.

"So, David, we were just talking about how to find invisible people, and then you showed up," Matt said, reading my wilting shoulders like a book. "Jonna was telling us about her troubles with an unhappy and untraceable church man."

I shot him a glare and suddenly felt protective of Jed.

"Oh, right," David said. "You're a reporter for the *Dispatch*. That must be fascinating."

"Fascinating?" I considered the adjective and determined it didn't quite fit the profile of my week. "Absolutely. Life is always fascinating at the *Dispatch*. But Matt says you're into American literature? That must be *fascinating*." I deflected, gulped the last of my drink, and wiped my lip with my hand.

"Actually, I'm only working in the American lit department's library. For the year. I'm on leave from a university in New York to study some of the college's literary archives," he said. I nodded, trying to look as though I cared. David's face softened and grew enthusiastic at the same time. "That's why I was late tonight. Came across a document that provides our institution quite a link to your brother's."

For the next fifteen minutes or so, David went on discussing something about New York writers who had gone west and left some of their creative works in the Denver College archives. Mary chimed in with curious literary questions, and Matt felt compelled to provide historic context to the discussion. I sat staring at the photo of Saint Agnes hanging near the dartboard. It was certainly a cheery academic discussion, but my mind jumped between Terry, cult members, and a real but invisible Jed Sundae.

Mick plopped our dinners on the table along with a round of coffee mugs. We spent the rest of the night much the same as we started: The three academics talking while I listened, adding an occasional interjection just to remind everyone I could keep up with them. I was a lot of things, but I was not dumb.

By the time we'd made our way to the street, David turned to me.

"I enjoyed myself tonight, more than I have in a while. Thanks for coming, Jonna." He took off his glasses and polished them against his shirt, blushing slightly under the streetlight. His eyes were definitely green. Something in my stomach shifted. I loved Mick's shepherd's pie.

"But I didn't get to hear about you. I'm sorry I talked so much." He smiled at me as he spoke. I looked toward the Denver skyline and moved out of the light. Matt was waiting inside for Mary, who was "fixing her hair." I hoped they'd emerge any minute. They didn't.

"I'd love to hear some more about *you*," David said, emphasizing the "you" in the same tone he used to describe his document discovery.

I shifted away from the streetlight, since I knew the heat in my cheeks would have given me away. I had to admit, David's comment was nice to hear. But when I looked back at him, I could not get Terry Choyce's face out of my mind. I thought of him on the steps of the Catholic Outreach Center, the sun on his blond hair, his gentle way with the children. Suddenly, the summer air felt dry and uncomfortable.

"So would you mind if I gave you a call sometime?" David asked, bringing me back to the moment. "Would that be okay?" he said again with a depth and sincerity in his voice that put me at ease. I wasn't sure how I should answer, but it didn't matter. At that moment, Matt grabbed me from behind and squeezed me in a bear hug.

"See, Rockley?" Matt said. "She's pretty swell, isn't she?"

I punched his gut with the sharp of my elbow, remembering the myriad times my brother had embarrassed me in similar moments throughout my life. I suddenly wished I knew Jed's secret to disappearing.

"It might be the first thing yet you've been right about, Professor," David shot back.

I made it to my car, safely dodging his question and Matt's teasing. I waved to them all, put the keys in the ignition, and hurried down the street.

When I got inside my apartment I kicked off my clogs and collapsed on the couch. But I felt something bumpy under me:

Gideon. I grabbed the little book and set him next to me. Then I did what I'd been wanting to do all night: I lit a cigarette and took a long slow drag.

Even that could not keep the tear from sliding down my cheek.

::Chapter Eight

Someone was pounding on my door. I turned over in my bed, cozy under the flannel sheets, too tired to get up. Even in the summer, I kept my flannel sheets on my futon—they were soft and therapeutic against my skin. I needed them year-round. This morning I pulled them over my ears hoping the noise would go away.

The pounding only got louder. I popped open my eyes and tried to make out the numbers on the clock. But they were as fuzzy as my head this morning. A little sliver of light came through the window.

"Juana! Juana! We go church, sí?" Mrs. Rodriguez was calling between pounds. "You there, Juana?"

Church. Was today already Sunday? How did that happen? I'd slept so hard I didn't even hear my alarm. Or maybe I'd forgotten to set it after I'd come home from dinner at The Pub of Saint Agnes with Matt, Mary, and what's-his-name. What was his name? I knew what it wasn't: Terry.

I rubbed the sleep out of my eyes, pulled my feet over the side of the bed, and stared at the door. I yawned. I was just about ready to tell Mrs. Rodriguez that I was coming down with something, when she called out.

"We go your church and other church too?"

I fell back against my flannel pillow and soaked in the comfort. Other church? Of course. This was the morning I'd decided to visit Into the Fields Fellowship after taking Mrs. Rodriguez to Capitol Pres. I glared at the door and dragged myself to it.

"Oh! You no look so good, Juana." I could always count on my neighbor to give it to me straight.

"Me no feel so good, either. Muy sleepy-do."

"We eat Jesus this morning, sí? That make you better. Make you no sleepy." My Catholic friend always associated church with Holy Communion, so she liked to say we were having a meal of Jesus whenever we went, feeding on him to keep us going for the day. I suspected she was right. But this morning I wasn't too hungry.

She smiled at me, patted my shoulder to get me going, and pushed her way toward the coffeepot. I hung on to the door, still open into the hallway, as she fumbled through the freezer for coffee beans.

"Pronto, pronto, amiga! I make you café, pick you up for Jesus."

I leaned against the doorknob, craving my flannel but knowing Mrs. Rodriguez's zeal would win this battle. I stared at the hallway floor and wondered when it had last been vacuumed. Christmas maybe? The smell of coffee drew me back inside, and I closed the door before heading toward the shower.

A cup of coffee was sitting on the sink when I got out. This was one serious church lady, I thought, swallowing most of the cup while trying to shape the wet loops on my head into some respectable form. We were out the door five minutes later.

We got to the second pew of Capitol Presbyterian in record time and sat beside the cheery faces of Matt and Mary just as the organist was pounding out, "Guide Me, O Thou Great Eternal."

I glanced around the small sanctuary and noticed that Mrs. Gildecek—who was sitting across the aisle—had a slightly brighter blue in her hair this week. I stopped staring, flipped open the hymnal, and held it for Mrs. Rodriguez, who was singing with more enthusiasm than I would ever manage even after a gallon of liquid caffeine.

Guide me, O Thou Great Eternal,
Pilgrim through this barren land.
I am weak, but Thou art mighty;
Hold me with Thy powerful hand.

I whimpered along, hoping the words would wake up in me that spiritual appetite Mrs. Rodriguez—and now the hymn—talked about, but my mind stayed back in bed. The cold shower and hot coffee had pushed my body out the door, but neither had been enough to get my brain moving as it needed to for worship.

Bread of heaven, bread of heaven,
Feed me till I want no more;
Feed me till I want no more.

After the final chords boomed from the congregation, I yawned and stared at the organ pipes as if the notes were still there. Mrs. Rodriguez grabbed me by the elbow and pulled me back into the pew. I passed the offering plate when it came my way and flipped through the bulletin during the sermon, hoping some Holy Spirit-generated energy would jumpstart my emotions in spite of me. I was too groggy to be an active Presbyterian this morning, but considering how our denomination was known as the "frozen chosen," I doubted anyone would notice anyway.

"A nice God-word, sí Juana?" Mrs. Rodriguez said to me as we strolled up the aisle toward the fellowship hall.

I hadn't the slightest idea what the pastor had just preached, so I decided simply to smile at my friend and hope that another cup of coffee would do the trick, even if it was church coffee. The powdered-sugar cookies and glazed donuts would help, too; I was sure of it.

We stood chatting, sipping, and munching with my brother, his wife, and the Sunday school women—average age sixty-seven—getting the latest news on casserole recipes and hospital visits. Just as Mavis Artenwild started to tell us her plans for a short-term missions trip to an Indian reservation on the Western Slope of the Rockies, I noticed a thin man I hadn't before seen at church. He stood alone in the corner. His black sports jacket was wrinkled, and his hair was smooth against his head. He wore black sunglasses, which I thought strange. I'd hated the fluorescent lights in the fellowship hall since my first visit three years ago, but I didn't think they were *that* bright.

Then it dawned on me: I knew this man. I'd spoken to him in the lobby of the *Dispatch* just days before. Suddenly, I was wide-awake, swerving in and out of clusters of Presbyterians as if I were late for a plane in the airport. I dodged Styrofoam cups held in pale hands, pointy purses dangling from elbows, and shiny metal walkers standing ready to take their owners anywhere they wanted to go. I blurted out, "Excuse me!" along the way, concentrating on the cups and elbows so as not to clobber some poor senior in the process.

But when I finally arrived at the corner of the fellowship hall, it was as empty as the computer searches I'd done on the guy. How did Jed Sundae become so invisible again? Hadn't that been him across the room, or was my mind playing tricks on me this morning? I knew I wasn't quite awake, but I could have sworn on Gideon that it was the same man who days ago had bravely visited me at the *Dispatch*. I rubbed my eyes. Then I stared at the empty space, at the emergency exit sign above me, and at the spots on the linoleum floor in case he'd dropped any clue to suggest he really had been here.

When I turned around, still baffled, I ran smack into Mr. Walker's walker. The ninety-one-year-old man had been a founding elder of the church and had never officially resigned his position on the welcoming committee, even after a hip replacement, a heart attack, and a recent bout in the emergency room with poison ivy. No one dared ask about that one.

"I couldn't catch him, either," he snapped. Mr. Walker's white eyebrows gathered in bushy heaps above his eyes, creating a cushion of sorts for his glasses to lean against.

"Who?" I asked, stepping a few inches away from the metal in case it smacked my shins again.

"Whatdoyamean 'who'? The visitor! The guy with the wrinkly jacket, that's who!" Apparently, he'd not been listening to the pastor's sermons on patience. Or the ones about kindness. Then again, I couldn't even tell him what the pastor had said fifteen minutes ago, let alone two weeks ago.

"So, you did see him? That guy in the sunglasses? I was thinking I was going nuts, Mr. Walker," I said.

"Course I saw him. It's not every week we get a visitor, so I try to snag 'em before they get away. Guess I'm losing my touch."

He looked up at the exit sign above, shook his head, coughed, and turned his walker around.

I stepped slowly—very slowly—beside him, silently commiserating our loss and wondering how either of us could have kept this man from disappearing. Jed Sundae seemed to have a knack for that.

Mrs. Rodriguez found me by the Walkers and pointed to the watch on her wrist. I shook Mr. Walker's hand and gave him a napkin. The powdered cookies he'd been gobbling as consolation for "missing the visitor" had turned his lips white.

"You'll get him next time!" I said.

"Darn right I will," he said, dabbing his mouth and blowing his nose with the same napkin. "Hey, aren't you two coming to the Stockade this morning? They've got a special on ribs."

"Tempting. But we've got another stop to make," I said, pushing up my hair to give it some shape, if only for a second. "See you next Sunday."

"Lord willing! Be careful now, Jonna," Mr. Walker said, right before he zeroed in on the last of the powdered cookies.

I took it as good advice considering where we were going, but hoped I wouldn't need to heed it. How bad could Into the Fields Fellowship really be?

When we got in the car, Mrs. Rodriguez was still singing, "Guide Me, O Thou Great Eternal"—only this time I didn't recognize the words. She was singing in Spanish. I wanted to join her, but I had two things working against me: I didn't know the Spanish version, and my head was still absorbed by the reality of spotting—and losing—Jedediah Sundae with an *e*. Instead, I hummed and went to start the car—but realized I'd left my bag back in the church, below the pew where we'd been sitting. I *was* tired. I told Mrs. Rodriguez to continue her worship while I hurried back into the sanctuary.

I ran down the aisle, found my bag, but slowed down as I walked back through the sanctuary, trying to catch my breath. This was more exercise than I'd had in weeks. I vowed to quit smoking once and for all. It was a dumb habit I'd picked up in my teens—before Mom and Dad had stopped rolling their own once they realized it wasn't the best way to serve God. Somehow I even managed to keep lighting up during college ski team competitions. But that was then, and this was the time to quit. And I *would* take up jogging. That was final. I made a pact with the Great Eternal when I got to the last pew, and this time I meant it.

Just as my lungs had calmed down and I turned the corner into the lobby, I could hardly believe how quickly God rewarded me: There was Jed Sundae coming down the other end of the hall!

But when he spotted me, he turned and ran. I went after him.

He bolted down the staircase behind the sanctuary, through the still-lively fellowship hall, and slammed open the emergency exit door where Mr. Walker and I had first spotted him, leaving it open to the parking lot. I stumbled down the steps behind him, caught a breath, and picked up speed, airport-style again, weaving in and out of coffee hour. This time I didn't bother with "excuse me."

"He's gone that way, Jon!" Mr. Walker was hollering and pointing. "Hurry, you'll get him! You'll get him!" I brushed past him, feeling his support as well as my burning lungs, and was just about to reach the door when Mavis Artenwild stopped right in front of it. I screeched to a stop.

"I have been telling people for I don't know how long that they are not supposed to use this door. It's an emergency exit only. Can't they read the sign, for heaven's sake?" She slammed the door shut and stood in front of it with her arms crossed. I smiled at her, thankful for the air, wiped the sweat from my eyes, and wondered how to make my next move. But Mr. Walker rescued me.

"Mavis, there's some of these donuts left. Come get some!" He was yelling to her and waving at me. Just as she moved toward the coffee table, I jumped forward.

"Sorry, Mavis!" I screamed and threw my shoulder into the door.

But when I got out into the parking lot, the only person I saw was Mrs. Rodriguez, who was now standing beside my car, still singing and enjoying the Colorado morning sun. I looked up the street, across the parking lot, and back again. There was no sign of Jed. At least I still had my bag.

"Did you see him, Mrs. Rodriguez? That man in black?"

Mrs. Rodriguez looked up suddenly at me, as if she were surprised to see where she was. She'd been lost in her reverie. "No, Amiga. I no see no black man. I have shut eyes with Jesus."

I smiled as I climbed in the car. I scrounged for the keys and drove toward the address I'd written in my notes for Into the Fields Fellowship.

I turned onto Colfax Avenue, its claim to fame being that it's the longest continuing street in any U.S. city. Colfax went from the eastern plains to the foothills of the Rockies right past the golden dome of the capitol and the homeless men who slept in civic Center Park across the street. That also meant it stretched across just about every neighborhood and economic pocket of the city, which always made Colfax an interesting ride. I kept my eyes open for Jed, just in case I spotted him on the sidewalk.

When we turned onto Colorado Boulevard, Mrs. Rodriguez was still singing. I hummed along but stopped as we passed the annex of the Buddhist Cultural Center. It still bothered me that their building was gone. I made a mental note to visit the monks again in the next week and call about the investigation.

We drove across the bridge above Interstate 25 and pulled into the blacktop surrounding Into the Fields Fellowship just south of the interstate. It looked to me as if the building had once been a store of some kind—grocery, hardware, maybe even one of those chain pet stores, but I couldn't tell which one. It had obviously gone through its own conversion—as I'd discovered in my job was pretty common whenever religious groups bought up some old shop that had gone out of business.

The IFF leaders had taken this modest square site and made it into a church with glass windows and nondescript colors outside. The only thing that distinguished it was an old marquee sign in front with big black letters that simply read: "A Place to Belong." If someone didn't know already that this was a church, it might have been easy to mistake it as a meeting center for Alcoholics Anonymous or an insurance office.

I pulled into a parking place and jotted down what I saw: about a hundred or so cars and trucks, most of them in the same condition as mine, very few newer models. I scribbled the message from the marquee and watched a few people get out of their cars and walk toward the makeshift sanctuary. They might as well have been walking into the mall. No one carried Bibles, no one talked with others walking past them, and no one was wearing a tie or formal dress. In fact, many men wore the kind of work pants you might see on a mechanic or deliveryman. The women were in simple skirts or stretch pants with matching tops.

"We stay here or go in, Juana?" Mrs. Rodriguez smiled at me and watched me write. She sighed, pulled two wintergreen Lifesavers from her purse, and dropped one on my lap while she popped the other in her mouth.

"Why we go here again?" she asked, rolling down her window when she saw I wasn't moving. She rested her elbow on the door and looked at me with eager brown eyes as she waited for my answer. I was glad she was with me. Her presence, as well as the mint, was refreshing.

I explained to her what the same man I'd just chased through coffee hour at Capitol Pres had told me about this church last week and that he'd seemed genuinely upset by what was happening here, though I had no idea why. I was sure he was not just another unhappy ex-church member who didn't like the music or who thought the preaching was boring. No, this man said something was really wrong at IFF, something that was not consistent with the religion he valued. I believed him.

"Then we go find out," Mrs. Rodriguez said firmly, rolling up her window and pushing open the door. I followed her to the building.

A plain woman with brown hair that flipped up on the ends and whose age was somewhere between my neighbor's and mine greeted us at the door. She handed us a bulletin like the one Dolores, the nail executive, had given me, and shook our hands weakly.

"Good morning. Welcome to Into the Fields Fellowship, a place to belong," she said without a trace of emotion. As we moved into the massive warehouse-like room, I heard her offer exactly the same line in the same way to the person behind us, and the next. I glanced over my shoulder at her and wondered how many times she'd said that this morning. I couldn't help but think she sounded like a telemarketer.

Mrs. Rodriguez found us a seat toward the back of the room—which felt like a huge grocery warehouse without the food. We were reading the bulletin when a tall, pale man with scraggly hair extended his hand. He was a few rows ahead of us on the same aisle.

"Goot morning. Velcome here Into the Fields Fellowships, a place to belong," he said, a trace of Europe in his speech and the same eerie tone that the greeter lady had used. "My name is, uh, Hank. Nice have you to us this morning." Two upright lines formed between his eyebrows and his shoulders were stiff.

I smiled, hoping he'd relax, and took his hand. I wondered how many times he'd said his broken sentence. His handshake was also one of those fishlike squeezes, which seemed odd to me given his size. He did the same with Mrs. Rodriguez, who shot me a glance that suggested she, too, thought it odd.

The church bulletin didn't offer any new clues about this nondenominational gathering, but I read it thoroughly anyway. Order of worship, Scripture reading, fellowship announcements. It all seemed pretty standard to me, and so far I still didn't understand what Jed was upset about. Maybe a couple of people were chilly, even kind of weird, but I figured the same could be said about the church we'd just left. I decided to stay open-minded, even if my reporter antenna was not getting any new signals.

Maybe Jed Sundae *was* just another disgruntled churchgoer. Lord knew, I'd met plenty of those the last few years at the *Dispatch*.

But when I watched the pastor move to the podium, saw

his smooth gestures, and heard the speed with which he spoke, I felt I was about to be sold a side of beef. I sensed Jed had told me the truth.

"Good morning, welcome to Into the Fields Fellowship, a place to belong," a thin, middle-aged man spoke from the microphone on a small stage in the front of the room, about where the meat section would have been.

As soon as he said it, Mrs. Rodriguez and I stared at each other. Zero emotion came through his voice. Behind him were six other men with equally serious faces standing with guitars or at an electric piano. Two women stood at microphones off to the side, one of whom was our greeter.

"Let's sing our praise to the God who has made each of us special and unique," the man said with as much enthusiasm as his greeting, yet all the people around us obeyed.

I did not recognize the first song, though everyone clapped and sang as though this was one they'd learned in childhood. The same thing happened with the next song, and the next. Though each chorus had different lyrics, they all sounded exactly alike to me. The clapping never changed, the sounds from the instruments up front never varied, and the faces in front of us all seemed frozen in their expressions.

My mind suddenly flashed back to high school English class with Miss Klem. We were doing a unit on science fiction, and she'd had us read Jack Finney's book, *Invasion of the Body Snatchers.* (Though my brothers never agreed, I always thought the book was miles better than the movie.)

In the story, alien creatures invaded earth in the form of plantlike pods and began to take on the form of whatever humans they encountered. Slowly, they began to suck the life out of the people, making them look and act the same, but without being exactly who they once were. The protagonist—a writer, I think, or was he a doctor?—began to realize something wasn't quite the same with Uncle Joe or Aunt Betty. When he stumbled on the truth behind the alien invasion, he refused to give in to their plot. His resistance saved the day—and Planet Earth—by sending these creatures back from where they came.

It was a funny image to have in my head at a Sunday morning church service, but I couldn't help but wonder if Aunt Greeter up front or Uncle Neighbor down the aisle just weren't quite the same as they'd always been, before they found this "place to belong." When we finally sat down, I jotted "Finney" on my bulletin as the next book I'd check out from the library.

"Good morning, welcome to Into the Fields Fellowship, a place to . . ."

"A place to . . . belong," I heard Mrs. Rodriguez say. My head darted her way, alarmed to hear her echo the man on the stage. But when I glanced at her, she winked at me to relax. I did.

Another man stepped to the microphone while the others left the stage. "I'm Pastor Jeff Whitman, and you're exactly where you're supposed to be this morning," he said, his tone a serious line in the air.

So this was the man whom I had just missed when I visited his office, the man who was making visits to sick members, his secretary had said. He had short brown hair and thick round glasses that made him look a bit like a professor. He wore black jeans and a short-sleeved Hawaiian-print shirt. I guessed he was in his forties, though I couldn't tell from where we were sitting.

He preached for the next thirty minutes, although I thought what he did was more like talking than preaching. Over and over he told the people "they were special," gave them one or two Bible verses to remind them how special they were, and then told stories the rest of the time that illustrated to his congregation just "how special each person here this morning really is." That was the extent of his sermon. It seemed harmless enough, positive and uplifting even, if you were the kind of person who liked things simple, and who needed to feel special.

While he talked, I looked around the room and discovered that no one—except me—was taking notes. Everyone nodded when he made a point and laughed at his stories. Clearly, this group had been together long enough to know how to respond to their minister, but I was beginning to wonder if something had in fact dropped from the sky and gotten *Into* the Fields Fellowship?

Pods?

As he finished his talk, Pastor Jeff told us about "a wonderful new ministry we've started, called 'Field Hands.' We're taking meals to or cleaning houses for our special elderly friends who live alone." His voice was smooth and easy to listen to. Bingo. I remembered searching on the computer for anything on Field Hands, but hadn't found a thing. This was interesting.

He told a final story and then asked several men to come forward for—what else?—a *special* offering.

Up and down each row of chairs, filled with the quiet lives of middle-class folks, they passed a red velvet bag with wooden handles. I couldn't believe my eyes—every single person in every single row put money into that velvet bag as it passed. I had never seen such a thing, not at any church, synagogue, or temple I'd ever visited as a reporter. At least a few people always passed it on without contributing. Not here. I began to squirm in my seat, a wave of guilt coming over me. How could anyone not feel compelled to give with that kind of collective generosity? I scraped a dollar out of my bag and dropped it in.

After a few more choruses and *special* words, we shuffled into the crowd of people making their way down the aisle and toward the door as the band played a final song—which by now even I sang along to, though I'd never heard it before today. We smiled at a few families beside us, who smiled dutifully back. I glanced up at the ceiling. It looked as if it hadn't changed much since they'd bought it when it was a store. At least they'd lined the sides and the stage with thick green plants throughout the massive hall to give it an earthy feel.

A queue formed at the door where the pastor stood shaking everyone's hand. Once the band stopped playing, I noticed how quiet it was. No one was laughing or joking with each other. No one seemed to linger over family updates or job news. So by the time I reached Pastor Jeff, I had a few questions I hoped to get answered.

"I'm Jonna Lightfoot MacLaughlin, religion reporter at the *Denver Dispatch*," I said, Mrs. Rodriguez at my side.

"Oh? Well, it's lovely to meet you. I'm sorry I missed you at the office the other day," he said, grinning. He stood barely six feet tall and nothing about him seemed out of the ordinary—in fact, he seemed like your average fortysomething pastor with a calming manner.

"Well, I was wondering if I could—"

"And who's this with you?" he interrupted.

I looked at my neighbor, whose eyes were fixed on the IFF leader. "Oh, she's my neighbor, Mrs. Rodriguez."

He extended his hand to her, and a full rich smile filled his face. "It's a pleasure to meet you. So glad to have you with us."

I was suddenly quite invisible as the pastor focused on the short Hispanic woman beside me.

Mrs. Rodriguez tilted her head slightly, grinned, and withdrew her hand.

"You will come back and visit us, won't you, Mrs. Rodriguez? We'd love to have you join us!" She shrugged.

I reeled him back in. "Pastor Jeff, I'm wondering if you could answer a couple questions for me," I asked, figuring this was as good a time as any.

"Absolutely. What would you like to know?"

"Well, for starters, how exactly does Field Hands work? Is it a nonprofit?"

"Why not come and see the work yourself? We meet on Wednesdays. You're always welcome at Into the Fields Fellowship, a— "

"A place to belong," I quipped.

He chuckled and glanced at the line of people behind me waiting to shake hands with their pastor.

"Sure, okay. One more quick question, about a former member of— "

"Tell you what. Why don't I give you a call at your office? Would that be okay, Miss MacLaughlin?" He leaned over and whispered in my ear. "I'm sort of working right now."

Something about his closeness burned the air in my lungs. I handed him my business card and said loudly so the crowd behind me could hear me: "I'm sort of working now, too, Pastor. That'd be fine if you called me at my office at the . . . *Denver Dispatch* newspaper. I'll look forward to talking with you."

He nodded and laughed a deep but sincere laugh, the kind that suggested such joviality was a habit. The joke was on me, though, because when I looked around, I realized not a single person appeared to have heard me. They were simply staring at whatever seemed to catch their attention, lost in their own "special" place.

When we got to the parking lot, Mrs. Rodriguez turned to me and whispered, "I no think I go back there, Amiga." I was about to ask her to explain what she meant more when she noticed another Hispanic woman about her age strolling toward the bus stop, an IFF bulletin in her hand. She greeted her in Spanish, and the two struck up what seemed to be a friendly conversation as we walked toward my car, though I couldn't understand a word.

Suddenly, I got an idea. "Mrs. Rodriguez, could you ask your new friend a question for me?"

She nodded at me and said something to the woman, and then they both looked back at me, waiting for my question.

I swallowed, almost afraid of what I might discover. "Could you ask her if she ever knew a man named Jedediah Sundae here at the Fellowship?"

When Mrs. Rodriguez explained the question and repeated Jed's name slowly, the woman's face went blank. A tight, pale shadow crossed it, and then she began to shake her head back and forth with more emotion than I had seen all morning. Mrs. Rodriguez asked her what was wrong. And the woman rattled off something so fast I was amazed my neighbor got it. Then she turned to me and translated the woman's response in English.

"She say the man, the Jedediah Sundae, he no more, he no more."

"What do you mean, no more?"

"Juana, she say this man Sundae is no alive." She paused. "She say he die last year. He dead!"

::Chapter Nine

"But I'm telling you, I chased the guy through coffee hour! How could he be dead?"

I was emotional this Monday morning as I sat in Skip's office. I all but inhaled the half cup of mocha in my mug, thumping my foot against the chair in a nervous rhythm. I felt wound up and exhausted at the same time, even though it was only 10 a.m. After the bizarre comment from Mrs. Rodriguez's friend in the IFF parking lot, I hadn't been able to relax the rest of the day. And although my flannels were as cozy as ever when I finally got into bed last night, I didn't sleep well. I'd wanted to keep my "objective reporter's eye," but I felt bad for the guy whose church friends thought he was dead.

"Well, maybe he's not dead," my editor said calmly. He leaned his head back as if he were looking for an answer.

"Of course he's not dead. I ran after him!"

"*Anything* that gets you running is definitely for real," he said, a tiny smirk crossing the bottom of his mouth. "Seriously, Lightfoot, let me get this straight. The guy tells you something's rotten in Denmark . . ."

"Yeah."

"But folks in Denmark tell you the guy's dead?"

"Right."

"Hmm," he grunted, putting his hands behind his head so his elbows stuck sideways. He studied the ceiling and asked, "Ever been in a bakery, Lightfoot?"

He had my attention. "Almost daily."

"Ever *work* in a bakery?"

"Nope. I was taught to try to avoid temptation, Skip. Working in pastry conditions would *not* be good for me."

"Point taken. But what's the first thing you notice when you visit a bakery?"

"Besides the chocolate éclairs?"

"Besides those."

"The smell of freshly baked bread, the sweet aroma of brownies, cakes, and pies in the oven. Oh, don't get me started."

"Exactly. You notice the smell for one simple reason."

I closed my eyes and imagined a chocolate cream pie. This was painful.

"Don't you want to know the reason?"

"The reason for what?"

"Why you notice the smell?"

"Isn't it obvious?" I looked down at the baggy shirt that I hoped hid most of the extra pounds I carried in my waist and hips as a result of too many stops at too many bakeries.

"Wrong question, Lightfoot. You notice *because* you don't work there. You only visit."

I stared at my editor for a minute. His dark blue tie matched his eyes and beamed against his starched yellow shirt. His beard was neatly trimmed, and not even a paper clip on his desk was out of place. Skip Gravely was born a professional. I was not. Maybe that was why I still wasn't tracking with him.

"Help me, Boss."

"They say people who work in a bakery sort of lose their sense of smell—"

"Perish the thought!"

"Their noses grow numb the more they smell bread in the oven. You following?"

I wanted to. I was still tripped up on the bread thing. And the pies.

"In other words, maybe those folks in Denmark can't smell the rotten eggs anymore because they've been there too long. They've become a little numb, if you will."

"Exactly! They were the numbest people I'd ever seen. It was spooky." I shook my head, thinking about the Sunday service at Into the Fields Fellowship before wandering back into the conversation. "So, you think that's part of what Jed's talking about? That maybe he's the one who's somehow managed to, well, stay *alive*?"

"That's what you need to find out," Skip said. "Do some checking with the Better Business Bureau and some of Hannah's contacts at City Hall. See what you come up with about who's for real and who isn't at Into the Fields Fellowship. This might be bigger than religion."

"Nothing is bigger than religion, Skip. You know that," I said in mock-lecture tone.

I grabbed my cup and started for the door at the same time his phone rang.

"Skip Gravely." I watched him introduce himself, but he waved me back into his office.

"Well, well, Frank Murphy. How long has it been?"

I hurried to the chair where I'd been sitting, anxious to hear why the Boulder detective was calling my editor.

Skip laughed into the phone and looked at me. "It's Jonna,

Murphy. Not Jean." He rolled his eyes and shook his head. I did the same.

A million questions ran through my head about why he might be calling: The suspect they'd captured on Saturday morning was now claiming he was my "God" after all? The annual Wicca Gathering in Boulder was getting rescheduled? Someone had called in again about the space aliens who landed in Rocky Mountain National Park? All of these were legitimate possibilities for a detective in Boulder County. Suddenly, I wanted a cigarette. I tapped my fingers on my notebook, remembering the pact I'd made yesterday morning with God. I would quit. No matter what.

"In fact, she's sitting right here," Skip said. "Let me put you on speaker phone."

We stared at the phone as if the man were sitting between us. Detective Murphy's voice was as wound up as mine this morning. He coughed and hurried through the news. My guesses weren't even close.

"So the guy's got a record a mile long," he said. "He'd jumped parole when we found him Saturday."

"What'd he do?" Skip said.

"More like what didn't he do? You name it: domestic violence, breaking and entering, even fraud. Stole some lady's credit cards and went on the town. He's had quite a career." He paused to yell at someone in his office. "Anyway, just wanted to call and, you know, say thanks for the tip. Skip, you want to keep that one."

Skip looked up at me and nodded, his eyes turning upward. "I plan to, Murphy. She's living proof that religion is good for us."

The two men laughed as though they'd exchanged these morning jokes for years.

I, on the other hand, did not feel flattered or relieved. In fact, my anxiety level was rising. "But, Detective, that was *not* the guy who called me. I told you I didn't recognize his voice. Which means that— "

"Yeah, well, we'll just call this a happy coincidence, okay?"

I remembered my father's philosophy about coincidences: God working anonymously. "Great, but the squeaky little guy who thinks he's God is still out there."

"And if you hear from him again, let me know. See ya, Gravely."

Skip shrugged and turned to his computer. I stood up for the second time that morning in his office, more stressed than when I had first come in. It was really nice and all that the stars had aligned on Saturday morning so they could catch some ex-con who'd broken parole, but it didn't exactly cheer me up about the state of the world.

Work was getting confusing, even slightly weird. Then again, where I grew up, weird was normal, so what was new? Then again, I reasoned with myself, I'd never seen anyone's weirdness actually hurt someone else when I was a kid. Then again, I'd never quite bargained for the reality that some people's spiritual ideas could get a little out of hand. Even a lot. To the point of indulging in some type of chainsaw madness or groovy drug-fest gone bad. Then again, the detective did have his officers looking out for the guy, even if they only had a "voice" to go on. I pressed my hair up, rubbed the back of my neck, and shook my head, baffled by the seemingly chaotic mess the universe was in.

"Remind me to give you a raise next year, okay, Lightfoot?" Skip said, bringing me back to earth. He was madly typing at his computer.

“A lifetime supply of chocolate will do,” I said as I walked past the flame coming out of his keyboard. He mumbled something about seeing what he could do.

Back at my desk I stared again at my notes and chewed on the end of my pen. Hannah was on the phone, so I thought I’d better wait before interrupting her.

If IFF members had in fact lost their “sense of smell,” as Skip suggested, what was it that had gotten them into the bakery to begin with? What sweet treat did they come looking for?

Welcome to Into the Fields Fellowship, a place to belong.

The phrase dropped into my ear as if someone were standing behind me. *A place to belong.* Was that part of the appeal for these people? Did Pastor Jeff and his leaders become like a family to them? Did IFF give lonely souls something they couldn’t find anywhere else? If that were the case, what was so wrong—or so evil, as Jed had said—with fitting in at a local church? Wasn’t that the point of religion: to give people something they could be a part of, some way to connect?

“Not if it steals their dignity, honey,” Hannah answered after she’d hung up the phone and I’d thrown the questions her way.

“What do you mean?”

“My grandma always said church folk were supposed to be the freest people in the world. You know why?” I opened my mouth to answer, but she kept going. “Cuz they know who they are. It’s in here,” she said, putting her hand on her heart and speaking in a matter-of-fact tone as if she’d just ordered her lunch. She picked up the phone book and flipped through it.

I thought about her words as I admired Hannah’s red and

black flowered-print blouse, which of course matched her linen black slacks. Neither had a wrinkle anywhere. My skirt, on the other hand, didn't have a visible unwrinkled patch.

"But these people seemed more like robots than anything else," I said, offering her a piece of my milk chocolate.

"Well, Lightfoot, maybe it isn't a *real* church." Her phone rang, and she held up a finger for me to "hold that thought and the chocolate." She wasn't the first person to wonder what was real in this story. I swished the Hershey's between my cheeks until it dissolved on my tongue, then wrote down the word "real." I clicked on the Internet dictionary and typed in r-e-a-l to see if its definition offered any clues.

> *Real: a.) Being or occurring in fact or actuality; having verifiable existence: real objects, a real illness; b.) True and actual; not imaginary, alleged, or ideal: real people, not ghosts; a film based on real life; c.) Genuine and authentic; not artificial or spurious: real mink; real humility. d.) Free of pretense, falsehood.*

When I read the last definition, I remembered something Detective Murphy had said about the ex-con: *Even fraud. Stole some lady's credit cards and went on the town.* That was interesting. Maybe the reason I hadn't been able to find anything on Jed Sundae or Jeff Whitman or Field Hands or any other part of Into the Fields Fellowship was because they were not "free of pretense or falsehood." Maybe they were acting as someone—or some*thing*—else.

I looked up another word.

Fraud: any act, expression, omission, or concealment calculated to deceive another to his or her disadvantage; a deception deliberately practiced in order to secure unfair or unlawful gain.

I had no idea what could be gained by it, but my gut told me that there was some sort of deliberate deception happening at IFF. I printed out the definition of fraud, wrote "Jeff Whitman" on it, and slipped it onto Hannah's desk. She read it while she talked on the phone, nodded to me like it rang true to her, and grabbed her pen. "I'm on it!" she wrote, which I knew meant she'd check with her sources in the Colorado Bureau of Investigation (CBI), who could process criminal and civil identification files and records.

I clicked on the Better Business Bureau's website and began searching for anything that might help me understand how a nonprofit organization or charity could stay off so many radar screens. I might be able to hold my own on anything related to Hinduism, crystals, Protestant denominations, or Bible games, but when it came to economics and business issues, I needed extra revelation. The BBB was a good place to start.

But just as I began surfing the site, my phone rang.

"Jonna Lightfoot MacLaughlin."

"Hi, Jonna. David Rockley here."

David who? I cradled the phone on my shoulder and continued to click and read on the BBB site, wanting to get some answers to my questions. I clicked under "Consumer Protection" and read silently, *Sometimes, you can be your own worst enemy.*

"Jonna? Is this a bad time?" The voice in my ear was low and familiar, but I couldn't for the life of me put a face to it.

"I'm sorry. Who is this?" I looked up from the screen and

massaged my eyebrows.

"David. Matt's friend. We met the other night at The Pub of Saint Agnes?"

Oh. Him. I scrambled around my desk for coffee or chocolate or any other form of edible fortification but came up empty under every paper pile and hiding place. Instead, I opened the drawer and found a stick of Juicy Fruit gum that I thought had been in there when I was first assigned this desk. It was a little hard, but it would work.

"Oh, sure. David. Sorry, sort of a busy morning."

"I could call back."

"No, no. Sure. Yeah. Okay!"

"So you want me to call back?"

I tried to crack the gum but it was too stale. "Would you mind? I'm sort of in the middle of something right now and . . ."

"Be glad to. Just wanted you to know I enjoyed meeting you."

Uh-oh. That was a phrase that sounded a little like there might be romantic inklings tucked behind it. My shoulders sank as I scrolled down on the website, not wanting to pay attention to the male voice in my ear. I stared at the moving cursor.

"Well, you can always count on Saint Agnes for a good time," I said, working the gum.

Silence.

"Wait, that didn't quite come out right," I said.

"I couldn't have said it better myself! Hey, I know you're busy now, so I'll call you later, okay, Jonna? No problem. Don't work too hard!"

Click.

I decided to forego getting depressed about my social life

and instead went back to doing what I did best. I kept reading on the BBB site.

> *Simply put, the easiest way for a criminal to steal your identity is to ask you for it. Posing as your bank, or your insurance company, or your doctor's office, the criminal calls you on the telephone, gives you a plausible story, and asks you for key pieces of personal information. This practice is called "pretexting," and you can learn more about the practice from the Federal Trade Commission.*

I picked up my pen and copied the word "pretexting" in my notes. Something about this seemed to fit with what I had observed at IFF and what I had *not* found on Jed or anyone else. Only problem was, I couldn't prove a thing. I needed verifiable evidence if I were going to run this story by my editor. Maybe that piece of paper Jed had waved in front of my nose when we talked in the *Dispatch* lobby would provide exactly what I needed, but I didn't know how to track him down. The phone rang again, and now I was annoyed at its intrusion.

"Lightfoot," I barked.

"Hi, Jonna. This is Terry. Choyce. You know, at the— "

"Of course! Terry!" I sat up straight and fixed my hair.

"Sorry to bother you, but— "

"Absolutely no bother," I said. "It's been a miserably slow morning." I sucked in my stomach and ironed out the wrinkles on my skirt with my hand, in case they could be transmitted through the phone line.

"What can I do you for?" I smiled innocently into the phone, though I wasn't sure that came out right, either. I knew it hadn't when he laughed.

"Just wanted you to know a little second-grade girl by the name of Keisha is expecting you on Thursday for the Reading Club here at the center. She told me so herself."

I flipped open my calendar and saw Thursday was empty. "It's already in my schedule," I said, writing it in my book.

"Great! Hey, mind if I ask you something?"

Ask me anything you want, Terry Choyce, I thought. *I'll say yes every time.* "Shoot," I said in my best Julia Roberts voice.

"Well, okay. Uh, I was wondering . . ."

"Yes?"

"Well, I hope you don't mind if— "

"I don't mind."

"I mean, okay, I'll just ask," he said.

I waited. I could feel my cheeks filling with Irish red.

He coughed. "Okay, here goes. How's the story coming? I mean, I know you only just finished our interview on Friday when Maddy came by, and it's only Monday, but . . ."

Maddison Jones. I'd tried to forget her.

So this was Terry's question? I had to admit that my Friday-night fiasco with him and Maddy had deflated my enthusiasm for the story. Besides, the Better Business Bureau's website was staring at me, as were the piles of faxes, newspaper clippings, and invitations cluttering my desk, the dozen e-mails screaming for my attention, and my notebook filled with scribbles about the Buddhist temple fire, the Unity Church, and the Boulder guy who seemed to confuse divinity with masculinity. I searched for a response. Terry persisted, and as he did, my interest in Catholic centers was suddenly renewed.

"You know, the story on the Outreach Center? How's it

going?" he asked gently.

How was it possible that a male voice could melt female fears? Hearing his question sent me to the image of his face and passion for his work, his bulging arms and gentlemanly style. Then I saw Maddy's beautiful face competing with my frizzy head. But before I could digress into loser status, a sudden burst of inspiration dropped out of nowhere. If I was going to hear Terry's voice more in the future, I needed to change strategies.

I needed to become glamorous. And I would.

"Of course. The story's almost finished," I said.

"Wonderful! By the way, sorry about Friday with Maddy. She loses objectivity whenever she's around celebrities."

"What do you mean?"

"You. She sees you as a celebrity. Really, she's a big fan of your work, and luckily for us, she's an equally big fan of our work at the Center."

"I'll bet," I said. I knew a competitor when I saw one, and this woman was no more interested in my work than the sports reporters were. And if she really cared about the Center, I was sure it had a lot more to do with Terry's muscles than with his mission.

"I'm not sure if I told you, but she's responsible for our fundraising, which was why she'd come over that day. She'd just gotten news of a grant that could pay for more computers."

"Is that right?" I said. Some women would use any excuse.

"In fact, you might want to talk with her about the story."

"Yes, I might," I said, though I was sure that would not be pretty.

"Of course. You're the reporter," Terry said, beautiful humility resonating in his voice. "Well, I'll look forward to seeing you on Thursday, Jonna. Bye."

"I will, too, Terry. Bye." I felt fortified for battle by his last sentence. Would he really look forward to seeing me? Or was I just another volunteer to him? What did it matter? He'd said it and that was enough. Oh, hope was a powerful medication for single women.

Whatever the reason he was looking forward to seeing me, I would go and somehow miraculously look good in the process, conquering the first hurdle for his attention. I'd buy lipstick. I'd wear real shoes. Even if Maddison Jones had staked her claim already, pretending to worship my work and his and looking ridiculously gorgeous each step of the way, I was all the more determined to rise to the occasion. And not for one second would I buy that she cared a lick about religion reporting or Catholic charities. Come on.

Boy, oh boy, people could stoop really low.

I noticed the colors on my computer screen and saw the information about pretexting. Wait a minute. Maybe *that* was what Jed Sundae had been trying to tell me, that some gutter-level deception was going on at the nondenominational center. Thank you, Maddy.

I grabbed the phone and pounded the number to IFF's main office. I tapped the chair with my foot while listening to the first, second, and third ring. On the fourth, a sugary female voice—which I immediately identified as Delores Watson, executive assistant and classy nail stylist—spoke in a recorded message: "Hello! You have reached Into the Fields Fellowship, a place to belong. For worship service information, times, and locations, press one; for all other calls, please hold."

I held. And tapped again. I grabbed a pen and started a list:

1. Buy lipstick. 2. Go shopping at real store. 3. Ask Hannah—

"Good morning, Into the Fields Fellowship," Delores said in a wispy breath. I could hear her nails clicking on the computer in the background.

"Watson, I presume," I said. Ever since reading Sherlock Holmes mysteries as a kid, I'd always wanted to say that to someone.

The clicking stopped. "May I help you?"

"Jonna Lightfoot MacLaughlin here. I'm wondering if Pastor Jeff is in."

"Oh, I'm sorry, Ms. MacLaughlin, he's on another call right now."

"I'll wait." I scratched the back of my head with the capped point of my pen and looked at my list.

Ms. Watson coughed. "Are you sure? He could be a while, and I don't think he'd mind calling you ba— "

"I'm happy to wait. No problem. I've got some urgent questions to ask him . . . you know, about Jed Sundae, the guy you'd never heard of."

She paused. "Oh, him. One moment please," she said, the wisp gone from her voice. She pushed some clicking button and sent me to that telephone holding world where happy little musical tunes play while you wait.

The first song I didn't recognize, but the second one was one they sang on Sunday morning, something about being God's special child. I jotted the word "special" on my list and spit out my Juicy Fruit. I clicked on a Denver news website to get the latest update on the weather: "Partly cloudy later in the afternoon with showers around 4 p.m. High around 93 degrees today with 0 percent humidity."

I didn't know why I liked knowing the weather forecast or temperature. It wasn't as if I was going outside to jog or plow a field or anything. Maybe it was one way of knowing how to plan what I should wear, though I never knew the weather until I was already dressed and it didn't matter anyway.

The phone and happy music stayed cradled in my ear as I clicked to another weather site, scoured a site on upcoming movies, ordered a new sweater for the winter through a mountain store my parents always took us to, read a review of a new Laura Lippman detective novel, and added to my list: 4. Fix hair. 5. Pray for miracles. I suddenly noticed no one was singing in my ear.

"Ms. Lightfoot?" a man's voice said. "Are you there?"

"Oh, sure. Sorry about that. I was enjoying the wait, Pastor."

"Look, I'm a little busy right now and— "

"Me, too. But this will just take a second. Ms. Watson probably told you it's about Jed Sundae. What sort of man would you say he was?"

"Excuse me? I'm not sure I know what you mean."

"Really? Well, you know, tell me how Jedediah fit into your congregation. Was he a helpful guy? An usher? Did he serve as a Sunday school teacher, because if he did I think that'd be classic. I can just hear the kids telling their parents, 'My Sunday school teacher's name is Mr. Sundae.' Don't you think that'd be funny?"

Pastor Jeff Whitman did not laugh.

"Listen, Pastor, I'm just wanting to get some feel about why this man would call me to tell me about your church. You know, I get calls all the time from disgruntled church members, and the way I see it, you pastors have it tough, trying to please— "

"He called you?"

"And I've met him. Seems like a nice enough man, though a little nervous. Did you find him nervous, Pastor . . . *Jeff*?"

"I'm sorry to cut this call short, Ms. MacLaughlin, but I have a meeting I need to get to." He now sounded more like he'd sounded on Sunday morning. "Could I call you later?"

"I'll be here." I hung up and looked at the phone, considering the conversation we'd just had. He'd all but admitted knowing Jed when he'd asked if Jed had called me. But seconds later, he'd seemed to reconsider his position and pull the reins in again. What was he up to?

I started down the hall for more coffee, my mind packed with possible theories. If something smelled in Denmark and folks in the "bakery" of Into the Fields Fellowship could no longer smell it—though I was mixing my metaphors—maybe Jed's problem had been that he did not belong in the "place to belong." Maybe he'd never lost his sense of smell.

What if people thought he was dead now because, at some point, Jed had begun stirring things up a little too much, reminding them that life was supposed to be tastier than rye bread? Maybe he challenged them to smell the bakery a little more than they were supposed to, and they—especially Jeff Whitman—did not like that.

I got to the coffeepot, still chewing on the ideas, when Tony Thompson, the sports guy, waddled in. He stopped in front of the refrigerator, opened it, and considered his options, as lost in his thoughts as I'd been in mine.

I stirred some sugar into my coffee and took a chance. "So . . . Thompson."

He spun around and stared at me. "So, Lightfoot," he said, sounding as if he'd just awakened. "What's new with the spirits?"

"The usual. But let me ask you a question, okay?"

"I'm not going to church. It's final."

"Not that. Suppose you went to the stadium to find out about a former player on the team."

"Yeah?" He poured himself the last of the coffee and put the empty pot back on the burner, ignoring the on button.

"Only problem was, when you asked the coach and a few of the other guys about this former player, they said they'd never heard of him. What would you do?"

"Check to make sure he'd really been there."

"You interviewed him yourself last year."

"I did? Do you know something about the Broncos I don't, Lightfoot?"

"Theoretically, Thompson. Theoretically. You know from your own experience, your own eyes, that the guy played there, but no one wants to admit it."

"They're lying to cover their butts. Sorry, I mean, backsides."

"Thanks, Tony. That's what I thought."

I heard him spit into the trash can as I hurried back to my desk. Hannah was not at her desk, but she'd left a note on my keyboard: *JLM, A lead on Whitman. Checking with CBI; should have more tomorrow. HXH.*

I spent the rest of the afternoon catching up with e-mail, planning my glamour makeover as best I could, letting the story ideas of the morning percolate in my head, and ordering lunch from BurritoCasa, who delivered.

When my veggie tostadas arrived, I dove into them and tossed some of the piles of old newspapers from my desk into the recycle bin at the same time. As I bit into my lunch, salsa squirted out, a straight line down my chest and on top of the front-page story I'd written on the Buddhist temple burning down. I wiped my mouth and shirt and decided I should pay another visit to the temple to chat again with my monks before heading home. When I finished eating and tidying, I grabbed my bag and keys and took the elevator downstairs.

But just as I was walking across the lobby of the *Dispatch*, Pastor Jeff Whitman was coming in, looking straight at me through the tinted professor-style glasses that rested on his nose. When I saw the hard glaze on his face, a nervous something or other rose in my stomach. Somehow I knew God would understand what I did next: I reached in my purse and pulled out a cigarette. Organic.

::Chapter Ten

I stood outside the entrance to the *Dispatch*, Pastor Jeff Whitman just a few feet from me, dodging my smoke.

"Making a pastoral visit?" I asked, enjoying the taste of tobacco and silently apologizing to the heavens for it.

"You could call it that." He spoke in a low voice, not at all like his special pulpit voice.

I tried to act confident, though I was sure my nicotine habit gave me away. "Thanks, but I have my own pastor. He's real nice. I've been a faithful member at his church for oh, let me see— "

"I'm happy for you, Miss MacLaughlin, but I didn't come to find out about your personal church habits."

"No?" I leaned toward him and exhaled again out of the side of my mouth, trying not to blow smoke on him. "That's a surprise."

A short, quick grin spread across his cheeks and just as quickly disappeared. He pushed his glasses close to his eyes and rested his hands in his pants pockets. "I did come to offer some friendly pastoral advice to you, if you don't mind." He turned his face to me when he said this, and I had to admit, the intensity of his gaze all but dissected me. I steadied my knees, determined to hang on to my instincts about him. "I'm sure you're a busy young woman, and I don't want to take more of your time . . ."

"Ah, I have lots of time, Pastor. I'd love to find out more about your *ministry*."

"Well, that's just it. We have a church policy not to talk with the media."

"Oh? And why's that?"

"Plain and simple: We don't want the publicity. We feel it distracts us from what we're supposed to be about."

"And what would that be?"

He pulled his head back in astonishment, as if he could not believe I wouldn't know their purpose. He shook his head at the question. "I'm not sure you'll understand, but we're offering people a place—"

"Oh, I know, a place to belong."

"That's right. Many of our members come from, uh, difficult situations, and Into the Fields Fellowship gives them a chance to start over." He paused, pulled out a handkerchief from his back pocket, and wiped the corner of his mouth before tucking it back into its slot. "The Bible says that if any man is in Christ he is a new creation. The old has gone, the new has come. That's what we're about, but we don't like to advertise it."

I dropped the butt of my cigarette to the ground, stomped it out with the toe of my clog, and considered what he had just said.

"Though we appreciate your interest in our work, we do not want you to write a story on us. You understand."

"What can you tell me about Jedediah Sundae?" I dropped the question like the cigarette I'd just finished and looked into his face as I said Jed's name, wondering how this otherwise normal-looking pastor would respond when he heard it.

He didn't. Not even an eyebrow tweaked. He simply pushed

his glasses back on his nose and nodded. Then he turned his wrist over and looked at his watch. It had big dark numbers on the face, as if he had trouble seeing it otherwise.

"I really must get back to the office, but I will tell you this." He sighed before he continued and stuck his finger under his glasses to scratch his eyelid. "We received a call about a year ago that Jed Sundae had died in a car accident somewhere in the mountains. That's why I was so surprised when you said you'd received a call from him. Perhaps someone's playing a joke."

"Why do you think someone would do that?"

"Well, Jed had been mixed up with some difficult people. But I can't help you any more than that."

"You've already helped me a lot. For instance, you just admitted knowing Jed Sundae, even knowing him well enough to identify the 'type' of people he'd been 'mixed up' with. So now I know the guy's for real. I am curious, though, to know what kind of people you find difficult, Pastor?" I tilted my head toward him to signal I was all ears.

He cleared his throat and pulled a pair of sunglasses from his shirt pocket. He exchanged glasses so that now when he looked at me all I saw were black lenses. "I'm glad to have met you, Miss MacLaughlin, but I hope you'll respect the sensitivity of our work so that you and I don't have to have any more conversations."

As he started toward the street, he stopped suddenly as if he'd forgotten something, turned back around, and grinned one more time before he spoke. "Oh, and do give your neighbor, Mrs. Rodriguez, my regards, won't you? She seems like a nice lady."

He stood still for a moment to make sure I'd heard him. Then he waved his hand and disappeared into the crowded crosswalk. I stared after him, blinking at the faces walking past us. Though the summer heat stung my cheeks, I shivered at the sound of Pastor Whitman's words on my ears. Did he just say what I think he said?

I hurried toward the parking lot. By the time I'd reached my car, my hands were shaking and my stomach had dropped like it did on the down part of a roller coaster. I punched the lighter into the dash and waited, scrounging around my purse for Gideon. I needed backup. And though I usually carried him with me, today I had everything in my bag *but* the miniature New Testament with Psalms.

"Help," I said, looking through the streaks on my windshield toward the sky.

I drove straight to my apartment and ran up the stairs to Mrs. Rodriguez's apartment.

Once I caught my breath, I pounded on the door and hollered for her, but she didn't answer. I ran into my apartment, picked up my phone, still shaking, and called her. No answer. I rummaged through the kitchen trash and found an envelope from an old electric bill. I grabbed a pen and wrote: "Mrs. R., SEE ME when you get home, okay? LOVE, Jonna." I taped the envelope to her doorknob and went to my couch.

There was Gideon, under two pillows and a pair of socks. I flipped open the miniature Bible to whatever page it fell on and read: "Yea, though I walk through the valley of the shadow of death . . ." I slapped it shut. I reopened it and read: "A thousand shall fall at thy side, ten thousand at thy right hand . . ." I shut it again and went for two out of three: "Peace I leave with you, my peace I give unto you: not as the world giveth, give I unto you. Let not your heart be troubled, neither let it be afraid."

That was more like it. That I could hang on to.

I spent the next hour alternating between listening to old CDs, baking chocolate chip cookies, scrubbing the bathtub, opening up the door to see if the envelope was still there, and closing it when it was. At 8:05, I called "Kung Fu Palace" for an order of sweet and sour chicken and fried rice, hoping that might calm me down as I waited for my neighbor to return home. I decided if she wasn't home by 10 p.m., I'd report her to the Missing Persons Bureau.

I was picking the fried rice off of my skirt—I'd never gotten the hang of chopsticks though I loved trying—when there was a knock on the door. I shot out of the couch, sending most of my uneaten dinner across the floor, ready to smother Mrs. Rodriguez in a big bear hug. I glanced at the clock—9:43 p.m.

But it wasn't my neighbor. I retreated a few inches when I saw skinny Mr. Fink standing there, examining his fingernails. He wore the same sleeveless T-shirt and jeans he'd worn when I saw him last week sweeping the sidewalk. He took a step back when I yelped and hung his head toward the carpeted hall.

"Sorry, Mr. Fink, I thought you were Mrs. Rodriguez."

"I ain't her," he mumbled.

"No, you're not." I smiled at him, but he didn't look up. I stepped into the hall and leaned against the door. My lungs and shoulders tightened.

"Yer shower still leaky?"

"Well, yes, but it's a little late, don't you think?" He kept his head lowered so I could see the balding spot on the back of his skull.

"Fine. You don't want it fixed . . ." He muttered and turned down the hall, the thin muscles above his elbows bobbing with each step. I watched him bop toward the stairs, guilt rising in my soul, when I suddenly realized this might be the only chance I'd have to get my showerhead on an environmentally friendly track.

"On second thought, Mr. Fink, that's a good idea. If you wouldn't mind fixing it. Now."

He stopped when I said this, nodded his narrow head, and shifted his way back to my apartment. "This is the time, yup. Now's as good as any," he muttered again, his lips barely moving as he pulled a wrench from his belt and shuffled straight to my bathroom.

I tilted my head as he passed and had the strange notion I'd heard him say that before, though of course I hadn't. It was equally odd that I hadn't had to point out where my bathroom was. But then he was the building maintenance man. He'd probably been in each apartment at some point.

I shrugged and left the door open to the hallway in case I heard Mrs. Rodriguez come in. The clank of metal against metal was a new sound in my apartment. I swept up the rice on my living room floor, tossed it the kitchen trash can, and checked in on Mr. Fink.

"How's it going?" I tried to be cheerful.

He grunted and kept fiddling with the pipes, so I returned to the kitchen to sample a few of my cookies to make sure they were okay. I couldn't tell from the first one, so I taste-tested another. By my fourth, Mr. Fink emerged.

"Douwwonnacwookie?" I mumbled, chocolate chips crunching in my cheeks.

He shook his head, wiped his hands across his stomach, and jammed the wrench back into his belt buckle. "That oughta do for a while," he said, the words barely audible as he shuffled toward the door.

I followed him, swallowing the last of my cookie with a quick sip of milk so I could speak intelligently.

"Well, I appreciate your help, Mr. Fink," I said. "Now I'll feel better about taking a shower and not wasting all that water. You know what I mean?"

"Nope." He sniffled and fidgeted back and forth as he stood at my door, as though he wanted to say something else but he wasn't quite sure what or how. Then he glanced across the hall, saw the note on Mrs. Rodriguez's doorknob, and shook his head at me as he turned and headed toward the stairs, where he met my neighbor—four bags of groceries dangling from her hands and arms—as she was coming up. He grunted and pointed his thumb toward me when he saw her.

"I am *so* glad to see you!" I said, hugging her and sliding two bags out of her grip while we squeezed through the door to her apartment.

She tilted her head at me, her eyes tired but serious, and she set her bags on the tiny kitchen table. "Mi amiga. Que pasa?"

"Hold that thought!" I dropped the bags next to hers, hurried across the hall, and grabbed a few cookies.

"Ah. Juana, you good girl!"

"I was worried about you."

"Me? Por qué? I be with grandkids all day. First day of week, sí"

"Oh, that's right. I knew Monday meant something."

She collapsed in the chair at the table and held a cookie in both hands, nibbling around the edges.

I poured her a glass of milk and sat down across from her. "Remember that preacher at the Fields church yesterday?"

"Me no like him. He not right, Juana."

I stared at her light brown face with its curvy wrinkles across her forehead and felt the wisdom it reflected. This was a woman who had labored all her life at making a home for her children in a country that was not hers. All the cleaning and cooking jobs she'd worked along the way had given her an education into human nature not many colleges could match. When I asked her to explain what she meant about Pastor Whitman, she bit hard on her cookie and leaned back in her chair.

"He no true."

"How so?"

"He say nice but he no mean it. He not right . . . in here." Mrs. Rodriguez put her hand over her chest and patted her heart in the same way Hannah had when she quoted to me her mother's saying about "church folk." I knew they were both right, but I also knew their intuition made my job harder. After all, a reporter was responsible to verify truth through solid evidence. I might have truth, but I didn't have much to prove it.

"Well, I talked with Pastor Whitman today, Mrs. Rodriguez. He visited me at work, and as he was leaving, he asked about you, which is why I was worried all night. I could never forgive myself if anything ever happened to— "

Mrs. Rodriguez's put her hand on top of mine.

"You no worry, Juana. I no scared a that guy." She raised her shoulders and pursed her lips, as though she had seen far greater challenges. "My Jesus big, yes? He help me and he help you. No worry, okay?"

"Okay. No worry." I smiled and held her hand.

"Okay. Now you go. Mis niños make me sleepy!" She rose from the table and began putting away her groceries. Her dress hung tired on her small body, and her long gray hair fell from her bun. She picked up the last cookie and held it up in the air before dropping it into her mouth. "Muchas gracias!"

The light was blinking on my answering machine when I got back in my apartment. I pushed play and turned off the lights in the living room.

"Hi, Jonna. David Rockley here again. Thought I might catch you at home tonight. Sorry I missed you. I'll keep trying! Have a good night."

I rolled my eyes at the pesty-ness of my brother's friend and got ready for bed, still worrying about my neighbor, even though I'd promised her I wouldn't. Maybe a night of solid sleep would help me think more clearly and worry less about this story. I had three good witnesses who believed something was rotten at Into the Fields Fellowship, but I didn't have a shred of evidence—yet—to help me know exactly how they were misusing their power. But one thing was sure: There was nothing I could do about it tonight. Flannel sheets, a firm pillow, and Gideon beside me on my nightstand were the best remedy for what ailed me.

The next morning, I ironed my skirt and used high-octane straightener *and* conditioner on my hair, small but important steps to my glamorous transformation. Despite Pastor Whitman's request to kill the story on his Fellowship, I had decided to drop by his office.

When I got there, though, the door was locked. I'd left my apartment around eight o'clock, bought my Java Pit mocha, and expected the IFF office to be opened by the time I pulled into its parking lot. But neither the Nail Lady nor the pastor had arrived yet, so I pushed my business card through the mail slot in the door and got back in my car.

Since I was in the neighborhood, I thought there might be one story I actually could put to rest on this hot Tuesday morning. I rolled down the window and turned up the radio as I drove, listening to "Colorado Country: All Country, All the Time." It was Oldies Week, and Patsy Cline was crooning, as only Patsy could, "Walking After Midnight." I tapped the steering wheel and sang along.

I didn't stop singing when the traffic light turned red, either. I'd long ignored the stares of fellow drivers who weren't sure what to make of my singing with my car windows open. My brothers had trained me well—I made them listen to me the times I thought I was Whitney Houston or Shania Twain. Besides, I had a new reason to sing—I was going to win over Terry.

As I pulled in front of the Buddhist Cultural Center and parked, Patsy and I were just finishing. I grabbed two bottles of Leadville Springs Water from the backseat and hopped across the street.

The younger monk, robed in brown, answered the door, his eyes wide with a blend of fear and longing. He stared at me, smiled, and then erased the smile with his hand as if he remembered he was not supposed to be nice to me.

"Mornin', Brother. It's a hot one, isn't it?" I said as I shoved a bottle of water into his hand and opened mine. I took a long, slow drink as we stood in the morning heat. He watched me swallow. When I finished the entire bottle, I wiped my mouth and shook my head at him.

"Must be hotter inside, huh? No air conditioning and all. I'm telling you, I admire your commitment to suffering for the sake of enlightenment. I'm not so good at it."

"It's a simple choice," he said quietly, a trace of his Southern accent wrapped around the words. "Comfort does not lead to the path of insight."

"No, but it sure can help sometimes. I mean, I just *think* better when I'm not so stinkin' hot, you know?" He stared at me as if he *did* know, but then he shook his head and looked at the street behind me. I glanced, too, to see what he was seeing: cars speeding by. I decided to act on my hunch, especially while I had him alone.

"I have a theory about your fire. If you don't mind, I'd like to test it on you, okay?"

He nodded.

"I'm guessing a particular young monk called Charged Up Electric Repair and Installation to order the air conditioning unit for the center. He even told people not to come the day they were sending out the work team. But when the Dharma found out about the order, this younger monk felt guilty for wanting to cool off during this ridiculous heat wave. And maybe he forgot to reschedule the Center's usual activities when they cancelled the order?" He kept looking beyond me, but I knew he heard every word. "He, being the Dharma, of course forgave the young brother, but the guilt—and the heat—were too much."

He cleared his throat but did not say anything.

"So maybe he thought if he fiddled with the electrical wiring on his own to reconfigure the cooling fans in the system when no one was looking and no one was conveniently there because he'd told them to stay home, the indoor temperatures might at least be controlled in the Center. But they were old and something went wrong, and before he knew it, a spark turned into a blaze."

Now he was staring at me. He opened the bottle of water and guzzled all of it.

"My brother did that once in a friend's cabin," I whispered. "Thought he was an electrician when, of course, he wasn't. Luckily they had one of those neat little extinguishers nearby before it got too bad. It was an accident, of course, but a costly one, a really costly one. Luckily, or providentially, no one was around to get hurt." I waited. "Of course, it's just a theory. Probably crazy, don't you think?"

His eyes filled. A tiny tear slipped down his cheek as sweat gathered across his brow. I braced myself, knowing how I could buckle around crying men.

"I never meant . . ."

"Of course not. But the robes, the building, the summer heat, well, it was all just too much, right?"

"I thought I could do this. I thought if I just yielded to this structure, to the enlightened ways, and if I had enough discipline for the daily meditation and devotion, I'd find the answers." The accent had returned entirely, and I saw the face of a man who once lived a very different life in a small town somewhere southeast of here.

"Maybe that's not your job," I said softly.

He shifted his focus on me. "What do you mean?"

"Maybe all the discipline in the world would still never be enough. Maybe it's someone else's job to help us be the people we're supposed to be, and maybe . . ."

But at that point the Dharma appeared, taking back control. "Ms. Lightfoot, this is not the time for newspaper interviews," he said, pushing the young man to the side.

"Is that what we were doing?" I said.

He ignored me and turned to the younger monk. "Brother, it is time for meditation."

"Well, sir, this monk, um, this *man* was just about to do some, uh, reflecting," I jumped in. "Weren't you?"

He stood silently looking at his feet, his shaved head shining in the morning sun.

I stared at the Dharma. "I think he might know how your fire got started."

"Things are not always as they seem, Ms. Lightfoot," the Dharma said.

"That's for sure. But I'm thinking you also knew how the fire started and, being the good Buddhist that you are, decided to make the most of a bad situation. Suddenly, the burning of the Buddhist Cultural Center was a great opportunity to—dare I say it—win a few new friends, perhaps?"

With that, he gently pulled the other monk back inside and away from our conversation, before stepping out into the sun with me. "Miss Lightfoot, your cynicism is not conducive to positive energy."

"No, I suspect it isn't. But how about tapping into the virtue of honesty with me and admitting that you used the fire to get a little free publicity for the Center?"

"Because I am committed to the ways of truth, I will say to you that we did view the tragedy of our building—a terrible accident, I might add—as divine direction."

"Excuse me?"

"For many months, we had been considering ways to better communicate the path of transcendence and enlightenment with our Mile High friends. This tragedy, this suffering, led us to a new opportunity for growth, as suffering always does."

I studied his face, slightly depressed that this religious man could be so savvy about public relations and so sincere about the ways of his religion.

"Well, you're certainly right about one thing," I said. He

tilted his hairless head as he listened. "Things are not always as they seem."

He bowed toward me, bid me good day, and stepped back into the annex.

I called Skip while I stood on the sidewalk in front of the Center, knowing someone from inside the temple was watching—and listening. I explained my theory to my editor, told him the young monk's reaction, and asked him if I should write a follow-up story, citing the records from Charged Up Electric. He said to call the fire inspector first to see where he was with the investigation.

"Good idea. I will call the fire inspector about my theory," I said as loudly as I could for the men who were eavesdropping.

As I started my car and glanced back at the Center, I remembered the leader's comments on suffering when we'd talked the last time I was here. He'd said suffering was the path to enlightenment, and certainly that was true enough. But it sure seemed confusing to me why anyone would sign up for a life of intentional discomfort when there was already so much of it in the world. I had no doubt this young Southern man was experiencing his own right now, without having to ask for more.

Back at the office, when Hannah sat me down in her chair and handed me a Godiva dark, I knew something big was happening. As usual, she looked the model of professionalism: a soft yellow short-sleeved jacket with small gold stripes lining it at an angle. Her skirt was an extension of the same and hung wrinkleless to her knees. Her gold pumps mirrored her fashion attitude. I was suddenly very aware of my baggy tank top, but hoped she'd noticed my calmer hair.

"Well, girl, you might have opened a juicy can of worms,"

she said, hand on hip and eyes beaming. Hannah loved investigative reporting; the bigger the challenge of tracking down information, the more she hunted and dug and scrounged until she got what she was looking for, which was good news for me this morning.

Then she glanced at my skirt. "Did you iron that? What gives?"

"New leaf," I said. "I'll be asking for detailed fashion advice later. First things first."

She nodded approvingly. "It seems your 'Pastor' Jeff Whitman used to be a dotcom executive, known by the old boys at the Denver Tech Center as 'Slick Whit.' I mean, the guy was notorious as a computer genius. He created software that most people couldn't even read, let alone use on their computers."

"So that's why I couldn't find anything on him! I didn't even think to look under the business directories." I let the Godiva dissolve on my tongue as I waited for Hannah to continue.

"Leave no stone unturned, Lightfoot. It seems the Colorado Bureau of Investigation has been looking for him, too, but couldn't find anything on him. You know why? Because there *is* nothing on him. At least not in the computers."

"What do you mean?"

"Well, as I said, he was a techno-genius. But after he went to trial for fraud with his first business—yes, you heard me—people were afraid to do anything with him. Apparently, he was acquitted, though the damage to his reputation was already done."

Hannah was pacing in our cubicle, a radiant Queen Bee among a swarming hive of reporters and editors racing past us.

"And?"

"And then he started a second software company for credit

card payments. The whole thing tanked when the industry went belly-up in the nineties. People said he wouldn't have survived anyway because he never seemed to recover from the fraud thing. One guy even told me he'd heard Whitman found religion when he was in the pits. Anyway, the messier your life becomes, the more you want to believe in God, I guess."

She grabbed her notepad and tossed a few pages back until she found what she was looking for. "One source said, 'Slick Whit knew systems so well that he could get into any computer, anytime, anywhere. But even that didn't help him after going to court.'"

"You mean he was a hacker?"

"Maybe. But it's obvious this guy could create anything he wanted with a simple keyboard."

"Which means he could also delete anything he wanted, right?"

"I guess so." She paused as if she'd not yet considered this. Then she peered up at me, her face filling with understanding. "If you're going where I think you're going, then this guy is very very un-church-like. In fact, I'd call him downright criminal."

I stood up and grabbed my notes from my desk, flipping through them to something Jed had said when he'd first called me. When I found it, I flicked the page with my index finger and zeroed in on the issue with a whisper. "It makes sense, Hannah. Jed said—and I quote—'The IFF leaders are taking the hard-earned money from their people and telling them all sorts of new ministries will come from it. Only problem is . . .'" I stared at my notes.

"Only problem is . . . *what*?" she prodded.

"That's just it. He couldn't finish. Got so emotional he hung up on me. But he said enough to make me realize that people who attend the church are, well, not in a good *place*." I laughed at the sound of the word considering how Pastor Whitman used it: "a place to belong."

"I've got another call in to a lawyer friend, Lightfoot, but I have to finish this mayor's story on the new tourism lobbying efforts. Tell you what," the gold queen sat at her desk and picked up the phone while she finished her thought, "you keep poking around. I'll do the same, and tomorrow morning we'll meet at Pete's for a power breakfast—and some fashion tips. Free of charge, except you buy. Agreed?"

"Brilliant. Thanks, Hannah."

I clicked on my e-mail, saw that tomorrow was already the second day of the regional Southern Baptist meeting at the Mile High Convention Center, and knew I'd better make an appearance. I grabbed my calendar and wrote it in.

After I poured myself another cup of coffee, I typed some of the things Hannah had told me in a document I named, "Field Questions." Then I typed my notes from the interview with Jed as well as the things Pastor Whitman had said on the morning Mrs. Rodriguez and I visited. I also wanted to make sure I wrote down what he'd said to me yesterday on the sidewalk in front of the *Dispatch*, every word I could remember, including the icy threat he'd implied for my neighbor. Then, like a word puzzle, I moved each detail around on the computer screen, trying to make the story fit together, but still knowing I didn't have enough.

The phone rang.

"Jonna Lightfoot."

"Hi, Jonna. David Rockley again. Bad time?"

I dropped my head and exhaled. "No. It's okay. Just, uh,

working."

"On a story?"

I stared at my screen, amazed at his question. "Yes, a story. How are you, David?" I'd learned to divert attention away from me when I needed to.

"Me? Oh, fine. Completely absorbed by this Mile High weather. I love taking my books outside and sitting in the sun. It's too good to be true for this East Coast native used to summer humidity."

"Well, be careful. You're closer to the sun, you know. It's easy to burn."

"Can't help it. I love calling folks back home to tell them that I'm sitting on a mile! It's really quite astounding when you think about it, being able to relax while you're 5,280 feet high."

My head shot up and I looked past my screen. That was it! Pastor Whitman was recruiting people by telling them IFF was a place to relax and belong, creating some sort of false community and making them feel special and elevated. But the closer they got, the more vulnerable they became. Burned. There must be some sort of trail of evidence to confirm the fraudulent front.

"David, I'm sorry, but I've got to go."

"Anyway, I called to see if you'd like to have dinner with—"

"Maybe you could call me later. Thanks a lot!"

I hung up the phone and decided to pay Into the Fields Fellowship another visit. I wanted to hear from the pastor himself just why he was pulling in members to his congregation only to take from them once they were there. I was sure he'd spiritualize it again for me with Bible verses and moral concern, but at least he'd know one person out there was questioning his practice.

I'd barely slipped on my clogs when the phone rang again. I stared at it and debated if I should let the voice mail pick it up. But something nudged me to grab the receiver. "Lightfoot."

"It's Jed Sundae here."

I slumped back in my chair. "Jed! How've you been since I saw you last— "

"Are you still working on the story?"

"Are you kidding? Of course I— "

"Need some help?"

"What I need is evidence. Proof. A paper trail I can follow."

"I've got one. But I have to be careful. I'm pretty sure they're on to me."

"I don't know about that. They think you died last year in an accident in the mountains."

"They told you that one too, huh?" I heard him breathe out a burst of anger before continuing, "You know where the new Martin Luther King, Jr., statue is at City Park?"

"Sure. But I hardly think now is the time for tourist— "

"Can you meet me there tonight? At midnight?"

Patsy Cline sang in my mind as he said it, though her song seemed much happier than the thought of City Park in the darkness of a hot summer night.

"You wouldn't want to meet any earlier, would you? Say at The Pub of Saint— "

"That's the safest time for me right now, Jonna. Well?"

"I'll be there. But, Jed, I need to know one thing."

He was silent, but I heard his steady breathing on the line.

"Why'd you make me chase you through coffee hour at Capitol Presbyterian yesterday morning?"

He let out a slight cough before answering. "I had to make

sure you . . . you were for real."

"For real?"

"I figured if you went to a church on your own, not because you were following some assignment, well, I figured I could . . ." He paused.

"You could?"

"Trust you. We have to stop them, Jonna."

"We will."

"Dr. King. Midnight." Click.

I hung up the phone, swallowed, and sat very still. The world of religion suddenly seemed much darker.

::Chapter Eleven

The moon was a white speck in the sky, no brighter than the stars and hardly the night-light I was hoping for during my mysterious City Park rendezvous with Jed Sundae. Then again, it was only 10 p.m., so maybe by midnight the moon would sparkle at least a little, like the psychedelic lava lamp Mom used to keep lit in the bathroom once she tucked us into bed.

I'd taken comfort in that lamp as a little girl every time I'd stumbled through the dark hallway for a late-night pee or drink of water. The bright glowing lava and circled peace sign had calmed my childish fears and kept boogie monsters and warmongers at bay—or at least in my brothers' room.

But tonight my fears were adult-sized, and I wanted a night-light I could count on. Long before I'd moved to the city I'd heard urban legends of thug gatherings or Wicca ceremonies that took place in parks throughout the city most summer nights. Rumor had it that the darker the night, the more criminal the activity, though the police blotter at the *Dispatch* rarely confirmed it. Never mind that my experiences living here hadn't confirmed the scary stereotypes of the city, either. Fear only needed a crumb to feed its appetite and make it bigger than the real world. Tonight I was chewing on it as though I hadn't eaten for days.

So at 9:59 p.m., I left the bright *Dispatch* office, where

frenetic reporters were putting last-minute touches on stories while copy editors harangued them with questions. I stood in the parking lot and noticed how dull it was in comparison to the activity inside. And dark. There was only a hazy gray ceiling above the earth, some white cosmic specks sprinkled across it, and, with the exception of a few street lamps and headlights, not much brightness anywhere.

I swallowed, wondering why I hadn't stuck with obituaries. They were at least predictable. Religion was supposed to be predictable and steadfast as well, or at least comforting. Why, then, did I feel as if a blender was switched on in my stomach? What if I suddenly had to run? The last time I'd exercised was when I hurried up the stairs to my apartment to see if Mrs. Rodriguez was there—and I'd almost had a heart attack on the spot. What had I been thinking?

Jed's shaky voice in my head answered my question: "We have to stop them, Jonna."

I climbed into my car, lit a cigarette, and stared at the flame on my match until it almost burned my fingers. If Jed could risk the boogeymen of City Park to uncover the truth behind Into the Fields Fellowship, I'd at least make a showing. If it got too creepy, I'd go home, eat chocolate, and hang out with Gideon.

Instead of driving directly to City Park, though, I turned onto the street in front of The Pub of Saint Agnes for the good blessing of a smooth pint, a hearty chowder, and the courage of the Scottish Maiden. I could use all the help I could get.

As I slid into my favorite booth by the window, Mick saw me and instantly brought over my ale. I'd barely gotten the words "Bowl of corn chowder, please" out of my mouth when the lanky Scotsman was halfway into the kitchen. I picked up my cell phone and dialed. Then I heard the voice that instantly infused confidence into my blood.

"Matt MacLaughlin here."

"Hey, Big Brother! How's academia this time of night?"

Matt laughed and coughed. I heard him say, "I need to take this call—see you in class!" and a door shut. "So what's wrong with the guy?"

"What guy?" I asked as I picked up my drink and swirled it around so the foam moved like a miniature wave.

"Whatdoyamean, 'what guy'? David? Rockley? Your blind date last week? Remember? I saw him in the library this morning, and he says you're avoiding him. Says you won't take his calls. So, what's wrong with him?"

Oh, *that* guy. He's not Terry Choyce, that's what's wrong with him. "Did David call me?" I said, gulping my Fat Tire.

"Jonna! This guy's for real. And he's interested. What gives?"

"Listen, Matty, I didn't really call to talk about my love life."

"You don't have a love life. That's why I'm trying to—"

"I'm working on it and making some changes. But point taken. I'll call the guy back."

"Yes, you will."

"Whatever. Listen, remember when I told you about the invisible ex-church member?"

"The who?"

"You know, the guy from Into the Fields Fellowship?"

"Oh, yeah, the one who doesn't exist?"

"Right. Well, he wants to meet me tonight. He wants to give me the scoop on IFF to expose them."

"So he's gone from being the Invisible Man to Clark Kent's Superman?"

Only my brother could merge protagonists from great literature with comic book heroes. I laughed. Mick set down my bowl and walked back to the bar. "That's one way of looking at it," I said as I picked up my spoon and slurped into the phone.

"Are you at Saint Agnes's? No fair!"

I slurped again.

"So when's he coming there?"

"He's not," I said.

"I thought you just said you were meeting the invisible man."

"I did."

"See?"

"But not here." I took a mouthful and paused. "Let's just say he's knocking at midnight with the dream king."

"Ooooh. Reporter code. Cool. You have such a fascinating career, Little Sis."

"Cut it out. I'm nervous, Matt."

"The dark thing again? Thought you got over that when Mom put that lamp in the bathroom."

"Have you looked outside? It's not exactly raining comets."

"You mean you're meeting this secret guy . . . outside? *Tonight*?"

He paused. "Whoa, Jon. Why'd you do that?"

"I didn't! He called *me*. Said the only time he could meet was midnight in a place he knew they wouldn't go."

My big brother coughed again into the phone and then went quiet for a full thirty seconds at least. "I'm coming with you."

"No, Matt, you don't have to do that. Won't Mary be worried?"

"She'd insist."

"But . . . no . . . I don't need you to . . . Well, would you?" I stuttered. I picked up my glass and drank. Then Jed's face filled my mind. "Matt, what if he sees you and decides to skip out? I'll never get an interview with him. He's pretty jittery."

"I'll ride my bike and hide out. The dream king, huh? You'll be at the Dr. King statue in City Park, I presume?"

"Well done, Sherlock. Man, I'd stink as a spy."

"You're right. Listen, I'll be there. Count on it. Let me call Mary and finish grading some papers. Then I'll hop on me harse and ride over thar, me lassie."

"I'll owe you one, Matt."

"You owe me millions. And tomorrow you'll begin to pay me back by calling David. See you soon. And Jonna, don't do anything . . . I wouldn't, okay?"

"Of course." I dropped my phone back into my bag and finished my meal, feeling better and stronger.

I looked over my notes to make sure of the questions to ask Jed Sundae. I didn't know if I'd have another opportunity to talk with him, so I had to get enough for a story. What did he know about Whitman's computer skills? How exactly was IFF illegally or even unethically taking money from its members? What kind of paper trail could I find to prove people were being ripped off?

If I came away from City Park without these answers, I knew Skip would doubt this story. But there was definitely something wrong at this church, and I had to find out what it was—even if it meant venturing into City Park when it was dark. If my parents taught me anything from all of their environmental protests and peace rallies, it was that sometimes you had to sacrifice yourself—or at least your comfort—for the sake of the truth. Besides,

Matt would be along for the ride.

I paid Mick and at 11:30 p.m. got into my car. I tossed up a last-minute prayer and drove. I turned on the radio, but decided "Colorado's all country music all the time" was not what I needed right now. I looked instead for a song in my head. Patsy Cline morphed into "Guide Me, O Thou Great Eternal," the hymn we'd sung Sunday morning. Suddenly, it had more meaning than it had during the service. "I am weak, but Thou art mighty; Hold me with Thy powerful hand."

Before I got to the refrain, I had arrived in the circle that surrounded the new statue of Dr. Martin Luther King, Jr. Last year, the mayor had commissioned a local artist to create the new sculpture and had then surrounded it with an interactive wall that chronicled the Civil Rights Movement in the U.S. By day, the monument was an awe-inspiring testament to the courage and work of the famous reverend and a movement that, thankfully, changed the direction of our country. By night, or at least this moonless night, it was a dark hallway with no lava lamp in sight.

I turned off the ignition and locked my doors. I took a deep breath and finished the hymn as loudly as I could, the notes vibrating off the glass, "Bread of heaven, bread of heaven, Feed me till I want no more; Feed me till I want no more!" The muscles in my neck relaxed slightly and a tiny burst of anxiety popped out of my mouth when I finished. I stared up at Dr. King, quietly comforted, and waited. It was 11:57 p.m.

But if minutes could be years, the next three took me into a new decade. A million images paraded across my mind: chocolate chip cookies the size of Texas, Hannah's yellow suit, Saint Agnes smiling from beside the dartboard, Mrs. Rodriguez with her grandbabies, Matt holding Mary's hand, words and sentences scrolling across my computer screen in the office, a new pair of shoes, coffee hour at Capitol Presbyterian with lively wrinkled faces, and of course, Terry Choyce's beautiful broad shoulders and glowing smile. I stayed on that image for several seconds, sure that if people could be night-lights, he was mine, as corny as it seemed.

I yawned and began to rub my temples. But I jumped off my seat and almost poked out my eyes when I heard a "tap, tap, tap, tap" on my window.

It was Matt, straddling his bike, his face sweaty and hair pushed out of the sides of his helmet. He smiled as I rolled down my window. "Hey, Lois Lane. I got you covered. I'll be behind the trees. Be careful."

"Okay." I sighed, glad to see something as familiar as Matt and his bike. "Now hurry. Don't want to blow my cover."

"You don't really have one, Jon. You're sort of obvious." He laughed as he waved his hand across the dark circle to show me there was no one else around, only a few shadows thrown from the streetlight off of Seventeenth Avenue.

I rolled up my window, watching him wobble behind a tree, and went back to my fantasy of Terry, hoping his blond wavy hair and blue eyes would dispel the shadows. I would call him tomorrow, about the Reading Club of course. It was an easy decision to volunteer to read to children, especially because the man who ran the club was a bronzed god and most likely my future husband—if I could fend off the likes of Maddison Jones with the new me. Tomorrow, I'd also schedule a hair appointment and research local gyms. I didn't want to limit the mysterious ways the Lord might want to work in my love life. I'd also start eating less, maybe join Divine Dieters at the . . .

Thump!

A knuckle hit the window above the passenger's seat. I jumped again, every bone and blood vessel trembling from my eyebrows to my toenails.

Thump!

"Jonna, it's me. Jed."

I peeked across the seat. His face was bent into the glass, and he was pointing to the lock on the door. I slid across, swallowed a sigh, and pushed up the T so he could get in.

"Who's the guy on the bike?" he said as he crammed himself into the seat. He smelled of hot days and old cologne, like a man who'd once been used to better things but hadn't been able to afford them lately.

"What guy?"

"Behind that tree. If you've called the police, I'm going to have to—" He reached for the door handle.

I grabbed the elbow of his jacket. "He's my brother, Jed. I admit it. I hate the dark, okay? He insisted on camping out to make sure I'd be okay since I wasn't sure what I was doing outside in the middle of the night, for Pete's sake! So, well, just ignore him. It was a dumb idea to have him come, but he's just my brother. That's all." I rolled down my window to let in some fresh air.

Jed dropped his hands on his knees, and for the first time ever, I heard him laugh. It sounded more like a slight chuckle, really, but it was definitely in the laugh category.

"Well, okay, then," he said, his voice the gentlest I'd heard from him. "We don't have much time, so let's get right to it."

I pulled out my notepad and pen and held it up to the dash-board, hoping the street lamps would give me enough light. Jed began to talk, and I began to scribble in big letters so I'd be able to make sense of the night-time notes later.

"You probably noticed when you went to the IFF service that most of the people were . . ."

"Smiling? I did. But it was like they didn't have any soul. Do you think that's because . . ." I stopped as soon as I saw Jed's hand in front of my face.

"I don't mean to be rude, but would you mind just listening? That's your job as a reporter, right?"

"Right. Yes, right, that is my job. Sorry. Go ahead."

He cleared his throat and continued, "Most of the people at IFF are not Americans. They've come to Denver from Mexico or Eastern Europe or Vietnam, looking for jobs or family or some friendly place to start over. That's why I first started going. I liked learning about the world from these other people. It felt right. Pastor Whitman even convinced me that he was helping with their immigration status."

He paused and sighed softly as if he were considering how to phrase his next sentence. "And I was a mess, too. Just lost a marriage and a job back east, and the church that I attended wouldn't accept divorcés. I'd almost given up but decided I'd come home to the mountains. They always inspired me as a kid. Anyway, Into the Fields helped me get through a dark spell."

He pulled out what he said was the same piece of paper he'd shown me in the lobby of the *Dispatch* and waved it up and down. His tone turned fervent again.

"But enough is enough. This is the form everyone has to sign to become a member of the Fellowship. Once you've gone through five months of membership classes, you fill it out. It asks for all the normal information. You know, name, address, birthdate, statement of faith. At first I didn't think much of it. Until I got to the line asking for my Social Security number and credit card numbers. When I asked the pastor why he wanted these, he told me it was just part of the process of joining the community and sharing everything in common, just like he'd taught us from the book of Acts. He said it made taxes easier, especially because the members could decide to give directly to the church through their computerized accounts or direct deposit."

I stopped writing when I heard this and looked up at Jed. I was about to ask him a question but thought better of it.

He unfolded the paper as if he were going to read it aloud, though it was too dark to see what it said. Instead, he cleared his throat. "I didn't question the pastor after that. I thought he was right and that I'd finally found the church community I'd always hoped for. You know, a place where people really care about each other, a place . . ." his voice cracked.

I finished his sentence. "A place to belong?"

He nodded and ran his wrist across his forehead like it was the hottest night all summer, though the air was cool and dry. Then my brother, hidden amid a bunch of trees and bushes, sneezed so loudly I instinctively hollered, "God bless you!"

Jed continued as if he hadn't noticed. "I thought it really was a place I could belong. But then . . . then there was the baptism service. And for the first time since turning in my membership form, it started to click that something wasn't quite right."

"Why? What's wrong with a baptism service?"

"Pastor called about a dozen of us onstage one Sunday morning and announced to the congregation that we were joining the church and getting baptized. He sprinkled our foreheads with water and prayed for each one of us. Then Delores, the pastor's wife, handed each of us an envelope and hugged us. Pastor said this symbolized our new identity in Christ. The worship band began to play, and everyone praised the Lord as we went back to our seats."

"Delores, the Nail Lady, is married to *Whitman*?" I asked.

Jed nodded, took a deep breath, and went on, "I hadn't opened the envelope until I got home."

I was writing so furiously, trying to capture everything he said, that I'd worked up a strong appetite for a cigarette. I knew I'd never hear the end of it from Matt if I lit up right now. I resisted the urge and listened.

"That envelope, Jonna, is why Whitman told you I was dead."

"What do you mean?"

"I mean he'd taken Jedediah Sundae and completely erased him. Just like that." He snapped his fingers. "Suddenly, I was Jerome Samson. Really. He'd given me a new driver's license with my picture and birthday, only a few years younger, and the name Jerome Samson with a new address. Know what else was in that envelope? A new Social Security card, along with a form to fill out for a new checking account."

I couldn't believe what I was hearing. Skip was right—this was getting much bigger than religion. "What happened to Jed?"

"Deceased. I found out the hard way when I went to use an old credit card one day to fill up my car. The system rejected the card—the gas station attendant said it came back expired. He looked at me suspiciously, so I paid cash for it and left."

"Why didn't you just call the card company and explain what happened?" I asked, breathing in the midnight air. It was getting thicker the more Jed talked.

"Have you ever called a credit card company?"

"No. I tend to hyperventilate at the thought of credit for anything. I'm a cash-only kind of girl. I blame my parents."

"Consider yourself lucky. Because if you *had* ever had a problem with a credit card and called your company, you'd find out just how hard it is to get a real person on the phone. And if you do, it's a miracle, let alone if you managed to get the right person who could help you get back an identity they think doesn't exist anymore. You know why? You can't do a thing without your Social Security number, and if yours is suddenly declared void because all the forms say you've died, they won't talk with you."

Matt sneezed again and again. Poor guy. Allergies were bad tonight. What a conspicuous bodyguard he was turning out to be.

Jed continued, "See, if someone steals your identity, your records, transcripts, you name it, and then racks up a new line of credit with it, it takes you a really long time to clear your name—and that's only *if* you have the time, money, and information it takes to win it back."

I stopped writing and stared toward the man in my passenger seat. My eyes filled up at the thought of how miserable this must feel for Jed. I couldn't help but pat his arm.

"Don't worry about me, Jonna. I'm still Jedediah Sundae."

"With an *e*," I added.

He chuckled for the second time that night. "Once I figured out what was happening, I started calling around. I began to realize he was acting as a guardian or a type of professional expert to help these new immigrants, *creating* all their identities and filling up the IFF bank accounts in the process."

"But couldn't they leave?"

"Why would they? He takes care of them, makes sure they have groceries and some sort of work and a place to sleep. Yeah, they're stuck. They can't get back their identities even if they knew how. The way I see it, he's building an empire on people whose identities aren't even real and who are now completely dependent on him. And the worst part is, he's covered his tracks. They've all signed their forms so it looks like they're consenting to his help."

Now I could barely keep up in my note taking—and breathing. My heart was a barrage of emotions and my brain was trying to calm me down. I scribbled and flipped page after page, trying to get down the general outline of this utterly amazing scheme as Jed relayed it to me.

"I'm pretty sure Whitman is on to me, Jonna."

"How?"

"I think he's still got connections in the banking industry. That's where he worked— "

"Before he became a *pastor*. Yeah, I know."

"You do?"

"One of my colleagues managed to track down a little dirt on him. It wasn't easy because he seems to be a very tidy guy, especially with computers. But the CBI has been interested for a while in where Mr. Jeffrey Whitman is, ever since he left his first job."

A deep grumbling sigh emerged from Jed's frame, and then he began to laugh. Hard. Loud. Not a cackle really, but more like a person who hadn't laughed in a year and was now getting rid of twelve months of fear or despair. And he let it rip, from the bottom of his belly into this moonless summer night.

I started to laugh, too, infected by the sound. Soon I heard laughter from behind the trees as well, blending in with ours, and the sudden three-part harmony surrounding the Reverend King seemed an appropriate song of victory.

"You have no idea how good it is to hear I'm not crazy," Jed said, finally catching his breath and wiping his eyes. "I'm not alone in hunting down this monster."

"No, you're not, Jed. But there is the annoying little detail of needing paperwork to point to Whitman. As you said, even if we could get some of the membership forms or new identity applications, I'm not sure they'd help since they have real signatures."

The laughter evaporated and his intensity returned. "There are at least forty-eight immigrants and a dozen other broken people—like I was—who are in his grip. Who knows how many more are considering it. He tells them exactly what to do, all while pretending to build a community around Jesus. It burns me up."

"So let me make sure I've got this straight. He ropes in newcomers, makes them believe he's helping them, and then steals their freedom at the same time he uses their identities to make IFF a bunch of money, right?"

"Right."

"And then they think they have no way to get out, so they give up . . . which gives him more power over them?"

"Exactly."

I let out a slow breath. I'd listened to Matt's unofficial lectures enough to know that these kind of tyrants throughout history were more dangerous and evil than serial killers—taking the hope of a man was far worse than whipping his body. I thought I'd seen my share of bad religion stories over the past two years, but from what Jed had told me, it had just gone to new depths.

"Tomorrow, Jonna, look for a Broncos fan in the business section of the Denver Public Library at two p.m., okay?"

"Why?

"You'll know then. Bring your notes. There will be a—"

Jed didn't have time to finish his sentence. Tires screeched into Dr. King's circle, and headlights beamed straight onto our faces. When the light pierced my eyes, Jed was already out of the car and running through the park. Matt jumped in front of the lights, positioned between the two cars and looking goofy in his helmet.

Someone got out of the car, but I couldn't see anything except a silhouette against the light.

"Nice evening, isn't it?" Matt hollered, looking up at the sky like an astronomer. "I was sort of hoping the constellations would be a little clearer, but you take what you get, you know? Anyway, you can see the stars better if you turn off the lights."

The person didn't answer. Instead, he jumped back into the car, laid on the horn, backed up, and sped away as quickly as he came. The big dark car was gone in a second.

I sat behind the wheel of my little car, stunned. What would happen to Jed? How could I confirm his story? He'd taken his paper with him. And what about the immigrants at IFF? Now more than ever I needed light for my questions.

But it would have to wait until tomorrow. Because my brother was putting his bicycle into the trunk and opening my door. "You okay?"

I nodded.

"Good. Slide over. I think we've had enough adventure for the night, don't you?"

I did. In fact, every inch of my body suddenly felt depleted, as if all the air in a balloon had just disappeared. I was tired. And worried. Though I risked a lecture, I couldn't help but pull out my last cigarette—I promised myself it really would be my last—light it, and suck in a long slow drag before blowing it out the window. I stared at the streetlights as we drove. And all the way home Matt didn't say a word.

::Chapter Twelve

I had been so worn out when I'd gotten home the night before that I hadn't noticed the blinking light on my answering machine. Once I'd stumbled out of the shower and into the kitchen for breakfast, I saw the flashing pink light and pushed play as I opened the freezer. Uh-oh—the bag of coffee beans was skinny. I stared into it, hoping more beans would magically appear, at least enough for a pot. I needed some strong brew this morning, so I shook the bag a couple of times. Maybe that would do the trick.

"Jenny, you are ignoring God, just like the rest of the world, and that is a very dangerous thing." The squeaky voice filled my apartment. I dropped the bag and looked at the phone. "God's" timing—as usual—was terrible. He continued, "I expected you to come to Boulder Canyon last Saturday to worship me. I am disappointed at your disobedience."

My eyes circled the room from ceiling to floor, and I had a sudden urge to escape by playing one of my parents' old Bob Dylan albums they had given me the first time they'd converted to the Presbyterian faith. What was it with this "God" guy? Why hadn't Frank Murphy, the Boulder detective, taken me seriously about him, and more to the point, why was he calling me at *home*?

I pushed stop, pulled the tape from the machine, and

dropped it into my bag to play for Skip. Maybe he could pressure his old pal into tracking down this creep so he would stop harassing me—and who knew how many other women he might be calling. At the very least, my editor would know the next step to take.

I took a few extra minutes in front of the mirror this morning, smoothing out my newly conditioned hair and blending black mascara into my eyelashes so that they were thick like spider's legs. I stopped at 7-Eleven for a giant cup of coffee, orange juice, and a tank of gas, but by the time I got to the office, Skip was nowhere to be found. Neither was Hannah, which I thought strange since she usually beat me into the office. I poked my head around to see if Skip's assistant had punched in yet, but he wasn't at his desk, either. I scratched my eyelashes and stared at Skip's empty chair as I had the empty bag of coffee beans in hopes he would suddenly appear. I poked my fingers into the back of my head and wondered how I would look after my salon appointment as part of my beautification strategy. I sighed, still staring into Skip's office, wondering what to do, waiting for my caffeine to kick in.

"You lost, Lightfoot?" Tony Thompson's voice boomed into my ear. He was looking ever the sports reporter—worn-out baseball cap, untucked and un-ironed shirt, gallon of Coke in his hand.

"No, I, uh, well, it's just. Hmm. See . . ."

He glared at me and stepped back. "You're scarin' me, Lightfoot. I mean, what's the world coming to if our one righteous reporter looks as clueless as you do right now?"

I tilted my head at him. Finally, his voice registered and I found some light. "Good point, Tony. Know where the boss is?" I gulped my coffee and tried to regain some composure.

"At some editor's meeting with the board. Rumor has it we're going to have to cut back on stories for more ads. I'm betting religion's the first to go." He chugged his Coke, wiped his mouth with his sleeve, and stared at my head. "Hey, what happened to your hair? Something's different . . ."

I ignored him. "Religion's always the first thing to go, Tony. That's why the world's a mess."

"Uh-oh, she's back, and she's kicked into preacher's mode again."

"Hey, I could be wrong, but I'd bet good money your Broncos will be saying their prayers this fall, am I right?"

"Well, they're going to need some sort of miracle if they think they can make the playoffs." He chugged again, glaring at my spidery eyelashes as if he'd never seen such a thing. I watched the dark liquid drizzle onto his shirt and sympathized.

Then I took a chance, desperate to talk through some of the information Jed told me last night. "What do you know about identity theft?"

Tony squinted at me and rubbed his chin. I wondered when he'd last shaved. "Is that a trick question?"

"No, really. Know anything that happens when someone loses his identity?"

"Let me guess, he gets reincarnated?"

"I'm serious. You know, losing your name, your Social Security number, your birthday, everything. Any idea?"

He tossed his head back and forth. "I think you're talking about billions of dollars lost every year by banks, companies, and consumers. Last year, a couple of car salesmen in Florida swiped the credit card numbers, Socials, and names of a bunch of customers, including an eighty-two-year-old widower. You know what they did with them? They bought cars for their friends. Pretty stupid if you ask me."

"Wow. Thompson, I'm impressed . . ."

"I didn't always do sports, you know, Lightfoot. I started on the cop beat and sort of got hooked, so I keep up . . . in between games. Anyway, it's the latest crime flavor of the month, and it's only getting worse cuz most police districts don't have the staff to deal with it, and the technology these thieves use is only getting more complicated. Nine times out of ten these scumbags never get caught, and if they do, they hardly ever get convicted. Know why?" He paused and looked away before squinting back at me. "Because the *victim* has to prove he's innocent. How crazy is that? But what's that got to do with religion?"

I was astonished. I'd always thought Tony Thompson was all scoreboards, beer belly, and defense. But now the Buddhist Dharma's words were echoing in my head: "Things are not always as they seem."

"Remember when I asked you about the invisible guy?" I asked. Tony nodded and I kept going, "Seems he'd been a part of a church where the pastor is stealing the identities of parishioners and banking up wads of money for himself."

Thompson pushed out his lower lip in disgust and shook his head. "Whoa, that's worse than pro wrestling." He knocked my elbow lightly with the side of his fist and shook his head again. "Well, Lightfoot, you got your work cut out for you. Want a little earthly advice?"

I didn't, but I decided it couldn't hurt. "Move to features?" I asked.

"Nope. Be careful. This is dangerous stuff, and we wouldn't want someone writing *your* obit, if you know what I mean."

"Ah, that's the nicest thing you've ever said to me, Tony."

"Well, who else would make the coffee around here?" With that, he turned and bobbed back to the sports department, chugging and whistling as he did.

I headed straight to my desk. Between Jed's eerie midnight confession, God's scary reminder of his existence on my answering machine this morning, and now Tony Thompson's friendly advice to be careful, I was feeling just a little bit tense. I breathed in, then out, formed an "O" with my index finger and thumb and tried to meditate the anxiety away. But the more I did, the closer I felt to hyperventilating. Yoga techniques had always been a little clumsy for me. I took another deep breath and filled my lungs with stale office air, but heard Jed's voice ringing in my head. So I mumbled, "Our Father which art in heaven . . ." and went to work.

Once I'd logged on to my computer, I did a quick search of "identity theft." I gulped some coffee and read from one identity protection website:

> *Identity theft is a relatively low-risk, high-reward endeavor for a criminal. Credit card issuers often don't prosecute thieves who are apprehended because the firms believe it is not cost efficient. Consequently, they can afford to write off a certain amount of fraud as a cost of doing business.*

That wasn't exactly encouraging. It sounded as if credit card companies were almost planning for at least a few "scumbags" (as Tony called them) to rip people off each year. I reached for my notebook to decipher my scribble marks from the dark rendezvous with Jed. I wanted to check what he'd said against what I was reading. But as I did, a smooth and mighty brown hand grabbed my wrist and spun me around.

"It isn't nice to stand up your only friend in the newspaper world." Hannah was looking down at me, her head jetting one direction while her shoulders bent the other. But it was her outfit, as usual, that got my attention. She wore a pale green suit with an African scarf flowing over her shoulders and eye shadow that matched. How did she do this so consistently?

"Morning, Hannah. You look great today."

"Don't even try, Lightfoot. I thought we were meeting at Pete's for a power breakfast and fashion advice?" She released my wrist, rolled her hand into a fist, and plopped it on her hip.

I gasped, threw all ten fingers across my mouth, and shut my eyes in shame. "I completely forgot. I am the queen of losers! I'm so sorry."

"It better be a good excuse, Girl, or I'm never helping you out on a story again, you hear?" She sat down at her desk. "And what did you do to your hair? It's flat. What's up with that?"

"Great conditioner, eh? Next week I'm heading to the salon to really go for it," I said, scrounging quickly through my bag and desk drawers for some sort of peace offering. Finally, I found a semi-recent bag of individually wrapped dark chocolate drops and held out a handful.

She accepted, staring intently at my eyes. "And are you wearing mascara? What is happening to you?" she asked, meticulously unwrapping a chocolate with her sculpted nails and then dropping it gently into her mouth.

"Let's just say I'm improving my chances at love," I said. She smirked and sucked on another chocolate.

"Whatever. So what happened last night?"

I told her the story of my midnight meeting with Jed and of

the details he'd unraveled about IFF stealing his identity, giving him a fake baptism ceremony, and trapping innocent foreigners by making them believe they belonged. I described what the pastor made his members do and even told her about the mysterious car screeching into the park while Jed had scrambled off into the night. All morning I'd wanted to talk it through—with more than a sportswriter, that is—but now as I did, each unsettling detail that spilled out of my mouth made me more and more disturbed by what I heard from my own voice.

Hannah nodded again and again, swallowed, and delicately dabbed her mouth with a tissue. She glanced out the window before looking back at me. "Well, Lightfoot, you're in it now."

"What do you mean?"

"I mean, this is no church potluck. This is white-collar crime at its best."

"And the creep is acting as a minister, for Pete's sake. I hate that!" I glanced down at my notes, disgusted by the details but thankful that I could read them at all. I was more amazed still when I remembered I'd actually written them in the middle of the night.

I looked up at Hannah, who was now staring at me, her teeth chewing lightly on her upper lip and her eyebrows pinched toward me.

"What?!" I asked.

"My lawyer contact? He said your best bet is to get to the police special computer crimes unit with everything you know and give them the heads up. Chances are those guys downtown wouldn't mind a little extra information from you."

"But—"

"You know why? Because they work with everyone from the U.S. Attorney's office and the Justice Department to the Federal Trade Commission and the FBI to nab snakes like him. We're talking federal offenses, Lightfoot, felonies and long prison terms *if* he's caught." She paused before she continued, "Not to mention journalistic respect for the reporter who breaks the story. It could be your ticket up the ladder—maybe even to a bigger paper." She raised an eyebrow at this last idea, always the career woman.

Once again I was awed by how her mind worked. I'd always figured I was lucky if I met Skip's deadlines, let alone thought beyond the next assignment. Hannah, however, was always on the hunt for the story of the century, the prizewinner and career-marker, as she called it. But the thought that a religious story could turn into a *big* one only meant one thing in my book: bad news. And that was enough to make me want to crawl back into bed.

Hannah jotted down a phone number and pushed it in my hand. "Call them soon. And be careful."

"Ah, not you, too."

"Think about it, Girl. If the guy can erase people like Jed Sundae from any legitimate form of identification, imagine what he could do with a nosy reporter who's all but accusing him of playing God."

I blinked at her. She finished her chocolate, twirled around in her chair, and logged on to her computer.

"And the mascara is all wrong for you, Lightfoot," she said over her shoulder. "Try a *little* light brown instead." Then she was off and running with her own work. Her lecture weighed on my shoulders. If I hadn't smoked my last cigarette last night, I might have lit up right on the spot, despite Hannah's disapproval, company policy, and city ordinances that relegated misfit smokers to the dark corners of the outside world on the sidewalk. But I was out of tobacco, as well as promises to quit, so I sat there staring at the back of Hannah's perfectly sculpted head, pondering my options and makeup choices.

I moved my line of vision out the window and toward the mountains that sat in the distance at the edge of Denver's suburbs. What if Hannah and Tony were both right and Jeff Whitman was already planning the end of any Jonna Lightfoot McLaughlin bylines? What if he'd gotten wind that I knew what he was doing and was somehow arranging my *disappearance* the way he'd done with Jed? And what if, after I was no longer a real person on this real planet, he kept on deceiving his members at IFF for years to come, all in the name of *belonging,* while he got richer and richer?

What happened to the good news in religion?

I was now on the brink of a really bad mood. I decided I needed a break, so I left a note and the tape from God on Skip's desk and drove to the Convention Center. Nothing like a good dose of sincere Southern Baptists with their nice hairdos to pull me back into the cheery realm of optimism. I'd been covering their regional conferences for the past three years and found myself particularly charmed by the apparent requirement Southern Baptists had for attaching "Bless your heart" to almost every sentence. And if the conversation turned a little gossipy, "Bless *his* heart!" was added at the end with a few chuckles to justify the claim: "I don't think he's much of a preacher, bless his heart!" So I was all but expecting this mob of positive souls to cheer me up on this Wednesday morning.

Of course, these were only the Southern Baptists from Utah,

Colorado, Nevada, and New Mexico, and I'd heard the folks in other regions of the country, especially Louisiana, Alabama, and Texas, were a whole different breed, bless their hearts. But that didn't matter: The *Denver Dispatch* always covered the Southern Baptists when they came to town, newsworthy or not.

Skip once told me it was because the founder of the *Dispatch* back in 1907 was also the son of a Baptist—or an S.O.B. as his competitors called him. He apparently insisted on the tradition of reporting each year on his church affiliation. Even after the *Dispatch* was bought and sold almost a dozen times since the S.O.B. owned it, no one ever challenged his policy, which was a good thing for the newspaper's Number One Religion Reporter all these years later. I knew my story would run tomorrow.

I flashed my press pass to the usher at the door of the Convention Center exhibit hall and wandered by a group of pimply faced teenage boys wearing "Jesus is the Bomb" T-shirts as they handed out bottled water. I took a few bottles for the road and headed toward the information booth. The general session had already started. Leaders were giving the latest update on the denomination's growth, which was exactly the information I'd need to write the small story. I already felt better.

"Praise the Lord, Brothers and Sisters! We have finished this fiscal year in the black, and now are in a position to give above our annual response to home missions. Turn to page thirty-one in the year-end report and follow along as we thank the Lord for his provision." The man speaking on the stage had thick black hair that rolled back high off his forehead like knuckles on a hand. He was as tall as he was thick around the ribs and wore a dark blue three-piece suit.

An older woman with puffy brown hair and bright red

lipstick grinned at me as I walked in and looked for a seat. She waved me into the nearest row, handed me the annual report, and patted my elbow.

"Hey there! Glad you could make it today," she said. Her smile filled her face and a tiny smudge of red colored her front tooth. She noticed my press pass, put her hand on my shoulder, and whispered, "Now, you let me know if you need anything else, Sugar, okay?"

"Sure will. Thanks," I said as I joined the eight hundred or so men and women sitting throughout the place who'd flipped open the report to page thirty-one. I was impressed by the meticulous accounting details on the page, which showed how these western Southern Baptists spent their money.

The fact that they could be so public about their finances told me they valued honesty. Which, of course, immediately made me think of how Jeff Whitman had apparently lied ten times over to his members about money and who knew what else. I jotted down a few notes in the margin of the report along with some quotes from the dark suit onstage and smiled at the lipstick lady as I left some fifty minutes later. She grinned and rolled her fingers up and down at me. I waved back.

I'd gotten enough information for a story and a nice way to stay in touch with one of the country's largest Protestant denominations while also honoring the *Dispatch* tradition. So I rewarded myself with two hot dogs from a vendor outside the Convention Center, squirted some mustard and catsup on them, and stood in the noonday sun to have lunch. The fresh air felt good, even if it was ninety-six degrees and climbing. But as the sun warmed my face, my mascara started to feel slightly baked.

I blinked and replayed in my mind the events of the last few days, trying to make sense of them. All of what Jed and Tony and Hannah said was troubling to me—stealing someone's identity and compromising his financial security were not supposed to happen, especially in a place like a church. Destroying the lives of real breathing people was just plain wrong.

I wiped off the mustard from the middle of my shirt and hurried back to the office. Skip was still not in, and my note and cassette tape were where I'd left them, which meant the Boulder detectives weren't any wiser about God on the loose. I hoped the guy wouldn't attempt any divine act, at least until the police knew he was out there.

I pounded out a short article, titled it, "Southerners Bring Religion West," and filed it with the copy editor. Then I drove to the library at exactly 1:54 p.m. to find the Broncos fan Jed told me to look for. It was 2:04 when I walked up the stairs to the third floor of the library, past the homeless guys wearing their three overcoats and playing chess in the reference section, and through the rows of fiction. But when I saw a display of mystery novels by Agatha Christie and Dorothy L. Sayers underneath a banner that said, "Crime Solvers!" I got temporarily distracted.

On the top shelf was Sayers' *Strong Poison*, one of the Lord Peter Wimsey mysteries, where the protagonist was a mystery novelist accused of poisoning her fiancé. I grabbed it. Growing up, my parents took turns reading these novels to us on Sunday nights. I loved trying to imagine who did it and how Lord Wimsey would solve the case.

I flipped through the pages of *Strong Poison*, absorbed by the story, and laughed out loud when I read Wimsey's defense of the novelist: "She writes detective stories and in detective stories virtue is always triumphant. They're the purest literature we have."

I smiled, digging in my bag for my library card as I walked over to the checkout desk. I never made it. A short person wearing a bright orange and blue T-shirt suddenly threw a football block into my shoulder, knocking me off balance and sending me sprawling to the floor. Lord Wimsey flew across the room, my bag landed on my head, and my clogs scattered under the library computer terminal. I looked up and saw the blue-orange blur race off down the hall. I scrambled to my bare feet, collecting my bag and my wits, and ran. Or tried to.

I followed him into the biography section, then in and out of the foreign languages. Just as I was about to catch up, the blue blob disappeared into the stairwell. I knew I wouldn't have a chance there, so I spun around and looked for the elevator. I found it tucked behind a Fourth of July exhibit and punched the down arrow. I tapped my fingers against my hip, caught my breath, and waited. Nothing happened. I punched the button again and looked at the numbers above the steel door. It wasn't moving. I hurried back to the door to the stairs, but when I reached for it, it wouldn't budge. It was locked.

Whoever pushed me across the floor was getting away and wanted to make sure I couldn't follow. My shoulders shook from lack of oxygen. I looked at my feet and decided to recover my clogs, but when I glanced up, I realized where I was—in the middle of the library's business section, exactly where Jed had told me to go. I stood there, glaring at the shelves and flicking my head back and forth to make sure I wasn't about to get tackled again. That was when I spotted it.

Sitting on the end of the shelf with its cover facing me—beside R. J. Jansen's book, *The Secrets of Successful Billionaires* and Tillie Jankowsi's, *Dress Codes for Entrepreneurs*—was a thin hardback called, *Brands, People and IDs Please.*

It was an unremarkable-looking book, the corners tattered and the cover plain black with green lettering. But the author's name struck me, Whitley Jeffries. It was too close to be a coincidence—especially if you believed there was no such thing as a coincidence, as my father liked to say when I was growing up.

I opened Jeffries' book and could hardly believe my eyes. There, tucked between the pages, were three pieces of paper, folded tightly into four tiny squares. My hands started to tremble. I unfolded the first: It was a membership form for Into the Fields Fellowship with the name *Jedediah Sundae* written boldly across the top and his signature on the bottom, underneath his Social Security number and two credit card numbers.

The second piece of paper was another photocopied membership form with the name *Ernesto Gonzalez* written across the top, a squiggly signature at the bottom, and only a Social Security number above it. I swallowed, trying to moisten my dry mouth, and remembered the Southern Baptist bottles of water in my bag. I pulled one out and guzzled the whole thing. When I unfolded the third piece of paper, I felt my knees almost buckle. Written neatly across the top of the form was the name, *Mrs. Maria Rodriguez.* Her address was the same as mine, except for the apartment number, which read #5A, directly across from mine.

I gasped when I read her name, shoved the forms and the book into my bag, and hunted down my clogs from under the computer terminal. Then I hurried down the front steps of the library to the first floor. I'd barely gotten to the central desk when I felt a hand tap my arm and whirl me around.

"Hey, Jonna!" David Rockley's face was one wide smile. His brown hair was tucked under a Yankees baseball cap, and he held a stack of thick books in his arm. "Imagine running into you here. You researching a story?"

My neck ached. "You could say that."

"Me, too. Researching, I mean," he said. Then he looked carefully at my face and turned serious. "You okay? You look a little pale, in fact, sort of different from the last time I saw you. Are you feeling all right?"

"Sure, well, no, I mean . . ." I didn't know what to say as I tried to hurry toward the desk. David hurried with me.

"Anything I can do to help?"

A librarian at the desk shushed us. We stepped away from her, and I thought about David's question, tapping my bag as I did.

I whispered to him, "Yes, David, there is. You could call my brother and ask him to meet me at my apartment as quickly as he can. I'll try him, too, on my cell phone, so at least one of us should reach him. It's an emergency. I'm on my way there now."

His eyes got wide. He brushed his nose with his fingers, adjusted his cap, and nodded at me. "You bet. I'll do it right now." He set down his books on a chair, hurried over to the pay phone by the newspaper section, and dropped in a quarter.

I handed the grumpy librarian my card, checked out the Jeffries book, and jogged to my car in the parking lot. I felt as if I was just coming out of an exercise class. Not that I knew exactly what that was like, but I could imagine it was as hot and sweaty as this bizarre summer afternoon. I decided to include aerobics in my new beautification regime. But right now, I just wanted to get to my apartment and check on Mrs. Rodriguez.

As I drove, David's face in my head reminded me that I hadn't called him back to answer his question about a dinner date. Maybe because I was holding out for someone else, which made me remember that tomorrow I was supposed to confirm with the Catholic Outreach Center that I'd help out with the afternoon Reading Book Club. I only had twenty-four hours to look better than I did today. And on this hot and harried day, even the thought of sprucing up for a gorgeous blond man named Terry Choyce didn't calm my nerves or prepare me for what I found when I finally pulled in front of my building and climbed the stairs.

Mrs. Rodriguez's apartment door was open, but she was not home.

::Chapter Thirteen

Mr. Fink almost knocked me flat as I poked my head around the door and into Mrs. Rodriguez's kitchen. He was darting out from under the sink, grease smudges across his cheeks, a wrench clenched in his fist.

"Need another washer," he mumbled, apparently to himself since he made no reference to my existence as I jumped out of the way.

"Where is she?" I charged after him. He flung open the storage closet in the hallway and scrounged through the shelves.

"Mr. Fink?" I looked at the back of his skinny jeans bent over as he searched for some gadget that would solve his plumbing problem. "Mr. Fink?"

He stood up, as if he'd just heard from above, and turned around.

"What?"

"I asked you where Mrs. Rodriguez was." I was shaking but tried to remember to breathe. To relax. To get centered. To release the negative energy into the cosmic atmosphere and implore the Almighty for help.

"How should I know?" He wiped his hands on his shirt and snorted.

"You're working in her apartment," I said.

"Fixin' the sink, is all."

"I see that. Do you know where she is?" I was firm now, though I felt a tinge of panic in my teeth.

"Nope." He turned back to the shelf, muttering something under his breath.

"Mr. Fink. This is important!" I couldn't help but pace between the closet and the door to my apartment. When I arrived back at the closet, the custodian grabbed something shiny off the shelf and bolted back into Mrs. Rodriguez's kitchen. I followed.

Then my stomach growled. Between the anxiety and muscle movement at the library, I must have burned off at least a hundred calories. Which was a good thing considering my Choyce strategy, but I was hungry. My throat was dry too. I needed sustenance. Instinctively, I opened my neighbor's refrigerator, but when I looked inside, I screamed. It was empty! Except for a half-full jar of jalapeños and a tub of margarine, there was no other sign of either Mrs. Rodriguez or her groceries.

"If you have any idea where she might have gone— "

"Fixin' her sink, that's all." Mr. Fink's voice squeaked out from under the sink, his head hidden and his legs stretched out on her floor.

"Well, it's obvious something's wrong. Her refrigerator is *never* empty. And she'd just gone shopping; she's always got burritos or tortillas or pie or milk or whatever."

Mr. Fink grunted and banged on a pipe. I licked my dry lips and decided to investigate the rest of her apartment. Her living room looked the same as it always did, including a stack of junk mail on the table beside the TV Guide and her grandchildren's school pictures. Her bedroom was tidy, but when I opened her closet, blouses and skirts and cotton knit slacks were strewn on the floor. Hangers were empty and piles of unfolded sweaters lined the shelves, as if someone had gone through them in a terrible hurry. Actually, it looked exactly like my closet on a normal day, but I thought Mrs. Rodriguez had higher standards. Something was not right.

My eyes began to tear up. If anything happened to my neighbor, it would be my fault. I was the one who dragged her with me that morning to Into the Fields Fellowship. I was the one who introduced her to Whitman, something I now understood all but guaranteed disaster and danger. I stared at the disarray of her clothes and wondered why on earth I'd let her come with me in the first place.

"Hey, Sis," Matt's presence was a chocolate caramel fudge bar for mc, full of comfort and hope and clarity. I blubbered to my brother about all that was wrong in the world. Or at least in my job. About how I'd been tackled at the library and how I'd discovered the membership forms tucked inside the business book. About Mrs. Rodriguez's empty refrigerator and messy closet, Whitman's comments, and how Hannah and Tony had both warned me to be careful. I rambled and sneezed and finally found a tissue in my pocket that absorbed most of my emotional leakage.

After a few minutes Matt lifted my head and wiped off a bit of the mascara from under my eye so his finger turned black. He blinked.

"Mary baked carrot cake last night," he said softly. "From scratch."

I blew my nose and tried to look happy. "Did she put chocolate chips in it?"

He nodded. At least one thing was still right in the universe.

We walked out and looked into the kitchen. Mr. Fink was finishing up. He'd left a greasy little stain on the linoleum floor.

"Did Mrs. Rodriguez happen to say when she'd be back, Mr. Fink?" My face felt a bit puffy, but I looked him straight in the eye anyway. He looked away.

"Nope." He collected his tools and headed toward the door. Then he stopped and, without turning around toward us, said, "But I reckon she'll be back at the right time." And he left.

Matt and I looked at each other.

We closed the door to her apartment and unlocked mine. Matt went to the freezer for coffee beans but found only an empty bag. He rolled his eyes at me, tossed the bag in the trash, and dug around the back of the refrigerator until he found a can of Coke. He plopped some ice into two Mason jars, pouring back and forth into each as light brown foam collected on top. He handed me a glass and sat down with his.

"You're sure Mrs. Rodriguez isn't visiting her family somewhere, right?" He gulped his drink, waiting for an answer.

"Sure, I'm sure," I said, leaning back on my couch. "Sort of."

"That's what I thought. Maybe you just need to wait for her."

"But, Matt, there *are* no coincidences! That's what Dad always told us."

"Yes, he did, but what's that got to do with where Mrs. Rodriguez might be?"

"*Her name* was on one of the three IFF membership applications I found at the library. One's considered dead, and I haven't had time to check on the other, though I suspect he's vanished, too. Now my neighbor's gone as well *and* her refrigerator's empty." I took one big sip and set down the empty glass. "Don't you think that's just a little too coincidental?"

"Maybe she hasn't had a chance to get to the grocery store."

"No, just a few nights ago she came home with four bags of groceries!"

"So maybe she was taking a long trip somewhere, and she was really hungry," he said. Then his eyes widened, as if some new observation had just registered with his brain. "Hey, what happened to your hair? You're not using that stuff on it again for some guy, are you?"

"Matthew BigBear MacLaughlin! Are you taking this seriously?" I stood above him.

He sat up and pushed his glasses back on his nose. "Uh-oh—I'm in trouble now. Haven't heard all three names since I set you up with that tuba player when you first moved here. He wasn't a bad guy, really, Jon. Who could blame him for trying to impress you with 'Ode to Joy'? Hey, we all have our faults."

The smirk now was out of control. I watched Matt's shoulders shake and his face contort in delight as he cracked up. I wondered how we could be from the same family. While I felt the weight of multiple galaxies, Matt moved easily in an orbit of sheer glee. It wasn't fair.

Suddenly, I reached forward and placed my hands on both sides of his neck.

"What did you just say?" I shouted.

He caught his breath and grinned. "I said, uh, relax, Jon. She's probably fine."

"No, about the tuba guy trying to impress me?"

"Yeah, well. We've never quite thought of Beethoven the same way since, have we?"

"I mean after that?"

"Let's see, we all have our faults?"

I squeezed his cheeks with my fingers. "Whitman might be smart enough to cover his tracks, but, for heaven's sake, he's got at least one fault. You know what it is?" I asked, back in the living room. Matt grunted, his hands above his head, surrendering.

"He required people to fill out membership forms."

"Huh?"

"That's the paper trail I need to break this story. Those forms! It's why Jed told me to . . ." The thought of Jed suddenly paralyzed me. I dropped onto the couch beside my brother and remembered our rendezvous in the park, the mysterious squealing car, and Jed running into the darkness. I turned to Matt.

"Can you stay here a while?"

"Jonna, I've got papers to grade."

"You brought them with you, though, am I right?" I jumped up and grabbed my bag.

"Well, yeah, but . . ."

"See? That's what makes you such a great teacher. You're always prepared."

"It's not working, Jonna Lightfoot."

"Just stay in case Mrs. Rodriguez comes back, will you, Matt?" I pulled out my cell phone and dialed Skip.

"You mean, *when* she comes back," he said. "But I'm only staying until then and only if . . ." He was about to present his conditions, but I held up my hand to wait when Skip answered the phone.

"Skip?" I said, "Lightfoot here. Can I meet you in your office in fifteen minutes?"

"Whatcha got?"

"It's the IFF story. I think we're ready to break it," I said, opening the door and looking into the hallway in hopes Mrs.

Rodriguez was coming home. It was empty.

"That would mean this is big, Lightfoot. You sure?"

"Nothing's bigger than religion. I'm sure. I'm on my way." I headed for the door. "Call me the second you hear anything, Big Brother," I said as I patted his frizzy head.

"You owe me. Again," he grunted. Then he shot up off the couch. "Hey, did you call David back?"

"Who?" I was out the door and down the stairs when I heard him holler, "This is the last favor I'm ever doing for you, do you hear me?"

"Nope. Can't hear you."

The late afternoon sky was pink and orange across the mountains in the distance. It was hot outside, yet my palms were clammy against the steering wheel. I turned onto Colfax Avenue and drove west. My mind was a mix of conversations, faces, and sentences. I pulled out a pen, found an old paper bag from the bakery on the passenger seat, and began to write on it as I drove in the thirty-five mile-per-hour zone. If I didn't get it on paper now, I might not remember exactly what I needed to say once I got to the *Dispatch.* Memory could be a tricky thing for the daughter of ex-hippies.

I stopped at a red light and focused on the notes on the bakery bag, concentrating on what I'd tell Skip. A horn honked behind me suddenly. When I looked up, the light was still red. What was the problem?

The horn blew again. I glanced in the rearview mirror. A small pickup truck was directly behind me, but behind him was a big dark car that began to look familiar the more I stared at it. It was, very possibly, the mystery car that screeched in and out of the park after midnight with Jed. I swallowed. Then I crossed myself like I'd seen Mrs. Rodriguez do as a sign of protection.

"Lordhavemercy," I mumbled. I looked both ways, put my foot to the pedal, and ran the red light. Sure enough, the car pulled into the oncoming lane, around the pickup truck, and sped after me. I tried to keep one eye in the mirror and one eye on the road until I realized this made me cross-eyed and hurt more than it helped. I opted for the road in front of me, with an occasional glance to see if the chase was continuing along Colfax, past the steak house and cathedral and thrift shops. It was.

At least, until I saw a day camp of at least fifty children crossing the street from the Capitol building and walking toward a yellow bus parked beside the sidewalk. They were barely twenty yards ahead of me. I slammed on my brakes, gripped the wheel with all my might, and tasted the caramel-carbonation of cola coming back up my throat. The children looked up with wide eyes at my car, giggling and waving at me as if this was part of their field trip. Then one little boy stopped in the middle of the line, pointed at my hair, and let back his head in hysterics.

When I glanced in the rearview mirror, the mystery car had completely disappeared. I looked over my shoulder, but he was nowhere. I looked in the mirror one last time, and instead of seeing an enemy in pursuit of me, I saw what the boy had laughed at. My hair was standing straight up off my head and clinging to the ceiling of the car; the electricity of the dry heat had pulled the frizz in a million directions, and I looked like a clown with an Afro. So much for taming conditioner.

The camp counselors hurried the kids along, and I drove toward the *Dispatch*, checking every few yards to see if the car had reappeared and spitting on my fingers to smooth my hair. I pulled into the parking lot and hurried toward Skip's office, still battling the static above and looking over my shoulder as I walked.

"So Frank Murphy thinks this guy's a problem," Skip said calmly, leaning back in his chair.

"Murphy?" I answered, collapsing into a folding chair across from him.

He held up the minicassette tape from my answering machine. "Boulder detective. Remember him? He listened to this and agreed with you—anyone who thinks he's God is scary and shouldn't be calling you at home."

"Nice of him to think so. I feel much safer." I flipped open my notes and looked at my editor. "Listen, Skip, let's forget about God for a second. I've got to . . ."

"Forget about God? Finally, you convince me to take him seriously, and now you want me to forget about him?" He adjusted his tie and took a sip of tea.

"Well, let's assume he'll still be there when we need him, okay? First things first."

I told Skip about the details Jed gave me in the park, about the information Hannah had found on Whitman, even the insights Tony gave me about identity theft. He sat perfectly still, his hands clasped together across his desk so that even the cuffs of his brown jacket looked relaxed. He had that look on his face that told me his mind was pushing words and facts around, shaping a story and weighing the news as I relayed it to him. When I came up for air, he cleared his throat, signaling to me that it was his turn to speak.

"Good reporting. I knew you'd find out what was wrong in the bakery. But . . ." He sighed and rubbed his chin. "But I'm still not sure it's enough to go to print. These are pretty lofty accusations without any . . ."

"Proof?" I asked, holding up the membership forms I'd found in the library book. "These three forms are the evidence we need." I handed them to him, introducing each and emphasizing the form for Mrs. Rodriguez. Skip studied the papers like a surgeon studying flesh before an operation, running his fingers across each line and turning the flimsy paper over and over. I waited, sitting forward, then back and forward again, watching Skip examine the evidence.

When he'd finished reading and handling the pages, he held them out to me. "You're right. It's exactly what we need to confirm this. Can you get me a story by Friday? We'll run it in the weekend edition, just in time for church."

I stood up and nodded.

He continued, "I want the pastor's response to these forms as well as Hannah's research. I'll talk to our legal department to get a heads up on this." He was scribbling some notes on his to-do list.

I cleared my throat. "Oh, and did I tell you I was followed here by some dark mysterious car?" He looked up. "Isn't religion exciting?"

He put down his pen and raised his eyebrow. "I'm calling Murphy on this one too, in case these stories are related. I don't think they are, but I want the police to know." He paused. "What kind of car was it?"

"A big dark one."

He stared at me.

"Well, it was!"

"Of course it was. They always are. But if it turns up again, see if you can get a make on it, okay?"

He punched the numbers on the phone with his pen and turned serious. "Oh, and I'll tell them about Mrs. Rodriguez,

Jonna. Did you call her family?"

"She's never given me their phone number and— "

My eyes began to fill at the mention of my neighbor's name, but the voice of journalistic wisdom, rammed into my head since college, reminded me that tears and editors were not a good combination—even if the editor was Skip Gravely, the kindest and calmest newspaperman in the business.

"We'll find her," he said, tapping his desk.

I nodded and mumbled something about "this summer's high pollen level." I poked my finger underneath my eyelid and turned toward the hall.

I was relieved to find the ladies' room empty. I blew my nose and stared in the mirror, looking for perspective, asking for divine help.

How would I feel if someone took away my identity? If they erased the wonderful name my mom and pop had conscientiously given me? What would it be like to wake up one morning with my entire history—everything that had shaped me and guided me—deleted in the push of a button? And how could I cope if, from that morning forward, I had to try to be an altogether different person with a new name and new details that defined my new identity?

Shame suddenly fell heavy on my shoulders.

That was *exactly* what I'd been doing lately: plotting to be someone else. I'd developed a crazy strategy for glamourizing this chunky, frizzy, secondhand, caffeine head who was always trying to quit smoking and love Jesus at the same time. I'd even come up with a list of steps to take that I'd hoped would make me . . . pretty.

If I could become another woman altogether—or at least try to look like Maddison Jones or my sister-in-law Mary or

Hannah X. Hensley—I'd thought I could increase my chances that beautiful men like Terry would take notice. Now, I was ashamed of the idea.

I grabbed a paper towel and ran it under the faucet. Then I stared at my round face, the Irish features, and overly zealous curls in my hair. I looked at my thrift-store tank top that revealed my flabby arms and chubby chest, and I thought of the people at Into the Fields Fellowship.

I remembered their faces in that drab converted grocery store where they really did *not* belong. That's when it hit me how much I'd been taking for granted. In fact, I'd never realized how much of *me* I actually liked until I imagined *not* being me at all.

One of the features reporters suddenly flung open the door and hurried in, her heels clicking across the linoleum tiles. She raised an eyebrow when she saw me but headed to a stall. I concentrated on scrubbing off the black mascara lines above my cheeks. Then a toilet flushed, the reporter reappeared, and she washed her hands in the sink next to me. She snuck a glance in my direction and said, "Whoa, Lightfoot, you look like you could use some help."

I blinked at her, then at my reflection.

"Yes, I could. Isn't it great?" I said, grinning.

She raised her eyebrow again before turning around and clicking her heels out the door.

I breathed a quiet apology. Then I stared back into the mirror for a few seconds. As I did, I felt the tiny ache of shame gently lifted from my shoulders. For the first time in a while, it felt good just to be me. And I smiled at what I saw:

There was the twenty-seven-year-old seminatural face of a woman with, well, dignity, because her parents had always loved her as she was, her brothers and friends adored her without expecting her to change, her boss believed in her no matter what, and her faith reminded her that she was no piece of dust floating through the universe hoping to find purpose. Her life was no accident. She was uniquely crafted, like the stories she wrote and the people she covered.

I took in a deep breath, the air smelling of ammonia cleanser, when my smile disappeared. I somehow knew I was still not finished. The blessings alone were not enough. My mind flashed to the morning Mrs. Rodriguez came over to ask about going to church. She'd looked at my hair and wondered why'd I'd straightened it. She'd told me I was perfect *as I was.*

Then she'd said, "Juana. God no make mistakes. You his, uh . . ." She'd paused, looking for the words and waving her hands around my face as if to describe what she'd wanted to say. At last, she'd found it: *"Tu eres la belleza de Dios.* "

I *was* the beauty of God. And it was true not because of any makeover I could ever plan or schedule on my own.

I blew my nose again and started to laugh. At first it was only a gurgle in my stomach. But then it grew and erupted into giddiness. Before I knew it, an untamed feeling dropped into my feet, shooting up through my legs and out of my arms. And I began to dance. Right there by the sink. I tapped in front of the mirror and jumped around the toilets and stalls, laughing and singing and shouting. I let my hair go and laughed at the stains on my shirt.

It was a spontaneous love-fest, and I didn't care who walked in.

When my feet finally stopped, I caught my breath and wandered back into the hall, by way of the vending machine. Back at my desk, I swallowed a few plain M&M's, still grinning when I realized that I'd just experienced something similar to what Pentecostals would call "getting the Spirit." Then again, philosophers would have called it "an epiphany," whereas some in Boulder might have referred to it as "a cosmic intersection." On the other hand, my Buddhist friends might have viewed it as "an enlightened moment," and Presbyterians would have stoically described it as "divine revelation."

Some might have even called it a mountaintop moment. I knew all the labels for transcendent experiences. But something more had happened to me, right there in the women's room of the newspaper.

I'd caught a glimpse of a holy truth I knew was not only alive and breathing, but personal and powerful. From that moment on, I referred to it as the Dance of the Toilet Stalls (or DOTS, in journalism code). And I knew if Terry Choyce was going to look my direction, it would have to be simply because of who I was, not who I tried to look like.

The night staff was putting tomorrow's edition to bed, so I ignored them, found my silly beauty list, and tossed it in the trash as I'd seen the sports guys do with wads of paper.

Next, I clicked on my computer and focused with renewed energy. I typed the name *Ernesto Santiago* into every database I could think of. Nothing came up. I remembered what Jed told me about foreigners and surfed my way through the immigration and naturalization services site. I found what seemed to be a thousand complicated forms immigrants were required to fill out if they wanted to attain permanent residence status. I realized if you didn't speak English or have a law degree to understand the jargon, it would be nearly impossible to live here with proper documents. No wonder Whitman could act as a guardian.

When I still hadn't found anything on Mr. Santiago, I shifted to an old-fashioned strategy—I picked up the phone book and flipped through the *Santiagos*. There were nine *Ernestos*. I began dialing each number, but the first four were disconnected and the fifth was busy. There was no answer with the sixth, but when I tried the seventh, a boy answered.

"Hola."

"Could I please speak with Ernesto?" I poured the bag of M&M's across my desk and heard the phone drop, the boy holler, and a television blare. A man picked up the phone.

"Sí"

"Ernesto Santiago?"

"No," he clipped. "I am Ernie *Sanchez.*"

"Hmm. That's funny. This is Jonna Lightfoot MacLaughlin from the *Denver Dispatch,* and I found your number in the phone book under *Santiago*—not *Sanchez.* Of course, it is last year's, and you know I never can find the most recent one around here. They must hide it in the . . ."

"What do you want?" he said, now whispering. I circled his phone number in the book and asked if he'd ever heard of Into the Fields Fellowship.

"I don't want to talk about it," he whispered.

"How about Jeff Whitman? Want to talk about him?"

"No," he mumbled. I heard children laughing in the background.

"Okay, well, how about Jedediah Sundae?"

He coughed before answering in what sounded like his regular voice, the tone of voice a man uses when he doesn't care who hears him.

"Jed Sundae is a good man." Then he hung up.

I took all that to mean this was *the* Ernesto Santiago whose membership form I held in my hand and that he was now supposed to answer only to Sanchez. Whitman must have forgotten about old phone books and apparently allowed some members to keep their previous numbers. If this was another of his faults, I reasoned he had more. Who didn't? I couldn't keep track of all of my ten thousand faults—but today I realized they were part of what made me me.

I popped a green M&M in my mouth and considered my next step. It was 6:07 p.m., and though I was sure no one would answer, I dialed the number for the church office. The voice of Delores, the Nail Lady and Whitman's wife, answered.

"You have reached Into the Fields Fellowship, a place to belong. If you would like to leave a message for Pastor Whitman, please press 1. For all other—"

I didn't press one, I punched it. When I heard the pastor's recorded voice, asking me to speak slowly, I shook my head, tossed a blue M&M into my mouth, and tapped my fingers on the desk while I listened to the rest of his message and waited. Finally, the beep came on and I spoke as slowly as I could.

"Hi, Mr. Whitman. Jonna Lightfoot MacLaughlin here from the *Dispatch*. I know your policy about not wanting any publicity and all, but I'm afraid I simply have to run a story on your, uh, work there. I've got some very interesting membership forms in my hand and just thought you'd like to comment for the record on what exactly they mean. I have my theories, but it's only fair for you to correct me if I'm wrong. Oh, and maybe you could answer some questions about how exactly you're funding ministries like, let's see here . . ."

I flipped through my notepad. ". . . like Field Hands, Fields of Green, and Field Works. Very creative names, but I can't for the life of me find any public information or nonprofit applications that confirm they exist. See the dilemma I'm in? Anyway, I hope I spoke slowly enough. Oh, and I'm looking forward to talking with you soon. Thanks."

I hung up and spent the next two hours typing the rest of my notes. When I tossed the M&M's wrapper in the trash, I locked the IFF evidence in my top drawer and drove home.

Matt insisted on taking me to stay at his house with him and Mary. He'd been such a sport about waiting for Mrs. Rodriguez—who still had not come back—that I didn't want to argue, though I wasn't happy about not being home in case she did come home.

That night, I got one of the best night's sleep I'd had in weeks. Though it'd been a hot night outside and my head had been buzzing, the muscles in my body had taken a beating—meaning they actually got used—and I'd been tired. I wasn't sure if it was my DOTS or the firm mattress in my brother's fold-out couch, but I slept more soundly than I had in months.

Armed with Mary's carrot cake and a big cup of real coffee, I spent the next morning calling Mrs. Rodriguez's phone number over and over, hoping she'd pick up. In between calls, I pored over the morning *Dispatch* on Matt and Mary's dining room table and found my story on the Southern Baptists buried underneath a truck ad on page thirteen. At least it kept with *Dispatch* tradition.

As I sipped my coffee, I felt thankful that we still *had* a tradition, one that hadn't been hijacked by some evil agenda to build an empire. This IFF story was getting into my skin, making me recognize things I had before taken for granted, like history and traditions and individuality.

I tried Mrs. Rodriguez's number once more but still no answer. By the time I got to the office, I was humming an old song we used to sing at protests with our parents: "We Shall Overcome." It seemed a good way to start the day, and it kept me focused as I put down on paper the story of the spiritual identity thieves living in our city. I wanted to give Hannah an update, but she was in a meeting. Skip was talking with the legal guys, and everyone else from sports to features seemed frantic, as usual. So I spent the next few hours shifting between my computer and the phone, leaving three more messages for Pastor Whitman, dialing Mrs. Rodriguez's number, and hoping, praying, Jed Sundae would contact me in between.

I ordered lunch from Wonton Dynasty, but stayed at my desk, cutting and pasting paragraphs and quotes in the first draft of my story. By 1:17, the phone rang, the first call I'd received all day, and I assumed it'd be Whitman. I bumped over my half-empty carton of fried rice into my lap, picked out a few peas off my lap, and grabbed the phone after its fourth ring, ready to confront the thief.

"Lightfoot."

"Hello, Joan, I mean Jonna. Stephano here."

I sighed in disappointment, scanned the Rolodex in my head, and shut my eyes to try to remember who *Stephano* was. I bluffed.

"Yes, Mr. Stephano. How can I help you?"

He sneezed. "Sorry about that. Allergies. Anyway, yeah, just wanted you to know about the fire."

"The fire?"

"The Buddhists. We've concluded it was caused by some

faulty wiring in the ventilator system. So it was *not* arson, just a sad accident," he said before sneezing again.

Ding. The light in the elevator of my brain went on.

"And it was not a hate crime, okay?" The fire inspector's voice boomed.

"Of course not. Is the case closed, then?" I asked, still picking at the remnants of my lunch.

"Like a book. Or something like that. See ya around."

I hung up the phone and made a note to visit the monks tomorrow. They might give me a follow-up interview, a few comments that could turn it into a nice little article. Maybe something on where to go after the incense was snuffed out. I thought about the young monk standing in the sun the other morning and how unhappy he'd looked, how the temple and the westernized Eastern religion seemed to require more from him than he knew how to give.

It suddenly crossed my mind that just about everyone was struggling to find out who they were supposed to be. And I realized that identity was something of a buried treasure that sent most folks looking for a map rather than simply digging in.

The phone didn't ring the rest of the afternoon. By four p.m. I adjusted the marvelous frizz on my head, drove by way of my apartment building to check to see if Mrs. Rodriguez was home yet—she wasn't—and pulled in front of the Catholic Outreach Center. It was raining, so by the time I got to the front steps, I resembled a zookeeper at elephant bath time.

Keisha was waiting for me at the door, eyes wide and tiny black braids shooting off her head. She jumped up and down as I rushed in, soggy and dripping and smiling. She grabbed my hand and led me into the gym where tables were set up with books on them.

The beautiful blond man, with whom I'd exchanged only a few conversations but enough to think we belonged together, was sitting at one of the tables. Maddison Jones was nowhere to be seen. Terry Choyce was reading Dr. Seuss's *Green Eggs and Ham* to two small boys who sat close to their hero. He towered between them on a bench, his white skin an artistic contrast to their brown. The boys were completely lost in the pages he held, hardly noticing the man reading to them.

Keisha yanked my hand, and for the next hour, she and I watched as Franklin, the turtle, encountered his fear of the dark. Then we followed him in other adventures. We laughed at each picture and sounded out words. Keisha flipped the pages and pointed to the colors, telling me about the pictures she liked to draw and talking in stories and details and descriptions with so much drama and excitement, it was better than any television show or movie.

"I'll draw you a picture for your office, 'kay?" She was off her chair now, enthusiasm bouncing out of her.

"I'd love that, Keisha. Bring it for next week, okay?"

"Yeah, okay!"

Someone announced from the hallway that Reading Club was over, and the room started to move. As Keisha and I put the books back on the shelf and stacked our chairs, Terry walked over to us. I stood up straight and Keisha darted toward him.

"There you are," Terry said, swooping up the girl to his shoulders and smiling at me.

"Hey, Terry. How'd it go today?" I felt the red in my cheeks rise and fall.

"I was hoping to see you today," he said, setting down Keisha and asking her to go help Momma O clean up. Keisha skipped across the gym to the older woman who was collecting dozens of children's books from the other tables.

"I made a promise to Keisha and the Reading Club."

"Yeah, it's a lot of fun, isn't it?" he said as he watched the children with almost parental pride.

"It is," I said, gazing at his perfectly shaped nose.

Terry turned toward me and suddenly became intense. He looked at me, then down at his feet.

"Uh, this is a little awkward, but I was wondering, Jonna, well, if you don't have plans tomorrow . . ."

"I have absolutely no plans tomorrow. Not a thing," I said, noticing the firm shape of his chin and the fine flow of his hair.

"Night." He glanced up. "Tomorrow night. There's a dinner at the Brown Palace Hotel downtown. Sort of a fundraiser for the Center. I'd like it if you could come." He paused. "As my guest."

The galaxies opened and a choir of angels sang sweetly in my ear as I stood a few feet away from destiny. I mumbled something about "loving to" and floated to my car parked out in front. I hummed as I turned the key and shifted into gear.

This had turned out to be a far better—make that blissful—week than I expected. I decided to celebrate with dinner at The Pub of Saint Agnes. I'd been reminded that there was something far bigger than all of us put together at work in the world, a glimmer of inspiration that lifted me out of myself.

At least until I looked in my rearview mirror three blocks later and saw I was being followed.

::Chapter Fourteen

I turned slowly onto Colfax Avenue and watched the needle in my speedometer settle onto twenty miles per hour. The sun had just fallen behind the mountains, and it was a quiet night in Denver. The streetlights were bright, casting few shadows across the four lanes of road as I drove toward The Pub of Saint Agnes. I kept an eye on the mystery car a few links back, determined not to let its eerie presence ruin my otherwise enchanting moment with Terry Choyce.

At the next intersection, I changed lanes and saw that the car did too. I flipped my signal up and turned right to test whether the other car would do the same. It did. When I accelerated to a cruising thirty-five miles per hour, it managed to as well. But when the stoplight up ahead turned from green to yellow, I got an idea. I slammed on my brakes in the crosswalk, threw the gear into park, unbuckled, and pushed open the door. I ran back until I reached the culprit.

"Hey, why are you following me?" I yelled as I slammed my fist on the hood of the car and glared into the driver's eyes. He suddenly sat up straighter than the windshield, his head almost bumping the ceiling. His face was pale but familiar, and the look in his eyes was one I'd seen before. Then I remembered. He was the man who'd sat beside Mrs. Rodriguez and me the morning we'd visited Into the Fields Fellowship.

"Hey, you're the guy . . ." I said, leaning in closer. He yanked his elbow off the door and tried to roll up the window, but I grabbed his wrist and hung on. He shot a look in his rearview mirror, then at the car beside him and in front of him. He was boxed in.

"Why are you following me?" I shouted again, still clinging to his arm. He looked again at the cars around him and yanked his arm away. But I hung on. His eyes darted and sagged.

"Leave me alone," he said shortly. Again, he tried to roll up the window and began to turn the steering wheel with his other hand toward me, as if he could maneuver his car and make a getaway into oncoming traffic.

That was not going to happen. At the same time I let go of his wrist, I opened the driver's door, reached across the man, and grabbed the keys from the ignition so fast neither of us had time to blink.

"Excuse me?" I yelled. "You've been following me through Five Points and Capitol Hill. You chased me down Colfax yesterday afternoon until I almost hit a bunch of kids on a field trip, and now you're telling *me* to leave *you* alone?"

He started tapping his fingers on the dashboard and shaking his head back and forth. The light turned green and a rental truck behind us honked its horn. I motioned for him to go around, and he motioned for me to get lost, loosely translated. I shrugged and looked back at the man who'd been following me.

"Listen, I'm not leaving until I know why you followed me." He started to moan. "And guess what? Neither are you," I said, dangling the keys in front of him. I looked up at the traffic jam we were creating and sighed. "It looks like this is going to make a lot of other people pretty mad."

He glanced in his mirror and moaned again. He swallowed so that his throat bulged, and he fidgeted in his seat. He rubbed his eyes. Another truck honked.

When he finally looked up at me, massive tears filled his eyes, slipping down his cheeks and onto his T-shirt. Oh, Lord. This was not good. A grown man crying in the middle of the street was all I needed. I knew it'd do me in if he got weepy. Another driver laid on his horn and shouted for us to "Move it!" I shook my head and gathered the resolve I'd discovered in the ladies' room.

"Now don't do that," I said to the man, looking in my pocket for a tissue to hand him but coming up empty. "I just want to know— "

"Pastor only say to scared you. Only scared." A trace of Europe hung in his voice, the same accent I had heard from him the morning we visited the service. He wiped his nose with his wrist.

"Pastor Whitman?!"

"Yes. But I not want make anybody mad, just scared." He rolled the "r" in *scared,* sniffled, and rubbed his eyes. "He tell me some people need help with fear of God."

"Well, tell Whitman it didn't work." I put one hand on my hip and leaned against the open door of the man's car as more drivers passed, gawked, shouted, and honked.

I noticed that the moon was almost full and bright at the same time I saw a police car turning toward us, his light flashing in circles. The driver heard the siren and started to shake. He looked across to the passenger's door as if he were considering running.

"Don't even think about it," I said, grabbing his elbow with the hand that wasn't still holding his keys. "What's your name?"

He began to sob and tried to wiggle out of my grip. I hung onto my resolve. "Tell me now and I'll go easy on you with the cops. Your name? Now. The one your mother gave you?"

"Hans . . . Mueller . . ." he mumbled between breaths. Then he sat up straight again as if something had just occurred to him and suddenly spoke clearly. He gripped the steering wheel, yanking his arm away from me. "I mean, Hank. Mullen. I am Hank Mullen," he said, staring straight ahead.

"Uh-huh. And I'm Madonna." He jolted his head toward me and widened his eyes as if Madonna really was standing beside him—which one, the pop singer or the Catholic matron, I wasn't sure. Lines creased between his eyes, and his face had that look in it that craved hope, that wistful longing for something far better than what he was experiencing right now. I suddenly felt sorry for him. I realized he would believe anything I said and probably would do anything I asked—if he could understand my English. Now I really was angry, mostly at Whitman for what he'd done to demoralize this poor man who was obviously far from home.

"So Hans, uh, I mean, Hank. When did you get baptized at Into the Fields Fellowship?" He ran his hand across his nose again and blinked several times in a row.

"How you do know that?"

"Call it divine intuition."

He paused, considering my source of knowledge and answered, "Last year. Last year when I become new man." He pushed back his shoulders in pride. "It was big deal."

"I'll bet it was." I smiled. "And how do you like being a *new* man, Hank? Is it what you hoped for? Do you like how Pastor Whitman treats you now?"

Conflict hung behind his eyes as he pondered the question. The lines on his face grew serious.

"I like good enough," he whispered, tilting his head. "Better than before."

"Better than before? Before *what*?" I asked. But he didn't have a chance to answer me as two police officers approached us, officially ending our conversation.

"Interesting place for an evening chat, isn't it, folks?" the younger officer said, looking over Hans, peering in his backseat with his flashlight, and then holding the light in my eyes as his partner walked around to the other side of the car. I squinted.

"Now that you mention it, Officer, it is," I answered, flipping my head up and down the street. "But you do the best you can with what you have, you know? Anyway, I'm Jonna Lightfoot MacLaughlin, religion reporter with the *Denver Dispatch*. My press ID and driver's license are in my bag." I nodded toward my car.

He looked at my Datsun and bowed his head forward as if I'd just been given official clearance. I ran to my car, grabbed my bag, and was back with the officer in seconds, handing him my identification cards.

"What's the trouble?" he asked, looking from my press pass to my face.

"This man's been following me for two days. I decided to ask him about it." I handed the officer Hans's car keys. He looked at them and then at the driver, whose conflicted expression of fear and pride had not changed.

"Is that true? Have you been following this young lady?"

"Yes," Hans whispered. The police officers exchanged glances.

"Well, sir, I'm going to need to see some identification."

Bingo. Hans reached for his wallet in his back pocket as the younger police officer held the flashlight on him, though the streetlights on Colfax were bright enough to see throughout the car. The other officer peered in from the side door, his hand resting on his holster. Hans pulled out a driver's license and held it up.

The laminated card had a recent photo of Hans on it, but the name read, "Hank Mullen."

"Ask him what his mother named him," I whispered to the officer. He raised an eyebrow at me, but asked Hans anyway. Hans didn't answer.

The officer poked and prodded him, even held the light right in his eyes until Hans finally blurted out, "Hans Mueller. But I am Hank Mullen."

The officer took a step closer, his eyes moving between the license and Hans. "When's your birthday?"

"May 5."

"What year were you born?"

He paused. "1963."

"Hmm, that's funny. Your driver's license here says you were born in 1966. Guess everyone wants to be young again." He appreciated his own sense of humor and winked at me. I forced a smile and suggested he call in the license to check out Mr. Mullen, though I told him I was sure they wouldn't find a thing on him.

A question mark formed in the young officer's face, so I answered him, "I'm writing an investigative piece on a religious organization he's been involved in. That's how I know. I'm going to bet you'll also find several interesting *new* credit cards in Mr. Mullen's wallet." I raised an eyebrow at Hans, who by now could not stop fidgeting, wiping his nose, and glancing at the passenger door.

"A church?" Junior Policeman exclaimed. "I knew there was a reason I didn't trust those guys in the collar!"

I wondered if I should try to defend the good guys in religion, but the young officer didn't seem too interested in spiritual matters right now anyway. He nodded to his partner and walked back to the patrol car while the other officer came up alongside us.

He smelled of tobacco. I sniffed to make sure. Suddenly, my fingers and lips tingled, craving the uplifting but health-defying taste and feel of a cigarette. A battle between flesh and spirit ensued. On the one hand, I reminded myself of the reason I really, really had quit, for the very last time: Dignity. Self respect. God's idea. On the other hand, what harm was there in a little creative imagining, a little whiff of cigarette smoke? I breathed in the cop's secondhand smell, careful not to inhale too deeply, and enjoyed the memory. If I had had a third hand, I wasn't so sure who'd win.

Hans suddenly shifted in his seat, threw his body out the door, and ran up the middle of the street into traffic. A car screeched its brakes and swerved around him. The smoke-scented officer elbowed me against the car and took off after Hans. For an older guy with a nicotine habit, I was impressed with how fast he ran. Within minutes, he had Hans on the ground under a streetlight, leaning over him and holding his arms behind his back. Mr. Junior Policeman ran up beside us—I was beside the two men by now—and flicked the license as if there was a dead mosquito on it. Another car slowed down to watch.

"Yup. You were right. There's not a thing on a Hank Mullen. Which means any credit cards in his wallet are probably fake and this driver's license is no good." Now he looked at Hans, squirming on the street. "Would you like to tell me where you got this?"

The other officer pulled him to his feet, handcuffs in place.

"He asked you a question, pal," Officer Number 2 asked, yanking the cuffs.

Hans yelped, then spoke clearly while gazing straight ahead. "A goot friend help me."

"A *goot* friend?" Junior asked. "Well, I don't suppose this goot friend explained to you it's illegal to use it, did he? See, you don't seem to have a Colorado driver's license, sir, and it's against the law to operate a vehicle without one. Guess what? You get a free trip with us."

Hans bit his lip, sniffled a last time, and walked toward the patrol car, Junior leading the way. I handed the tobacco officer my business card. He studied it, smirked, and gave me his at the same time I asked how long they might keep Hans.

"He probably won't be released until tomorrow," he said.

"Please go easy with him, Officer. It's not exactly his fault, which you'll see the more you dig," I said as I watched Hans duck his head into the backseat.

The police car drove off as the other officer got in to drive Hans's big dark car. A brown four-door Ford Crown Victoria with Colorado license plates, to be exact, and a broken taillight, right side.

I gave up the idea of dinner with Saint Agnes—it didn't seem right to celebrate after this poor guy had been handcuffed for believing his pastor a little too much.

So, I drove home to a still-empty apartment building, no neighbor across the hall. I told myself it was all in my head, that Mrs. Rodriguez was a grown woman and could take care of herself. Besides, I had no cigarettes, caffeine, or chocolate to ward off any worry. Only Gideon and a quiet living room. So within minutes of hitting the pillow, he'd put me to sleep. I dreamed of dark cars, Spanish children, and cookies.

I barged into Skip's office the next morning and interrupted his phone call. He held up an index finger for me to wait a minute, glanced at his watch—7:45 a.m.—grabbed a pen, and scribbled down a phone number. I paced and yawned. He hung up the phone and looked up at me.

"Well, Lightfoot. What inspiring news have you got for me this morning?"

"It's not *good* news, that's for sure," I said, marching in front of his desk, shaking the mass of nice hair above my shoulders, and recounting the events of the last evening. Today's black cotton dress with tiny flowers hung just above my knees, a sleeveless summer thing I proudly found at Second Threads consignment. I loved wearing it on Denver's hottest days but hated whenever I came inside the air-conditioned office of the *Dispatch.* My flabby arms were full of little bumps from the frigid indoor temperature. Pacing kept me warm and awake—until I could get a refill on coffee.

"So?" Skip said. He sipped his coffee, rubbed his beard, and seemed as calm as I was intense.

"So? So here's the deal." I sat down to focus and told him about confronting Hans on Colfax—in his Ford Crown Victoria—and how Whitman had sent him to scare me. I told him about Hans's fake ID with the name "Hank Mullen" on it, how he told the officer his "goot friend" helped him get it, and how it confirmed what Jed Sundae had suggested all along: Into the Fields Fellowship was in fact stealing the identifications of some of its members and creating fraudulent ones in their places.

"Where's the guy now?" Skip asked.

"Safe. Thankfully, he's away from Whitman and in the

temporary care of the Denver Police Department since he couldn't exactly drive home on a bogus license." My voice sounded jittery, as if the goose bumps had jumped onto my vocal chords.

Skip heard it, too, and did what he did best. "Good work, Lightfoot. Now let's get this thing in print. I want you to try one last time to get Whitman's response. Because of the membership applications you found at the library, our legal team is ready to go with this, but I think the pastor needs the chance to explain his side. If you can't get him on the phone, pay him a visit . . . with one of the photographers." He paused as he considered the next step, as if he were already reading the pages in his mind.

"This is a series, Lightfoot. Page one tomorrow outlining the gist of the story. Once it's in print, you'll have an easier time talking with IFF members who will probably come forward. Let's tell their stories. And let's get some police experts talking about how easy it is to steal someone's identity."

"Right. And I'll get a seminary professor as well to talk about religious abuses." I took out my notepad and scribbled, "Seminary PROF." But when I looked up, Skip tilted his head, raised his shoulders, and pushed out his palms.

"Because . . . ?"

"It's the whole point of the story. Whitman quoted Bible verses to me as the basis for his work at IFF, but since it's leading to criminal activity, well, he's obviously just clipped the sections he thinks would benefit him out of the Good Book," I said and tapped my pen on my paper.

"And what's the problem with cut and paste?" Skip pushed out his jaw and rested his hands behind his head, like a college instructor who'd thrown out a grenade to his students.

"You can't do that, Boss. It's not how religion works, anymore than if someone ripped out a few paragraphs from one of your editorials and claimed that was all they needed to start some radical antigovernment group. You're supposed to respect the whole message, right? From start to finish. It's not like shopping."

He nodded his head, which was still leaning back against his palms, and raised an eyebrow at me. "You sound like Whitman is guilty of more than breaking the law."

"Absolutely. You just can't take bits and pieces you like from the Bible or the Torah or the Koran for that matter, paste them together, and do whatever you want with them. But that's what Whitman did—he ripped out the central message of Christianity . . ."

"Which is?"

I blinked at him and realized he wasn't interrupting me to be sarcastic, nor was he merely being tolerant. No, the look in his eyes and the slight curve on his mouth told me this was indeed an opportunity to clarify what I'd come to believe.

I paused before proceeding, wanting to get it right. "Which is, well, Christians would say it's that people get a second chance in life to become brand new because Christ died on the cross for them. He took the punishment for their sins so that they could come to God clean and new. Weird paradox, I know. That's what it is, though. But Whitman used that same message to build a sorry little empire for *himself*. And do you know what?"

He lifted his glasses and waited.

"I'll tell you what. That means he's broken a much bigger law than any in all of Colorado, or the whole country for that matter. See, Whitman hasn't just stolen something you can replace on earth, like a credit card or a car. He's taken the two most valuable things in the entire world of religion—people and the Holy

Word—smeared them with his lies, and claimed them as his own. Now do you see what I mean?"

He smiled. "So you should call a seminary professor to comment on the story."

"Good idea," I said as I slapped the edge of Skip's desk with both hands.

He stood, a tower of instant calm over my anxious breathing, and nodded toward the door.

"But first I want you to track down Whitman. I'll meet with the other editors and prep them on the story." He took off his glasses and rubbed them with a handkerchief.

I jumped from the chair, my brain swirling around the events, conversations, and faces that were shaping this series, and headed toward the door.

"And, Lightfoot?"

I turned.

"This is why you're the Number One Religion Reporter in town."

Irish red charged across my face, pushing me down the hall toward my desk. It was 8:07 a.m. I picked up the phone, pounded out Whitman's number, and once again got his answering machine. I told him I was looking for him and gave him the number to my cell phone. Then the perfumed aroma of Hannah X. Hensley floated my direction, and I swiveled my chair around to my colleague.

"Top of the morning to you, Hannah," I said. She was just coming into the office, her denim Friday jeans creased perfectly down the middle of her legs and her linen blouse hung neatly around her frame. At the same time I was noticing her outfit, I saw Hannah's eyes roam from the top of my frizzy head to the scuffmarks on my clogs. I suddenly couldn't remember if I'd brushed my hair that morning. But she just smiled and tossed me a chocolate bar.

"Nice dress, Lightfoot. It's so . . . you," she said, dropping her bags and plopping into her chair. I took that as a compliment and proceeded to tell her about the latest developments with the Into the Fields Fellowship scandal.

"Well, Girl, this might be the one." She raised a Black Power fist above her head as she said it. I knew exactly what she meant, how that tiny three-letter word "one" carried enough ambition and career accolades to last a lifetime. I stretched my neck, more interested in unwrapping my breakfast treat than in the idea of something beyond filing this story by the end of the day.

After a stop at the coffee machine, I called the photographer's desk and relayed Skip's order for a camera to meet me at Whitman's office. I hung up, hurried to the elevator, and was on my way out the *Dispatch* door and across town. Habit forced me to glance in my rearview mirror just in case anyone else had the inclination to follow me. But all I saw was the slowness of the morning rush-hour traffic, which suddenly struck me as really funny. Rush hour? Miles and miles of anonymous cars crawling along Interstate 25 heading south at a pace slower than mountain snow melting in the springtime—and this was *rush* hour!

The chuckle felt good, I had to confess. And I wasn't sure if it was the laugh, the chocolate, the conversation with Skip, or a memory of my DOTS mixed in with a little divine protection—but my shoulder muscles relaxed, my heart slowed, and my head quieted. I breathed softly. Jed's face blended in my mind with Mrs. Rodriguez's and now Hans's. Something was right about this drive, about taking this road to this place at this moment. I knew it—and I didn't need to worry about what I was about to do next.

I pulled off at the Colorado Boulevard exit, turned right, and drove another mile or so before parking out in front of the renovated grocery store now known as Into the Fields Fellowship. The sign said the same as it had the morning Mrs. Rodriguez and I visited—A Place to Belong—and I clung to the prayer that my neighbor was safe. I dug in my bag for Gideon and thumbed through the miniature New Testament. I decided I couldn't wait any longer for a photographer, so I locked my car and opened the door to the office.

"Morning, Mrs. Watson-Whitman. I'm hoping Pastor Whitman is in," I said with as much cheer as I could muster.

She looked up from her computer. Her hair was pulled back tight in a brown clip and her face was lined with heavy makeup this morning. Delores glanced at me several times and rubbed her eye with one of her beautifully sculpted nails.

"I'm sorry, Miss Lightfoot, but he's not in this—"

"I'll wait. I'm expecting a photographer anyway." I sat down as I made my announcement. The room had the same corporate office flavor as before, with Bible verses hanging in the pictures on the walls.

"No, I'm sorry, he won't be coming in for a while," she said, standing up, not a drop of emotion in her face.

"That's okay. I'll wait. Like I said, a *Dispatch* photographer will be here any minute."

"I don't think you understand—you're not welcome to wait here."

"But I thought this was a place to belong?"

She glared at me.

"Hey, maybe you could help me. I was wondering about those applications your members have to fill out. Why would you need their Social Security numbers and credit card numbers?"

Her glare creased her hard face. Her lips squeezed inward.

"I mean, I think it's sort of a strange request for a church, don't you?" I stood up, walked directly in front of her, and pointed to her desk. "Do you use that lamination machine for the ID cards you make for your new members? I noticed that the last time I was here but thought it was just something you'd use for Sunday school. See, the Sunday school teachers at the church I go to always laminate neat little charts and pictures of Jesus and stuff like that for the kids, you know, so they don't rip them up, and so they'll last forever and— "

"I don't know what you mean." She blushed, even through the makeup.

"No? Maybe someone else uses the lamination machine." I smiled. "Well, okay, what do you know about Hans Mueller? Oops, I mean Hank Mullen?"

"Miss Lightfoot, our policy is not to talk with reporters."

"I know. But I'm going to write a story anyway about Into the Fields Fellowship, so I thought you wouldn't mind helping me get some things straight. I could quote you if you like. Everyone likes to see their name in print, right?"

Her lips went tighter. I continued, "So about Hans? Where exactly is he from? I'm thinking Germany, maybe the Czech Republic. Can't quite tell by his accent but— "

"Hank's been a member since last year," she said softly. "He is— "

"Oh, I knew that already about Hans, I mean Hank. I don't know why I keep calling him Hans. Do you?"

Silence.

"Anyway, Delores, I met him last night. We were both downtown. A beautiful night, but boy, it was sad to see what happened to Hank." I fiddled with her paper clips, straightening one and bending it back and forth, back and forth, back and forth.

"What happened?" she snapped.

"What happened? The police took Hank to the city jail, that's what happened. In handcuffs, poor guy—he was scared stiff. Something about using a fake driver's license and having fake credit cards in his wallet and running away from the police. Not to mention the fact that he'd followed me all over town for some crazy reason," I said, flicking another paper clip across the desk. She gasped as she watched it fly, then took a step back from me.

Jimmy Larson, the young *Dispatch* photographer, opened the door. He fumbled in his camera bag, smiled at Delores and me, and pulled out a wide-angle Sony.

"I'll be right back," she whispered as she hurried around the corner and opened a door.

"Jimmy, snap the pastor when he comes out."

"You got it," he said, setting his features.

I glanced to see what Delores had been typing: an immigration form for a Sylvia Stibeowich. I jotted down the name and snooped a little more around the desk. There was a pile of envelopes beside a stack of files, most of which were addressed to credit card companies. Underneath one of the papers, I noticed a blank membership application for IFF, identical to the three I'd found in Whitman's book in the library.

A door slammed and I jumped back to my seat across the room. Jeff Whitman was standing over me within seconds, squinting behind his glasses and adjusting his tie. Jimmy clicked.

"Mornin', Pastor," I said as I held up my hand to wave.

"What do you want?"

"You mean you haven't gotten my messages? That's strange. I've left at least a hundred asking for your help with—"

"I told you the last time I saw you we do not talk to the media. The publicity is a distraction from our work." He paused and turned to Jimmy. "Stop that immediately."

Jimmy snapped a few more before answering, "If you say so."

"I hate to tell you this, but you're about to get a lot of publicity, or distractions, depending on your perspective," I said as I cleared my throat. "In tomorrow's *Dispatch*, page one, we're running a story on how you and Into the Fields Fellowship have stolen the identities of at least four members, forged countless credits cards to get money for ministries that don't seem to exist, and even issued false drivers' licenses for these same members, one of whom is now in the custody of the Denver Police."

He stood completely still, staring at me. I took out my notepad and pen. Jimmy snapped a photo of the wall of Scriptures as Whitman's face turned red and blotchy.

"So, my editor thought it'd be polite to see if you would like to make a comment on any of these issues?" I held pen to paper, ready to write.

Delores now also stood in the doorway, her eyes bouncing between the three people in the office. A slight breath escaped out of the sides of Whitman's mouth. Besides pushing back his glasses he did not move.

"I don't expect you to understand," he said in a low, hard voice.

"Try me," I said. "How about for starters you tell me

why you've applied for immigration status on behalf of certain members?"

"All members consent to our services."

"So you're confirming that you have in fact filled out these applications?"

He ran his finger across the top of his lip.

"I'll take that as a yes. Next question: Why would you require members to consent to your services, and then create new identities for them, even fill out bank applications for them, if it's not just to fraudulently acquire funds?"

"Many people come here unable to help themselves in adjusting to life in this country. Or they're coming to us from desperate situations. We offer them a place to . . ."

"I know the line, Mr. Whitman, with all due respect."

"Many of our members go through a conversion experience."

"Hey, I'm all for spiritual conversions, but that doesn't usually mean you get a new Social Security number, a new birthdate, a new driver's license, a new— "

"I'm surprised a religion reporter would not know the Scriptures, or the biblical promises that anyone who comes to God can become an entirely new creation, a whole new person. The Bible goes on to say they will receive a new name."

"That's funny," I said. "I always thought the Bible said that was God's job."

"I am his servant."

Jimmy captured his face just then.

"So you *are* giving these people new names and new identities?" I looked at him before I wrote it down. I heard a tiny whistle from his nose. Delores coughed.

"We are only helping people here."

"And becoming rich in the process while they stay stuck under your control?"

His jaw flinched, and he turned his wrist over to see his watch. "I believe our time is up."

"All right. We're leaving. But before we do, I suppose Delores told you about poor Hans, I mean Hank. That's going to take some getting used to. Anyway, guess what? He's talking. He even told me why you had him follow me. And just so you know, it didn't really work because I was already afraid of God. But you, now you're a different story . . . you are *not* God."

I wondered if flames might shoot out of his ears at any moment—he looked that angry. The blotches on his cheeks and forehead reappeared, and suddenly he grabbed for my notebook. I punched his hand away and bolted toward the door. Jimmy stepped behind me and Delores jumped in between him and Whitman, to stop her husband, I suppose, from doing anything he might regret. Just before I pushed open the door, I turned back toward him.

"Answer this last question. Where is Mrs. Rodriguez?"

A low guttural laugh emerged from his throat when he heard her name.

"She came here on her own accord, looking for help. Just like the rest of them. Print that in your godforsaken newspaper!" He flung his hands in the air as if he were disgusted with me, spun around, and skittered back toward the hallway, Delores looking after him like a child following an angry parent.

"You okay, Lightfoot?" Jimmy asked, more for his sake than for mine, I thought. "That was like walkin' into a snake pit!"

"Isn't religion exciting, Jimmy?" I proclaimed. "Hey, thanks for coming. See you back at the office."

I watched him drive off before I settled back in my car. As I did, my palms grew sweaty and my stomach tight. What did Whitman mean that Mrs. Rodriguez had come there on her own accord? How could she have filled out that form? I couldn't believe it. I *wouldn't* believe it. She was not that type of woman. But that didn't account for the fact that I still had no idea where she was.

My cell phone rang just as I pulled into the parking lot of the *Dispatch.* I parked, turned off the car, and found the phone underneath a pile of chocolate wrappers in my bag, realizing I hadn't checked my messages.

"Lightfoot."

"Yeah, Frank Murphy here. Listen, we've been able to trace some of the calls from this *God* character to a specific address."

"Really? Well, that's good news," I said, walking across the blacktop, my dress swaying across my knees.

"Good news? Well, not really. See, the address is from one of the apartments in *your* building. We believe you're in danger, Ms. Lightfoot."

::Chapter Fifteen

It wasn't exactly the inspiration I was hoping for as I stumbled back into the *Dispatch* lobby. I pushed the phone to my ear in case I hadn't been listening right.

"*My* apartment building? What are you saying, Detective?" I dug around in my bag for something to put in my mouth and ripped off the foil of an old Hershey's kiss.

"I'm saying that until we can find God, we think it's too dangerous for you to go home."

I sucked on the chocolate and stared at the spots on the floor, shaking my head at what I was hearing. It was a strange day in the world of religion reporting when a detective told you not to go home until he found God. True, my beat covered a lot of ground—potlucks, burned temples, dictatorial pastors—but how had it suddenly come to include danger?

He went on, "We haven't been able to trace the calls to any one apartment—seems like this character has tapped into each line to deliver his messages to you. We're sending out a team to interview your neighbors and see what we can find out. In the meantime, stay put, okay?"

"Stay put?"

"Yeah, that means do *not* go home under any circumstances until I call you back."

"But . . ."

"Don't make me call your boss on this, Miss Lightfoot."

"I hear you. Thanks."

No sooner had I hung up and dropped the phone in my bag than I felt a hand on my elbow. I jumped back, tripping out of my clogs and falling into the wall.

"Whoa, Lightfoot, a little jittery today?" Tony Thompson had barged through the lobby and I hadn't even seen him. He lifted the bill of his baseball cap as he gawked at me against the wall, then set it back on his head so that his hair shot out sideways.

"Tony! Yeah, nice to see you, too. How's the sports world?" I tried to recover and found my shoes.

"On hold. Didn't you hear?" He pointed to the elevator.

"Hear what?" I asked as he pushed the button.

"Skip's called an emergency meeting." He looked at his watch. "Right now. Whole staff has to be there. Heck, I was snooping around the stadium when I got the call to come back to the office."

Ding. A green arrow lit up, the steel doors slid apart, and we stepped inside. Tony punched the number and shoved his hands in his jean pockets. His gray T-shirt hung loosely over his belly.

"Any idea why?"

"Why what?" he said, scratching what looked like at least two-day-old whiskers on his chin and neck.

"Why Skip called a meeting? Hello!" I widened my eyes and leaned my head toward him.

"Oh, that. Something about the network crashing. It's a wonder it doesn't happen every other day—that thing is so old. Anyway, I'd suggest you say your prayers, Lightfoot. Sounds like we're gonna need 'em."

"Always do, Thompson, always do."

We stepped out of the elevator and into a frenzy of newspaper people rushing down the hall, shouting over each other, and hurrying to the conference room. I joined the crowd and found a seat by the door. Skip stood up, his gray suit a perfect reflection of his demeanor: smooth, fitting, professional.

"Okay, people, thanks for coming. I'll make this quick. In case you haven't already noticed, our entire system is down. The main server crashed about an hour ago."

A collective moan bounced around the room until Skip thwarted it and continued his speech, "Listen, folks, it's not the end of the world for us. We have been known to put out newspapers in the past without the aid of computers—though most of you are too young to imagine such a possibility." He smiled at the rookie obit reporters lined against the side wall. "It'll be a bit of a headache, but you need to go ahead and assume your deadlines have not changed. That means you might want to find a laptop, a friend's computer, or—here's a concept—a pencil and paper to get your stories done. If we have to be here all night to get tomorrow's paper out, we will. Understood?"

Another groan started until Skip waved his arms like a conductor to quiet us.

"I know it's Friday, and you probably all have big plans . . ."

Hey, I *did* have plans, big plans . . . for me. And with all due respect to my editor in chief here, I was not about to let a technological crisis keep me from my first date with Terry Choyce. No matter what the newspaper business was supposed to be—

". . . and normally I'd be the first person to tell you to keep those plans. But if we have to compromise our personal lives to get out the news, well, that's what we do in this business. It's what we signed up for when we entered journalism. The people in the Mile High City have a right to know what's going on. Besides, we're this close to catching up with the *other* daily." He squeezed his fingers together in front of his face and squinted. A few people laughed, others shifted in their seats.

Hannah, who'd been sitting in the front row, raised her hand. Skip nodded at her.

"Any idea what exactly happened with the system, Skip? Rumors are flying, you know, especially at that *other* paper." She asked the question loudly but confidently as if she were at one of the mayor's press conferences.

Skip grinned and turned toward me.

"We're pretty sure this is the work of a hacker, probably someone who's a little nervous about tomorrow's paper, if you know what I mean. Our tech team is tracking that down, the police have been called, and our systems team is working like mad to get things running normally again. But the bottom line is, we *are* going to print, even if it kills us."

"Why would someone want to hack *our* system?" one of the features writers blurted out from behind Hannah.

"Probably because we have some information he doesn't want the public to know."

I swallowed at the sound of his words. Skip was still looking at me, and I was still looking at him. Our editor was referring directly to Jeff Whitman, implying *he* was the number one suspect. That meant Whitman's schemes were now effectively targeting the entire *Denver Dispatch*, not just its religion reporter. I knew he was not happy about this story, but I never imagined he'd resort to using his old computer skills for something like this.

"So that's it, folks," Skip went on. "You know what's at stake, and since we have the best reporters in the entire Rocky Mountain region . . ." He paused so the compliment could settle in as he took off his glasses, wiped them with a tissue, and pushed them back on before finishing his sentence. ". . . because we have the best, I feel confident the city will have its newspaper tomorrow. Thanks for your patience. Now, get to work."

A buzz rose in the room as people pushed out chairs and headed toward their respective departments. Two obit reporters elbowed by me. I envied them for the simple fact that their stories would never be dangerous or risky to print. In obituaries, after all, you could leave out the poor guy's dirty laundry as a means of respect. But in every other section of the paper, the dirty laundry *was* the story. Even religion. I sighed and made my way past them to the man who'd run the meeting.

"Is it true, Skip? You think it's Whitman?"

"The crash is too coincidental, Jonna."

"Well, there are no coincidences, that's what my dad always said."

"He might be right. Remember when Hannah checked Whitman out with her business contacts and found the dirt on his companies?"

I nodded.

"I thought it was interesting he'd been known as this great computer genius. So I checked out the court records, and sure enough, the same thing happened to the systems of the companies he worked for. One even accused him of intentionally erasing all of their files." He snapped his fingers. "Poof, completely gone and no backup."

"Do we have backup?"

"You're the *religion* reporter. We have all kinds of backup, right?" He smiled as he led me out of the conference room and down the hall.

"Good point. I must admit the timing *is* intriguing. I mean, I just came from interviewing him."

Skip stopped in the hall to listen.

"And?"

"And he wasn't exactly warm and fuzzy. Jimmy got some good shots of him."

"Great. And what else?"

"And he never denied filling out forms for his members or asking for their credit card numbers and Socials on their membership applications. He told me they consented to his help, and, of course, he threw a few Bible verses at me to justify his actions."

"Sounds like it's enough for the first story, right?"

"More than enough."

He patted my shoulder and headed toward the computer center to see about the progress. I went back to my desk and stroked the frozen computer sitting on it as if it were a wounded pet. Nothing happened. All the work I'd done on the story the other day was frozen, maybe even gone. I tapped the computer again, just in case a miracle might happen. It stayed dead, so I picked up a pen and the phone and called a New Testament scholar from Western Theological Seminary I'd relied on for commenting on other stories.

"Professor Peterson? Jonna Lightfoot MacLaughlin here." I explained the situation with Whitman and asked for his insight.

"I can always count on you to challenge my thinking, Jonna. Hmm, let's see." He paused before continuing. "Well, I don't need to tell you there's nothing new about religious leaders who latch on to one aspect of the Bible at the expense of the rest. But because the Bible is considered both an historic document as well as God's sacred Word, it just can't be reduced to fit our likes and dislikes. It's a whole book with a whole message, so you can't take a part of it to create a rationale for doing something that is inconsistent with the rest of it."

"So if Whitman is taking a verse and using it for his own gain, he—"

"That's the problem, Jonna, we *all* do that. It's why we have so much division among Christians. I guess human nature likes things neatly categorized and denominational. But whenever we create these selective theologies, you know, when we build belief systems or doctrines around only a few Scriptures, it's always dangerous and harmful to the Christian message. Why? Because basically we crown ourselves God in the process." He cleared his throat. "Does that make sense?"

"Perfect." I scribbled his insights onto my notepad and thanked him for his time.

"Hope it helps," he said.

"It already has," I answered and hung up. I stared at his response in my notes and understood for a second why I had so much trouble reporting any good news on the religion beat: Human nature tended to get in the way. We were messy beings. Dark. Corrupt. Needy.

Then again, I figured that was the purpose behind every religion. It automatically required a story bigger than ourselves to guide us in knowing how to live *with* ourselves.

I fished out the "IFF evidence" I'd locked away in my drawer, shoved it into my bag, and turned to Hannah who was pounding on her laptop.

"Hannah, I'm heading to the library."

The fury stopped and she shifted my direction.

"Book club? *Now*?"

"Free computers. Always." I gave her a thumbs-up. "Call me if the system is resurrected, okey doke?"

She raised her hand, nodded, and dove back into her story on her backup laptop. I drove quickly to the library, checking in my rearview mirror for mystery cars while mapping out paragraphs and sentences in my head.

I parked, still scanning the cars around me just in case, and hurried across the parking lot. But when I walked into the library, all the terminals were filled. Between a few homeless guys, a couple of frantic-looking college students in summer session, and three older men working on résumés, there wasn't a single computer available. Where was the good karma when I needed it? I put my name on the waiting list with the librarian, sat down at the magazine rack across from the computer room, and pulled out my notes.

I couldn't help myself, either—Skip's challenge to use real paper and pens rang in my mind. I tore out some blank pages from my reporter's notebook, picked up a pencil, and started to write:

> *When Jedediah Sundae went looking for a new start at a Denver church, he never expected to be handed a new identity, complete with a fraudulent driver's license, Social Security number, and credit cards. But he says that is what happened once he decided to join Into the Fields Fellowship (IFF), a nondenominational Christian organization located at Colorado Boulevard and Interstate 25.*

> *Sundae says IFF required his Social Security number and credit card information on its membership application, and he supplied it without thinking much about it. This was a church after all, a religious institution that he thought was the answer to his spiritual quandary.*
>
> *That is, until Pastor Jeff Whitman baptized Sundae and gave him a brand-new identity—as Mr. Jerome Samson. That's when Sundae says he became alarmed, especially once he learned his old credit cards had been cancelled and his bank account wiped out, and when he went to verify his other financial records, he was surprised to learn he'd been declared deceased.*

I added details about Jed's life since then, profiled Into the Fields Fellowship's nonregistered charities, and highlighted Whitman's past as well as his response to my questions this morning. And I expanded on the other members who'd been affected by the man's treachery:

> *The* Dispatch *has obtained records for at least three other members besides Sundae who have also completed the application, providing IFF with personal financial information and in exchange, given new "spiritual names" and identity cards, which they believed represented their conversion experience. The Denver Police took one member Hans Mueller—who identified himself as "Hank Mullen"—into custody Thursday night for operating a vehicle with a false license. Another prospective member has been reported missing.*

It dropped like a bomb on my head, that last sentence about Mrs. Rodriguez. I still would not believe she'd asked Whitman for his help. She told me she didn't trust him, and Mrs. Rodriguez never went back on her word. But where was she? And more importanly, was she safe?

I grabbed my phone from my bag and called her number again. Still no answer. Then I pulled out the three applications I'd found in Whitman's book, picked up the one that had her name on it, and stared at it. Maybe something in it would give me a clue. It looked like her handwriting, and each detail about her seemed accurate. But then I noticed that she'd only provided the information on a solitary credit card number, one that included the expiration date, 07/03. It seemed strange to me to provide information on a credit card that was about to expire unless you suddenly didn't care if it did. After this month, it couldn't be used. Maybe that was the point. Maybe Mrs. Rodriguez had given a bogus number that Whitman couldn't access, just to throw him a curve.

I smiled at the thought and scribbled some more of my story, careful to incorporate Professor Peterson's comments as well as Whitman's to give balance and perspective. If the librarian ever called my name when a terminal became free, I didn't hear him. I was completely lost in the story and in the sheer catharsis of pen on paper. Until my bag rang. Several heads looked up from their books and magazines toward me, scowling at the intrusion. I whispered a hello. It was Hannah.

"Lightfoot, the techno guys have been able to access a backup system. It's limited, but we have enough to file stories by five."

"Fine. I'm almost done, just need to type it."

"Well, you better hurry up. Oh, and your phone's been ringing off the hook. It was getting on my nerves so I finally answered it."

"The man of my dreams?"

"Didn't say. I just told him you weren't here but you'd be back soon. Then he slammed down the phone. You do get some wild ones, Lightfoot."

"Tell me about it," I mumbled as I glanced at the clock on the wall. It was 3:55 already. "Holy smokes, it's almost four! I'm on my way, Hannah," I said, loud enough to bother the library visitors again and apologizing in the process. I crammed my notes and paper into the bottom of my bag and headed for my car.

Outside I shot a glance up and down the street, noticed some rain clouds starting to form, and felt the pressure of a summer storm as well as the "page one" expectation. I didn't want to disappoint my boss or Jed or Mrs. Rodriguez. I rolled down my window as I drove and pleaded for divine help again. Then I checked again in my mirror—just in case. But when there was no one behind me, let alone following me, I relaxed.

By the time I'd reached the *Dispatch* parking lot, the sky had darkened and raindrops the size of chocolate-covered almonds began to fall. Thunderstorms before dinner were a common summer occurrence in the Mile High City, and I felt the curls in my hair frizz beyond my skull. I parked, slid my bag over my shoulder, and grabbed an old newspaper from the backseat to hold over my head as I dodged across the lot, glancing up at the sky as if I could avoid the gushes. I was almost to the sidewalk in front of the *Dispatch* when I smacked straight into a live body.

It was Whitman.

I screamed. He reached to put his hand across my mouth, but I punched his arm out of the way, flung the newspaper at him, and ran toward the *Dispatch* door. He jumped in front of me, pulled my arm toward him, and stood inches from my face, rain drenching both of us.

"Where is it?" he muttered, a low guttural sound not at all like his pulpit voice, his grip on my arm piercing.

"What?"

"The application."

"Which one?" I yanked my arm out of his hand and jumped sideways. He did the same, slipped on the wet pavement, but recovered so fast that he snatched my arm again and dug in.

"It doesn't matter," he mumbled into my face. "You can't get this story anyway, can you? Awfully hard to write when the computers are down, isn't it?" An ugly crease pushed his lips into a smirk.

"You would know, wouldn't you, Whitman? First you bankrupted companies by crashing their systems, now you rip out people's souls by stealing their identities."

"You can't prove a thing." He clawed his fingers into the flesh above my elbow as if to prove his point.

"No? I've got enough for a page-one story," I said, blinking from the raindrops and pointing up to my office. "And after the first story comes out, I'm sure all sorts of people will want to talk with me."

His eyes contorted wider than any I'd seen. "The Lord sent me to *help* these people!" he screeched. He raised his foot and stamped it on the pavement, twisting my skin in the process.

"The *Lord* had nothing to do with it. You wouldn't know the first thing about real religion, you pathetic little man. I think our time is up here, *Pastor*."

I pried his fingers off of my arm and charged toward the door, but as I did, he lunged at my throat and my bag, gripping both with equal strength. I tipped to the right, then the left and hung on to my balance, trying to remove his hands from my neck and the strap of my bag. We swayed back and forth until finally I kicked out my foot so hard, throwing all my unexercised weight behind me, that it landed on his kneecap with a thud and sent my clog flying off my foot and across his face. He fell back, groaned, and staggered to the ground, cradling his knee, rain soaking him like a flood.

At exactly that moment, Tony Thompson and a group of sportswriters descended from the office door. He saw me drenched, coughing, and struggling to find my breath and my clog just as he heard Whitman's yelps a few feet away. His face shot from mine to Whitman's and back again. He brushed away the rain on his eyes and looked again as if to make sure he was seeing clearly.

"Lightfoot, you surprise me."

"Nice timing, Tony."

"Friday Afternoon Club is always good timing," Tony said. Whitman by now was collecting himself and trying to figure out how to walk in the rain with a bum knee and a bloody nose.

I breathed in a deep pocket of air and afternoon showers, adjusted my bag, and pointed toward Whitman. "Remember our invisible man, you know, the identity-stealing, system-crashing scumbag?" I asked Thompson.

"Ah, yes." He looked at Whitman, who was now limping toward his car.

"That's the guy," I said.

"Well, boys, duty before pleasure. We have an errand to run first, a delivery to make to our friends at police headquarters. You okay, Lightfoot?"

But he didn't wait for my response. He rallied the sports guys around Whitman, pulled his arms behind his back, and pushed him in by the head to the back of their car. Whitman yelped again.

I watched them drive away, the rain sliding down my cheeks and the reality of the moment dropping into my brain. My lower lip quivered. I poked my toe back into my clog, wobbled inside, and leaned against the elevator wall as it carried me upstairs. I found a tissue in my bag and wiped my face before I found Skip.

I told him what had just happened, that Whitman must have been the one who called when Hannah answered and was waiting for me to come back.

"The slimy little leech," Skip whispered as he brought me a cup of coffee. "Jonna, now more than ever we need your story."

I reached into my bag, found my papers on the bottom, and held them out to Skip. He sat down and pushed his glasses close. I sipped. He nodded. I sighed and finally, he stopped reading. He rubbed his beard.

"This is it," he said. "We've got a backup system that will work for now. How fast can you input this?" It was almost 5:37. We had to get stories to the copy editors by seven so they could paginate the paper and send it off to the presses by ten, in time for morning deliveries.

"I'm on my way," I said, pinching the story out of his hand. He picked up the phone while I wobbled back to my desk. Hannah was in the same place and mindset as she was when I left for the library. I wanted to tell her about Whitman's attack, but neither of us had time. I logged on to the computer and went to work.

By 6:45, I typed the last sentence, reread the story one more time, and dropped it in Skip's system folder. I turned toward Hannah, but she wasn't there and I hadn't noticed her leaving. The phone rang.

"Hey, Little Sister, are you still working on a Friday night?" Matt's voice was soothing. Then I remembered where I needed to be and panicked.

"No! I'm on my way out. I'll call you later, Matt!"

I darted out the door. I caught a glimpse of my reflection in the car window and laughed: My hair shot off my head in every direction. I marveled at its creative flare. But my eyes were as dark as the sky had been two hours ago—a combination of leftover mascara and weariness. The storm had passed, and I was a mess, albeit a tired, bruised, but grateful-to-be-alive mess.

Still, I could not go to the Brown Palace like *this*. I had to go home to change before meeting Terry Choyce.

I parked out front, ran up the stairs, and pounded on the door to Mrs. Rodriguez's apartment, wondering when I'd see her again. No answer. When I turned the doorknob and flipped on the light to my place, Frank Murphy's orders about not coming home until I heard from him popped into my head. Now I knew why. Someone was sitting on my couch.

Oh, Lord, I thought. *When it rains, it pours.* I considered quietly sneaking back to my car, but it was too late. When he heard the door open, he sprung up from the couch and swirled around at me, his skinny little arms flailing around his frame. My ears perked up.

"Mr. Fink!" I gasped. "What are you doing here?" I dropped my bag on the table and stood at the door. "Does something need fixing in my apart—?"

"The whole world needs fixing, Jenny!" His high-pitched voice registered in my memory. Murphy had said "God" had called from all of the units in my building, and as the custodian, Mr. Fink certainly had access to each. But he was hardly the prototype of a scary cult leader. I'd known him since I moved to the city four years ago, a cranky old man who swept the sidewalk and repaired my showerhead. He could not possibly be the kind of deranged creature who'd spray paint my building and send me secret messages about canyon revelries.

There was no way I had come face-to-face with God.

But the Dharma was right: Things were not always as they seemed.

"You have been ignoring me, Jenny, just like everyone else, and that ain't right." He rocked back and forth as he stood in front of my bookcase. "So now is the time. The world is doomed, but you have a chance, Jenny, if you'll only listen to me!" He jumped on top of the couch and started to beat the air with his fists, coming close to knocking off a lamp or two.

"Whoa, Mr. Fink! I've had sort of a rough day, and I think maybe we should get you some help because . . ."

He flicked his head back and cackled so loudly I was sure the whole building would be at my door in seconds. But he stopped as quickly as he'd started. His face turned white and his eyes got misty.

"I don't feel so good," he whispered.

"I can see why. Listen, maybe I should call someone to . . ."

"NO! I am what I am." He sprang off the couch and pushed me against the door with so much force I lost my footing and slid to the floor. Mr. Fink dashed into the hall, cackled again, and ran back into my apartment, hurdling over me and slamming my door shut in the process. He jumped back onto the couch. I was dazed; the room was spinning. And God was going wild in my living room.

Then my bag rang. Mr. Fink skittered to the window like a

spider and peered out from an angle. *Ring*. He bolted over to me, stood still, and tilted his head. *Ring*. I made a move toward my bag, but Mr. Fink slapped my wrist as if I'd been reaching for a cookie jar. I fell back against the wall and watched as he turned, swooped up my bag, and plopped it on my lap. I felt for the phone inside and flipped it open.

"Hello?"

"What did I tell you?" Murphy was not happy. "Thought I'd pay you a visit here at the paper but Skip tells me you just left and . . ."

"You were right. SO right. Like right here, right now." I smiled up at Mr. Fink, who now was inches from my head examining a few strands of my hair like he was as confounded by them as I was.

"Right," Murphy said. "We're on our way." I dropped the phone back in my bag and threw out a prayer.

"Mr. Fink, would you like to sit down on the couch?"

He considered this and walked slowly to the chair instead. His face turned white again.

"I'm not well. No one believes me," he mumbled.

"Really?" I managed to pick myself up off the floor and walk toward the kitchen. He lunged again at me, but I held up my hands in front of me and managed to stay on my feet.

"What are you doing? Did I say you could do that? I give you the orders and you obey!" he screamed.

"Getting you a drink of water, okay? You can come with me if you like." He ran to the sink and back again as I approached slowly. I poured him a glass of water, and he guzzled the entire thing. He poured another and threw down the glass.

"Okay, Mr. Fink, I believe you. I believe you!" My shoulders tightened. "Mr. Fink, I said I believe you. Please."

He looked at me suddenly with the saddest eyes I had ever seen and collapsed to the floor.

"Mr. Fink!" I screamed, and bent over him, turning his face toward mine. He was out cold, breathing loudly but completely unconscious. Something bulged in his shirt pocket, and I reached in to find a small plastic bottle of prescription pills. I read the label: "Paxil, antidepressant, a Selective Serotonin Reuptake Inhibitor (SSRI) may cause nausea, headache, anxiety, dry mouth, insomnia . . ."

"Oh, God," I whispered, setting the pills up on the counter and trying to make Mr. Fink as comfortable as possible for someone sprawled on a kitchen floor in a small apartment. I felt terrible for him. Not only was he on medication for depression, but the medicine itself seemed to be having equally depressing side effects.

Murphy and his team rushed in within seconds.

"Call an ambulance, Detective, he's having a reaction to some prescription drugs," I said as I cupped Mr. Fink's head with my hand and waved Murphy toward the phone. He flipped open his own, called for assistance, and drilled me on paying attention to officers of the law from now on. I nodded as my neighbor lay shaking on the floor.

"How about a blanket?" I asked. One of Murphy's men grabbed my bedspread from the floor and wrapped it gently across Mr. Fink.

"So this is God?" Murphy said, staring at the pale skinny custodian lying between the refrigerator and the stove. "Doesn't look too dangerous to me."

"I guess that's the point, huh?" I said. The paramedics arrived and took over while Murphy led me into the hall.

"Just when you begin to think you've got it all figured out, something like this happens," I said softly.

"So you're going to press charges, right?" He took out a pad of paper and a pen.

"Me? Press charges? Against God?" I laughed at my own joke. Murphy did not see the humor. "Sorry, Detective, but why would I press charges against my own neighbor? Because some doctor gave him meds that flipped him out? Who would sweep our sidewalk?"

"Listen, Lightfoot, it could be more serious than that."

"Well, then, let's wait until the hospital doctors evaluate him, okay?

He turned over his wrist to see the time: 8:15. An irrational thought plopped into my brain, and considering the week I'd had, I decided to follow it. Forget about vanity and changing clothes; spontaneity got the better side of me.

"Detective, would you mind if I got going? I sort of have, um, a date at the Brown Palace, and I need to get going." I poofed up my hair as if that would help.

"Yeah, okay. We'll take him to Saint Joseph's, just so you know."

"Perfect. Thanks a bunch," I said, patting his arm and skipping down the stairs. "Tell Mr. Fink I'll stop by St. Joe's later."

I rubbed my cheeks, trying to look a little less like the day I'd just had and more like a date. I found a meter in front of the Brown Palace, parked, and hurried inside. The concierge gasped when he saw me; between the dirty clogs, wrinkled dress, flabby arms, and frizzy head, I was sure he thought I belonged anywhere but this five-star historic hotel. I didn't care.

"Hi. I'm looking for the banquet for the Catholic

Outreach . . ."

"That way," he said, pointing through the lobby and looking the same direction to hurry me along.

I found the banquet hall, a massive room with chandeliers, round tables, and people. I stood on the side looking for Terry. I scoured the faces, up and down the rows of guests, but could not find my date. Then I saw someone waving at me from across the hall. I waved back until I recognized who it was: Maddison Jones. And she was inviting me to her table. She looked as stunning as she did that day we met on the steps of the Catholic Outreach Center. I swallowed, knowing I could never compete, and at the same time, something inside told me I didn't have to.

So I bumped my way across the room and sat down at the empty seat beside Maddison and across from Momma O, the grandmotherly Olivia Sampson who led my tour at the Outreach Center. She grinned at me.

"Jonna! So nice of you to come," Momma O said.

"Terry will be thrilled," Maddy added, introducing me as "the Number One Religion Reporter from the *Dispatch*" to the rest of the stunning people around the table. No one seemed to pay any attention to my appearance.

"Sorry I'm so late," I said, smiling at everyone. "Had to finish a story." They nodded politely at me as they went back to their desserts. I poured myself a cup of coffee and whispered to Maddy. "So where is Terry?"

"He's the guest of honor, didn't you know? He's up front." And sure enough, there, on the stage in front of us all, was the beautiful blond man of Catholic purity, one who seemed to understand the good news behind his actions and devotion, one who would be a perfect husband, faithful friend, and spiritual example.

I imagined future dates at nice restaurants, hikes in the mountains, walks around the park, teaching Sunday school together, or tutoring kids at the Center. I imagined our home, a big couch in the living room with tables of books on both sides and a couple of children coloring at the dining room table. I sipped, sighed, and drooled slightly.

Maddy nudged me with her elbow. I wiped my mouth.

"Isn't this a great send-off?" She motioned around the room. I followed her hand and returned to her face.

"Send-off? Help me understand," I said, admiring the absolutely perfect placement of her hair and makeup. She giggled as if my sense of humor was equally admirable.

"For Terry. Isn't this great? All these people coming to support him?"

"Fantastic." I nodded. "He does do good work for the Center."

"The Center? Well, you're right about that. But that's not the only reason for the banquet."

"It's not?" I brought my cup to my lips to finish my coffee.

"No. Didn't he tell you? Terry's decided to enter the priesthood. He's leaving for seminary next week and will start preparing to take his vows as soon as he arrives. We'll miss him, but we're all thrilled."

Coffee almost spewed out of my mouth onto Maddy. Terry Choyce, my future husband, a Catholic priest? The father of my children a father of the church? How was that possible? What was he thinking?

For the second time that day—or was it the third?—I felt as if a bomb exploded on my head, leaving me dazed and the room spinning.

But Terry stepped to the microphone, confirmed to the entire crowd what Maddy had just told me, and was greeted with applause and cheers from around the room. My fingers tingled and went numb, that feeling you get when you've been clinging to something too tightly and then you let go.

I told Maddy and Momma O I hadn't felt very well all day and asked them to give my regards to Terry. Then I slipped out the side door and through the hotel kitchen, stopping long enough to lean against a cart of dirty dishes and catch my breath. That was when I lost it. I began to sob. Tears gushed from my eyes and off my chin.

How could I have been so dumb? Terry hadn't asked me out on a date; he had invited me to a banquet along with half of Denver's Catholic population to showcase the work of the Outreach Center and to announce his ongoing commitment to it—as a priest! My heart tore in half and every muscle and blood vessel in my body throbbed and shook and shivered.

I stumbled to my car, drove myself home, and collapsed on my bed, where I stayed for most of the weekend. I didn't get up to shop at Food-a-Rama, visit Mr. Fink in the hospital, or attend worship services at Capitol Presbyterian. I didn't answer the phone when Matt called and left a message. I didn't pick up Gideon or flip through Oswald Chambers—though I did skim a P. D. James mystery after I'd read my page-one story in the *Dispatch* and tossed it in the recycle bin.

About the only other thing I did was worry about Mrs. Rodriguez because she still had not come home. I'd even flipped through the phone book thinking I might find her family's listing, but there were so many hundreds of Rodriguezes I knew I'd never track her down that way.

So in between worrying and flipping and trying to forget what an idiot I'd been with Terry Choyce, I smoked half a pack of cigarettes I'd found hidden in an old backpack in my closet. Jesus knew I'd quit again next week.

I stayed in bed all weekend because it was just easier than moving or thinking. I'd had enough of the depressing side of religion to last a while.

::Chapter Sixteen

Someone was pounding on my door. I raised my head an inch or so off the pillow, opened an eye, and saw it was 7:34 a.m. Was it Monday? I shut my eye and lay completely still. Even after two days in my flannel sheets, everything from my ankles to my fingernails to my pride—especially my pride—still ached. Getting up to answer the door would require effort, and that was something I still wasn't much interested in.

The pounding continued. A groan started to form in the back of my throat, but I pushed it down with my tongue and swallowed the sound. If I were quiet and did not so much as twitch an eyelash, maybe whoever was at my door would think I wasn't home. At least *I* could pretend I wasn't here.

It didn't work. The thump on the door was steady, as persistent as my leaky showerhead had been before Mr. Fink fixed it. Poor Mr. Fink. I imagined him lying in his hospital bed at St. Joe's, looking every now and then at the empty chair in his room while he waited for his neighbor to visit—the one who never came. I listened to my stomach growl. My head throbbed as the raps on the door continued.

Then the phone rang. Actually, both phones rang, first the landline then the cell in my bag. In between rings, the knocks continued, like drumbeats keeping rhythm for the horn section.

A fly buzzed around my room, zipping into lampshades and over my head, as the reminders of the world beyond my sleep got more and more annoying. I hung on to my resolve.

But when my alarm clock screeched at 7:35 a.m., I rolled over and punched it with my fist, sending it flying across the room. The knocks got louder and the rings kept ringing until finally I threw back the sheets, stretched as long as the bed, and plopped my feet on the floor. It was hot. Already. Dry summer heat forced sweat across my forehead.

I wasn't sure which annoyance to confront first, so I opted for the path of least resistance. My bag was a few feet away, right where I'd dropped it when I came home Friday night and collapsed of a broken heart. I still couldn't believe it: a priest, for heaven's sake! I'd been so stupid for believing something that was clearly unbelievable.

I snatched the bag, tracked down the pest, and flipped it open.

"What?" I snapped, pouting on the edge of my bed, tempted to lie back down.

'What do you mean what?' Hannah's voice was loud in my ear. "Listen, Girl, I don't know what's up with you, but you better get it together."

"Why?"

"What do you mean why?"

"Why do I need to get it together?"

"Because I said so," Hannah said firmly.

"Not good enough."

"Since when was what Hannah X. Hensley said not good enough?" she preached the words at the same time I heard a thud from the door and the click on my answering machine. "Seriously, Girl, you okay?"

"Seriously, no. But hold that thought, Hannah, someone's on the other phone," I said, tossing the phone on the pillow. I staggered toward the kitchen and listened for the message about to come over the answering machine.

"Hi, Jonna. It's David Rockley again." I rolled my eyes and rubbed my temples. I never had called this guy back. Matt was going to pound me with a lecture about my nonexistent love life, and I wouldn't be able to argue. "I'm sorry I'm calling so early on a Monday morning, but I wanted to catch you before you went to work. Guess I missed you. Again. I'll keep trying. Hey, and congratulations on your front-page article on Saturday! What a story. See you later." Click.

This guy was certainly determined; so was the obnoxious person at the door. I wobbled toward it.

"Who is it?" I hollered above the thuds. My stomach growled again. Still no answer but more knocks.

"Listen, whoever you are, if you don't tell me who you are, I'm not going to answer."

Thump, thump, thump.

"Fine." I went back to Hannah.

"Who was it?" she asked.

"Some guy. Who cares?"

"Whoa, Girl, you are having a serious attitude."

"So?"

"So it's not cool. What happened?"

"Oh, the usual. I went to meet the man of my dreams and he . . ."

"Don't tell me. He decided to enter the priesthood, which is certainly a noble and admirable vocation but not too encouraging for anyone interested in a future life with him, right?"

I sunk onto the bed. "How'd *you* know?"

"I'm a reporter, Lightfoot! I can't reveal my sources, but I can get on your case. May I remind you that there are other men out there in the universe who . . ."

"Don't even go there, Hannah. They'll all either marry women more beautiful than me—which I'm okay with—or they'll sign up for a life of celibacy. Then again, they might all become cult leaders in some— "

"Enough of the pity party, Lightfoot. I'd come over there myself and whup your behind except I have a press conference downtown in twenty minutes."

"Oh, darn."

"Snap out of it, for Pete's sake. You have a job to do. And for your information, Miss Pitiful, you've got two gentlemen sitting here at your desk waiting for you to come in. That's why I called."

"I don't care."

"Well, you better care. One says his name is Sundae—who I think is now pretty famous thanks to you and your Saturday story. And the other is . . ." She turned her voice away from the phone and toward the other man. "What's your name again? Oh, right, Santiago."

That woke me up.

"Tell them I'm on my way, okay, Hannah?" I said as I threw my heartbroken, pitiful self around the bedroom looking for something to wear.

"That's more like it, Girlfriend. I'll tell them," she said. "And, Lightfoot, good work on the page one."

"Yeah, yeah," I answered, flinging skirts and T-shirts in the same direction as my alarm clock before I settled on a black denim skirt with only minor stains and a paisley cotton blouse with the bottom button missing. My stomach growled again, so I hurried to the refrigerator in search of anything. I found a half-eaten brownie and a grapefruit in the back. I pulled out both and started in.

Thump. Thump. The knocks rose in irritation level at least ten degrees. I finished peeling the grapefruit, popped a section into my mouth, and walked to the door. It was sour.

"Whoisit?" I stammered, sucking in my cheeks and swallowing the fruit. Another thud and I'd reached my limit. I yanked open the door, ready to pelt someone with a flying grapefruit, but saw a tiny gray-haired Mexican woman standing in her housedress, her hands gripping a plate of steaming sopapillas, her tongue licking the white sugar off her lips. She'd been knocking with her shoe.

"MRS. RODRIGUEZ! Where have you been?" I threw my arms around her, careful not to damage the pastry plate, and kissed her cheek.

"I be here knocking on your door all morning but you no answer. I hear you call out, Juana, but I no could answer cuz of this." She nodded to the plate she was holding. I glanced down but kept rambling.

"I mean, before now. Where have you been before this morning? I've been so worried about you, thinking it was all my fault and hoping, praying you were safe because I could never forgive myself if something happened and I don't know what I would do if . . ." She kicked my shin as if it was the door.

"Ow!"

"You want breakfast?"

"Oh, yeah! Come on in," I shouted, bringing her inside and ushering her to the couch where she set the plate between us. I took a bite as powered sugar sprawled across my skirt like snow on a mountain and realized I hadn't even attempted making a pot of coffee.

"Tell me everything while I make us coffee." I jumped from the couch and watched the sugar snowball down my skirt, over my kneecaps and onto the rug. It didn't matter, though, now that my neighbor was home. And safe.

She smacked her lips and began, "Remember when you tell me to ask that lady about that Sundae guy? And she say he no alive? She also say she scared of pastor. I think that pastor, he no treat my people right; he no good guy for Jesus. Then you say he maybe want to give me trouble, sí?"

"Sí," I said, digging through the freezer for some signs of beans. Nada. I put on the kettle instead and got out the tea bags.

"I want bad pastor no there no more. So I go to him for to help me. But I no dummy, Juana." She grinned at me, powdered sugar coating her mouth, a sparkle dancing in her eyes. "I go trick bad pastor."

"Mrs. Rodriguez, did you go *undercover*?" I poured the tea and sat down.

"*Hee, hee, hee!* He no smart as he thinks, Juana." She chuckled as she sipped. "He say he no help me until I become member of Fellowship. I say I like that mucho so he give me Bible talk and say I got to write on paper."

"A membership application?"

Her eyebrows shot up. "Sí! I write on paper and give many información."

"Like your credit card number? The one that was about to expire?" I asked as I inhaled the first cup of caffeine I'd had all weekend.

"Good girl, Juana!" Mrs. Rodriguez laughed again and patted my knee. Then she pulled a piece of paper and two laminated cards from the square pocket on her housedress and held them out to me.

"He give me this." The paper was a copy of the membership application I had seen stashed in Whitman's book at the library. One of the cards was a fake Colorado driver's license with her picture on it as "Mary Ramos," and the other was an immigrant's green card that looked so real I thought she *was* Mary Ramos.

"Wow. You could go all the way to Mexico on these," I said, pouring more tea.

"Juana! I no need these to go Mexico. I take these to help you help my people. Besides, I got real passport for me, Maria Louisa Rodriguez, from United States of America. I am citizen. I pass the big test and everything seven years ago."

She was beaming at her accomplishment and pulled out her U.S. passport to show it off. As long as I'd known her, I'd never thought to ask about her residency status. And apparently, Whitman hadn't either since, in spite of providing other information for him on the IFF application, she was left with her American identity very much intact. He hadn't thought to erase her past records because he had never considered she might have any. I shook my head at the courage of her trick.

"After I visit bad pastor, mi hermana teléfono to say come quick. She say she about to give new baby niece so I hurry to go visit. And Mr. Fink say he want fix mi kitchen for two days and . . ."

"Mr. Fink?"

"Sí. He say he gonna make big mess to make sink better. I got to take bus all night to hurry to mi hermana. I sorry I no call you, but my new bebe, she come too quick. I almost no make it in time. Oh, but she is muy bonita!" She fished in her pocket for another picture and showed me one of a giddy newborn girl with brown fuzz on her head.

I held the photo out in front of me and something clicked inside me, "*Tu eres la belleza de Dios.*"

"Sí, Juana! She is God's beauty!"

"And she was born in Mexico last week?"

"No, Juana. Mi hermana is in Omaha, Nebraska!"

We laughed and demolished the rest of the tea and sopapillas. After a weekend of moping and sleeping, I had to admit it felt good to laugh. When we'd collected our breath, Mrs. Rodriguez turned to me.

"Why you not know where I go? I tell Mr. Fink to tell you. He no say?"

I recounted for her the strange day I'd come looking for her, finding him under her sink but him not responding to my questions. Then I told her that things hadn't been quite right for Mr. Fink lately, either, that he wasn't feeling so well and was now at St. Joseph's Hospital. Her face grew serious.

"Qué lástima," she whispered. "And what about the Sundae man? You find him?"

"Holy cow!" I hollered, bolting into my room for my bag and sliding back into the living room inches from my neighbor. "Jed Sundae's waiting for me at the office! I've got to go, Mrs. Rodriguez!" I leaned over to her, squeezed her neck, and kissed her cheek. "So glad you're back. I'll see you tonight, okay? Don't go anywhere!"

"Okay, okay!" She laughed as she let me pull her up from the couch and hurry her out of my living room into the hall. She opened the door to her apartment and watched me skip down the steps. I waved up at her, feeling a strange blend of relief, ache, and hope tumble through my bones. At least one of my prayers had been answered.

By the time I arrived at the *Dispatch,* it was almost 8:30 a.m. and at least ninety-five degrees outside. I parked, wiped my forehead, scrunched my hair, and made my way through the lobby then the elevator and around the maze of the newsroom to my desk. Jed was not there. Hannah was not at her desk, either, and I had the sudden urge to return to my pity party—as she'd called it. It just seemed easier and my body was still tired. Then a healthier idea popped into my head that sent me looking for Skip.

I was glad I did—because Jed Sundae and a small man wearing a blue Denver Broncos T-shirt, jeans, and a cowboy hat were sitting in two chairs across from my editor. All three men stood up quickly as I barged into the office, and I felt blood gush behind my cheeks at their gentlemanly gesture.

"Jonna! Just in time," Skip said, glancing at the clock on the wall and pointing to another chair. "I was just hearing from Mr. Sundae and Mr. Santiago what happened when your story came out on Saturday."

"Great! I'd love to hear," I said, shaking hands with the man beside Jed. "I'm Jonna Lightfoot MacLaughlin. Don't believe we've met." He tipped his cowboy hat and nodded.

"I'm Ernesto."

I turned toward Jed, smiled, and gripped his hand. He smiled back and we sat down.

"Sorry I'm late. Had an unexpected visitor—Mrs. Rodriguez is home!" I blurted it out as if it were the best news of the day. And so far, it was.

"And?" Skip asked, leaning forward and adjusting his glasses as if they helped him hear better.

"And she's fine, thank God. In fact, more than fine. She's sneaky. You know what she did? She pulled a fast one on Whitman and gathered more evidence from our 'bad pastor,' as she called him, than I could have." I dug through my bag for her paperwork and cards and set them on the desk like a lawyer setting up an exhibit before a jury.

"Before we continue, I need to apologize for . . ." The man with the cowboy hat cleared his throat and fidgeted in his chair. ". . . for hitting you at the library. I didn't have much time that day—had to pick up my son from school before getting back to work at the Fellowship office—and you, uh, seemed a little distracted, so I needed to hurry you up."

Skip looked at me, his eyes wide but his gaze firm.

"That was you?" I blinked. "Well, I guess we *have* met. Hey, before you guys decide to sneak me any more secret documents, you should know I *always* get distracted in libraries!" Their faces filled and the air in the room relaxed. "Isn't that the point?" I added.

The thought of libraries made me think of books, which made me think of Reading Club at the Catholic Outreach Center, which reminded me of Terry. I felt humiliated again. Until I thought of Keisha.

But when I leaned back in my chair, the stiffness in my muscles returned. I stared at Jed and watched his mouth start to move, his hands rolling through the air in slow motion, but no sound was entering my ears. Somewhere in a fog or a dream I heard voices. I pressed my thumb against the top of my shoulders and breathed in, then out, then in, trying to get it together. But Terry's face at the banquet dropped into my mind, and I was standing on the street in front of the Brown Palace heaving and sobbing. Sleep pulled on my joints, and all I wanted to do was . . .

"Jonna? Everything okay?" My eyes popped open at the sound of Skip's voice.

"Right. Sure. Sorry. Long weekend," I said, brushing off some of the white powdered sugar spots on my skirt. "Now we were talking about . . . what again?"

"About what happened when the *Dispatch* came out on Saturday," Skip said.

"Oh, right . . . What happened again?" I stared at him as if I'd find the answer hidden in his beard or his glasses.

"What happened? More like what *didn't* happen," Jed responded. A tinge of relief trailed his voice. "My phone didn't stop ringing. It was like having my name in the paper suddenly declared me 'resurrected' to other members of the Fellowship. A couple of old timers said I'd disrupted the community, but at least a dozen called to say they'd been terrified for so long that they'd become paralyzed, which, of course, was just what Whitman wanted. They hadn't known what to do except listen to him. It's like the story helped them know how to move again."

"It's true," Ernesto whispered, then increased the volume in his voice as if realizing he no longer needed to be afraid. "I wouldn't have gone along with this, either, that's how scared I was of what Whitman might do. Until Jed kept stopping over and over and over, helping my wife and me see through it. I was working in the Fellowship office last week—part of my job was keeping the place clean—when I saw *my* file out on Delores's desk. I figured there must be others, so I told her I was coming back later that night to vacuum. That's when I decided to make a few copies."

I sat up straight.

"When the story came out, people were worried, frantic even, but relieved at the same time, you know? Then everyone heard Sunday morning services were cancelled, which Whitman has never done," Jed said.

"No, it'd be tough to lead worship from jail," I told him.

"Whitman's been arrested? How did they ever find him?"

"Not quite as hard as you'd think." I thought of Tony and the sports guys carting off the fake preacher to the police. Jed unfolded a piece of paper he'd pulled from his shirt pocket and flicked it open.

"Well, just to make sure he stays there, here are the names and phone numbers of members who said they'd talk with you—on the record. Maybe it'll help some of them get back their lives and their identities. It's a start at least. No one wants this to go on, you know. No one wants to lose their freedom to be themselves."

"No one," Ernesto affirmed.

The words hung in the room for a few long seconds. None of us moved. We just sat there, struck by the possibility of what could have happened if Jed had not come forward, if Ernesto had not provided those forms, if Skip had not taken me seriously, and if I had not written the story. We each knew our part, and felt a humbling acknowledgement that something bigger had coordinated our efforts, sort of like those times you stand on top of a mountain and find the comforting perspective that you are small but not insignificant.

It was Skip who finally broke the silence. "Jonna will get right on it, gentleman," he said quietly, rising from behind his desk. "But in the meantime, I'd like you to talk to our legal team.

And you might want to get legal help yourselves, in part so you can get back your identities and clear your credit reports. No telling where else this could lead."

We walked back to my desk, and I turned to Jed.

"So, what are you going to do now that you're, uh, alive again?"

"Ernesto and I want to try to help the others. We're starting a little group in his house, maybe we'll look for a real pastor, but our main objective is to get back a piece of who we really are. Let's hope it helps us get our feet back on the ground." He and Ernesto followed Skip into the hall, but halfway down Jed stopped and spun back toward me.

"Jonna?"

I looked up.

"Thanks for believing in me."

"Likewise, Jedediah Sundae with an *e*. Likewise."

I spent the rest of the morning alternating between cups of coffee, the Catholic Outreach Center story, and interviews with some of the IFF members on Jed's list. Hannah came back from the press conference with the news that the mayor's office had announced a formal investigation into the works of former-Pastor Jeff Whitman, and local authorities were holding him without bail at the Denver County Jail. She slapped my back and handed me a Godiva dark as a sign of her pride. I didn't realize just how hungry I was until I peeled back the wrapper and bit.

So by lunchtime I ran down to the hot dog stand in front of the *Dispatch* and ordered two wieners with the works. It felt like an oven outside with the temperature probably close to one hundred degrees by now. I was squirting on extra mustard when I noticed a nearly bald man about my age standing beside me buying a bottle of water. His forehead was shiny with sweat. He looked familiar, but I couldn't place him. I dumped more onions on my hot dogs and hurried back toward the air-conditioned building.

"Miss Lightfoot?"

Where had I heard that voice before? I turned around, bit into my lunch, and waited at the door.

"I don't know if you'll remember me," the young man said, stepping toward me, his eyes scouring the ground. He wore what looked like brand-new slacks and a white button-down shirt. I wondered if he was a Mormon missionary. He twisted his bottle cap.

I tilted my head and swallowed. "Should I remember you?" I asked, trying not to let hot dog juice drip down my blouse.

"No, I don't suppose you should. I mean, y'all must meet a lot of people every day, so I don't know why you'd remember someone like me," he said softly. I noticed the Southern accent. But something wasn't right. Until he guzzled his water—that was when it hit me.

"The Buddhist Cultural Center! That's where I met you, right? What happened to your robe?"

He grinned sheepishly. "I've decided to leave the Center. The Dharma agreed it was not my destiny, and so I'm heading home to Alabama. A better man for having tried."

"It didn't have anything to do with the fire, did it?"

"I was never real good at suffering, you know? But you helped me understand the ways of enlightenment."

"How'd I do that?"

"You respected me. That's why I came to see you, and that's what I am taking home with me."

I wiped my forehead. "Listen, it's hotter than hades out

here. You want to talk some more inside?" I nodded toward the *Dispatch*. He laughed.

"No, thank you. I have learned to embrace the heat," he said. "I was simply hoping to run into you to say good-bye."

"You mean you've been waiting out here in the heat to tell me that?"

"Only since ten a.m." I looked at his watch—12:45.

"Well, I think you're right. You *are* going back a better man, or at least a patient one. You could have come upstairs, you know, to my office."

"I didn't want to disturb you from your important work." He put out his hand and I shook it. When he let go, he turned and walked slowly across the street to the bus stop, his face red from the sun but relaxed at the wait. I waved, finished my first dog, and went inside. I'd had enough heat; I wanted to embrace the cool, man-made temperature of an office building.

And that was where I stayed most of the rest of the week as the heat climbed to record numbers. I wrote four more page-one stories, profiling IFF members and exposing Whitman's methods for stealing identities while creating new ones and spiritually manipulating immigrants and vulnerable citizens in the process. I talked with several detectives and federal agents who were now involved in his investigation, and who had discovered he was the ringleader of a gang of identity thieves who were said to be one of the saddest and worst cases the feds had seen this side of the Mississippi. From everything they told me, Jeff Whitman was not going anywhere—except prison—for a long, long time.

By Friday morning, though, I was ready for a break and a change. I could only write so much about stolen identities and false spirituality before it started to bog me down. I finished the piece on the Catholic Outreach Center, with a final mention of Terry's decision to come back to run it after seminary. It would be a *good news* story—for most people.

And I'd finally agreed to set up a dinner foursome with Matt, Mary, and Mr. Persistence, David Rockley, for dinner at The Pub of Saint Agnes, not really caring so much about the date—especially since Terry's crushing announcement a week ago—but knowing chowder, ale, and light conversation would be a good diversion from the bad news I'd been reporting.

It was another hot July morning, and I was also ready for a change of temperature. I felt restless. So I spent the morning trying to ward off the uneasiness by thumbing through Gideon, consulting Oswald Chambers' devotional, and enjoying some coffee and one of Mrs. Rodriguez's brownies before heading out to my car by nine a.m.

Mr. Fink was sweeping the sidewalk. His face was pale and taut, his arms still skinny and a little slower this morning as they pushed the broom carefully across the cement pathway.

"Hey, Mr. Fink! When did you get home?" I asked as I unlocked my car.

"Wednesday."

"Sorry I didn't get to visit you at St. Joe's, but I, uh, well . . ."

He grunted loud enough to make me stop, then waved at me as if it'd be better if we didn't talk about it. I agreed.

"Well, it's real nice seeing you this morning. But you take it easy in this heat, okay? Don't you work too hard." He nodded as I got in my car. That sidewalk never looked so good.

I had five messages waiting for me when I got into the office. My second oldest brother Mark was the first message. He was calling from his office in Mobile, Alabama, to tell me he had a new girlfriend, "a beautiful brunette with the funniest sense of humor and a whole lot of brains. You'd like her, Jon. She even teaches Sunday school at a small Lutheran church and, get this, bakes her own chocolate cakes from scratch. See?"

"Show off," I mumbled, sipping a fresh cup of coffee and debating whether I'd call him back, knowing he'd ask me about my love life after he gushed about his. Nope, he could wait, I thought, though I did want to catch up with him.

Mark worked for some marketing research firm in Mobile that I never quite understood but he seemed to enjoy. It was hard to believe it'd been almost five years since he'd moved south, just after our parents headed for the mission field of Central America to work with coffee farmers. Not long after that, Luke moved his family to New Jersey, Matt and Mary came to Denver College, and I finished my journalism degree, joining the *Dispatch*.

I stared at their pictures on my desk, until the cheer dissolved to nostalgia and my eyes got misty. I missed the cushion of my family. With them, I could always be sure of our identity, and certain that no one close to me would enter the priesthood, though they'd probably entertained it at one time or another. With them at least, life had made sense.

I pushed out my lower lip and sulked a little more before listening to the next messages. All four were from a woman who identified herself as Hattie Lipsock, the managing editor of the *New Orleans Banner*. I had no idea who she was or why the editor of a newspaper I knew had won its share of Pulitzers would be leaving me messages, but my curiosity was piqued. I punched in her number, and she answered right away.

"Thanks for returning my call, Miss MacLaughlin. I know

you're busy and Lord knows I am too, so I'll get right to the point." Her voice was easy and familiar, like a favorite aunt's at a family reunion.

"Here's the scoop: I'm an old Denver girl from way back, so I read the *Dispatch* regularly online. That means I've been reading your stories, especially this latest series on that *scumbag* of a pastor." She punctuated the word, and I smiled as I listened to the spunk and rhythm in her tone. "Anyway, what I'm getting at is this: We at the *Banner* pride ourselves on our daily coverage of all things local in New Orleans and the grand state of Louisiana. We've got ourselves some of the country's most religious folks you'll ever see—and I mean we've got it all, Catholics, voodoo priests, Baptists, Mardi Gras maniacs, Episcopalians, Jews, you name it. Fascinating place here for anyone interested in worshiping just about anything you want!"

She laughed at herself, snorted really, before she continued, "So here's my question: What would it take to get you to come here and work for us?"

The phone slipped out of my hand and hit the top of my desk with a thump. I fumbled for it, finally latched on to it, and put it to my ear.

"Sorry about that. You sort of caught me off guard this morning," I said. "Let me get this straight: New Orleans? You want me to move to New Orleans? Louisiana?"

"Well, Sugar, that would make reporting for the *Banner* a lot easier, don't you think?" She laughed as she said it, a full-framed hoot, and I imagined her jiggling as she did. I got the impression that this was the type of woman who drank every drop of life out of each day and collapsed each night enormously satisfied.

"Well, I don't know if . . ."

"I've already talked with Skip about this and— " she said.

"You talked with Skip?"

"Sure did. He and I go way back. Course he doesn't want to see you go—why would he? An ace reporter like you doesn't come along every day. Then again, that man knows the newspaper business, which means he understands that sometimes you need a change of temperature to move your career forward. Or, you know, a new place to strut your feathers, as they say down here."

"They do?"

"Sure do. So I'm prepared to increase your *Dispatch* salary by 15 percent to have you come on board as our number-one full-time religion reporter. We'll give you whatever else you need, and I will personally show you around the Gulf Coast, Cajun country, the Arts District, you name it. I think someone like you could find lots of great stories in a town like New Orleans."

She said the name of the city as if it were one word and infused it with such magic and adventure that I immediately thought the Mile High City was small and normal in comparison. I gripped the phone and the side of my desk.

"Well, Hon, what do you say?"

"Uh, well, I, see, the thing is . . ."

"The thing is you don't know the first thing about me or this town! And you're a reporter. I know that. You need to snoop around a bit, see what you find out. It's in your blood. I understand that, and we're willing to wait to get you here, okay?"

"You are?"

"You bet. Now, I gave you all my phone numbers so you can call me whenever you want with any questions you might have. Better yet, come on down and visit. Hey, you don't happen to have family in the area, do you? Biloxi, Baton Rouge, Birmingham,

Mobile? They're all in spittin' distance."

"They are?" I could spit on Mark in Mobile? Surely it was no coincidence he'd just called this morning. After all, there was no such thing.

"I'm tellin' you the truth, Jonna. Can I call you that? You got kin nearby?"

"A brother in Mobile."

"Perfect. Pay him a visit and have him bring you on over. Our treat. See what you think." She hooted again and continued, "But I need to warn you, Jonna Lightfoot MacLaughlin, I'm going to call you every week for the next year until you say yes. You know why? Because I want the best reporters I can get for the good people of Louisiana. How's that sound?"

"Well, I guess if . . ." I gulped my coffee.

"I think it sounds divine, of course. Allrightie then, talk to you next week!"

Hattie Lipsock hung up, and I stared at the phone as if I couldn't believe someone had really invented such a contraption. Or that such a person as the woman I'd just listened to was not some character in a novel but was a real, breathing person who'd just offered me a job. A change of temperature. A new place to strut my feathers. A chance to move my career—and my heart—forward.

I swiveled my chair toward Hannah, who in perfectly matched scarf, suit, and shoes, was writing frantically at her desk.

Without looking up, she said, "If you just got offered a job, you better take it, Girl."

"How did you know?" I gawked at her.

"I know everything. And I think it'd be good for you," she said, her fingers still pounding the keys.

"You do?"

Finally, she stopped and looked right at me.

"Lightfoot, every reporter knows you've got to keep moving to find the stories that mean anything. The more you do, the more you have a shot at the big guys."

Her voice was so stern I had to listen. But just as I was about to respond, she continued, "Besides, you're good. They'd be lucky to get you."

I blinked at my friend and tried to swallow. Nothing went down. Hannah simply looked back to her computer screen and typed, signaling to me that I had better not interrupt but I had better pay attention to her advice. I guzzled my coffee and searched for the *Banner* online.

I read every article, even the sports stories. I tried to imagine myself walking around the French Quarter, dipping my toe in the Mississippi River, and exploring the cathedrals and churches and history and who knew what else of this city that before now had barely registered in my brain.

When I told them that night at The Pub of Saint Agnes, Matt and Mary said they'd always wanted to hear *real jazz* in New Orleans, and if I took the job, that'd give them a good excuse. Even David Rockley said it sounded "exciting!" But then again, he also said I looked "beautiful tonight" in spite of the tangles on my head and the stains on my dress. So I wasn't exactly sure I could trust his judgment. Then again, my brother and sister-in-law could smell a dumb idea a mile away, and reporting for the *Banner* seemed to them to have the right scent about it.

"Remember what Dad used to say, Jon, about major decisions?" Matt asked.

"Which time?"

"After he finished *The Confessions of St. Augustine*. 'Love God and do what you want.' He loved quoting it—in that order." Matt chugged and then continued, "So the question is, do you want to go?"

I finished my Fat Tire as we sat in our favorite booth by the window. I stared at the streets outside, and suddenly the lights of the Denver skyline seemed to dim. When I glanced back at Saint Agnes on the wall, I was sure she was nodding at me.

I spent the rest of the weekend chewing on Augustine's words as though they were a caramel chocolate bar, talking them through with friends at Capitol Presbyterian, and browsing the travel and geography section of the library.

By Monday morning as I sat in my car at the Java Pit, I pulled out my cell phone, found the scrap of paper with Hattie's phone numbers, and dialed. She picked up on the first ring.

"Hi, Hattie, it's Jonna Lightfoot Mac . . ."

"Hey, Dawlin'! Give me some good news, will ya, and tell me you're comin' on down!"

"Good news? If you've got some, I'd love to find it. When do I start?"

bonus content includes:

- Reader's Guide
- Denver Gets Religion: 12 Sacred Sites to Visit Next Time You're in the Mile High City
- The Lighfoot Amateur Reporter Instruction Kit
- Book Two in The Lighfoot Trilogy
- Acknowledgments
- Author

::Reader's Guide

1. Why is religion reporter, Jonna Lightfoot MacLaughlin, in search of good news? Why do you think she is ideally suited to be a religion reporter?

2. What makes names so important to Jonna? How do you think names affect our sense of identity, if at all?

3. Consider the cast of characters in Jonna's life: her brother Matt, her colleague Hannah, her editor Skip, her neighbor Mrs. Rodriguez, and her new young friend Keisha. What role does each of these people play in Jonna's life? Do you know individuals who might be similar, and if so, how could you encourage them today?

4. Jonna has a "thing" for coffee and chocolate. What does this say about her? (Take a minute to indulge in a cup of coffee or a piece of chocolate to better understand her situation.)

5. Why do you think Jonna is attracted to Terry Choyce? How is he different from other men in her life? And why is she avoiding David Rockley?

6. Though Jonna's job as a religion reporter is to engage with a variety of religions in an increasingly pluralistic culture, she is able to navigate her way without compromising her own Christian convictions. What religions in Denver does Jonna encounter that are different from her own? And how does her commitment to her faith and her local church influence her perspective and the way she interacts with people who come from different faith traditions? What can you learn from her?

7. When Jedediah Sundae first confides in Jonna about Into the Fields Fellowship, she is not sure what to make of him and his situation. What does she eventually learn of the truth there, and how does it affect her as a person and as a reporter? What makes her Dance of the Toilet Stalls so significant?

8. In what ways does Jonna show compassion? Professionalism? Integrity? Weakness? Growth?

9. What surprised you most in *A Mile from Sunday*? How has the story affected your perspective of the role newspapers and journalists play in our lives? What themes and issues surfaced for you throughout Jonna's journey in the Mile High City, and what made you laugh?

10. What do you think will happen to Jonna Lightfoot MacLaughlin when she goes to work for the *New Orleans Banner*? Will she find good news? Or a good man?

::Denver Gets Religion: 12 Sacred Sites to Visit Next Time You're in the Mile High City

(in no particular order)

Mother Cabrini Shrine: Located beyond the foothills of Golden, Colorado, the Shrine was established by Saint Frances Xavier Cabrini as a summer camp for orphan children and for the purpose of spreading the gospel. With her beatification in 1938, the property became a place of prayer, pilgrimage, and devotion to Mother Cabrini and the Sacred Heart of Jesus. The shrine is one of many missions served by the Missionary Sisters of the Sacred Heart of Jesus.
Address: 20189 Cabrini Boulevard., Golden, CO
For more information: www.den-cabrini-shrine.org

Trinity United Methodist Church: Established in 1859, this is the oldest church in Denver and is one of the finest examples of "Modern Gothic" architecture in the United States. According to definitions of design, "The church is an auditorium clothed in a Gothic shell." What made the building "modern" in 1888 was the marriage of Gothic detailing and a rococo theater with the latest technology. Today, the church offers a welcoming and transforming experience: the love of Jesus Christ.

Address: 1820 Broadway, Denver, CO
For more information: www.trinityumc.org

The Cathedral of the Immaculate Conception serves as the Mother Church of the Catholic faithful in northern Colorado. The Cathedral was consecrated in 1921 and elevated to a minor basilica on December 25, 1979. On August 13 and 14, 1993, His Holiness John Paul II celebrated Mass at the Cathedral as part of the World Youth Day celebration held in Denver that year.
Address:1530 Logan Street, Denver, CO
For more information: www.denvercathedral.org

Corona Presbyterian Church is a 280-plus member congregation committed to serving Jesus Christ in the city of Denver since 1904. Corona is a member of the Presbyterian Church (USA) denomination, "evangelical" in its theological commitments and progressive in applying the gospel to its diverse, urban ministry environment in the Capitol Hill area of Denver.
Address: 1205 E. Eighth Avenue, Denver, CO
For more information: www.corona.presbychurch.net

Saint John's Episcopal Cathedral: Before Colorado became a state or even a territory, before the City of Denver was incorporated, this congregation was founded during the Colorado gold rush as the Church of Saint John in the Wilderness. Today Saint John's remains a vibrant congregation rooted in history and continues its tradition of living on the frontier. A grand architectural feat, the cornerstone for the current Cathedral was laid on January 24, 1909, and the first service held within on November 5, 1911. The nave was completed of limestone

with a "temporary" brick chancel, and its ceiling is 65 feet in height,185 feet long, and 52 feet wide. It contains much artwork of significance.
Address: 1350 Washington Street, Denver, CO
For more information: www.sjcathedral.org

Riverside Baptist Church, affiliated with the Southern Baptist Convention, is a family of born-again people from many different cultural and ethnic backgrounds, united under the lordship of Jesus Christ for the purpose of glorifying God by developing Spirit-born disciples of Christ and planting reproducing churches. The church sits on a hill overlooking the Platte River Valley, and the view from Riverside Baptist of downtown Denver is breathtaking.
Address: 2401 Alcott Street, Denver, CO
For more information: www.riversidebaptist.com

Assumption of the Theotokos Greek Orthodox Metropolis Cathedral of Denver was established in the early decades of the twentieth century for newly arrived immigrants from traditionally Orthodox countries. In 1979 the Holy and Sacred Synod of the Ecumenical Patriarchate of Constantinople established the Greek Orthodox Diocese of Denver; in 2002 the Diocese was elevated to the status of Metropolis. In the spirit of Pentecost, and in recognition of these origins, it has become the common practice in most parishes to read the Lord's Prayer in Arabic, Latin, Slavonic, Ukrainian, Romanian, and Spanish languages, as well as in Greek and English. The Cathedral is a striking building, dating back to the early twentieth century. Famous for its large golden dome, other attractions at the Cathedral include a vast, decorated interior and regular guided tours.

Address: 4550 East Alameda Avenue, Denver, CO
For more information: www.assumptioncathedral.org or http://denver.goarch.org

Shorter Community African Methodist Episcopal Church, organized in July 1868 by Bishop Thomas M. D. Ward, was the first African-American church established in Colorado. The church has grown from a log cabin erected in lots at the corner of Nineteenth and Holladay Streets (now Market Street) to its current location, "Freedom Crossroads," Martin Luther King Boulevard and Richard Allen Court.
Address: 3100 Richard Allen Court at Martin Luther King Boulevard, Denver, CO
For more information: www.shorterame.org

Congregation Emanuel, the oldest Jewish congregation in the state of Colorado, was founded in 1874. It is the largest Jewish congregation between Kansas City and the West Coast. It had its early beginnings in a burial and prayer society that was organized in 1866. By 1874, two years before Colorado became a state, the congregation was officially incorporated by twenty-two members. Within the first year, membership was almost doubled, and on September 28, 1875, its first synagogue was dedicated. This was located at what is now the corner of Nineteenth and Curtis Streets. Early in 1876, the congregation engaged its first full-time rabbi.
Address: 51 Grape Street, Denver, CO
For more information: www.congregationemanuel.com

The Zen Center of Denver, a Zen Buddhist community (sangha) offers Zen Buddhist practice and training. The

Zen Center of Denver is part of the Diamond Sangha, an international network of centers and teachers in the Harada-Yasutani line of Zen Buddhis, descended from Western Zen pioneer Robert Aitken Roshi.
Address: 3101 West Thirty-first Avenue, Denver, CO
For more information: www.zencenterofdenver.org

Denver Catholic Worker: Catholic Workers live a simple lifestyle in community, serve the poor, and resist war and social injustice. Most are grounded in the gospel, prayer, and the Catholic faith, although some houses state that they are interfaith. Each Catholic Worker house is independent and there is no "Catholic Worker headquarters."
Address: 2420 Welton Street, Denver, CO
For more information: www.catholicworker.org/communities/commlistall.cfm

Colorado Community Church is an evangelical Christian church with multiple campuses. Each campus is unique and reaches out to its community in its own distinctive way. The goal is for each to connect and cooperate with each other in order to broaden the impact of Christ's gospel in our community and beyond.
Address: 3651 South Colorado Boulevard, Englewood, CO
For more information: www.coloradocommunity.org

::The Lightfoot Amateur Reporter Instruction Kit

Grab your notebook and pen and look around! What do you see in the world of religion? Whether a cathedral or storefront church, a temple or mosque, an annual event or regular meeting, what religious sites or groups in your community, town, or city catch your attention? There's probably an interesting story there worth pursuing!

Step One

To be a religion reporter, you first need to do some homework. You'll want to find out what time services are, attend a few if you can, and pay respectful attention during the gathering. Ask for visitor's information and read it. Perhaps arrange to meet the pastor, rabbi, or leader. Chat with members. Take notes on all that you notice or hear (never trust your memory!).

Most people are willing to talk about their religion *if* you politely ask the right questions and sincerely want to learn.

Remember, too, that religion reporters don't pursue a story to challenge what people think or believe, but simply to understand. A religion reporter's role is to gather information and report their discoveries, *not* to change people's minds, or try to get them to convert.

So try to stay as open-minded and unbiased as possible—you never know what you might learn or what unique story possibilities might arise!

Step Two

Be prepared. Once you've decided what your story is, dig into it with questions. You might want to follow Lightfoot's typical questions for reporting, especially because the answers will shape what you end up writing.

The following should get you started:

- WHO is the story about? Who are these folks?
- WHAT do they believe? What have they had to overcome to arrive at their religious conclusions, and what is unique, distinctive, or inspiring about their beliefs or ministries?
- WHERE specifically do they meet, and what is the surrounding area like?
- WHEN do they meet and how often?
- HOW did they come to be (history), and how do they practice their beliefs?
- WHY do they meet together?

Step Three

Once you've gathered as much information as possible, grab a cup of coffee or some chocolate and get ready. Read over your notes so your thinking is clear. Your goal is to introduce readers to the experience you had and provide them with the information you gathered so they can draw their own conclusions.

Now, write *only* a 400-500 word story that answers your questions clearly and objectively. Be sure to use words that anyone could understand and provide details that help outsiders get an accurate picture of the religion or group.

Writing Tips: Use complete sentences, short paragraphs, and interesting quotes from some of the people you've interviewed, making sure to properly attribute their titles. You might want to linger over a few religion stories in your local newspaper to see how stories are written and covered. Pay attention to the language, details, and structure of how the reporter has conveyed the information.

Step Four

Once you've finished your story, give it a good headline, put your byline underneath the headline, and consider submitting the story to your book club or friends. Take their feedback graciously, edit your story so it's as clean and strong as it possibly can be, and consider submitting it to your local newspaper (if they haven't covered this story yet). Editors often need good stories from freelance writers in their community.

Finally, consider submitting it to the Lightfoot Amateur Reporter Award (LARA) Contest at www.lamppostmedia.net where we'll post the best stories. *All* posted LARA reporters will receive the next Lightfoot book in the trilogy *free*!

So pick up your pen and start exploring the world around you as an amateur religion reporter!

Coming April 2007

:: the lightfoot trilogy

book two

a quarter after tuesday

A***uthor's note:*** *The Lightfoot Trilogy was born in my head in January 2003. I knew then that Lightfoot's career would take her from Denver in Book One to the enchanting city of New Orleans in Book Two (and ultimately to New York City by Book Three).*

But when Hurricane Katrina hit in August of 2005, I joined the world in grieving for the people there. I wondered what would happen to all of the stories, actual and fictional, that included New Orleans as a backdrop. At first, I thought it would be too emotional to write about it. Like so many, I was deeply saddened by the storm's tragedy. And then I realized I had to write it. Jonna was always meant to go to New Orleans, to experience the magic, culture, and faith of one of America's most unique cities.

This is a tribute, then, to the people of New Orleans, to the memory of what was and to the hope of what could be.

Summer 2004

::Chapter One

Big Wendall tossed two beignets on the counter next to my coffee and stretched his lips from side to side, laughing the whole time as if my breakfast were a source of great joy for him. I smiled back.

"There ya be, Dawlin'," he said. His voice was so deep it echoed inside his rib cage before erupting throughout the tiny café he ran. Then the man—who stood at least two heads above me—snatched my dollar bills with a child's tease, slapped them in the cash drawer, and dropped a few quarters in my hand, still laughing with each motion. Big Wendall was as happy as he was big.

"See ya tomorra!" he boomed before sending me off and waiting on the man behind me.

I nodded and laughed at the same time I stirred a few packets of sugar in my chicory drink that looked more like milk than coffee. I grabbed the beignets from the counter and inched my way through the crowd that gathered each morning at The Big 'n Easy Café before work. The combination of this fried pastry, powdered sugar, and creamy coffee had become a staple for me ever since I discovered Big Wendall's little diner around the corner from the office where I worked.

I sipped my coffee—which was lukewarm—as I headed outside. No matter. The morning temperatures had already soared to a scorching ninety-eight degrees—plus humidity—so I didn't mind a cool shot of caffeine to get me going.

I rounded the corner on St. Peter's Street but stopped short when I saw a thick piece of pale yellow tape stretched from a building to an orange cone in the road. A handwritten sign dangled in the middle: "Workin' on banquette. Please use street." I studied it, my eyes jumping from the words to the gaping holes in the sidewalk as if the Man in the Moon had spit rocks onto it, until I knew what I needed to do. I set my coffee on the ground for a second, reached for my little brown book and pencil in my bag, and scribbled: "B-a-n-q-u-e-t-t-e." Though I'd settled into a city just a few states down and over from where I grew up in Colorado, sometimes I felt like I had packed up and moved to Belgium or Haiti. This place had another language and a way of life I'd never seen in the Rocky Mountains.

It was New Orleans, after all. Home of beignets—which was also in my book with the pronunciation "ben-yay" beside it—jambalaya, po'boy sandwiches, and crawfish. Not only had my eating life taken a radical—and wonderful—turn, my survival skills had required the purchase of a little notebook so I wouldn't be lost whenever new words came my way.

Like now. I recovered my coffee, gulped it all, and wandered up to my desk on the third floor of the *New Orleans Banner,* the Crescent City's number two daily newspaper. I'd barely logged on to my computer when Harry, the mail guy, darted by and flung a skinny brown envelope onto my desk.

"Here, ya," he mumbled as he kept up his pace, flinging

envelopes and packages to reporters along the hall.

"Thanks, Harry," I responded, though he was well into the sports section by the time the greeting left me. I picked up the envelope, noticed there was no return address, and saw whoever sent it got my name wrong. I sighed and opened it anyway at the same time I took a bite of my beignet. Powdered sugar fell like an avalanche down my black T-shirt as a piece of paper from a Big Chief notepad dropped from the envelope, folded unevenly in half.

It was a message from God. Correction: It was from one of her representatives, and it read:

> *Jennalou, Mother God's 'ligned Her celesteel powers and come to the Bayou. We seen her and She mad! Only She can help a hard and horrable town like ours. Tell 'em in the paper. Ya chosen to deliver this message that God, She live 'neath the waters. Do it. Cuz if ya don't, a gris-gris be on ya!—ExpectAntly, God's Kith and Kin.*

I pressed my index finger against my forehead to help put the sentences in clearer focus. It wasn't even nine a.m. yet, and even though it was only Tuesday, I was suddenly as groggy as I felt at the end of a week. July humidity—and bizarre messages—did that.

I re-read the lines, tried to brush away the "snow" on my shirt, and reconsidered my view of God. He was a she? A mother? Who spelled worse than I did before spell check? And now She was alive and apparently madder than hades in the Bayou, just waiting to wreak havoc on those of us who lived in the *horrable* city across the way?

"Oh, Lord," I said out loud. "Not again."

First things first. Why did God always seem to get my name wrong whenever he—or she—contacted his—or her—local religion reporter? Sure, Jennalou was a nice enough name for these parts, but it was quite a deviation from the byline that represented all of who I was, the same grand name my socially conscious hippie parents—Maggie and Ron—christened me with almost thirty years ago: Jonna Lightfoot MacLaughlin.

Jonna rounded out the musical foursome of my brothers, Matthew, Mark, and Luke; Lightfoot was in solidarity with our First Nation American neighbors (my brothers, too, boasted Native middle names like BigBear, RunningWind, and EagleWing). MacLaughlin was the gift of our Irish ancestors who shipped over from County Clare sometime after the Great Potato Famine.

Obviously, names meant something in our tribe. They mattered, and we could get a little testy when someone—who claimed to be in the naming business after all—didn't get it right.

As I thought about it, though, most human folks around here hadn't bothered with it, either, preferring either "Dawlin'" like Big Wendall, "Hon" like the name my neighbor Madame PennyAnne used for everyone, or "Hey" if they called me anything at all. And if anyone did attempt Jonna, they'd add another syllable entirely, drawing it out to a long slow Joohhnna. At first, I confess, it made me nuts, but after almost a year of reporting in this town, I had to admit I was becoming charmed by the rolling hills of a Lousiania-ian accent.

But that did not mean that Jennalou first thing in the morning—and in the middle of my breakfast—touched the charm-spot in my soul. I scratched my head at the name as well as the reference to Mama God and looked around the newsroom for another brain to bounce this letter off of. The City Hall reporters were looking quite serious on their phones and laptops, the sports guys were shooting paper wads toward the trash can like they were at the free-throw line, and two of the feature writers were comparing shades of nail polish while the other two were poring over the "competition's" stories. I saw through the glass wall of her office that Hattie Lipsock, my editor, was meeting with someone, and Red, the real estate reporter who sat across from me because they apparently alphabetized the cubicles and religion was closest to real estate, hadn't yet come into the office this morning. He usually wandered in by the crack of noon.

So I glanced back at the old family photo I'd propped up on my desk, the picture taken when my brothers and I were still in high school. Most of what I knew about the world's religions I'd learned from my family, and try as I might, I just could not remember ever hearing my parents talk about Mama Almighty when we were growing up in Colorado's mountain country. Buddha, yes. The Transcendent Self, the Dalai Lama, Moses and Elijah, and even the Baha'ullah—these divine heads (and others) my brothers and I met at various detours on our parents' soul journey to Jesus.

But God as Mother? That was a new one for me. Only the earth was our parents' spiritual mother, and then only on the occasion when she needed protecting. Those times, we'd join hundreds of other "peace activists" at Rocky Flats Nuclear Power Plant just outside of Boulder to protest its abuse on our Mother Earth.

I picked up the Big Chief message again and stared into my empty cup, suddenly aware that no amount of coffee—or flower-child know-how for that matter—could help me translate what a gris-gris was. I pulled out my brown notebook and added it to my vocabulary list. Clearly, I needed New Orleans expertise for this one, to know just how seriously I should take this latest message from God. And Lord knows, I was not excited to hear again from him. Or her.

After all, the last time God was on the loose was when I was the Number One—and only—Religion Reporter at the *Denver Dispatch*, the Mile High City's number two daily newspaper, my previous job. Eventually, we discovered God had gotten his meds very mixed up. Though his messages as the Almighty were admittedly a little wacky, they were at least relatively polite and safe in their tone. This morning, however, God's maternal counterpart and her representatives were making threats. In fact, she sounded downright mean.

Which called for a cigarette.

I picked up my bag, headed downstairs to the street, and lit the end of my National Spirit, the organic cigarettes I'd ordered from www.natural-cigs.com. My prayers to quit so far had not been answered, though I was sure they would be one day. I believed the Almighty would someday have mercy on my nicotine habit. Again.

After a long lung-infesting drag, I flipped open my cell phone and punched the numbers.

"Mornin', Madame PennyAnne," I exhaled. "It's Jonna. What's a gris-gris?"

"It's gris-gris," she said, wrapping the French pronunciation around the words so I couldn't hear the s's.

"Yes, that. What is it?"

"How much time do you have?"

I looked at what remained of my cigarette.

"Couple of minutes."

"Why?"

"Because that's all I have for a cigarette break."

"That's an evil habit!"

I nodded my head in agreement and waited for her to "get recentered" as she called it.

"I meant, why are you asking?"

I told her about the Big Chief letter. I figured if anyone could interpret this cryptic message it would be Madame PennyAnne Trusseaux, New Orleans born and raised bartender and jazz expert by night, psychic reader and official voodoo tour guide of the French Quarter by day. And full-time single mom of Ruthie, my nine-year-old neighbor. They lived upstairs from me in the tall converted garage that now held three boxlike apartments.

"Well, it's not pretty, Hon."

"No? Should I be worried?" I sucked hard on the Spirit.

"Oh, yeah, and very afraid. See, a gris-gris is like, shoot, what would you Yanks call it? Reckon it's like a curse, or a spell. It'll mess a girl up. Who put one on ya?"

"No one yet. Just threatened to if I didn't tell readers of the *Banner* that Mama God was alive and mad in the Bayou!"

"Everyone knows that."

I coughed as I exhaled. "They do?"

"Sure, she's been living in some gator ever since I was Ruthie's age."

"So I shouldn't run a story on her?"

"Old news, Sugar. Besides, if they do put a gris-gris on ya, ya can always run down to Voodoo Heaven and get ya a gris-gris bag to wear 'round your neck."

"I can?"

"Yup, they're real nice over there. Cost ya about twenty bucks, and it'll give ya all the protection ya need. Hang on, Hon . . ."

I heard a bell jingle as PennyAnne greeted a customer. She was in her tiny storefront "office"—the one she called Psychic Light—a space she rented on St. Ann Street just around the corner from our apartment building on the edge of the French Quarter. She was hoping to get a little closer to Bourbon Street where the tourists always seemed to pay good money to know their futures, but Madame PennyAnne just couldn't afford the rent there. Yet.

"Gotta go, Hon. It's Psychic Light Time."

"Yeah, go, go. Thanks for the help."

"Sure 'nough. See ya tonight for dinner, right?"

"Absolutely."

I folded my phone and dropped it in my bag at the same time I dropped my cigarette to the ground and stomped it out with the toe of my clog. I looked at the buildings around me and thought about what a different place this city was compared to Denver. For one, Denver was a mile high in altitude and sometimes, it seemed to me, in attitude as well. Denver was an upbeat, energetic town where bike trails and ski racks were as ubiquitous as art galleries and restaurants. New Orleans, on the other hand, was below sea level, and below the radar screen of anything I'd known as familiar back home. The sky this morning was a smoke-colored haze—complete opposite of a

Colorado blue—and the heat reflected it. I used the back of my hand to wipe the sweat that had formed across my forehead during my five-minute break.

No dry western heat here, I thought as I climbed the stairs back up to my desk, thinking, too, that back home even God was different. There, he never threatened you with spells or curses. But then again, coffee was just coffee and there were no beignets to be found in the Mile High City. Not to mention the fact that there, handsome Catholic men had a tendency of snapping your heart in two. Or one did anyway.

I caught my breath from the three flights of steps and decided I'd take a gris-gris and beignet over a broken heart any day.

By the time I got back to my desk, I noticed the person in Hattie's office was just standing to leave. He was a thin, tall man whose suit jacket fell neatly down his back like it was supposed to and whose dark brown hair was smooth against his head. From where I was sitting, I figured he was somewhere between Hattie's age and mine and probably one of the local business owners she met with often so she could keep her "finger on the pulse of the Crescent," as she liked to say. The advertising department loved her.

When I saw him reach across Hattie's desk to shake her hand, I brushed the remaining snow tracks from my shirt, scrunched the tips of my hair in hopes of giving it some order, and grabbed the Big Chief notepaper. Hattie was another good source for All Things New Orleans. She was bound to have some piece to this puzzle.

I stood at the edge of her glass office, tapping the letter with my pencil, waiting for Hattie's meeting to end with an opened door. I re-read the sentences and spelling errors and considered PennyAnne's take on the threats. She was probably right; this was not worth pursuing. But religion reporters had to take seriously all messages from God. That was our job.

"Lightfoot! Good timing," Hattie said, pushing open the door. Her eyes—like most Southern women's I'd discovered since moving here—did a quick perusal of my outfit, makeup, and hair. Usually, it was clear that my secondhand clothes, frizzy hair, and naked face deeply disappointed them. Hattie, however, always seemed to catch herself, apparently deciding I was fine the way I was and today, tossing out a broad smile to encourage me. "Well, Sugar, I've been wanting you to meet someone."

"Uh-huh?" I said, looking from her smile to the man's. As I did, I felt my blood stop circulating. I gawked. I couldn't help it; this guy was a perfectly crafted male, a model straight out of the Sunday Style section. My Irish blood immediately filled my cheeks, and I let my eyes drop to his left hand. When I didn't see a gold ring, I swallowed and extended my hand.

"Jonna Lightfoot MacLaughlin," I announced, a lilt of availability in my voice.

"Our finest religion reporter ever," Hattie boasted to the handsome drink of water standing beside her. "And Sugar, this here's Reginald William Hancock the Third. One of the city's finest swindlers, I mean, developers."

"Don't believe a word Hattie tells ya, Ms. MacLaughlin," he said, his voice a rich blend of mocha and rum, his eyes a pool of chocolate sauce. "The pleasure's mine. But please call me Renn."

"Renn." I stared. "Renn. Renn."

"Lightfoot here's come down from Denver last fall," Hattie said, slapping my elbow and my sense back into reality. "Been here almost ten months now and is downright miraculous at getting some of the best religion news the *Banner*'s ever had."

"Religion?" said the voice. "You must have some real good connections."

"Not nearly as many as you do, Renn Hancock!" Hattie said to him. Then she looked at me. "This boy's family goes back to the days before New Orleans was French and Spanish and everything in between."

He laughed and smoothed the sides of his hair with his index fingers. "Ah, Hattie, don't go embarrassin' me! I suppose the next thing you'll say to this pretty young thing is that my family also owns half the city!"

Hattie tilted her head and winked at me. "Oh, no, Hon, I knew you'd do that yourself!" They laughed again like two people who shared a history of fancy dinner parties, corporate events, and campaign strategies. When the joke was over, though, he focused his eyebrows in my direction as if he'd just remembered something. I was still trying to decide if I'd heard right.

Did he just call me pretty?

"Hey, you're not the one who wrote that story about the two lawyers in town who do some kind of ancient body-mind meditation thing to redirect their anxiety in the courtroom, are you?"

"Yes, I . . ."

"'Om Control,' that's what we called it. Yup, that was Lightfoot's story, Renn, a real gem, didn't you think?" Hattie said. "Maybe you should try that 'meditation thing' considering the stress that family business gives you." Hattie winked again.

"Maybe I should. You know I went to elementary school with one of those lawyers you wrote about. Funny, we were good Baptists together, so I was a little surprised to see he'd switched to another religion."

I blinked at him. "But, Mr. Han . . . I mean . . . Renn . . . meditation isn't exactly a religion," I said.

"No?" he said, leaning toward me so close I could smell his cologne. "As much as I'd like to find out a little more about . . . it, you'll have to excuse me, Ms. MacLaughlin—can I call you Janie?—I'm needin' to get to another meeting."

Renn chuckled, picked up his briefcase, and squeezed through the door, looking at me with each step.

"I hope to see you again, Janie," he whispered.

"Okay," I mumbled, barely audible in front of this beautiful man. "Uh, it's Jonna."

He stopped and turned. "Excuse me?"

"It's Jonna, my name. Not Janie. But don't worry, everyone gets it wrong." I coughed. "Anyway, very nice to meet you . . . Renn."

He grinned when I said his name. Then he waved as he strode down the hall like he owned it, past the sports department, my desk, and the mailroom until he disappeared into the stairwell. Finally, I looked up at Hattie, who was shaking her head at me, the corner of her mouth turned slightly up and a lecture in her eyes.

"Careful, Sugar, that man'll steal muffin tins from his own grandma," she said as she spun around and walked back to her desk.

"Well, it doesn't hurt to look, does it, Boss?"

"Everything about that man could hurt," she said, settling

into her chair like a queen. "Now, whatcha got for me?"

I filed away her comment about Renn Hancock the Third in my brain and set the letter on the keyboard in front of her. I sat down in the chair where Renn had just been. His aroma still floated around me and I took a deep breath.

"Old news, Hon," Hattie said as she looked over the Big Chief letter. Her head bounced when she looked up, and the red streaks she'd colored into her hair glistened under the florescent lights. I noticed her lipstick matched her blouse as it usually did—both bright and bold like the woman who wore them.

Hattie Lipsock was a "seasoned" newspaperwoman—divorced and middle-aged—who'd grown up thirty miles from here, but after climbing the career ladder across half a dozen cities (including Denver), she'd finally settled in back home as managing editor of the *Banner*. She believed diets and magazines were for sissies, hard work and kindness for real professionals. I thought of Hattie as the type of woman who drank every drop of life out of each day and collapsed each night enormously satisfied. She was always in the office when I arrived and still there when I'd wander home—while somehow managing to take in every new jazz band, fundraiser, or exhibit in between.

"Old news? That's what someone else told me. But I'm always a little nervous about messages from God."

"Well, if you are, I reckon we all should be," Hattie said, shaking out the letter like it was laundry. "Tell you what. Make a copy of this for me, okay? And let's keep an ear to the ground about any new cults in the area, just in case Lord Mama decides to do something she shouldn't. Or . . ."

She stopped suddenly and flicked the letter like there was a gnat on it. Then she pursed her lips and studied the page.

"Or what?" I asked.

"Or I might want to throw this over to an old friend on the police force. One of the good guys, just so you know."

"It's that serious?"

"Maybe. This sort of reminds me of someone he told me about a while ago. Let's keep it low-key," she said, handing back the letter while she swiveled around to the phone. She picked up the receiver and was ready to make her call when she realized I was still sitting across from her.

"Something else, Lightfoot? How's the story coming on the cathedral repairs?"

"No. Fine. Good," I said, still sitting.

She lifted her eyebrows and shrugged her shoulders.

"Is Renn really that bad?" I asked.

"Only to those who like him," she said, rolling her eyes while pressing the numbers on her phone. "I know you're lookin' for a good man, Hon, but trust me on this one. Keep your distance from him and you'll die a happy woman. Now let's get to work, okay, Lightfoot?"

"Right. Sure." I picked up the letter and hurried back to my desk. Three voice mails were waiting for me. The first was from the assistant to a city council member inviting me to the mayor's prayer breakfast next week. The next was from the "social coordinator" for the local chapter of Scientology inviting me to their monthly lecture and dinner of organic cheese dishes. If I had a dollar for every potluck dinner I was invited to as a religion reporter, I'd all but own the paper. I was never sure why religious folks thought these gatherings were newsworthy, but one thing was certain about all of them: They liked to eat. No matter which God they worshiped or what spiritual persuasion they espoused, food seemed a natural starting point.

I could appreciate that. In fact, it was almost time for lunch. In an hour.

The third voice mail was from my second oldest brother, Mark, calling from Mobile, which was within "spittin' distance" of New Orleans, according to Hattie. Translated: about a few hours' drive (depending on how fast you drove). But before I had a chance to listen to all of his message, someone tapped me on the shoulder. I turned around in a whirl.

"Red! Well, it's not noon yet, what are you doing here?!"

"Morning, Lightfoot," he said, setting another beignet and cup of coffee on my desk before sitting at his. "Didn't know if you'd made it over yet to Big Wendall's, but thought I'd cover you, just in case."

I glanced from the bag to the man and back again before taking my second course of breakfast. This was strange: Red never came in this early, and he'd rarely offered me anything from Big Wendall's.

I bit and the snow fell. "Whatdyawant, Red?" My mouth was full of sweet pastry.

"What do you mean what do I want? Can't a real estate reporter show a little kindness to his colleague?" He drank his coffee as he leaned back in his chair.

His light brown skin was still shiny from the heat outside—it was supposed to get up to one hundred degrees today. He wore creased blue jeans and a baggy white shirt, looking more like a sports reporter than the real estate agents he often profiled. Red—or Rufus Ezekiel Denton to his wife and family—was a local, and one of the few African-American reporters on the desk. He was also one of the few friends I'd made in the office since I'd moved here—I guess we both felt a little like outsiders compared to the rest of the staff, and it helped that our desks were next to each other. Red was a friendly but quiet guy. Though he was a few years older than I was, his facial features often reminded me of a teenager. Youth became him, and he used it whenever he needed a source to open up.

I swallowed, chased the beignet with a swig of coffee, and brushed again at the sugar on my chest. "Sure, you can be kind every single day as far as I'm concerned, especially with food, but I can smell a deal a mile away."

He stared at his shoes, very seriously. Then he gulped again.

"Everything okay, Red?"

He looked up, his dark brown eyes wide with worry.

"It's my auntie, Lightfoot. She's in a home and her health isn't what it used to be, but her mind's sharp." He paused and pointed to his temple to punctuate his comment. "Anyway, I just came from visiting her, and I thought, well, maybe you could do a story on her and the folks at the home, you know, to cheer them up."

I wiped my mouth and tried to imagine his auntie.

"You have an aunt?"

"Course I do. Don't you?" He didn't wait for me to respond. "She all but raised me, Lightfoot. I hate seeing her in there, but she says it's not so bad. She seems to like it."

"How old is she?"

"Ninety-four. And she's sharp," he said, pointing again.

"I'll bet," I said and took out my notepad. "Hmm. Sounds

interesting. But I'm not sure what the religion angle is."

"The home itself. It was started back in the sixties by a bunch of churches—black and white, Protestant and Catholic. They wanted to take care of their old folks. Together. Maybe you could profile it as a modern success story? You know, 'Churches unite across race to care for their elderly' or something like that?" Red put his arms behind his head and stared at the ceiling as if he saw a story writing itself above him.

"Are you telling me this is good news?" My stomach perked up, and I leaned toward Red's desk. Too often I had to write stories on the darker side of religion—which seemed as wrong as aerobics after a big meal. Religion was supposed to be good for people, and so I was always looking for something inspiring or even uplifting to report. Red knew it. For heaven's sake, he'd heard me whine about it every day since I first plopped my books on the desk beside his.

He nodded. Then he reached into his pocket and handed me a piece of paper.

"I knew you'd get it. Here's the contact info." He unfolded it carefully and held it out to me. "Thanks, Lightfoot."

"Well, I haven't done anything yet," I said. I grabbed the paper, scanned it, and tossed it, on a pile of press releases. I nodded at Red and we spontaneously turned toward our computers. But another idea popped in my head.

"Red, since you're the real estate expert, ever heard of a developer named Reginald William Hancock the Third?"

He sighed, and his shoulders instantly sagged. "Renn? Who hasn't? His family's been around . . . in lots of ways." He looked up. "Why?"

"Oh, just wondering," I said, and picked up my phone.

::Acknowledgments

I'm grateful to my agent and friend, Don Pape, at Alive Communications; the good folks at NavPress, Terry Behimer, Jeff Gerke, and Traci DePree; my atomic engineer editor friend, Marlene Satter; novelist Vinita Hampton Wright; my parents, Jack and Nanci Kadlecek; and my husband, Christopher Gilbert, all of whom helped make Lightfoot's first installment a far better story; and to my editor and friend, Steve Wike, who first taught me the value of religion reporting.

And many thanks to you, the reader, for coming along on the adventure . . .

::Author

JO KADLECEK is a former waitress, soccer player, and high school debate coach who's always loved a good story. She grew up in the Mile High City of Denver before heading to sea level, first in Mississippi, then New York City, and most recently the Jersey Shore, where she and her husband live. She has worked as a full-time writer, reporter, retreat teacher, and adjunct writing instructor. In the fall of 2006, she joined the faculty at Gordon College in Massachusetts as an assistant professor of creative writing. Please visit her website at www.lamppostmedia.net.

Other Books by Jo Kadlecek

Desperate Women of the Bible: Lessons on Passion from the Gospels

The Sound of My Voice: a Novel

Fear: A Spiritual Navigation, a Memoir

Reckless Faith: Living Passionately as Imperfect Christians: 8 Studies on the Life of Peter

Feast of Life: Spiritual Food for Balanced Living

I Call You Friend: Four Women's Stories of Race, Faith, and Friendship